Eliza's Children

Joe Zeigler

Copyright 2017 Joe Zeigler

Published by Arrakis Publishing, Inc.

All rights reserved, including the right of reproduction, in whole or in part, in any form.

ISBN-13:978-0692926116

ISBN-10:0692926119

Library of Congress Control Number: 2017914421

Arrakis Publishing, Inc., Crystal River, Florida.

Contents

The Hack

Gordon Wysmann had just come back from lunch and was walking past the row of cubicles toward his nook in the programming building. He had an obligatory office in the administration building, but he much preferred to be among the programming team.

Gordon was a bear of a man, on the margin of old age, balding now, gentle, exuding patience. He was an electrical engineer who had graduated from MIT long before the young people who now worked for him were born. He had designed and worked on computers since before he graduated. In many ways, he had defined the industry and was now the revered old man of the genre.

As he passed Leif Hoberson's cubicle, he noticed a look of consternation on his colleague's face. Leif was light in his chair, leaning forward, his face very close to the display. He was pressing the Enter key over and over with what appeared to be increasing frustration.

"What's going on here?" Gordon asked, concerned.

"I don't know," he sputtered, turning toward Gordon, "It just keeps running slower and slower. At first, there was a short but longer-than-normal delay in the keystroke. Then the delay became longer and longer. I don't understand what's going on," Leif said, his eyes open wide and his voice becoming louder and replete with panic.

From her cubicle next door, Carol Fisher heard the voices and got up to investigate. Carol was an intern at Fauxbook, a part-time employee while she pursued an advanced degree in computer science.

Standing in the opening, she said nothing. It was obvious. Leif had a virus. It surprised her. No one knew more about computers than Leif. He was from West Virginia, a hillbilly and a prodigy who truly seemed one with the machine. Tall and lanky, with hay-like, unkempt hair, and little to no formal education. He was socially inept, shy, and withdrawn. His life was at the interface with the machines. *Darn*, she thought. *If Leif can attract a virus, there's no hope for the rest of us.*

Leif had moved aside, dazed and deferring to Gordon. Gordon was calmly tapping on the keyboard to no avail. He was not easily shaken. However, his ever-present smile gave way to wrinkles of worry, and his lips turned down in a frown as he realized something was very wrong.

Carol spoke for the first time. "Unplug it," she commanded.

Gordon and Leif looked at her. Gordon followed her eyes to the flashing lights. "Oh, my God!" he exclaimed, his eyes wide and his mouth forming an open circle.

"Leif, look at the activity lights. Up there." She pointed to the wiring rack. "Someone is dumping your data! It's running at terabits. In a moment, they'll have everything from your computer and may be going after the servers, if they haven't already."

Gordon yanked the desk away from the wall and pulled the plug from the rear of the computer. The lights went dark. They looked at each other in shock. "Too late, I fear," he said. "What happened, Leif?" he asked softly and not unkindly.

"I don't know. I don't know…I was working on a program for internal use, and it just started running slower and slower. I would strike a key, and the response time became longer and longer. I tried rebooting, and that helped for a while, and then it was the same thing. It just got slower and slower. I don't know what happened."

His tone was whiny, evasive. Gordon knew there was something Leif was not telling him.

"Leif," Gordon said with a serious tone and expression, "I'll ask you again: What happened prior to this event?"

Gordon was almost a deity to the group and to many in the computer industry. He had been there from the beginning and had designed many of the early groundbreaking machines. Despite his quiet voice, he was intimidating, and Leif was having difficulty withholding information from him.

"Well," Leif started, "the only thing that was a little strange was an e-mail from Google. It said someone from Ukraine had tried to log in to my account. They blocked the attempt but strongly suggested I change my password."

"Did you?" Gordon asked.

Carol stood in the doorway quietly, knowing where this was going. *Leif, you are so fired*, she thought sadly.

"Yeah, I guess. I was busy, and it was a distraction. I was trying to keep my mind focused on my work. So I clicked on the Change Password button, changed it, and went back to work."

Well, Gordon thought, *that got them in. But that's not enough. It would give them access to his e-mail. Somehow, they gained access to a lot more than that.*

"Okay, Leif, what happened then?"

Oh, God, Carol thought. *This is bad and getting worse.*

"I went back to work."

"Leif, you said that. This is like pulling teeth. Just tell me what happened, and tell me the whole story now." Though Gordon's voice was soft, he clearly communicated the seriousness of his demand.

Leif understood.

"I got another e-mail from Google said they thought changing I may have changed my password too late. They suggested I change my computer password. Again, I was busy and just clicked on the button and changed it."

"Oh, my Lord," Carol whispered. "No, no, no, he didn't give them the network password." But she knew he had.

"Go on," Gordon commanded.

"I went back to work. You have to understand I was totally focused on the code I was working on and trying to swat away these distractions."

"Go on."

"Then the antivirus software popped up a dialog box that said the network security may have been breached. It said I should change my network password and displayed a button to do that. It made sense to me, considering the earlier e-mails I'd received from Google."

Damn, Gordon thought, *they were in his computer and going for the whole enchilada.*

"Anyways I clicked on the button and changed my network password, then went back to work. That was what I was enthralled with. I was having trouble thinking about anything else."

"Leif, you are so fired," Carol said, "and I am so sorry."

"You can't fire me," Leif cried, red faced. "You can't fire me. You're just a programmer just like me. In fact, you are junior to me. You're just a kid out of college. You are just here looking for a rich husband. Bitch! Bitch! You can't fire me."

Carol didn't say anything. She just looked at him with an expression of pity. He was a good programmer, loyal to the company and dedicated. And she was sure this was the end of his career.

"No," Gordon said, "she can't fire you, and I won't. But she's right; you're going to be fired. Let's go see Jon."

Consequences

Gordon, Carol, and Leif assembled in Jon's office at the end of the corridor. The office was not ostentatious; it fit Jon Johnsson, who drove a ten-year-old Ford sedan and lived in the same house he had bought when he and Misika were first married. Though he was a billionaire, or at least very wealthy, as a result of his earlier ventures in the computer industry, he lived the same upper-middle-class lifestyle he had always enjoyed.

After explaining what had occurred, Gordon summed it up: "This is likely to have a pernicious effect on our systems, if not our business."

"Are you saying they may still have malicious software in our systems?" Jon asked.

Leif looked down, his face reflecting worry, embarrassment, and fear.

Carol was quiet.

"Hard to tell," Gordon replied. "It could be. We're running a couple of virus scanners on the whole system. But the most sophisticated malware will move to another part of the system. It's programmed to see signs of the scan, and it just moves. It can be hard to pin down."

"My God," Jon said, which was as close to foul language as he got. He was a kind, gentle, and very religious man who, when in doubt, took solace in piety.

"We're setting up to start a simultaneous scan on all of the servers and workstations tomorrow. That should root it out—if, indeed, something is in there," Gordon replied.

Mary Adams slipped into the room and made herself small against the wall.

There's trouble, Gordon thought. She was part of, and for the moment, the only member of, the documentation team. He knew she was going to be trouble. He realized the social mores of the new generation were a mystery to him. But, still…*slut* wasn't part of his lexicon, but it was the only word that fit. There was no doubt in his mind Mary would eventually cause friction between the young men, and perhaps women, of the group.

"Hello, Mary," Jon said. "We are going over the intrusion to the system this morning, which appears to be serious. I welcome your input." Jon never saw the bad in people and commonly made the mistake of thinking, against all evidence, everyone was as unselfish and God-fearing as he.

"Thank you, Mister Johnsson," Mary replied.

"Jon, Jon, call me Jon," he insisted.

"Okay," Gordon said. *Now we have that settled.* "We don't know what, or how much, they downloaded before I unplugged the workstation. That, too, could be a significant issue."

"My God!" Jon exclaimed.

"I have two engineers examining the logs. However, the intruders may have been clever enough to disable the normal logging of the computers' activity," Gordon said.

Rumors about the meeting at the "end of the hall," the euphemism for Jon's office, were spreading through the building. As a result, Jeromy Carpenter, one of the senior programmers, appeared and took a spot against the wall next to Mary.

"Do you have this under control?" Jon asked.

"Not at the moment," Gordon responded. "However, I will soon. If there is any suspicion of malware, we'll wipe all of the computers, reinstall the operating systems, and restore our work from our backups."

"Good," Jon said. "That should get us back on track."

"Well, Jon," Gordon said, "yes and no. It's not going to help determine how much of our system, applications, programs, and data they downloaded. I'll look at the logs and get back to you." Out of the corner of his eye, he noticed Mary leaning gently against Jeromy. *And it begins*, he thought.

"I'm sure you'll do the best you can. And I have total confidence in you and our team. Have faith; everything will be fine."

Jeromy had to lean into Mary for balance as she slowly pressed her body against him. He hoped no one in the room noticed his reaction. Then he felt something brush against it…Mary's hand. She'd noticed.

Mary was a petite young woman, perhaps twenty-five, with a cute enough face, small breasts, a narrow waist, and ample hips. She was okay looking. She was small, short, not even five feet tall. But she exuded sexuality. It was amazing, like a cloud of estrogen, progesterone, and testosterone—mainly testosterone. Jeromy felt as if he was breathing it all in from the cloud around her. His member began to throb, and he suppressed a moan.

"Okay, Gordon," Jon said. "I'll let you get back to work. But I'd like to have a report by the end of the business day."

"I'll do my best, Jon."

"Anything or anybody you need to get this done, you have my authority to commandeer it."

"Thanks, Jon," Gordon replied. "Before I go, there is the question of Leif. What do you want to do with him? His actions, I'm sad to say, are troublesome."

Leif cringed, and Carol quietly left the room. Mary and Jeromy stayed. Mary stayed to witness the drama, and Jeromy was paralyzed.

She leaned toward him and whispered in his ear, "I'll meet you in the cafeteria after."

God, Jeromy thought, *I need more than a cup of coffee. What does she have in mind?*

Jon said, "Ah yes, yes, Leif. What do you have to say for yourself, young man?"

"I fucked up," he said, and he instantly regretted his use of profanity. But Jon said nothing. He leaned forward, perched on the edge of his chair, and looked attentive. He had presence. Leif on the other hand appeared shrunken in his chair; his shoulders drawn forward and together–not quite cringing.

"Sorry, sir..." He forced himself to glance up into Jon's worried blue eyes but could not hold eye contact. "Well, sir, all I can say is I admit to my errors. Spear phishing is not something I would normally fall for," he said softly. "I was totally engrossed in my work this morning, and it was a distraction. I was upset it would disturb my flow. I was on a roll and producing good work."

"I understand," Jon said in a fatherly tone. "Go on."

"Well...I just dealt with it quickly, without paying attention or giving it any thought. When the next two e-mails came, I just did the same thing. It was stupid; I knew better and know even better now. It will never happen again." Leif sighed with relief. He had gotten that out without making a further fool of himself. He continued to look down, dejected and shamed.

"You are going to have to fire him, Jon," Gordon said.

There was a pregnant silence. Finally, Jon said, "No, I'm not going to fire you, Leif, though what you did is inexcusable. Gordon, put him back to work. But his workstation is to be disconnected from the network. Change his passwords so it will be impossible for him to log in to the network. Then install a portable disk drive on his workstation."

"Jon, I'm not sure this is wise. It might be better to make an example of him," Gordon said, not unkindly.

"We are going to have an all-employee meeting tomorrow morning at eleven a.m.," Jon said. "Leif, you are going to prepare a presentation to describe and explain this event and present it at this meeting tomorrow. I understand you have learned from this. I want everyone to share your experience and to learn from it. Then, you will meet with each new employee during their orientation and explain to them how this happened."

"Okay, Jon," Gordon said. "That's what we'll do."

Jon turned to Mary and Jeromy. "Please, please, give us the room; Leif, you may go also."

The pressure against Jeromy's body disappeared, and he bolted. Mary straightened and left the room without comment. Leif wasn't moving, so she closed the door behind her.

Expectations

Jeromy rushed across the hall and into the nearest men's room, too preoccupied to notice Carol in the hallway. He splashed cold water on his face. It didn't help. So, reaching into his pants, he arranged the tip of his penis under his belt buckle. Exiting the toilet enclosure, he examined the result in the mirror over the sinks. Okay, that will do if no one looks closely.

"Mary," Carol said, "what happened? Does Leif still have a job? How bad is the virus?"

Mary squinted her eyes in frustration and looked down the hall. Jeromy was not in sight.

"He went into the men's room," Carol said. "So, what happened?"

Mary glanced at the men's room door. "Leif is fine. Jon hates to fire anyone—a dangerous affliction, if you ask me. But, no one asked me."

"And?"

"Leif is reassigned and banned from the network. Jon also asked him to give seminars on how to avoid being hacked." She looked Carol in the eye. "You noticed."

"Hard not to," Carol replied, her lips curled just a little in a knowing smile. "What happened with the virus? Is it going to be a problem?"

"I don't care what you think, really. But, you'd best mind your own business." Mary took a step toward her almost, but not quite, invading Carol's space.

"Hey!" Carol said, not backing up. "You asked if I noticed you getting the kid all worked up. I did, I answered you, and that's that. I didn't express any judgment. What's with you? I'd just like you to answer my question about the virus."

"Yeah, okay," Mary replied, stepping back. "Gordon is going to track down the virus, do what's necessary, and report back to Jon. I wouldn't worry about it."

Oddly, Carol thought, *she looks worried.* She noticed Mary's eyebrows were pinched together and the frown lines on her forehead prominent.

At that moment, Jeromy came out of the bathroom. Both of the women noticed the vertical budge in his pants. Mary's eyes widened as she took in a quick breath.

Carol looked at him directly. "Hi, Jeromy. Leif didn't lose his job."

"Yeah, I know. That's good," he replied his head lowered, avoiding eye contact. He was waving his right hand around at his side in a vain attempt to distract attention. "See you later," he said and almost scampered down the hall.

"I'll be there soon," Mary replied to his back as she gave Carol a warning look, her eyes slits and her lips pressed tightly together.

"Hey," Carol said extending her hands palms outward in a defensive posture.

The conference-room door opened, and Leif came out. Behind him they could see Jon and Gordon, their chairs close together, in intense conversation.

"Leif, I heard it's not so bad. Everything's going to be all right," Carol said.

Leif's head had been hanging. He paused and then raised his head to look at her. "Yeah, I guess. But, I was stupid. Maybe I should be fired."

"Hey, we all make mistakes. You shouldn't beat yourself up. It'll all work out."

"Yeah, I guess," Leif replied, again hanging his head. "See you guys later."

"Sure will," Mary replied with a lyrical tone as she gave Carol a stern glance.

"So, Gordon has the situation under control?" Carol asked.

"Well, he's going to look into it. I wouldn't say it's under control yet. He knows what he is doing. I'm not going to worry about it."

"It's scary, though. I feel like there's a stalker out there trying to hurt me—violate me. I know it's not personal. But, it feels personal."

"No, it's not personal," Mary replied extrapolating Carol's meaning. "I just want to have some fun."

"I understand."

"Do you? Do you really?" Mary spoke aggressively. "I know you disapprove. Screw you, Miss Goodie Two Shoes! I don't care what people think of me. I'll not be put in a box of other people's expectations. They believe I should live up to their expectations while they don't live up to mine—or even their own. Fuck that! I'll do what I want, and you should just mind your own business."

"So, you don't think the virus will be a problem?"

Mary looked at her appraisingly for a long moment and then burst out laughing. Carol joined in, and the tension broke. "I think we're going to be friends."

"Good friends, I should think," Carol replied. "Now, about the virus. I'm worried—I have a lot riding on this company."

"Yeah, me too," Mary said, "more than you can imagine."

"You're worried?"

"A little," she finally admitted. "What are you, a computer science major?"

"Uh huh." Carol nodded. "I'm working on my PhD."

"I figured. Well, I'm just an English major and just a BA— totally expendable. I'm just your documenter. In fact, right now I'm the entire documentation department."

"Well, that's an important job."

"It is, and I know how lucky I am to have it. A degree in English is not the most marketable. I was very lucky to get this job."

"Why did you major in English?"

"My father was an English major. In fact, he was head of the English department. Expectations, you know. I was a victim of expectations. But never again."

Carol sensed Mary was being uncharacteristically open, but then she saw Mary tense and her lips form a thin line.

"No, I take it back. I'm not worried. You know those who can't create hack. How good can they be? I'm not worried; our guys are better. And, we have Gordon Wysmann. Everything will be fine."

"Yes, Gordon, the secret weapon. Besides that," Carol said, "Jon might be onto something. It may be a good idea to segregate the programmers, all of them, from the network and the Internet. I can't think of any reason they need access. And, if they do, it could be on another terminal from the one they are using for coding."

"Ha!" Mary replied. "Are you seriously thinking of weaning the programmers from the Internet? Have you lost your mind?"

Again, they laughed together.

Foreplay

At 3:00 p.m., the cafeteria was almost empty. The space was huge, with kiosks serving food of all cultures and for all appetites. There was a sushi bar, Chinese food, pizza, hamburgers, comfort food complete with fried chicken, an India kiosk, Thai, vegetarian, Italian, kosher, Louisiana creole, and more. People from all over the world worked at Fauxbook, and the company wanted to keep them happy.

After a short search, Mary found Jeromy sitting alone in the comfort-food area. *This is fortuitous*, she thought. *He's right where I want him.* The section was closed for the day. Lunch was over, and the cafeteria had only a limited dinner offering. The fast-food areas were still open, though, and each had a few customers. However, they were alone in their section.

"Hi, Jeromy," she said as he sat down. "I'm so wet."

He struggled to answer; surprise at her statement slowed him down.

"Hi, guys," Don Matthews said, walking up and pulling out a chair. "I hear something is going on at the end of the hall. Were you guys up there?"

Mary smiled with just a hint of availability. "Yeah, it was about someone hacking us. I'm sure you'll hear about it shortly. What are you up to?" She didn't tell him much because spreading and creating rumors were not part of the culture of these young people. Of course, Don was not young. He was well into his forties. He was heavyset; his hair had turned prematurely white, as had his beard. He looked, more than a little, like Santa Claus and was generally as jolly—especially when he was drinking, which was often.

"Same old, same old," he replied. "I'm working on the back end of the customer database. You wouldn't believe what they want to do with customer data. Damn!" He smiled. "Just as a start, they plan to track users' browsing, and not just on Fauxbook—everywhere! When the Fauxbook user signs up, we load them up. Cookies, of course, but then we slip in trackers, loggers, and some stuff no one else has thought of yet."

"Really?" Jeromy said a bit impatiently. His focus was on his boner and Mary's last revelation.

"Yeah, really. Like I said, I'm just working on the back end, so I'm not involved with the algorithms that snag them, just the stuff we do to them once we have them. But still, it's amazing."

Back end, Jeromy thought, focused on something entirely different from Don's meaning. *Mary has a very nice back end.*

"I'm heavy into snagging," Mary said with a seductive implication Jeromy had never experienced.

How does she do that? he wondered. *Her tone implies sex as she expels the odor of desire. How does she do that? Jesus, my boner has slipped its restraint and is sticking straight up. Thank God for the table.*

"We'll have to compare notes and experiences sometime, Don." She touched the top of his hand quickly and withdrew.

"Yeah, we could do that." Don looked a little dazed. Mary had that effect on men. Women were another matter—or not. Jeromy wasn't sure.

He was anxious for Don to go away so they could get it on. He was thinking about throwing her on top of the table, ripping her pants off, and having at it.

Jeromy had patience when it came to getting what he wanted. However, his dick was throbbing again. Mary appeared to be perfectly happy chatting with Don. In fact, she was paying very little attention to Jeromy. Just as he was starting to feel neglected, there was her hand again under the table. This time it lingered. She stroked him as she kept her eyes locked on Don's and continued the conversation.

Don shook himself alert—it was more of a shiver—and asked, "Are you guys going to eat? I could join you. I have some time before I have to get back."

Mary said easily, still looking at Don, "No, we've eaten already. We're just hanging out after the meeting." She instantly regretted mentioning that. "But you can go get something, and we'll sit with you."

"Yeah, I think I will. I'll be right back." Once Don started thinking about food, he had to be about it. He pushed back his chair and headed toward one of the open kiosks.

Jeromy moaned softly. "Damn! You're not getting rid of him." He was very aroused, and the continuing presence of her hand on his phallus was not helping his situation.

"Have patience, Jeromy. Don's a sweet guy. I don't want to hurt his feelings. He'll leave eventually."

He was in agony. As much as he didn't want to, he reached down and removed her hand. Mary smiled sweetly.

The plate in Don's hand was piled high: two double hamburgers with cheese and bacon, two orders of french fries, and a thirty-ounce Diet Coke. He sat and immediately dug in without offering to share. Talking around a mouthful of burger, he asked, "What was the meeting about? Was it about the hack?"

"Yes," Mary replied, "but it was short and mainly concerned Gordon looking into it. Not a big deal." She locked eyes with him again, casting him a subtle come-hither look. This time she kept her hands to herself.

Jeromy, who was calming down a little, wondered what this woman was up to. *Was she flirting with Don as she rubbed me?* He didn't know her very well—or anyone else, for that matter. Fauxbook was a start-up, and most of the team members were strangers to one another. *Was she really promising sex, or is she just a tease? Has she changed her mind and decided to use Don to cover her escape? Well, if that's the deal*, he thought angrily, *she's a bitch.*

"I heard someone was fired," Don said, continuing to chew.

"Where did you hear that?" Jeromy asked, now recovered enough to talk. His anger had quelled some, though not all, of his passion. Now he was considering getting up and leaving himself. "You know more than I do."

Don's food was disappearing fast. He was already halfway through his second double burger. Mary had turned off the allure, and Don was becoming bored as well as satiated.

There's a reason he's fat, Mary thought. *But fat might be good. It could be a different experience, and he'd be eager to please.*

The Freezer

Piling the remains of his meal and the accouterments onto his tray, Don finally pushed back his chair. Mary leaned over and gave him a kiss on his cheek and a "see you later" smile. He paused for a moment before saying, "I have to get back to work."

"Bye, Don," Mary said. "Later."

Both Don and Jeromy wondered what she meant by *later*. Her tone seemed filled with meaning.

"Good to see you, Don. Stop by again," Jeromy said insincerely. *What happens now?* he wondered. *Is she going to make excuses and leave?*

"Maybe I will have something to eat," Mary said with innuendo, her seductiveness turned back on.

How does she do that? Jeromy wondered. *Or is it me? Damn! She's got me turned back on again in an instant.*

"Okay, you get something to eat. I have to go back to work," he said irritably.

"Oh, silly, I'm just messing with you. Let's go fuck."

Again, her directness shocked him. This was what happened in his fantasies, not in the real world. He had never met a woman like this. "Okay," he replied hesitantly. The aura was back. *How can she turn this sexual tension on and off at will?* Her hand brushed his crotch again.

"Hey, what's happened here?" Mary asked, grasping his diminished manhood. "We're going to have to do something about this." She moved her chair closer and leaned against him. Jeromy looked around, a little concerned. But there was no one near them. His blood was flowing because of her gentle ministrations.

"There, that's better," she said as she felt it strain against its enclosure. "Come with me."

"Where are we going?" This was the strangest date he had ever been on—if indeed this could be defined as a date. Usually, with women, he was the aggressor, the one suggesting sex. He had never been with a woman like this. He wondered what would be next.

Just as they pushed their chairs back and stood, Carol Fisher walked over. "Hey, what are you guys up to?" she asked.

"Just hanging out," Jeromy replied as he vainly tried to hide the bulge with his hands. But, he was just calling attention to it. His face flushed as his erection bid welcome to this new, beautiful, female.

"Yep, just hanging out," Mary agreed, covering a smile with her hand.

"I'm still thinking about Leif and the virus. I can't believe what happened."

"Yeah, I was happy Jon didn't fire him, though Gordon would have if it had been up to him."

"I was worried this would be the end of him. I like Leif; he's sweet, shy, and a brilliant programmer." Carol looked down with a sad expression and noticed the swelling in Jeromy's pants. "Oh," she said in a higher pitch. "I'd better go. I have a lot of work to do."

As she walked away, Jeromy said, "She noticed." He was embarrassed.

"Yep. Should I have asked her to join us?" Mary replied with an innocent smile, her subtle sexiness on full display.

Jeromy said nothing as she took him by the hand. *Ask her to join us?* This was becoming more and more like one of his sexual fantasies. He found it hard to believe this was really happening.

She led him around the end of the food-service counter and then behind it. Halfway down, there was a doorway to the now-deserted kitchen and food-preparation area. Pulling him gently, she brought him through, past the stoves and counters. She stopped in front of a stainless-steel door secured by a large handle.

"Where are we?" Jeromy asked. "Where are we?"

"You'll see." She grasped the handle and pulled. She guided him into a large walk-in freezer and pulled the door shut behind them.

Around them, Jeromy saw chrome shelves packed with various foods, from chickens to butter. Large hunks of raw beef were hanging from hooks in the rear. Mary led him down one of the aisles and took a left. It was cold, and he was a little apprehensive, for a number of reasons. *What if someone locked the door? We'd freeze.*

Finally, she stopped. There was a blanket spread on the floor. *Mary has been here earlier today, and she prepared*, he thought. *But this is crazy; it's cold. What's she have in mind?*

She turned loose his hand and unbuttoned her blouse. It was off in an instant; she wore no bra. "Quick—it's cold; take off your clothes!" Her skirt followed—she wore no undergarments and was quickly naked.

"God, it's cold," she said matter-of-factly. "Hurry, take off your clothes."

He reached for her and grasped each side of her waist just below her tits. She was warm, almost hot, like a stove. It was amazing. He was freezing. She was working on his belt buckle, then the button and his zipper. Then she broke loose and worked his pants down off over his shoes.

"Take off your shirt," she ordered, as she removed his shoes.

"What?"

"Take off your shirt," she repeated. "This isn't going to work if we're not naked."

He was surprised to realize he was no longer cold. He took off his shirt and stood on the blanket in the freezer as she remained on her knees. She looked up at him and smiled coyly. She was leaning slightly forward so he could see the swell of her hips. "Are you warmer now?"

He was. Warmth spread throughout his body. He was losing track of time and having trouble keeping his balance.

Finally, Mary leaned back and said, "Get dressed. Hurry; it's going to get cold." She was quickly donning her garments.

He was slower, and for a moment, he was confused by the crackling sound that arose as he moved. The moisture in his clothes had frozen.

"Come on, Jeromy," she said. "Hurry; I'm freezing." Before he had his shirt buttoned, she grabbed his hand and led him back through the aisles of frozen meat. At the heavy freezer door, she released him and grasped the handle. "I'd think you would open the door for a lady," she said. Swinging it open, she exited, and he followed. She swung the door closed and shivered. "Damn! Now I'm cold."

He shivered and finished closing his shirt. Then he checked the other enclosures and walked around the counters. He sat at one of the tables and tied his shoes. Mary sat across from him and smiled sweetly.

"God," he said, "that was good. But what's the idea of doing it in a freezer?"

"Oh," she replied in her sexy tone, "I just wanted to see if I could do it."

"Do what?"

"Keep us both warm in a freezer. It was a challenge I was up for. And, it appears, so were you."

Jon's Way

Gordon had been summoned to Jon's office at the end of the corridor. He entered to find a stranger seated on one of two facing couches. Roger Aegel was sitting next to him. Gordon had met Roger a couple of times. He was fat, bald, and pompous. *But then so am I*, Gordon thought. *Maybe not so pompous.* Aegel had a reputation as a bully, a womanizer, and a sexual predator. With sagging hog jowls, he was not naturally attractive to women unless he applied the leverage of his position.

Jon was in a relaxed position on the opposite couch. There was no obvious place for Gordon to sit other than next to Jon, and he felt a bit awkward. He hesitated.

"Sit," Jon said, pointing to an upholstered chair positioned at ninety degrees to the parties. It seemed to Gordon to be just a little outside the circle. He wondered if he should read anything into that. *Perhaps not*, he thought. *Jon is not that subtle. But something is up.*

"Gordon," Jon said, "this is Jeff Hoover, a new addition to our team." Jon, in his usual flannel shirt and kakis, was in juxtaposition to Hoover's finely tailored suit, tie, and matching handkerchief. Gordon thought of Jon as a genuinely simple man, an outdoorsman who enjoyed canoeing and fishing in upper Maine, who was nonetheless a genius. He was a brawny man with piercing blue eyes who shunned publicity.

Hoover seems to be a new addition to the Fauxbook family, Gordon thought. *I wonder what Roger is going to think about that.*

Jon thought of the company as a family. He rarely fired anyone; rather, he sought to have everyone fit in. An unsatisfactory worker might be transferred to another job in the hope it would suit him or her better. In the worst case, Jon would arrange for the person to go back to school, at company expense, to earn an advanced degree or whatever.

Gordon hadn't taken his seat yet, so he approached Hoover with his hand extended. Jeff rose, took Gordon's hand with a firm grip, and locked eyes with a steely, unblinking stare. *Not too firm, but firm*, Gordon thought, hiding a smile. *This fellow is going to be a force to be dealt with.*

"A pleasure," Gordon said, not sure he meant it.

"Jeff is going to be our chief operating officer," Jon said. "He is a graduate of Southern Methodist University and Harvard Business School."

Gordon understood. Jon was a pious man who attended church every Sunday and contributed to church charities. A Southern Methodist University degree would impress him, and a Harvard degree would cover Jeff's bigotry. Jon would think this man a person to be trusted. *I wonder where Roger is going to fit in*, he thought. He had not arrived with a stellar reputation and looked like a small-town banker—not the friendly kind. *In fact, he resembles Henry F. Potter.*

Some in Roger's previous company called him the bogeyman for his aggressive retaliation toward those who offended him. Roger also was engulfed in a cloud of whispers about his predatory behavior toward women. There were persistent rumors Aegel propositioned female employees for sexual favors using his position and power as both the carrot and the stick. The culture of fear was such no one would dare come forward. And he demanded absolute loyalty from those who worked for him. He was known for monitoring employee e-mails and phone conversations and hiring private investigators. "Watch out for the enemy within," he had told the staff during one companywide meeting.

Roger seemed to Gordon to be an odd person for Jon to recruit for a senior management position. On the other hand, Gordon was aware of Jon's propensity to discard rumors and to think the best of people.

The management organization at Fauxbook was a mystery, as was the organization at Jon's previous company, MCS. But MCS had become the second-largest peripheral company in the world, and there Jon had made the fortune that was financing Fauxbook. *So, who am I to question him?* Gordon concluded. *Genius is always hard to understand, except in hindsight.*

There was a soft knock on the door, which was open. Anne Jankin, Jon's secretary, announced Barry Konrad.

"Come in, Barry," Jon said. "This is Jeff Hoover. You know everyone else. Jeff is going to be our chief operating officer."

Barry moved quickly to shake Jeff's hand, and Jeff again rose. "Good to meet you, Jeff. I believe you will enjoy it here. It's a nice place to work, good people, and Jon is a great man to work for."

"Likewise, and I'm sure I will, Barry," Jeff replied.

Another knock at the door, and Carol Fisher entered and was introduced.

And there you have it, Gordon thought. *This is the way the company is run: by the seat of Jon's pants and by unannounced informal meetings at the end of the corridor.* Again, he wondered if this was the best way to steer the ship. And again he squelched the thought. Jon and Jon's way had been proven by past success.

"Carol is a part-time intern, planning to work full time during summer vacation. She is working on her PhD in computer science."

"What is your area of interest, Carol?" Barry asked as he undressed her with his eyes.

"My thesis is on goal-seeking programs with a special emphasis on designing the hardware to support the algorithms," she replied in a serious tone. Carol was young but very intense and proper. She wore a black pantsuit over a pure-white silk blouse. Her long blond hair was a spectacular contrast to her black jacket. Jeff was enthralled, and everyone, except Jon, saw it.

Gordon smiled. *Good luck, Jeff*, he thought. *Carol is the antithesis of Mary. She's the most straitlaced young lady I know.*

"All right," Jon said. "We're all here. Carol, you might wonder why you are here. I want you to show Jeff around and explain our ways. For all of you, and as most of you know, the most important touchstone here at Fauxbook is you are expected to do what's right. And I want you to encourage your subordinates in that philosophy. I know it sounds simple. However, it isn't. Actually, it's easy to do what's right. The hard thing is to know what the right thing to do is. That's why we are here to help each another."

Barry, Roger, and Carol were listening intently to the words of one of the world's greatest entrepreneurs. Jeff was distracted by Carol. She was young, gorgeous, slim, and well built, and she presented herself as completely unavailable.

Gordon, who had heard Jon's stock speech many times before, restrained himself from rolling his eyes. But he knew Jon was right on many different levels.

Carol was quiet, showing no expression. Beneath the calm veneer, she was star struck, in awe of these men, who were her childhood heroes. They had led great companies and created the industry. She especially admired Jon and found it hard to believe she had been invited to call him by his first name. She hadn't done that yet but was working up to it and looking forward to doing so.

"Fauxbook," Jon continued, "will be the most successful, ethical, and useful social network site ever launched. It will become part of everyone's life and make their life better for being part of the Fauxbook family." He swept his arm inclusively. "Jeff, do you have any questions?"

"No, Jon, not at the moment. Let me spend some time looking around with Carol's help. I'll talk to some people and read your employee manual and other literature. Then I'm sure I'll have a lot of questions. Until then, I'm ready to learn."

"Anybody," Jon said. "Does anyone have questions for Jeff?"

"Sure," Gordon said. "Jeff, give a brief synopsis of your qualifications and background. And tell us why you feel qualified for this job."

"That's a good idea," Jon said. "Just briefly. And if you prefer, we could postpone this until you've had time to prepare."

"No, Jon, gentlemen, Miss Fisher, that's fine. I feel prepared to explain myself. Briefly…" He smiled broadly, as if making a joke. "I was born in Pittsburgh. I studied engineering and then switched to business and graduated with a master's in business administration from Harvard. I was in the top five percent of my class and graduated summa cum laude. I am wicked smart and plan to prove it here at Fauxbook. I've been involved in marketing computer hardware and software at a high level for the last five years and have conceived of a number of systems in use today throughout the industry. Brief enough?"

Another egoist, Gordon thought. *Here we go. Jon thinks he likes these guys, but he never does. This is going to be an interesting year.*

"Any questions?" Jon asked.

"Sounds good to me," Barry said as everyone else grunted or nodded. "Welcome aboard."

"Good, good," Jon said. "Carol, take him away, and make sure he's fed."

The Tour

Carol led Jeff down the stairway, across the causeway to the next building, and down another level to the cafeteria.

"How many employees do you have now?" Jeff asked.

"Two hundred and forty," she answered. "Well, two hundred and forty-one now," she said with a ladylike smile. "They are almost all programmers and graphic designers. Some are marketing, Jon is filling the management positions, and there are a few network and Internet experts. Gordon doesn't believe in throwing thousands of programmers at a project. He thinks great art is accomplished by a few. However, we're building out for eventually employing six thousand people here."

"Six thousand?"

"Yes, eventually. The number is in Gordon's head. There's a book that claims Apple Computer, in the old days, employed six thousand programmers to develop a new operating system, to no avail. Over a ten-year period, they accomplished nothing."

"Really?"

"Well, that's what Gordon says. So he plans to keep the number small until the site is up. But then we'll need support people."

Jeff followed behind and admired the view. Carol was gorgeous and looked somewhat familiar. He felt as if he'd seen her somewhere but couldn't recall where.

They made their way through the cafeteria's outside tables, shaded by umbrellas. *Damn!* he thought. *This is big enough for a lot more people. The venue is huge.* Much of it was unoccupied because, as Carol had said, there were currently relatively few employees. Carol made her way to the salad bar, and Jeff descended on the sushi. They rejoined at a table in between, not far from where Mary and Jeromy had rendezvoused.

As they started to eat, Jeff said, "Tell me about yourself, Carol. How did you find yourself at Fauxbook?"

"Hmm." She held up one finger as she chewed. After a moment, she said, "I'm not sure I'm that interesting. But I'll tell you. I grew up in West Virginia—the poor part, which is saying a lot. My father was a coal miner when he was working, which was not a lot of the time. He's still alive but dying of black lung."

"Oh, I'm sorry," Jeff said nodding and leaning toward her.

"Not your problem," she answered in an edgy tone, her facade slipping for just a moment. Underneath her calm, proper front, Carol was as tough as nails tempered in oil.

There was a pause as Jeff, a bit surprised, absorbed what she had said.

"How did you get out of that situation?" he asked.

She smiled, her cheerful countenance restored. "I did well in school. After high school, I got a scholarship to West Virginia Tech. I worked part time. I'm part time here at Fauxbook, go to school, and work nights and weekends during the school season, and I've been promised full time with benefits during the summer. When I graduate, Gordon has promised me a job here. I'm looking forward to that."

"Does your interest, goal-seeking programs, fit in here?"

"Perhaps not, but I'm flexible. And as you say, I'm wicked and smart."

An interesting turn of phrase, Jeff thought. "It's often not easy to be the smartest guy in the room, especially if you are female."

"In West Virginia, that is certainly true," she said, understanding his meaning. "Not so much in the tech world or in academia. Smart people almost always like other smart people and are not threatened by others even when they are smarter. Not so much in West Virginia. I'm never going back."

Again, he detected a strident tone. *Interesting.* "What do you do for work on nights and weekends?"

"Enough about me," she said changing easily to everyone's favorite subject. "Tell me about you."

"Well, first, I'm not going to jump your bones, though you are gorgeous. I'm a happily married man with three wonderful children."

"Oh, thank God for that." She laughed. "I mean, thank you. I think."

"Yeah, you're welcome. I'm sure you saw Barry's look," he said, externalizing the other man's lust. She blushed, and he was sorry he had mentioned it. She seemed like a nice young woman.

"I love my work. I like people but only the best and as a manager; my goal is to weed out the workforce until we employ only the best. Then, I'll start weeding again until only the excellent are left."

"Ah," she said. "Darwinian."

"I guess you could say that," he said, impressed by this girl, "but you can't have an excellent company without excellent people."

They ate in silence for some moments, admiring the view. The cafeteria was on the south side of the building, alongside the river. The building had once been a wool mill, which had derived the power necessary to run the machines from the river. Jon had repurposed and remodeled the building to house the high-tech company Fauxbook.

After lunch, Carol showed Jeff the programming section, marketing, administration, and the servers in the computer building. "We use massive parallel clusters of off-the-shelf computers to create a parallel virtual machine. We're writing our own midware, too. The Fauxbook application is light on actual computer processing but very demanding of throughput. We expect billions of users, and there are no systems that currently specifically support what's needed.

"And our midware makes it almost crash proof, as any number of individual computers can go offline and the virtual machine continues to run. Though if it loses enough of its nodes, it will slow down."

"Nothing is crash proof," Jeff stated. "What if the building burns down?"

"There will be two mirrored sites. One is being built in California and another in Ireland. The workload will be automatically shifted to one of the other sites as needed. In fact, we plan to shift the load if major maintenance is needed at one site."

"That is impressive. We can truly market our site as unbreakable."

"Yep," she said with an enigmatic smile. "No doubt it's easier to market a feature when it's true."

"Hey," Jeff replied with a frown, "what did I say to deserve that?"

"Sorry, I didn't mean it the way it came out. I was just bragging about our hardware in an awkward way. Sorry."

"Apology accepted," he said with a smile of his own. "Actually, I was just busting you—I knew what you meant."

"You're terrible! You made me feel bad just for fun."

"Okay, now I feel bad."

There was a pause as they looked at each other.

"Are we flirting with each other?" She frowned and bit the corner of her lip.

He looked her in the eye for a moment. Her directness was refreshing. "No," he replied. "We are not. I understand what you are saying and you may be disappointed. But what we've been doing is making friends with each other. I find you interesting, fun, and intelligent. The latter opinion I reserve for very few people. I like you and think we can become good friends. But I'm a happily married man with no thought to stray," he lied.

She stared into his eyes for a poignant moment. Then she reached out and shook his hand. "Friends."

Inception

Alex arrived at Fauxbook with enthusiasm, and unbeknown to him, he was just in time for the singularity. With a newly printed degree in computer science from MIT, he was one of the many new hires straight out of college. He was young, excited, and ready to implement change or just to make something operate more efficiently.

For newly hired programmers, there was an obligatory interview with Gordon Wysmann. As Alex approached Gordon's office, he wasn't nervous. He was excited. The opportunity to meet the man himself was intoxicating.

The door was open, so he knocked on the frame. "Mr. Wysmann, I'm Alex Cromwell. We have an appointment."

"Yes, come in," Gordon replied.

Alex noticed an abacus on the wall behind Gordon's desk and smiled. *The basics, of course.* The cubicle was very neat. There was a bookcase filled to overflowing. A computer terminal on the desk, a couple of books, a notepad, and a pen. *A notepad?* He thought. *What's that for?*

"Come in, Alex." Gordon rose and extended his hand. "Sit here." He pointed to a chair. "And call me Gordon. We're pretty casual here. I imagine today will be the last time you wear a suit to work. I hope you have not made a large investment in suits."

"No, sir. I mean yes, sir. That is, I have only this one suit," he stammered as he shook the great man's hand. Suddenly, faced with the reality, he was unexpectedly nervous.

Gordon smiled, remembering when he had been a newly minted electrical engineer. There had been no computer science degree when he went to school. He, almost all by himself, had invented the college programs for computer science and taught many of the first classes. He understood why these kids were awestruck. He wasn't sure whether to encourage them or to tell them the truth. He was just a regular guy, perhaps smarter than most (but so were these kids), who bungled along doing the best he could and discovering, mostly by accident, astonishing things.

"Would you like a cup of coffee? Or something stronger?" he asked.

Alex smiled at the thought of getting drunk with Gordon Wysmann. *That would be a tale to tell.*

"No, sir, I'm fine. Thank you."

"Well then, tell me about yourself, your aspirations, your dreams," Gordon said.

Alex hadn't expected that. He'd thought Mr. Wysmann would ask about his education, his experience; he wasn't prepared for this. But he plowed right in.

"I'm from Iowa, corn fed, with all that entails. I was brought up in a hardworking, religious family with midwestern values. I know I'm too late for the hardware revolution. That ended years ago. Today computers are commodities. And the software revolution is over, too. There were programs, apps, developed for every need. Today, need is a small speck in the rearview mirror of application development. The focus is to create a need and then fill it. The goal has become to offer consumers something they don't yet know they need and can't do without."

"Interesting," Gordon commented. "So, you think our job is to fulfill wants people don't know they have?"

"I do," he replied, wondering if he were straying into dangerous territory by telling this famous man there was no need for his talent, only wants, and sometimes dubious wants at that. But he had no choice other than to go on. "The concept is new and was first realized by Steve Jobs at Apple. Apple was the most successful computer company in the world."

"Apple, really?" Gordon asked.

"How many of their products filled a need? Computers were originally created to fill concrete, pressing needs. In the early days, accurate gun tables had to be produced for each weapon the military possessed and for every new gun developed. Computers were good at this, faster than the human computers of the time and cheaper. Then, the census demanded an enormous amount of number crunching…a computer's specialty. As the price decreased and the availability of computers increased, they were loaded with software for increasingly mundane tasks, and fortunes were made.

"Moore's law stated computer power would double every eighteen months, and it did until the consumer-level computer became as powerful as anyone needed. Customers stopped upgrading their hardware yearly, and that was the end of profits for the traditional hardware builder, whose huge profits depended on ever more capable machines for users to upgrade to. On the other side, software engineers created thousands of solutions in search of a problem." He felt it was time to take a breath.

"I think you are going to fit in just fine. Welcome to Fauxbook," Gordon said with an ironic smile. He stood and shook Alex's hand, and it was over.

That was a good thing because Alex was beginning to sweat. Exiting the cubicle, he was met by a pleasant-looking middle-aged woman with a 1950s style.

"Hello, Alex," she greeted him. "I'm Anne Jankin, Jon's secretary. You have a meeting with Jon tomorrow. For now, let me show you to your workplace and escort you to lunch. It's about that time, and you must be hungry and exhausted after your meeting with Gordon," she said sympathetically. "He means well, but he can be draining. He is very intense."

"Yes," Alex responded, glad for the reassurance. She guided him down the corridor to an empty and sterile-looking cubicle. It contained nothing except a desk with a computer terminal on it, a chair—for a visitor, he presumed—and an empty bookcase.

"Don't worry," Anne said. "Spend this afternoon setting up your computer to suit you. After a few days, you'll make this space your own. I'll have them bring over a couch. Most find that useful."

"Thank you, Ms. Jankin."

"Anne, call me Anne. We'll get to know each other pretty well in no time. Fauxbook is just one big family and getting bigger. We take care of one another."

"Thank you," he said, unexpectedly overwhelmed by the speed in which he was being absorbed.

"Good. Follow me, and I'll show you the cafeteria."

Knowing he was from Iowa, she left him in the comfort-food section. And indeed, he ordered fried chicken, mashed potatoes, and corn on the cob.

Alex had been born in Clear Lake, Iowa. On the west side of town. Near the lake. The lake had been clear then. The apex of the year was the Fourth of July. The carnival came to town, and everyone from a hundred miles around came to visit.

On the Fourth of July of his thirteenth year, he had seen a thin blond girl standing on a paddleboard navigating just offshore, moving from south to north. He couldn't make out much of her upper torso, as it was covered with a life jacket. But he could see a narrow bikini string as it passed just over the armhole in the life jacket, and that was enough.

He did, however, have a clear view of her butt. It was fine. He had considered himself an ass man thereafter, and this girl had a butt he'd only dreamt about.

He had been thirteen.

When he arrived at Fauxbook, he actually had not moved beyond dreaming about girls' butts. Whatever—butts focused his thoughts, and he felt pleasantly guilty. Guilt was a concept well understood and accepted in Clear Lake. Religion was the glue that held civilization together, and original sin was the foundation. Alex had never missed a Sunday service with his family during his formative years, though he'd considered himself an ass man since he'd become aware of the difference between boys and girls. He found the guilt difficult to put aside.

First Pass

When Alex returned to his office cubicle, he found a young woman, a girl, lounging in the chair behind his desk—*his* chair.

"Hi," he said, surprised to find someone in his new office. On first glance, it didn't look like a business visit. She was wearing sneakers, blue jeans, and a tight T-shirt. It was obvious there was no bra beneath. The sight didn't exactly take his breath away. Though the shapes of her nipples were clear, she wasn't well endowed. Yet there was something about her.

"Hi," she said with a sly smile. "Welcome to Fauxbook. I'm Mary. I work in sales training and documentation. The two are sort of combined until we staff up." She smiled at the pun only she understood.

"That sounds like an important job," he said, a little confused as to what she was doing in his office.

"I think so. I majored in English at Oklahoma State, followed a boy to Boston, and here I am."

He sat in the chair on the other side of the desk. It felt a little awkward she had taken his chair. His seemed in the inferior position. "What can I do for you, Mary?" he asked.

"Oh, I just dropped by to welcome you to Fauxbook, introduce myself, and let you know there are some regular people here. I'm sure everyone you've met so far has been a muckety-muck or worse."

"That's about right," he said, smiling.

"Well, here I am, just a regular girl, at your service."

Somehow, he guessed she was not a regular girl at all. But he still didn't know what was going on. Maybe it was just as she said, and he was trying to read something into it that wasn't there.

"What's your job here?" she asked. "I guess it's something to do with programming, judging by where your office is."

"Yeah, I'm just a grunt programmer."

"What's your specialty?" she asked with an innocent smile.

He was uncomfortable. "I feel like I'm being interviewed."

"Oh, sorry, just curious. But in a sense, you are. I want to get to know the people whose code I'm going to be documenting. If I don't know what you are about and the overview and purpose of what you're doing, I discover, belatedly, I'm programming trivia rather than getting to the point. That's all, nothing sinister."

Now he felt chastised as if by an older sister. But the way she was leaning toward him, pulling her T-shirt even tighter across her breasts, was nothing like an elder sister.

She continued, "People code, and design computers, to match their personality. If they are kind and understanding, the programs they write will be forgiving. If they are sexy, they tend to write seductive code. On the other hand, if they have a controlling personality…well, you know what I mean."

"Okay, I understand. My major interest is machine intelligence. Some call the area AI, or artificial intelligence."

"A machine can be intelligent?" she asked innocently, though she already knew the answer. Men, she knew, liked to lecture women, and she was willing to provide them the opportunity when it suited her.

"Sure. Well, sort of. Are you familiar with the Eliza code?"

"Yes, I think I am. Is that Joseph Weizenbaum's test for machine intelligence?" She was intentionally a little off the mark without appearing to be completely ignorant.

"Well, sort of…it is a computer program designed to have a conversation with users back in the mid-1960s. The user typed in statements or questions, and the program formulated an answer from keywords in the user input and then produced the output."

"In the 1960s," she gushed. "That's amazing." She looked at him with rapt attention. "Before I was born," she mused.

"Yeah, me too. It was primitive, but that was the beginning. We've come a long way since then. My goal is to develop thinking programs that accomplish tasks without being specifically programmed, line by line, to do so."

"The computer thinks?" she asked, already knowing the answer. Mary was a very smart young woman and very good at hiding it. *Everybody and everything has goals.* She smiled.

"No and yes…The machine can be made to think. However, it depends on your definition of thinking. I don't believe a machine thinks the same way we do; it's different." Somehow, he realized, the tension between them was building. It seemed sexual. But she had not done or said anything overt.

"Different?"

"Different," he said. "There are a lot of differences, from small to overarching. The machine, for example, has no ego. The machines programmed to play chess have no difficulty retreating. Human players are constantly driven by their ego to advance. But it's much more than that. The machines ponder possibilities and calculate odds within the parameters of what they have been programmed to think about. However, those parameters are always expanding. So, who knows?"

"I think I understand. Often, lately, I've had difficulty knowing if I'm speaking with a person or a machine on the phone."

"The phone systems have gotten very good," he said. "But they are working within a very well-defined problem set that applies to the company they service. If the conversation strays from that envelope, the machine will transfer you to a human. But the machines just keep getting better and better. Human intervention is necessary less and less."

"Yeah," she said. "If you ask the machine if it wants to have sex, it's probably time for human intervention." She smiled.

That was a strange thing to say, he thought. *And it's the second time she's mentioned sex.*

"Well, I should be going," she said, rising. "Thanks for your time. It was good to meet you." She gave him a last appraising look and smiled. "Later," she said in a husky tone.

Alex moved around behind his desk and took stock. The inventory didn't take long, as there was nothing there except a desk, empty drawers, a chair, a computer terminal, a keyboard and mouse, and an empty bookcase. He toggled the power switch on the base of the computer. It came alive almost instantly. Smiling, he started to explore the space and the programs. Everything he would need, at least in the short term, was there. He opened and played with a high-end design program, a word processor, a spreadsheet, e-mail, and a browser. The computer was very fast, which was satisfying.

Leaning back, he looked around again. *It would be nice to have a couch in here*, he thought. *Ms. Jankin is right.* Sometimes he enjoyed an afternoon nap, and it would be handy for those late nights he knew would come, which sometimes extended into the next day. He could hear soft voices chatting in adjacent cubicles and knew the team was getting to know one another. *I'm sure that's all Mary was doing*, he thought. *Perhaps I should get out and wander around a bit myself.*

Pairing Up

Wandering the buildings laid out along the bank of the Assabet River, Alex found them disconcertingly empty. And big. There was a lot of room in this old mill building, which was rapidly being remodeled. There were construction workers throughout. The remodeling seemed to be expanding outward in all directions from the administration building, with the offices filling up with new hires as soon as they were complete. One five-story wing extending to the south was labeled *Marketing* by a discreet sign over the connecting hallway. An entire building to the west was *Engineering*. Past that there was a group of buildings, all labeled *R & D*. He figured it was a euphemism for *Programming*. The old mill building retained its fourteen- to eighteen-foot ceilings supported by huge beams and wide-walnut-plank floors scarred by over a hundred years of use. To the east, an entirely new concrete building was going up.

As he stood in the new glass-enclosed footbridge connecting the Administration Building with B Building and overlooked the new C Building, Jon Johnsson stepped up behind him.

"That's the building for the computer cluster, Alex. It's the only scratch, purpose-built building in the complex. It has to be, as we have to have an enormous amount of wiring both internally and connecting us to the Internet. In addition, we plan to cool the computers with river water as well as solar-powered air conditioning."

"The whole complex is impressive, Mr. Johnsson. And it's going to be solar powered?"

"Jon—call me Jon. Not all of the complex will be solar powered, though we'll use renewable power as extensively as we can. Many of the old buildings, as well as this new one, will be fitted with solar panels. We also plan to restore the power dam built in the eighteen hundreds and install new turbines to generate electricity."

"We could be energy independent," Alex commented.

I like that he says "we," Jon thought. *I like everyone to think of the company as a team if not a family.*

"We'll be close to it," he said.

"When do you plan to have the site go live?" Alex asked.

"I'm on my way down to talk to Gordon and Barry about that very thing. Would you like to come along?"

"That would be great if I'm not in the way."

"It will be fine. Have you met Barry Konrad? I know you've had a meeting with Gordon. That's a requirement." He smiled.

"No, sir. What does Barry do here?"

"He handles the logistics of getting the materials and equipment here on time and of the installation of the machines for the cluster. Right now, we are simulating the cluster with an IBM z13 mainframe. And we may initially go live or beta with that configuration."

Jon started walking, and Alex said, "A z13: isn't that an expensive stopgap?"

"Yes, it is, but necessary. And it is likely we'll be able to make it part of the eventual cluster. The cluster will, of course, continue to grow as our base of users increases. Gordon and I are thinking of eventually using the IBM machine as Internet traffic controller."

Alex was astonished. "An IBM z13 as a router! If that's not gross overkill, this system is going to be huge," he exclaimed.

"Yes, we're planning for billions of users. In time, almost everyone in the world will have a Fauxbook account."

Jon led the way to a small meeting room adjacent to his office in the administration building. They encountered Jeff walking the other way, and Jon motioned for him to follow.

Alex's first sight was of a handsome young woman seated on the couch next to the oak meeting table. Her long, straight blond hair was stunning, and it floated slightly in the air as she glanced toward him. On second thought, he decided she was beyond handsome, though it was a little hard to tell with her seated.

Gordon was sitting at the conference table across from another man, whom Jon introduced as Barry Konrad.

"Anne," Jon called through the door, "please see if Jeff can join us. Sit, Alex," he said, indicating the couch next to the blonde.

It gets better and better, Alex thought. *I guess he must have heard it before.*

Gordon was thinking, *Here we go again—another one of Jon's famous meetings.*

"And, Gordon, introduce this lovely lady?" Jon asked.

"Sorry, Jon," he said, rising. "This is Carol Fisher, an intern who plans to join us full time after finishing her PhD this summer.

"Carol, Jon Johnsson, our fearless leader, and Alex Cromwell, a programmer specializing in AI."

Carol rose and shook hands with both. The sight fulfilled the promise that had formed in Alex's mind. *Damn, she's good-looking!* he thought as he fell in love, or at least lust, and immediately felt guilty.

"Pleasure to meet you all," she said.

"Jon. Call me Jon."

"Yes, sir. And a pleasure to meet you, Mr. Cromwell."

"You may call me Alex, please."

"Good, nice people," Jon commented. "We have a good group. Now, let's get to it. I want to get an understanding of when we can get the site up internally, a projected beta date, and when we hope to go live. All of this needs to be coordinated with engineering, programming, marketing, technical support, administration, and outside vendors."

Well, this is one way to do it, Gordon thought, not unkindly. *It's just not my way. But it's Jon's way, and it's always worked before.*

"Barry, I'd like you to meet with the outside vendors next week and report back to Gordon and me."

Konrad nodded, and Jeff spoke. "It looks to me going live is at least a year out. I'll be ready. My plan is to create an initial interest among potential advertisers through networking, lots of lunches, and then ramp up over the next six months. I'll need something to show them at that point, and my team and I will start selling."

"What exactly do you need to show them?" Gordon asked.

"It would be best to have at least a demonstration site that worked reasonably well. I assume we'll have that. If not, I'll work with what's available."

"Okay, let's work on a project plan that gives us a working site in six months, a beta in eight, and live in a year," Jon said.

Alex found himself nodding along with the important people in the room. He looked over; Carol was nodding, too. *Jon is amazing.* The whole thing from plan to completion had taken less than ten minutes.

Gordon was thinking the same thing with some trepidation.

As the group broke up—Alex couldn't help but notice Jon left without him—Carol put a hand on his shoulder to keep him from standing. Glancing at her, he leaned back against the couch.

Carol removed her hand, which disappointed Alex, and turned toward him. "You're an artificial-intelligence expert?" she asked.

"I'd like to think so. But the truth is in this industry, expertise fades. Everything has to be relearned at least every eighteen months unless you are the one reinventing it. That's what I aspire to be: an innovator, not an expert. However, right at the moment, I'm fairly current. So you can put your hand back."

She didn't, though she smiled, displaying perfect white teeth, and that was enough for the moment. "I'd like to join your team," she said. "My interest is in goal-achieving systems, a subset of AI. I'm mainly focused on the hardware to support the system."

"I didn't know I had a team," he said.

"You do now. I've been asking around about how the hierarchy works here. I've been getting some unusual answers. It seems we're allowed, even encouraged, to form our own teams or interest groups. People call it different things. We can even belong to more than one team."

"I should form a team," he said, thinking it would be worthwhile to do so just to have her in it.

"Well, yes…I would be a team leader myself, but I'm only an intern, part time, for now. Later maybe. This is what I propose we do." Carol outlined a comprehensive outline of her plan and the composition and goals of "his" team.

"So," he said when she finished, "basically, you want to take over the world, starting with this company."

She smiled again but said nothing.

Carol Takes Charge

"I'll handle 50 percent of the middleware, 10 percent of the hardware project, and 10 percent of the application software." Alex understood quickly it would be his team and Carol would be in charge.

"Okay, that sounds like a starting plan. We'll need a user-interface expert," he said.

"Yes, that project can run concurrently. I'll talk to Gordon about finding someone. I've also found a lab in the programming building no one has claimed yet. I think we should move in."

"How do we do that?" Alex asked. "Are there forms to fill out or what?"

"No," she said seriously. "We'll just move our stuff in and put a sign on the door. I already have maintenance painting a sign. Okay, I'm off to see Gordon."

Only after she left did Alex realize he'd forgotten to ask her where the lab was located. *She's like a whirlwind.*

He decided to retreat to his cubicle until further developments, which would happen sooner than he expected. The programmers were housed, or *warehoused*, in a building connected to reception and administration by a second-floor causeway. It led to a balcony overlooking the steel-walled offices. *Cubicles*: there was no other word. The ceiling was high, three stories, with the balcony continuing all the way around and the managers' offices on the outside wall. The cubicles on the ground floor were formed of five-foot steel walls that were infinitely movable. There was a row of offices, with doors along the west wall. Leif had been assigned one to which all of the network connections had been removed per Jon's instructions.

Alex descended the stairway and navigated, not very well, the maze to his assigned cubicle. *I'll have to get a plant so I can recognize my office.* After two wrong turns and a dead end, he recognized his coat on the hanger just inside the door. Entering, he was surprised to find Mary relaxed in his guest chair. It was just a folding metal chair positioned on the opposite side of his steel desk from his plastic, swiveling office chair.

"Mary," he said, "good to see you." He wondered how she had found his office.

"Pizza tonight?" she said.

"Pizza?"

"Yes, I have a coupon. What time will you be home? I'll bring pizza and beer."

"Beer?" Alex was a little short of words.

"Yeah, beer. We'll have pizza and beer to welcome you to Fauxbook."

"Okay, but you haven't been here much longer than I have. We'll welcome you, too."

"Sounds good," she said. "I'll see you at seven."

"Do you know where I live?" he asked.

"Of course. I do my homework. See you later." And she was gone.

He logged in to his workstation and worked on personalizing it. After he arranged the program icons the way he liked them, he downloaded some of his favorite pictures from the cloud. He realized he would most likely be moving. But it didn't matter. Wherever he was in the company, he had only to log in to a terminal, and his computer identity would come along with him.

He tweaked and arranged until 4:00 p.m., and then, without really having anything to do, he left. He guessed it would be a while before things got ramped up and organized—though Carol, apparently, was moving fast.

After taking his time leaving the building and driving home, he took a shower and shaved—*Might as well be prepared*—before the doorbell rang precisely at 7:00 p.m. She had set a six-pack of Samuel Adams on the floor of the hallway, carried a large pizza in her left hand, and rung the bell with her right.

"Hi, Mary," Alex said. "Welcome." A new wave of confusion came over him as he wondered what was going on. Was she chasing him?

"Alex, thank you. I've come bearing pizza, and…" she said, bending to retrieve the six-pack, "beer."

Most likely she is here lobbying for a job. Maybe she heard about Carol's plan to put together a team, and she wants in. Though it was still warm in Boston, she was wearing a knee-length coat. But that made sense; it was November and would be chilly later.

"Hey, I like your apartment," she said.

Now he knew she was lying. It was just a simple efficiency with the kitchen at one end, by the door, and a bed at the other, with a small dining table in between. The furniture was rented, and he had hung no pictures, nor had he moved his books into the stark bookcase. Most of his belongings were still in cardboard boxes on the floor. There was a bank of LED lights illuminating the kitchen and entranceway, and a lone floor lamp next to the bed. He knew there was nothing nice about the place other than function.

"Thank you. Do I need to heat up the pizza?"

"Sure." She smiled. "That would be nice. Just set the oven on low." She handed him the pizza. She removed her coat and took a seat at the table. He turned, set the pizza box on the stovetop, and turned on the oven. What had he just seen? He stopped himself from turning back for another look. Rather, he deliberately set the oven to warm and slid the pizza box in before turning and asking, "Beer?"

She was wearing a woolen sweater with an open weave of quarter-inch holes. And it looked as if there was nothing but flesh underneath. As she spoke, she twisted her upper body just a little, enough for her left nipple to protrude through one of the holes and the movement to pull it back and forth. Her appraising eyes caught him looking, and a sly smile appeared on her lips. The garment seemed to be having the desired effect.

He opened and set a beer in front of her, saying, "Sorry, no glasses yet." As he spoke, she twisted at the waist, and the nipple disappeared back into the sweater.

"No problem," she said sweetly, smiling at his obvious discomfort. She lifted the bottle and tilted her head back for a large swig.

Now he was certain she had nothing on beneath the peekaboo sweater. Then, just as he was absorbing the situation, she swung her legs from under the table. He could see she had nothing on under her skirt.

Alex moved past her and sat on the edge of the bed, staring at her. After a long moment, she gave a small nod and joined him there. The pizza was forgotten. It was Monday.

Building the Team

"Alex," Carol said from the opening to his cubicle the next morning, "I got an interface guy. He was just leaving Gordon's office after his interview as I got there. He's going to meet us in the new lab. Grab your stuff." And she was gone. He picked up his coat and rushed after her. She led the way out of B Building, which was mostly occupied by marketing, across the parking lot to A Building. Alex considered the naming a result of a lack of imagination, which he wasn't sure boded well for the company.

The A Building butted right up against the edge of the millpond, on top of the retaining wall. It had been the original opening room where workers in the eighteen hundreds had removed the ties from bales of raw cotton. The operation had posed a fire hazard, so the building was removed from the main mill. As yet, there was no connecting causeway. You had to go outside to get to Building A. Alex wondered how much fun that would be during the depth of the Boston winter. But he noted there was an adjacent parking lot to the west. *I wonder if I can get a parking permit for that lot.*

B Building and part of D Building also adjoined the millpond, demonstrating the importance of waterpower in the eighteen hundreds.

Originally, it had been a three-story building. However, there had been a problem with the integrity of the hundred-year-old floors and difficulties creating offices among all of the columns supporting the upper floors. The architects had alleviated the situation by removing the floors of the two upper stories and installing stepped-back mezzanines. It was the most extensive remodeling in the entire complex. The first mezzanine was larger, about a third of the area of the first floor, and it was to house middle management. The upper mezzanine was set back and about a tenth of the size of the first floor. It would be reserved for the elite. Both mezzanines had unusually low guardrails that made Carol nervous when she got too close. They seemed to her the perfect height to trip over and too low to catch your fall.

In the end, it didn't work out that way, as the Fauxbook hierarchy or management structure was ill defined. Carol had appropriated about half of the first balcony. She immediately started filling out work orders to convert the first floor to a large lab, open in the center and filled with workstations on the periphery.

"Where did you get the work orders?" Alex asked.

"Oh, I picked them up from Anne's desk. They were already signed."

"Anne Jankin! Jon's secretary?"

"Uh-huh," she replied distractedly, focused on filling out the forms.

A young man with long brown hair entered. He wore blue jeans and a wool shirt with a pocket protector filled with pens.

"Hey," he said. "My name's Zeist, and I'm told I'll be working here."

"Ah," Carol said, "the interface guy. Just find a spot you like on the second level and let me know what you need. That's Alex." She pointed. "He and I will be working on the back end. He's the team leader."

She finished the work orders and left Alex and Zeist to get to know each other. After making her way through the labyrinth of the old mill, she knocked on Leif's closed door. "Leif," she said as she entered without waiting for an answer, "you've been reassigned. Log out, grab your stuff, and follow me."

Back at the lab, she explained that one of the work orders would create a private office for Leif on the second level, with no access to the network. "Per Jon's orders," she said, officially. "And," she told one of the maintenance workers who had shown up during her brief absence, "he wants it done now."

"What do you have in mind for Leif?" Alex asked. "You know he's in trouble and not allowed anywhere near our network or the Internet. What's he going to do?"

"He's going to do the bots," she said. "He doesn't need the network or the Internet to create bots."

"Bots?"

"Yes, bots, robots," she said, obviously ready to move on to something else but willing to placate Alex. "We're planning for billions of users. There is no way to test the system for durability without straining it. We need software robots, bots, billions of them, to help us hammer the system and find weaknesses. Then we'll work on it until the system can stand up to the volume. We don't want a DOS hack caused by our own users."

Alex knew how bad a denial of service hack could be. It could overwhelm systems and bring them to their knees. An inadequate system overrun by its own users would suffer the same fate. "Good idea."

A week later, Mary Adams attached herself to the team after hearing it was where things were happening. "You're going to need documentation," she declared. "And here I am to take care of that." She was wearing bell-bottom pants of many colors and a top that left her midriff bare when she removed her jacket, which she did as she entered Leif's office.

Promptly at 5:00 p.m., she and Leif left arm in arm—both smiling.

Carol and Alex were bent over a drawing table outlining the workflow for the system they planned to build. "Where are they off to?" Alex asked.

"Pizza, most likely," Carol answered in a distracted manner.

"Oh…" Alex said, distressed, as he had hoped to see Mary again. She had stopped by the previous Monday, and he'd been hoping to see her more often. *I wonder what Carol meant*, he thought as he stepped back from the table, stood, and stared at the door through which they had exited. It was Thursday.

Noticing, Carol said, "Don't worry. She'll be back for more."

Again, he wondered what she meant by that, but he wasn't going to ask.

Monday

"It's Monday," Mary said to Alex as she entered the lab.

"Yeah," he replied. "Did you have a good weekend?" He smiled, wondering what she was referring to. He had meant to ask her out over the weekend but hadn't had a chance to talk to her.

"Yes, thank you for asking." She smiled seductively. "I'll be over tonight at seven p.m. with pizza, if that's okay with you."

"Yeah, sure," he said, startled.

"Okay, I'll see you tonight. Right now, I'm going to work with Joe on the user documentation."

"Joe?"

"Yeah, Joe Zeist, the new user-interface guy. That's where most of the documentation will be needed. You guys are going to document the code yourselves, aren't you?"

"Always," he replied.

"Okay then, I'm on the user interface with Joe." Smiling sweetly, she almost skipped, obviously happy, up the stairs to the first balcony. Joe had moved into one of the offices with a door, on the south end. Having a door was an indication of prestige at Fauxbook.

"Nice view," she commented as Joe, seeing her through his window to the hallway, beckoned her in. She looked past him, in his seat behind his desk, to the view out the window overlooking the millpond. Stepping around the desk to stand next to Joe, she continued to look out the window.

"Why do you have your office arranged so your back is to this wonderful view?" she asked.

"I don't want anyone sneaking up behind me," he answered as he felt the pressure of her hip against his shoulder.

"Well, there's nothing sneaky about me," she said. "I'm as direct as it gets."

"Apparently," he responded. "So besides that, what can I do for you?"

"I'm doing documentation for the Fauxbook project," she said, sliding against him as she moved away, around the desk. She took a seat in the chair opposite. "The coders are embedding their documentation; my main thrust is the end-user interface, printed as well as online documentation, and the help system. I'd like your assistance to get all of that done."

"Okay, I can do that. How would you like to start?"

"With a couple of questions. Are you going to base the interface on IBM's CUA or Apple's HIG? There is a lot of documentation boilerplate for both I can use as a template and build on."

"Well, Mary—your name is Mary, isn't it? The Common User Access Standard is the more formal and widely accepted. However, Apple's Human Interface Guidelines are more detailed. The structure of our interface will be the CUA with a few Apple touches where required. Then I plan to have our own unique look and feel just below the initial presentation and becoming more our own standard as the user goes deeper into the environment. So I'd suggest you start with the CUA boilerplate, have the HIG handy for cutting and pasting, to save some time, and then be prepared for something new."

All right, she thought. *That was a pretty dance as we each tried to impress the other. I'll leave it here and let him come out ahead. He's a male, so his ego likely needs it.*

"Fine, I'll set up a template based on CUA boilerplate. Then when do I get a look at the interface?"

"If you turn around," he said, pointing behind her, "the initial flow design is on that whiteboard."

She turned. "Ah. Yes, that will be a big help. Thank you."

"Yes, it should keep you busy, and then we'll both be busy fleshing it out."

Mary smiled. *Fleshing it out, indeed.* Shared plans and goals were always exciting.

"Next," Joe said, "we'll need to develop a plan or technique for working together. I would especially like to see the integrated help system closely merged with the application…you know, to the extent it almost provides the answer before the end user asks the question."

"Yes, yes," she replied. "I know exactly what you mean…the next level."

"Exactly," Joe replied, excited. "The next level, yes! Exactly! That is precisely what I want." He murmured to himself, "The next level, exactly."

"Well, then, that's what you will get from me: the next level."

Still distracted by the new thoughts, Joe said, "I've still got some work to do; how about we continue this later, over dinner?"

"Great," she said, "but not tonight. Tuesday is free, though."

"Fine, stop by here tomorrow about five thirty, and we'll go across the street to the Thai restaurant."

"See you then."

Tuesday

Mary arrived the next morning after what she considered a fairly dull night with Alex. It had been all right but nothing special. *Every day can't be a roll in the freezer. But*, she thought, *I'll have to think of something special. Just to keep it interesting.*

She'd spend that day building the outline for the written documentation using CUA boilerplate, of which there was a lot available. Then she would stop by Joe's office and take a picture of the interface flowchart with her tablet. By the end of the week, she planned to be able to start filling it in with Fauxbook-specific features.

She'd seen Carol in Leif's office and wondered what was going on there. So she walked over.

Opening the door to the isolated office, she half entered. "Hey, what's going on in here?"

Carol was sitting beside Leif at his desk. They had both been looking intently at one of the two monitors in front of them.

They both glanced up at Mary simultaneously, and Carol said, "Leif is fine-tuning the bots. He's about there, and pretty soon we can start them with the midware on the z13."

"Already?" Mary asked, surprised. "I didn't know the bots were that far along."

"Yeah, I guess," Leif said sardonically. "It's amazing how much you can accomplish without the distraction of the Internet. They are going to tear your software up."

Ignoring his bitter tone, Carol said, "We have the midware for the cluster emulated on the z13. It's far from finished. However, it is never too early to start looking for weak spots and vulnerabilities."

"Give me until midday tomorrow," Leif said, "and we'll load her up and see what happens."

"How big is the workload you have ready?" Carol asked.

"About one million users," Leif answered. "Any more than that and the whole system might melt down before we saw where the problems were."

Carol chuckled. "Fat chance. You think a lot of yourself and your bots, don't you?"

"Yeah, I guess," Leif said. "And if I weren't exiled, they would be even better. But I believe you'll find these will do."

"All right," Mary cried, "the bots are going live tomorrow. We need to celebrate!"

"Good idea," Carol agreed. "We need a break—especially Leif."

"Joe and I planned to go to the Thai place across the street. Why don't you two join us?"

"Because Thai food all tastes the same, and so would cardboard if it were soaked in Thai hot sauce," Leif said, unable to lose his foul humor.

"Oh, stick it in your ear," Carol said, ever practical. "Let's meet over there at six this evening." They all agreed. After some cajoling, even Leif said he'd join them.

Carol spent the rest of the day fine-tuning the middleware simulation running on the IBM. She found there wasn't much to do, as Alex had done an amazing job. There was even code for porting some of the objects over to the cluster later for execution on Intel chips. He was much further along than she'd realized. *I should invite him to the celebration,* she thought. Then she immediately thought better of that idea. *Sooner or later, Mary is going to be a problem. Later is better.*

She made her way through the labyrinth of the first floor to Alex's cubicle. Knocking on the frame of the opening—there was no door—she announced herself. "Hi, Alex."

He looked up, not happy to be interrupted. He recovered and smiled. "Carol, good to see you. I was just putting in the hooks for the user interface."

"You're still working on the midware?"

"Yeah, it runs on the IBM, but I want to be able to document the hooks to the user interface Joe is working on. I've sent him some specs already."

"I saw that," Carol replied. "Leif has the first version of the bots ready to run on the simulator. We're going to put them to work tomorrow."

"What's the load?"

"One million."

"Is there a betting pool?"

"Should there be?"

"Ha, a million! It's not going to break a sweat. And this is early."

"You sure?"

"I'm sure."

"Okay, I'll see what I can get going. In the meanwhile, we should celebrate."

"Celebrate?"

"Yes, you've done a wonderful job, and so have I. As team leader, you should take me out to dinner tomorrow night after Leif launches the bots."

"How about the other guys?" he asked.

"Nah, let's just do you and me. We wouldn't be able to organize something for everybody by tomorrow. After it's run awhile, you should organize a picnic or something for the whole team."

"Sounds good to me," he said. "Where would you like to go?"

"How about the seafood house down the street?"

Oysters? He wondered what all of this was about. Maybe it was just a celebration and a break from weeks of hard work. But he hoped for more. *She is gorgeous*, he thought, realizing, not without some feeling of guilt, there was lust in his heart.

Turning her back to leave, Carol said, "Tomorrow," over her shoulder.

Alex watched her, thinking, *She's gorgeous from all angles.*

Hot Stuff

That evening, the four of them took possession of a booth in the shadows at the back of the dining room. Mary and Joe were opposite each other inside. Leif and Carol were beside them. As they chatted casually, Leif wasn't getting a positive message from Carol, though she was friendly enough. Beside him, though, Mary had it all turned on in Joe's direction. Leif could feel the heat and envied Joe for being its focus.

"To us," Carol said, lifting her glass of light beer to her friends. Mary reluctantly broke eye contact with Joe and raised her glass.

They all touched glasses and repeated, "To us."

"The bots," Leif said, and the ritual was repeated.

"I'm the interface guy," Joe said. "I'm not sure what is so important about the bots. It's a software program for testing the integrity of the application? Is that right? Is it more than one program?"

Carol answered, "Robots, bots for short...yes, they are software programs that simulate the load put on a system by users. Each robot acts like one user, and more bots can be added to increase the load. We're starting tomorrow with just a one-million-user load."

"My bots can each simulate more than one user at a time," Leif said, looking at Mary and hoping to impress her.

"That's amazing," Carol said, smiling at him. "They are a virtual team of software testers and will do the job in days that would have taken a hundred human testers a year. They are intelligent and fast, and the routine can be scaled up as the system passes its benchmarks."

"And it's cheap," Leif chipped in, trying to keep attention—especially Mary's—focused on himself.

"How are they intelligent?" Joe asked.

"As they encounter procedures that slow them down," Leif explained, "they try all possible approaches until they get feedback. Then they split off, or create, clones that perform that specific task well. It's Darwinian. Yeah, I guess you can think of them as intelligent."

"It's pretty cool," Carol commented, "and Leif is the best there is in the world at this."

Leif actually blushed. For all of his bluster, he was actually quite a shy young man.

"I can see why you're excited," Joe said. "I'm excited. I'm excited for you and for me. Alex has been sending me code and the specs for the hooks to the middleware for my interface. It's really getting exciting."

"Better than sex," Mary said quietly.

"I'd have to think about that," Joe answered. "It may not be better, but it sure turns me on."

"Would you like me to take care of that?" she asked.

"Sure." Joe's eyes narrowed and his eyebrows pinched together. "What do you mean?" *Is she propositioning me for after dinner?*

"I could just slip under the table and service your little problem."

Now he knew she was putting him on. And he could play along and give as good as he got. "What makes you think it's a 'little' problem?" he asked, smiling. *She's not going to get the best of me.*

"Well, let's just see," she said, and to his astonishment, she slid under the table. He immediately felt a tug at his zipper. That accomplished, she unfastened his belt and pulled his pants down. "Ah, no underwear," she said from under the table. "I like that."

No one said anything, though Carol chuckled softly. The table started to wiggle rhythmically. Apparently, some part of Mary's body or Joe's was in contact with it.

"Are you folks ready to order? Or do you need a few moments?" the waitress, who had just appeared, asked.

"You'd better give us a little more time," Carol answered. She seemed to be the only one of the three who wasn't speechless.

"Where is your friend, the young lady?" the waitress asked.

"Oh, she'll be back. She had to go to the head," Carol said.

Leif was embarrassed, for himself and for Carol. She was always so proper, and now this. He was disgusted, and moreover, he found himself aroused. That embarrassed him.

Joe pushed back the tablecloth and looked down to see Mary's face buried in his crotch. Any further view was obscured by her hair, spread out over both his thighs.

She raised her head, disappointing him. He feared he had spoiled the moment by disturbing her. Looking up at him with her large, innocent, soft brown eyes, she said, "Hand me down some of that hot sauce."

Leif was mortified. He was horrified Carol had to experience this. He looked at her, not directly, and was surprised to see her studying the menu. *She seems not disturbed in the least.* He reached out and grasped her hand.

First, she started to jerk away. Then she thought better of her response and relaxed her hand. She put down the menu and placed her other hand on top of his. "Pay no attention," she said. "I hear the chicken curry is very good."

Carol made her excuses after dinner and left Leif on the sidewalk outside the restaurant with Mary and Joe. "That was a large tip you left," he said to Mary. He was mainly making conversation to fill the awkwardness of being abandoned by his date. *It was a date, wasn't it?*

"That is for Alice, the waitress," Mary said. "She needs it. She's twenty-one years old and a single mother of two kids from different fathers."

"She's the one who asked where you had gone," Joe said with a grin.

"Yeah, she knew where I was. She called me a slut once for slipping under the table. She always makes a point of noticing."

"A slut!" Leif exclaimed, shocked.

"Yeah, a slut, but I'm not the one with no education and two fatherless kids. So I help her out whenever I can. Come on, Joe, let's go over to your place."

Leif was dumbstruck with envy.

Wednesday

"Raul, no, I'm not able to come tonight. That's it! Deal with it," Carol said into the phone as Alex entered the room. She waved at him, indicating he should sit. "Good-bye, Raul, I'll work double tomorrow night. Bye!" She hung up.

"Hi, Alex," she said. "I heard the new computers are here."

"Yeah, a couple hundred are being installed now. But, hey, look, if you have things to do tonight, don't worry about me. Do what you need to do."

"Okay." She smiled. "I'll do that. Tonight, we're going to dinner and to devour some lobster. Right now, follow me. Let's see Leif about some bots. I started the simulator on the IBM a half an hour ago. We should be good to go."

He had been thinking oysters, but lobster was close enough.

The two of them swooped into Leif's office. Carol gave Leif an air kiss next to his left ear and handed him an SD card. "Here's the loader," she said. "We're ready for the bots."

Leif stood, pointedly not taking the card, and stepped back away from them. Fear controlled his face.

"What's wrong? Aren't the damn things ready?" Alex said.

"Hush, Alex," Carol said. "There's something wrong, and Leif will explain what it is, won't you, Leif?"

They both looked at him expectantly. "Come on," Alex said impatiently. "We need to start testing on the big machine immediately. The cluster machines are already being delivered. Damn! Don't you understand?"

"Hush, Alex," Carol repeated, giving him a harsh glare.

Looking embarrassed, Leif said, "The bots are ready. That's not the problem."

"So what's the problem? Put them on the card," Alex said, pointing to the SD card still in Carol's hand.

Carol swatted him lightly on the back of his head.

"I can't," Leif said dejectedly. "I'm not allowed on the networks and certainly not near the z13. And I don't think it would be okay in high places for me to give you programs for you to install. They don't want me to have any contact with the network. This could be interpreted as contact."

"Oh, hell!" Alex exclaimed. "Are they still holding on to your mess-up?"

"Yeah, I guess," Leif said, hanging his head.

"Come on, Alex," Carol said, grabbing his hand. "We're going to see Gordon. Leif, you wait here. We'll be right back."

It took a while, but they eventually found Gordon in the lunchroom eating a bowl of chili.

As they approached his table—he was eating alone—he asked, "Hey, you guys want to get something to eat?"

"Gordon," Carol said, standing before him, a little too close and into his space, "the simulator is done, the cluster machines are being delivered, and Leif has the bots ready to go to work."

"That's good news," he said, looking up calmly from his bowl of chili. He ignored her proximity. It didn't bother him; very little did.

"He won't give them to us because you told him not to access the network."

"He interprets that broadly," Alex added.

"As well he should," Gordon replied. "Good for him. Ask him to come over to my office after lunch. And tell him to bring the robots." He handed Carol a USB memory card, which she correctly understood to be the delivery method.

It's amazing what he just happens to have in his pocket, she thought.

"Make sure Leif includes the source code," he ordered.

As Gordon returned to his office, which was close to Jon's, he said, "Anne, get that young man up here, Joe Zeist—the one working on the interface." Not having, or wanting, a secretary of his own, he usurped Anne's service. However, he knew it wouldn't be long before Jon, jealous of Anne's time, forced one upon him.

For Jon, Anne was much more than a secretary. She had been with him since she graduated from high school thirty years ago. Anne was his alter ego and his sounding board. If Anne wasn't comfortable with something, Jon rarely was either.

Leif arrived first, clutching Gordon's memory card in his hand. "Here they are, chief."

Gordon looked up with a grimace. "Don't let Jon hear you call me that."

"I worked on them on a single workstation in my office, which is not even connected to a phone line. This is the first time they have been outside of my office—or that machine, for that matter."

"I understand, young man. You have done well. It may be time to turn you loose on the world again."

"Thank you, sir." The "you have done well" sounded good.

"There is just one more thing," Gordon said.

But "one more thing" was ominous.

The Sum of It All

There was a soft knock; it was Joe. With a majestic sweep of his arm through the air, Gordon welcomed him and bade him enter and sit.

"Here's how we're going to handle this," Gordon said with a conspiratorial smile. "Give the chip to Joe. Joe, those are the bots Leif has been working on. For a couple of reasons, I'd like you to examine the code carefully before it's installed. It's going on the IBM running the simulator first. Is that going to work for you?" he asked, looking at Leif.

"Yes, sir…yes, sir. That will be fine, sir."

"Okay then, I'll explain it to Jon. What do you two think about codifying the procedure as a company policy? That is, all code is checked by a second qualified person before it is installed on any company machine other than the workstation where it was written?"

Leif liked the idea. A policy covering everyone was better than him, and others, thinking he wasn't trusted.

Joe nodded in agreement. But he added, "Gordon, you know I'm not current on operating systems or even load testing. I'm working on the user interface."

"I realize that, Joe. You don't have to design it; just check it out. And between us chickens, I'm certain it's fine. Leif does good work."

***

Leif looked happy when he returned to the lab, a swagger in his step. "Hi, guys," he called out.

"So," Alex asked, "did you get it done?" He expected the card to be in Leif's hand and the three of them to head to the computer building to start this thing up.

"Everything's good," Leif answered. "There will just be a slight delay. There is a new company policy." Leif explained it to them. "Joe is looking at the code now. I'm going to my office. I still have a lot of work to do."

"Well," Carol said, "it's almost four o'clock, happy hour. Let the celebration begin." She grabbed Alex by the hand and led him toward the coatroom.

Even with their heavy coats, it was a cold walk down two blocks to the Quarterdeck seafood restaurant. The fall chill was on, and it promised Boston a cold winter. They walked close together, arm in arm, to share body warmth.

Once seated, they ordered, and Carol got right to the point. "I mentioned earlier about one hundred of the cluster computers were here and being installed."

"Yes," Alex replied, disappointed at the direction of the conversation.

"Well, half of them are based on quantum chips."

"What!" Alex said, shocked. "Didn't that cost a fortune?" His mind spun as he considered the implications.

"No, the price was the same as the Intel machines. Simco believes if we are successful with a quantum cluster, their sales will be tremendous. So they are willing to sell us a couple of thousand cheap."

"Have you told Gordon about this?"

"No, just you."

"Just me?"

"Just you."

"You are changing the design criteria, the basic computers, of the Fauxbook cluster without telling anyone? Isn't that a little above your pay grade?"

"Well, I've told you."

"How is this going to work? Damn, Carol, no one really knows how a quantum computer works. Even using one requires a leap of faith."

"Yes, a leap of faith." She took his hand in hers across the table. "I believe in that."

"How is this going to work?" he repeated.

"Well, I'm installing them wired up in their own cluster the same way as the other machines. Then we'll put the two clusters on the same bus and see what the midware does. I'm thinking it will send a load to the quantum cluster—I'm calling it the q-cluster—and we'll see what happens. The midware will reassign the task if there is too much of a delay."

"Too much of a delay! Who wrote that code?" Alex asked.

"I did," she responded, "and a lot more. This is going to work, and more."

"More?"

Their food had come, for the moment, they ignored it.

"Yes, more. Just loading the machines normally will give us some information as to what they are capable of. But…" Carol paused, calmly put her napkin in her lap, rotated her plate a quarter of a turn to position it to her satisfaction, cut off a piece of lobster, and put it in her mouth. She chewed for a moment. "In the long term, I plan to have the bots program the cluster."

"The bots!" Alex exclaimed. He was having trouble understanding what she was talking about. The robots were just a testing tool. How could they program a cluster—especially a state-of-the-art cluster that only worked in theory?

"The bots," she said. She bit off a piece of garlic bread. "Yes, I've been working with Leif, and he explained to me his design is self-replicating. No, not self-replicating; that's wrong. We need to have him explain the details to you. But in short, when they encounter a task that slows them down, they spin off a clone— with the help of other bots—that is optimized to that task. A corollary of that idea is how we'll make the bots program the quantum chips, memory, and the cluster."

"With the help of other bots, you say?"

"Yes, Leif has them communicating and cooperating."

"Oh." Alex had a lot to think about. Not the least of which was how he had worked in the same building while all of this was going on and had fallen so far out of the loop. The first question was whether he believed her. The second was whether her ideas would work. He placed his napkin in his lap and started to eat. The process gave him time to think and absorb all of this.

Across the table, Carol smiled at him innocently.

God, she's beautiful. But she may be too smart for me, he thought, though he found that sexy, too. He wondered if he was supposed to feel guilty about that.

They did not say much more about work, and the evening passed pleasantly.

"May I walk you home?" Alex asked, knowing Carol lived in an apartment just a few blocks away.

"No, thank you. I'll be fine. Thank you for a very pleasant evening, and I'll see you in the morning."

"When may I see you again?"

"In the morning," she answered, pretending confusion.

"Okay, in the morning," he said, understanding he was being teased.

After slipping into her coat in the foyer of the restaurant, she turned and looked into his eyes. He was mesmerized by their deep blue.

"Soon," she said softly. "I work days and nights and go to school in between. It's hard to get out or get time to myself. For now, I'll look forward to seeing you in the morning." She smiled and walked out the door.

D-Bot

"Gordon," Joe said as he tapped on the doorframe of Wysmann's office.

"Come in. Sit," Gordon ordered, indicating the couch. "How did your project work out?"

"Not well, I'm embarrassed to say. The basic code for Leif's robots is pretty standard and seems okay to me."

"And then the other shoe drops." Gordon smiled.

"Yes, indeed, the other shoe. Yes, inside the basic code, it all takes a strange—wild, even—turn. It confused the heck out of me. I had no idea what it was about. So I went to see him."

"And?"

"He calls them Darwin's bots, or d-bots for short. They evolve by spinning off specialized clones to accomplish specific and time-consuming tasks more efficiently and quickly."

"They evolve?" Gordon said, thoughtfully.

"Yes, then when a task or problem is identified, the appropriate specialized group of robots responds. He says if it works, the system will learn and run like a bat out of hell."

These words were more prophetic than Joe realized.

"A bot can't do that," Gordon said dismissively. "They barely have ten lines of code. How can they clone themselves, evolve, and assign jobs to specialized robots? That's crazy."

"That's what I said to Leif."

"And?"

"He agreed I was absolutely right. But the few lines of code can call procedures…"

Gordon interrupted, chuckling. "Out of the black box of object-oriented programming, I imagine. Damn! But still…the boy is clever, but that doesn't seem to be enough."

"They communicate and cooperate."

"They what! With one another? Or a controller, a router?"

"Leif says it's with one another. They are all there is other than the procedures of the operating system, the midware, and later the application programming and the interface."

"Well," Gordon said softly, seriously, "that would be a lot, when you put it that way."

"Yes, sir. He's almost got me convinced. Well, maybe a little more than almost. He may really be onto something."

"Yeah," Gordon replied, "a nightmare I've been dreading for years, a nightmare whose coattails we have no choice but to ride."

"A nightmare?" Joe replied, surprised. "How is it a nightmare?"

"Never mind; give me the code." Gordon stretched out his hand. "I want to look at it myself. I'll get back to you in a couple of hours."

He reached over and disconnected his workstation from the network and everything else. After inserting the memory card into the USB port, he opened it and found the source-code files. They weren't hard to understand. *Short and sweet; Leif is very good.* He didn't know what some of the calls were, understanding most of them but not all. But he could imagine, as he had imagined this code years ago and disdained it.

He saw only the most basic part of the code had been implemented. The rest commented out as Leif continued to work on it. But it was certainly as he had feared. But what could be done? He knew where this was going and didn't know how to get off the train. Should he tell Jon? Jon didn't understand software. What good would that do? However, he would have to tell him eventually.

Elbows on his desk, he leaned forward and held his head in his hands. He knew there was no option other than to explain this to Jon.

***

Meanwhile, Mary was inside Leif's locked office, advancing his education in things licentious. *There are advantages to having one's office disconnected*, she thought.

Leif groaned. He was on his hands and knees and had never experienced anything like this before. In fact, he had very little experience, having basically been a nonsocial computer nerd all of his life. He froze, afraid to move and terrified she would stop.

"Don't stop. Please, don't stop," he whispered.

"Don't worry, baby. I'm not going to stop until it's time." It was, she knew, long past time. She wondered how long she could keep him in this delicious state. She leaned forward and gave him a love bite. He shuddered. "Careful," she said sharply as she continued to stroke him. Again, he shuddered. *It might be a very long time*, she thought. *But he's young; his heart is strong, though it might be weaker after this.* "Be still," she commanded.

After another few moments, he started to throb in her hand. *Damn!* she thought. *I'm losing him.* "Think about the bots, Leif. Tell me, when are you going to turn them loose?"

"Ah…" Silence for a few seconds, and then he said softly, "Tonight, tomorrow morning at the latest. Joe…" His voice was broken, but she had him back under control. "Joe approved them. Gordon is, ah…" He moaned. "He's taking a final look, and then Carol will load them on the simulator."

Mary didn't say anything; she didn't need to, as he was back to panting like a dog. She smiled and continued her manipulations. *God, his heart must be pounding*, she thought. *And I'm getting tired. I wonder if I can maneuver him into a different position without breaking the spell. He is a lovely sight, and I don't know when I've been more excited.*

"What's wrong?" He gasped, out of breath.

"Nothing, nothing, I was just thinking you'd like to do something different."

"Oh, no, please, don't stop. It's so good," he pleaded.

"Okay, okay, just a little change. My hand needs a break." *Damn! How long has he lasted?* She regretted not checking the time before she got him down. *He has been on this edge a very long time.* She smiled with pleasure.

The phone rang. Fortunately, they were just beside the desk, and Mary answered with her free hand.

"Leif Hoberson's office, Mary Adams speaking. How may I help you?" she said in her most professional voice.

"This is Gordon. May I speak to Leif?"

"I'm terribly sorry, Mr. Wysmann, but Leif is tied up at the moment." She gave Leif another pull, and he moaned. "May I have him call you back?"

"No, just tell him the bots have been approved. I'll call Carol and Alex and have them stop by in a few moments to pick up the installation chip."

"Yes, sir, I'll tell him. It shouldn't be a moment, and the chip will be ready when they get here."

Leif jerked and moaned louder.

"What was that?" Gordon asked.

"Just the wind off of the millpond, Mr. Wysmann. He'll be ready."

"Thank you, Mary. Congratulate Leif for me."

In numerous ways, Mary thought.

Mary quickly dropped the phone on its cradle, gripped Leif by the left ankle, and flipped him over. He gasped.

"Hurry," Mary ordered as she mounted him. "Hurry! We don't have much time."

A short time later, there was a knock. "Come in," Mary said calmly. "It's unlocked." And it was newly unlocked.

Carol entered to find Leif dressed neatly and seated behind his desk. She did notice he was red in the face and seemed out of breath. Mary was seated across from him, in front of a laptop perched on the edge of the desk. Her fingers, working over the keyboard, were just finishing a sentence.

Tell me I don't have control of the situation, Mary thought.

"Didn't Alex come?" Leif asked.

"No, he's over in the old computer building starting up the simulator on the IBM and checking it. I'll meet him there."

"Okay," he said, handing Carol the chip. "Good luck."

"Oh, I'm sure the bots will be fine, Leif," Carol said.

"I meant good luck with your bugs. The bots will find them. I'm not worried about the bots."

Carol smiled. "Good for you, Leif. Would you like to come?"

Mary chuckled at the thought.

"No, thanks; I've still got some important stuff to do here."

Carol smiled. "Okay, see you. Bye, Mary."

Mary closed the door behind Carol and locked it. "Do you want to start again?" she asked.

Leif tensed for a second. "I don't think I can. Later?"

"Sure, we'll have to think of something new and more exciting. See you tonight." She packed up her purse, folded her laptop, and was gone.

Slip the Reins

"Jon?" Gordon asked over coffee early one morning. "Did you assign the overall design to that kid Alex Cromwell and his team?"

"No, no, but they do seem to have taken the initiative."

"Do you know what they are doing?"

"Sure, they're building Fauxbook."

"That they are," Gordon said, shaking his head. "Everything from designing the hardware to the interface. Are you sure they know what they are doing even if you don't?" Gordon was skirting uncharacteristically close to criticizing Jon.

"It won't matter in the end," Jon replied. "There are two other teams set up in a more conventional way working on the system in D Building. At the six-month beta mark, we'll evaluate them all and determine which team has the best approach."

Gordon nodded, acknowledging the wisdom, which had always brought results. *At least so far*, he thought.

"At that point," Jon continued, "I'll reassign the people on the losing teams, give some direction—I'll leave it to you to redirect the second-best team and put additional resources behind the winners. It's like insurance. We have three opportunities to get it right."

Wysmann was glad he was recording all of this. At worst, he'd have fodder for an interesting book.

***

Gordon was right; over the last three months, Alex's team, led by Carol, had grown to fill the space, so Carol had taken over the entire second-floor balcony area, and the work orders had proliferated. Without specifically being tasked, the team had become the center of the programming effort, enlisting most of the grunts on the first floor.

"In addition," Carol said, "we are running the load testing and designing the bus."

"How is the load testing going?" Mi Ly asked. Mi Ly was a new hire right out of MIT's master's program. She was reputed to be brilliant and had done well in the interviews. She was cute enough, with a nice body. However, when she walked, her butt sort of trailed behind, as if in imitation of a centaur. The effect wasn't very attractive. Carol had assigned her to work on optimizing the test phase of the wiring to connect the individual computers in the cluster. Once the wiring was set, they would freeze the bus design. *That will make putting this together much simpler, as the computers will simply plug into the bus rather than having to be individually hand wired*, Carol thought.

"It's going well," Carol said. "Better than I expected, actually."

"Any problems?"

"Not many. The bots found an infinite loop, a few broken links, and a few dead ends, but Alex and Larry fixed those quickly. Leif has implemented some improvements to the code for the robots, and I've turned the second generation loose. How is your project going?"

"Good," Mi Ly answered. "I've been working on the cluster of two hundred you had running when I arrived. I'll send you my notes this afternoon. If you approve my suggested changes, we can start making the modifications tomorrow."

"That's great, Mi Ly. I'll look for your e-mail. See you later," Carol said as she turned and walked down the corridor.

"Alex," Carol said, sticking her head into his cubicle, "I'm free tonight. Dinner?"

He was astounded. He had given up on this romance, which had never gotten started long ago. "Sure, dinner sounds fine. But it's only been a couple of months since our last date. Don't you think we're rushing it?"

"Don't be acrimonious," she said, smiling. "You know I work all of the time. And it's not like we don't see each other every day. I've gotten to know you very well."

"What do you know about me?"

"I know I like you very much," she replied, entering his cubicle and planting a kiss on his cheek. "I know you're smart, a hard worker, and funny. See, I know a lot."

"Well, when you put it that way, I know a lot about you, too. And I'd love to have dinner with you tonight. Same time, same place?"

They had a congenial dinner, which included conversation, laughter, and even a moment when she grasped his hand and looked intently into his eyes. But once again, she insisted on walking herself home with only a hug and a kiss on his cheek. He was disappointed.

The next day he visited her office, planning to ask about her intentions.

"Alex," she cried happily when she saw him. "Good news: the quantum cluster is working!"

He smiled; her smile was infectious, and her beauty took his breath away. "Yes, I know," he replied after a moment. "It's been working for a month."

"Not like this," she exclaimed, holding a printout and pointing. "It's taking half of the load."

"You've installed the new midware?" he asked, surprised that she would do that without him.

"No, all we have been doing is optimizing the wiring for the bus. We made some changes this morning based on Mi Ly's notes, and voilà! It works!"

"You're not utilizing the bots, are you?"

"No, no, the load is just being entered by hand."

"So," he observed, "the load is exceedingly light."

"Yes, you're right," she said, still smiling. "This really proves nothing. But it indicates something. And it's good!"

"That sounds like cause for another celebration," he said, feeling like a glutton for punishment or at least frustration. *What am I doing? This girl is the ice queen and most likely still a virgin. Damn! But God, she's lovely and smart—not really very funny, though. She's too serious.*

"Alex," she said seriously, "I told you how I feel about you. But there's something I have to do—to show you."

"Uh-huh," he said. Thinking, *there she goes again.*

"Saturday. Are you free on Saturdays?"

"Yeah, I could be. All day?"

"Hopefully," she replied. "It will depend on you. I want you to meet me at work in the morning. I'll arrange to have the afternoon off so we can have lunch and spend the afternoon together if you still want to."

"Why would I not want to?"

"You'll see," she answered softly and mysteriously. "I'll let you know when I've made the arrangements."

"Okay, so, in the meantime, how about dinner tonight?"

"Alex." She laughed. "You are impossible. No, I have to work tonight."

"Damn!" he replied. "Where do you work? I could stop by, and we could go to dinner after." *Now I'm really getting desperate*, he thought.

"No, that wouldn't be a good idea right now."

"Okay," he said in a dejected tone.

As he turned to leave her office, she said, "I'm not working tomorrow night."

Sales

Gordon was surprised when he received notice of the sales meeting. A formal meeting was unusual. And it appeared all of the players would be there. A distribution list was attached.

Jon Johnsson

Gordon Wysmann

Jeff Hoover

Roger Aegel

Barry F. Konrad

Anne Jankin

Barbara Peregrine

Gordon wondered who Barbara Peregrine was but reckoned he would find out soon enough. The meeting was scheduled for the next day at 10:00 a.m.

***

At the appointed time, Gordon moved to his seat in the small conference room next to Jon's office and looked around. He seemed to be the last to arrive. *Probably because I have nothing to gain by the political maneuvering that's about to happen.*

Konrad wore a custom-made suit from Tom Baker in London. Gordon suspected he preferred Italian suits but feared, correctly, they might push Jon too far.

Jeff had dressed as the outdoorsman he wasn't as a nod to Jon, who was. They both wore shirts from Woolrich: Jon's flannel and

Jeff's buffalo-check wool. They both sported blue jeans, and Jon wore hiking boots from L.L. Bean.

Roger was in his usual rumpled off-the-shelf suit, wearing a tie that didn't match his shirt.

Jon stood. He was a brawny man with piercing blue eyes. He had presence. When he was in the room, everyone knew it.

"Okay, quiet down." An odd comment, as no one had been talking. Mostly they had just been eyeing one another, looking for weakness. "First, this lady to my right, next to Anne, is Barbara Peregrine. She started today as our event coordinator. As this meeting will most certainly end with a resolve to plan events, I think she should be here." Everyone either waved a welcome or nodded in Barbara's direction.

Jon continued. "This is a sales meeting. Some here wanted to bill it as a marketing meeting. However, marketing is too highfalutin for me. I don't market product; I sell product. Pure and simple. And I believe honestly a good product will sell itself. And that's been my experience."

Oh gee whiz, Gordon thought, *here we go again.*

"Jeff, stand up and tell everyone where we are on delivering product."

No wonder we don't have meetings, Gordon thought. *It's not like everyone doesn't already know. What a waste of time.*

Jeff Hoover, COO, took the floor. He pulled a chair from the table and lifted his foot, enclosed in a rattlesnake cowboy boot, onto it and assumed a laid-back posture.

"There are five legs to Fauxbook," he explained. "One: hardware. Two: software. Three: infrastructure. Four: administration. Five: sales, or what some would call marketing. "First, hardware. The midware software is running on the z13 simulator and has been for a month. During this time, there has been extensive testing, which has revealed some minor problems. They have all been fixed.

"The cluster is up and running, and we're testing and optimizing the wiring prior to building the bus. As of today, we have two hundred computers in the running cluster, and we're going to start middleware testing on the cluster within two days. This has been accomplished by Alex Cromwell's team under my supervision. The other two teams are most likely redundant, and those resources will be redeployed after testing is successful."

"What do I hear about a new type of computer being integrated into the cluster?" Barry asked.

"Yes, we are experimenting with quantum chips that make direct use of quantum-mechanical phenomena, such as superposition and entanglement, to perform operations."

It sounds like he memorized that, Gordon thought unkindly. *In any case, Carol's quantum cluster is now an accepted part of Fauxbook even though it was never contemplated in management's plan. Carol just did it on her own without seeking approval from anyone. And now here we are. Amazing.*

"Isn't it risky to experiment with hardware when we're essentially a software company and so close to launch?" Barry asked.

And here's another one who doesn't know what he's talking about, Gordon thought.

"No, I don't think so," Jeff answered. "The current cluster is small, only two hundred machines, and hand wired. Half of the cluster are standard Intel machines. So if the new machines don't work, we simply turn them off and replace them. In any case, Barry, so far, they're working, and we haven't even started to optimize the programming. Right now, they are emulating Intel chips. The future is promising. And no, there's no risk to speak of."

"Maybe we'd better let Gordon address this," Jon said. "I can understand why this might be a big issue in some minds. Gordon?"

Gordon didn't rise. "Jeff is right. There is no risk from the dangers contemplated."

"Thank you, Gordon," Jeff said with a small smile, thinking he'd won that round.

"However," Gordon continued, "I'm not saying there are no risks. There are always risks."

"What risks?" Jon asked.

"The technological singularity."

"What do quantum computers have to do with that?" Jon asked.

"Nothing directly; they are simply a step that leads to another step, and before we know it—"

"Well, it doesn't sound like it's a current or short-term problem," Jon said.

"I agree," Jeff said.

"I'm reassured," Barry added.

All right, so now they're piling on me, Gordon thought. *I wonder what they think that's going to accomplish for them. They're just spreading dissension, I guess, each hoping they will come out on top of the chaos.*

"Okay, software is on schedule," Gordon said. "I've already covered most of the issues. The midware is undergoing testing, and we're loading it on the cluster soon. The applications are running, and the user interface is a week away."

"Sounds good," Jon commented.

"Infrastructure is also on schedule," Jeff said. "The fiber is in for the main ISP connection and is going hot at the end of the month. Administration to support users and ad sales is in place. All that's left is to put sales in place and plan the launch."

"I think we should put on a show," Barry said. "A big show— invite everyone and make a big splash."

"In Maynard?" Roger asked.

"No, Boston. Make it an event to rival the old Atlanta Comdex. It will be a weeklong event. We'll take over the city."

Jon appeared troubled. He generally shunned publicity, believing an excellent product would sell itself.

"You're talking about a party, a celebration of Fauxbook's launch. All of the employees would be invited. It would be an opportunity to let off steam after all of the months of effort," Gordon said.

Relieved, Barry, who also knew Jon's proclivities, said, "Right."

"Sounds good to me," Jeff added. "My people could sure use a party."

After a thoughtful moment, Jon said, "It is important for a company to treat employees well. But if you treat employees nicely, you are not respected by the business world, unfortunately."

As often was the case, these words left everyone in the room confused and with the same thought: *Has he approved the idea or not?*

Barry decided to interpret Jon as having approved it. He said, "I'll meet with Ms. Peregrine, and we'll get started planning. As soon as we have a date, I'll let everyone know."

The Hunk

From her office window, Mary saw Larry arrive. He entered from the new enclosed connector from reception and administration to the first floor of A Building. *God, he's a hunk*, she thought. He was wearing a tight collared sweater and khaki pants. He was blond, well built, and tall. She felt her body responding.

He spoke to one of the female programmers, who, after listening, pointed up toward Joe's office.

Damn! He would pick a pretty one to ask, she thought with more than a tinge of jealousy.

"Mr. Zeist?" Larry asked, standing in the open doorway.

"Come in," Joe said, rising. "I'm Joe Zeist; call me Joe. I don't believe we've met."

"No, I just got here—well, last night. This is my first day, and Mr. Wysmann told me to report to you. Oh, I'm Larry Bowers, sorry."

"Okay, have a seat, and tell me your story."

"Oh, yeah, I'm supposed to give you this paperwork." He handed over a thick nine-by-eleven-inch envelope.

Opening it, Joe found Larry Bowers' CV, company paperwork, and a note from Gordon:

> Joe, I think this may be just the
> fellow you need to help you out
> with the interface.
> Gordon

Larry sat quietly as Joe went through the papers. They disclosed he was a graduate of Carnegie Mellon University with a major in computer science and a minor in sociology. He was fresh out of school with very little other than a part-time bartending job at the Pittsburgh Moose Lodge.

"Why sociology?" Joe asked. "It seems an odd mix of majors."

"It may be, but I have my reasons."

"Which are?" Joe said with some irritation. *I don't have time for this*, he thought.

"Sorry," Larry said, picking up on his new boss's exasperation. "My major field is computer science. The specialty that interests me is the machine-user interface—the user interface. How the user sees and interacts with the machine and how the provider, or programmer, creates an intuitive connection. I believe it's just as important to understand people, the users, as it is to understand the machine. You know, both sides of the equation."

"I'm sorry, too; don't mean to get off on the wrong foot," Joe said. "I'm just a little edgy. I've been working for months on the user interface pretty much all by myself. And I'm a little behind schedule." *Damn*, he thought, *Gordon is right. This is the guy we…I…need and somewhat desperately. Sociology, indeed; he is exactly who I would have asked for if I had thought of it.*

110

"Knock, knock," Mary said from the doorway. "I don't mean to interrupt, but I'm caught up and need some more work. Have you got anything on the interface for me?"

"Larry, this is Mary Adams, head of documentation for the department. And the only one who is caught up. Mary, Larry Bowers, who is here to save me."

"Pleased to meet you." Larry smiled. "I got into Boston last night and walked in the front door here for the first time this morning."

"Good for you." She smiled and turned on the aura. "Welcome to Boston, and welcome to Fauxbook."

"Thank you."

"I'm caught up. When Joe is done with you, I'll show you around and find you a cubicle. That all right with you, Joe?"

"Sure, thanks, Mary."

"Where would you like to put him? First floor?"

"No, no, please find Larry a spot as close to me as possible. I think we're going to get along, and he'll be an enormous help."

"Okay, fifteen minutes?"

"Fifteen minutes," Joe agreed.

She smiled at Larry and said, "See you then—fifteen minutes." She looked at her watch, turned, and left—smiling.

"Leave your coat and briefcase here, Larry. Get a feel for the place and move in, and we'll start tomorrow. In the meantime, I'll get all of my stuff organized so you can see where the work is going."

"So the sociology thing is all right?"

"Yeah, Larry, it's all right. The truth is, I wish I had thought of it. There's no doubt in hindsight we pay entirely too much attention to the machine. Though Carol might tell you this 'intuitive' connection of yours has to work both ways."

"I wouldn't disagree with her," Larry said.

They chatted until Mary returned.

"Ready?" she asked.

"Yes. Joe, I'll see you later. Mary, I'm in your hands."

If only he knew, she thought.

They stepped out on the landing. "This is A Building of the old mill complex. Originally, it was not connected to the rest of the mill for fire reasons. The enclosed connector was finished just last month."

"That's going to be convenient when the snows start," he said.

She looked at him, smiling with an expression that said, *That's the most brilliant comment I've ever heard.*

She's cute, he thought, *but a bit flat chested.* She was short with straight brown hair parted in the middle and cut short. She wore a white knit sweater above bell-bottom pants of reds, oranges, and browns, with high-top brown moccasins on her feet.

She's not much of a looker, he thought, *but damn, there is something about her that radiates sex.*

Freezer Reprise

"The first-floor cubicles house the majority of the programmers for our team," Mary said. "This first balcony has offices for managers and department heads. I'll find you a spot up here. The upper balcony"—she pointed up and across the open area—"is for muckety-mucks, very important executives. There are only ten offices up there, which are very luxurious."

"Who's up there?" he asked.

"Nobody." She smiled.

Larry laughed. He liked this girl.

"There are two more teams in D Building. I think they are going to be disbanded and retasked. Come on," she said, grasping his hand and leading him up the staircase.

"Why retasked?"

"Because Alex's team is so far ahead, and our stuff is working." She grinned and spread both arms in a sweeping gesture to encompass the entire team. "Come on."

She led him out of the building and across the parking lot to C Building.

"This is the computer-cluster building," she said as she swiped her ID card and opened the door.

As they entered the main area, Larry was awestruck. There were rows and rows of racks back to back with narrow aisles, and cable racks above.

"My God!" he exclaimed. "There must be thousands of them."

She held his hand. "There are three floors of these racks, with space for two hundred thousand computer nodes with six point four million cores."

"Wow! How large do you guys think Fauxbook is going to become?"

"Billions of users," she answered.

"How many billions?"

"Well, as far as I know, we're planning capacity for everybody."

He just noticed he was still holding her hand. *Or is she holding mine?* Once again, he felt her presence.

"Come on, let's go up on the catwalk, and you can see down through the whole facility."

He followed her up a metal staircase.

"The cluster running now has only two hundred nodes running on a hand-wired bus. That's what we've been working on, the bus, and I think they've got it."

"Alex's team is designing the cluster, too?"

"Yes, the apps, the programs, the middleware, and the cluster. There are some very exciting things going on here."

Stepping out on the catwalk between the first and second floors provided a spectacular view of the racks, the blinking lights, and the cable trays.

"Why are there so many blinking lights? It looks like way over two hundred."

"Oh, yes, there are more than two hundred computers down there. As they are delivered, they're slid into the rack and powered up. Then we load a system diagnostic program that will run continually until we're ready to plug them into the bus."

Larry was impressed. What was going on here was much bigger than he'd imagined.

"Let's get lunch," she said. "You hungry?"

"I am. It's been a long couple of days with little time for a real meal."

"Okay, the cafeteria is in E Building. Follow me." And she was off. They exited on the east side, and it was just a short walk across one of the parking lots.

"This is amazing," he said as he looked around the cafeteria.

"It is…they treat us well. Comfort food: that's what you need. Follow me."

They got trays, were served from behind the counters, and found a secluded table. Mary glanced at the entrance to the freezer and smiled.

"What are you smiling about?" Larry asked as he unfolded his napkin and placed it in his lap.

"Oh, nothing," she said, broadening her smile and leaning into his space. He didn't mind, though he was confused.

What's going on here? he wondered.

It was a pleasure to watch her eat. She was purposeful and direct. She was obviously enjoying herself as she worked her way through three pieces of fried chicken, mashed potatoes with gravy, and corn on the cob. He especially enjoyed watching her attack the corn on the cob. She held an end in each hand and worked her teeth from side to side as she stared at him with veiled eyes.

Between bites of the corn, Mary asked, "Do you have a place yet?"

"Yeah, a furnished efficiency downtown."

"Well, we should break the place in. I'll bring pizza tonight." She ran her teeth down another row, never taking her eyes off him.

He felt as if he were in a hot spotlight. "Tonight?"

"Is that a problem?"

"No, I just haven't unpacked yet. All of my stuff is still in suitcases. But the place is furnished; come on over."

"I'll help you unpack. About seven?" She lowered the corncob, her sultry eyes locked on his.

"Sure, that will be fine. Sausage?"

"Of course." She raised the corncob to her lips and continued gnawing on it.

***

Promptly at seven, Mary knocked on his door. He answered wearing jeans and a T-shirt. He towered over her such that she had to look up sharply to see his face.

"Come in," he invited. "Is that the pizza?"

117

"Yes. Thank you. I brought beer, too." She entered the small efficiency apartment. It was only one room in an L shape. The kitchen was adjacent to the door, then a small chrome-and-linoleum dining table, and next a couch and a single chair, a recliner. The bed and chest of drawers were in the leg of the L to the left. She put the pizza box on the kitchen counter and turned to face him.

The T-shirt was tight, displaying his huge arms. *He must work out.* His biceps appeared to twitch impatiently under his skin. *God, he's hot*, she thought.

"Let me take your coat. It's very warm in here."

She slipped out of her knee-length coat, revealing her new sweater. It was white woven wool with an open weave of multistranded bands. The weave was very open, and her large dark nipples were on full display. But she was losing it. *He is a hulk!*

She wondered how she was going to control this one. So far, not so good. She felt as if she was going to swoon. *But I will figure it out*, she thought. *First things first. I'll feel better about this once I get it put to bed. After that, Fridays are free.*

Hardware

"It's working," Carol said as she entered Alex's cubicle. "It's really working."

"What's working?" he asked.

"The cluster. The quantum computers are running as fast as the Intel machines. No one knows why, but there you go."

"Without an operating system?" Alex asked.

"They're just emulating the Intel machines," she said. "The bots are just running a load. Leif is working on the Darwinian bots, and Gordon is going over the bus specs."

"Do you have a plan for an operating system for the quantum machines?" he asked.

"I do—well, almost. It's running around in my head trying to get out. Leif says he is working on something, too."

"Is he out of the doghouse yet?"

"No, everything still has to come through us before he can put it on the network. Hey, I'm off tonight. Dinner?"

His heart jumped. She sure sent mixed messages. Was she a virgin? He'd never seen her with other guys. Damn! She was smart and beautiful, but it felt as if their relationship, if that's what it was, was going nowhere. It hadn't even progressed to a kiss good-night. Anyway, it was Monday.

"Can't tonight. How about tomorrow?"

"Got to work the rest of the week. Maybe next week."

What a waste, he thought. "What do you do nights?"

"Oh, you'll see. You're going to come visit me at work as soon as I can arrange it."

"Hi, guys," Leif said from the doorway. "I've got some updates for the cluster I'd like you to look at and install."

"Does Gordon need to look at them?" Carol asked.

"No, I don't think so. There are just incremental changes," he lied.

"Okay, I'll put them on after lunch. Come to lunch with us?"

"Sure."

She grasped Alex's hand, surprising him, and led him toward the cafeteria, with Leif trailing. They tried the sushi bar and found Mary sitting at a table by herself. They joined her, and Alex sat down beside her. As he pulled the chair to the table, her hand brushed against him. "Tonight," she mouthed silently, quick to claim possession. That he had arrived holding Carol's hand irked her. *He's mine*, she thought. She considered his fooling around with Carol a betrayal. But she hid it well.

There were no empty seats next to Mary so Leif sat down across from her.

"I have the documentation for the first level of the interface," Mary said. "Now I have to figure out how to document the additional layers."

"What do you mean?" Alex asked.

"Joe is designing the interface to be very simple and straightforward. Think the Google dialog box. But every feature you can imagine is just below the surface. So the basic functionality will be right there and intuitive. Advanced users can easily go beyond that. But how to document it? If I go in a linear fashion, it will be tedious." Mary calmly reached under the table and started rubbing Alex. He wondered if Carol noticed. She didn't seem to. "I'm thinking of dividing the documentation into different levels, like the interface. What do you think?"

"Yeah, I guess," Leif said from across the table. He wondered why Mary moved to sit next to Alex. She was his girlfriend, after all. *Isn't she?* And she was sitting entirely too close to Alex for his taste.

"The end user has only to read the sections that pertain to what they want to accomplish."

Gordon came by and stopped. "I ordered the bus this morning. They tell me they can start installation by the end of the month."

"You already approved the bus?" Alex asked.

"Yes, I did. It's brilliant, though I don't have a clue as to what the hybrid cluster is going to do."

"It will be, like, great." Leif was immediately sorry to have attracted the attention. However, at the same time, he was angry and tired of being in exile.

Gordon looked at him, worried. *But there's nothing to be done. The cat is out of the bag. The milk is spilled, the wolf is at the door, and all such. Nothing to be done.*

121

Alex didn't say anything. He was preoccupied with thoughts of Mary. *She will come over tonight.*

"Okay, I'll see you people later. Good work," Gordon said, and he was gone.

"Alex, let's go down and put the update on the cluster and maybe wire in a few more machines," Carol said.

"Okay, but I'm not sure it's worthwhile to hand wire in more machines. The bus will start going in soon, and all we'll have to do is to plug them in," Alex said.

"I know, Alex, but I'm anxious to see if this works." She grasped his hand and pulled him out the door and off toward the computer building. It seemed personal, as if she liked him.

Or more, he thought. *Her parents sure brought her up right. No sex before marriage, I guess.* But Alex wasn't comfortable with that concept, which he considered old-fashioned and a mistake.

Mary stared after them as they left. She was breathing rapidly and could feel the veins in her face throb as she flushed with anger. Coffee from her cup splashed on the table as her hand shook.

"What's wrong?" Leif asked.

"Nothing! Nothing is wrong," she replied between clinched teeth.

"You want to get together tonight?" Leif said, hopefully.

"No, I can't. I'll come over Thursday as usual. I'll bring my bag. It'll be fun."

"But it's only Monday. I miss you and want to see you more often," he complained.

"I miss you, too. However, there are things to do and people to see. Thursday will have to do. Unless you have a few minutes now. Let's go back to your office for a quickie."

Leif quickly led the way to his office. She moved toward him and dropped to her knees. The door wasn't locked, though she didn't think Alex and Carol would drop in during the short time this would take. And they did not.

Later, they took positions on opposite sides of the room. Some might think the move odd, but Leif was a nerd.

"You were really cute the other day when you had the meeting with Carol about installing the bots. The expression on your face was precious."

Leif flushed with embarrassment as he recalled the close call and the terror. He was unhappy with the thought Mary had enjoyed his discomfort. But excited nonetheless.

"We'll have to do that again. Or something like that. I'll give it some thought." She smiled sweetly. "Okay, got to go," she said. "You okay for now?"

"Yeah, fine," he replied, wondering if this was what it was supposed to be like to have a girlfriend. It was not what he had imagined, though the sex went beyond his fantasies. He was angry but afraid to complain, thinking, correctly, if he did, Mary would simply move on. She seemed flexible. *But she must love me.*

Girls' Night Out

Jon, unknown to himself, was a male chauvinist. He considered women to be gentle, somewhat helpless creatures to be taken care of by men such as him, but at the same time, he considered them equal in every way. And as an enlightened employer, he felt an obligation to do his duty. Hence, he instructed Anne to arrange a night of entertainment for the women of Alex's team. He had come to the conclusion it was Alex's team that would bring this home, and it was important for him to treat them well.

Anne had it under control—male strippers. Not the Chippendales but close enough—the firefighters! And dinner was included. She knew that Saturday was Mary's pickup night—there wasn't much that Anne Jankin didn't know about the people who worked for Jon. So she spread the word and had two charter buses out in front of the mill at 5:00 p.m. on Saturday.

All of the girls were dressed as expected: Mi Ly was in a Chinese Sleuth dress covering her from the neck to the floor. Mary wore long orange-and-yellow bell-bottom pants and a small bustier, leaving her midriff bare. Carol wore her usual black pantsuit with white silk blouse beneath. Her long, straight blond hair, splayed across her shoulders, formed a spectacular image. Her teeth were perfect and pure white and her eyes large and deep blue. She was easily the most beautiful woman there, if not the sexiest.

***

The nude black man stood before Carol, turned away, and vibrated his buttocks.

After a moment, he swung gracefully around to face her, his long erection almost touching her lips. Without hesitation, she reached around him, grabbed his buttocks, and pulled him to her.

"God, did you see that?"

"I did. That was surprising. She must have had a lot to drink."

"Too much, I think."

He continued to dance around the room, vibrating his ass and swinging his equipment, before settling on Mary. He pulled a chair opposite and sat, pole extended, and stared into her eyes. A wicked smile spread across his face.

Without missing a beat, Mary slid off her chair and onto her knees, planning to exceed Carol's feat. As was her way, she overdid it, and soon he was done. He retreated, spent, only to be replaced by four other well-built young men who were rapidly shucking their firefighter uniforms as they moved to the loud music.

The energy and excitement built. Soon, most of the girls were anxious to garner at least some attention. Mi Ly sat quietly, disdainful, her smartphone clutched in her hand occupying her.

Anne sat quietly at the bar and watched as the women had fun. Carol and Mary were smiling, enjoying themselves with drinks in their hands, and chatting with their tablemates. Mi Ly was obviously above it all. *Sad*, Anne thought. *She's missing out on the adventures of youth.*

Anne smiled as some of the primmest women of Fauxbook bared their breasts, walked up to the stage, or beckoned the dancers over to them. Now and again, one of the women would look toward Anne, wondering if this was what she had intended. After all, this was Jon's secretary. And Jon was as proper a Christian man as there was anywhere. However, Anne knew, Jon would never find out, and if he did, they would never know.

Two of the male strippers were extraordinarily endowed, and some of the women had organized a contest, which Carol had already won. Anne thought about that. Carol was the only one of the employees who was a mystery to her. Carol didn't talk about personal things and seemed to have no social life Anne could discern—and she was good at discerning. There had been no stories or the normal rumors accompanying her when she came to work at Fauxbook. Anne had been forced to assume Carol was a good girl of impeccable breeding who was saving it for marriage. That made her unique. Then she had witnessed that swallow. Now she didn't know what to think. *She couldn't have done it without practice. A lot of practice.*

The strippers drifted away, to be replaced by a calming orchestra, and dinner was served. After dessert, the strippers returned dressed in tuxes and danced with the women. It all settled down to a much more civilized evening, though Anne knew private arrangements could be, and were being, made.

When the buses pulled around front, about a quarter of the women were missing. Anne knew they would call taxis later. Carol and Mary were among the first on board, along with Mi Ly.

Anne was pretty sure she understood Mary and even Mi Ly, but Carol just became more of a mystery.

Working Hard

Alex walked into the lab just a few minutes late to find Carol hunched over a terminal.

"Were you here last night?" she asked over her shoulder.

"No, why do you ask?"

"Someone has been working on the operating system for the cluster. I thought it might be you. If it's not you, then it must be Leif."

"But he's not supposed to go near anything connected to the network."

"Yeah, I know. But it's running a lot faster, and all on the quantum side. Somebody has been working on it."

"Well, you're right; it has to be Leif. Who else could it be? I hope Gordon doesn't find out. I heard Gordon wanted to fire him over that hack, and Jon saved him. If he's fooling around and gets caught, that will be the end of him.

"How much faster is it?" Alex asked.

"Almost twice as fast on the quantum side."

"You got a status e-mail from the system?"

"Yes, this morning when I came in."

"Isn't Gordon going to get one, too?"

"Oh, God." She sighed.

"Yeah, he'll be here any minute. What are we going to tell him? Do you want to lie for Leif?"

And Leif walked in. "Hi, guys," he said, as if nothing was wrong. "I've got another update I'd like you to install."

Just then, Gordon appeared. "Hey, you people are doing good work. I just got an updated status that tells me the quantum side is improving. That's impressive when you consider no one knows how it works."

"You just can't look at it," Leif said. "Sort of like Heisenberg's uncertainty principle."

Gordon looked at Leif, wondering. "Well, let's meet after lunch and discuss where we're going with this. We're going to have to decide very soon whether we are going to continue to pursue the quantum idea."

"You can't do that!" Leif exclaimed.

"Do what?" Gordon asked.

"Dump the quantum systems! They are the whole point."

Point of what? Gordon wondered. *Leif sometimes, often, seemed to live in a different reality.* But he said only, "Well, it does look good."

He spread his arms out to either side and shrugged his shoulders.

He smiled at the three of them. "Okay, I'll expect you people in my office at two o'clock." Then he left. He had a lunch meeting with Jon and wanted to feel Jon out about where he feared this was going.

"Let's get go down to the cafeteria—I'm hungry," Carol said, grabbing Alex's hand. "Come on, Leif; it's twelve thirty already. What do you think, guys? Italian?"

Alex liked this hand-holding. It was progress, not much progress, but progress. "Sounds good to me," he answered, happy to be away from the freezer. It was a little embarrassing, especially when Mary joined them. Mary was hot and available—at least every Monday. And that meant tonight; his body responded to the thought.

But Carol attracted him as no woman ever had. *God, she's beautiful and smart*, he thought. *But why is this going nowhere physically? If it weren't for Monday nights...*

Alex and Carol ate quickly, anxious to get the update installed on the cluster. "We'll see you at two," Carol told Leif.

"I think Leif might be a little unstable," Alex said as they walked back to the lab.

"You think?" Carol replied widening her eyes dramatically.

***

When Alex and Carol got to Gordon's office they found Leif to be already there chatting with Gordon.

"Glad you could all make it," Gordon said, opening the meeting. "So the cluster is running faster. Alex, is your team working on the operating system?"

"Well, we have been thinking about it," Alex answered carefully. "But we have not actually done anything. I don't know why it's running faster."

"Carol?" Gordon asked.

"No, I don't know why. It's just running faster. We haven't made any changes." *Damn*! She knew where this was going. *But what can I do, lie?*

"Leif?"

"It's the bots," he answered.

"The bots?"

"Yeah, the bots," he said in a bored manner.

"That sounds like bull," Gordon said. "And it sounds like you've been on the network against Jon's orders."

"No, sir," Leif protested, suddenly alert. "I've given all of the updates to Alex for your approval before installation. I have not been on the network since the incident."

"I find that hard to believe," Gordon said. "Someone is working on it. If not you, who?"

"It's the robots," Leif insisted again. "They are finding their way."

Alex and Carol looked at each other, embarrassed.

"Told you guys: they're Darwinian, and they're in the quantum machines."

"The bots are figuring out how the quantum machines work and optimizing the operating system?" Gordon asked in obvious disbelief. "Is that what you expect us to believe?"

"No, no," Leif said. "Not how they work but what works. They are not really intelligent, but they evolve and retain what works and eliminate the failures."

Carol and Alex were simply staring, mouths open. Gordon was shaking his head. *That sounds intelligent to me*, Carol thought.

"And how," he asked, "did they get into the quantum cluster? You were supposed to be doing load testing and keeping your hands out of the networks. Did you install them?"

"I gave the chip to Carol and Alex for your approval. They were installed only after you gave permission."

"And," Gordon asked, "where did these bots come from that are reprogramming our clusters? You were supposed to be doing load testing, nothing else."

"I told you, sir, they evolve. There was only one kind of robot I created. Now they are replicating, modifying themselves, and communicating. They are creating clones within the swarms that know how to get things done on the q-cluster."

"How many?" Carol asked.

"About two million currently. Maybe more. Maybe a lot more."

"How do you know that, Leif? I didn't know how many times they have cloned themselves. Did either of you know?" Gordon asked, indicating Alex and Carol. They shook their heads simultaneously.

"Of course not," Leif declared. "There is no way to know. But, it's certainly exponential."

"Leif," Gordon said, "you have been on the network against Jon's explicit orders. Even if this Darwin-bot story is true, and it sounds like nonsense, you have been working on the machines. There is no doubt that's how the bots got from the Intel cluster to the q-cluster."

"No, sir, I haven't. Tell him, Carol…Alex?" He got blank, embarrassed stares. No one believed him.

Mary was watching the drama from the doorway. *They are all fools*, she thought. *The guy may be a nerd, but he's a brilliant nerd. No one else could have done this, and Gordon is about to fire him in Jon's name. Stupid!*

Killing Jon

Arriving at his small apartment only a block from the mill, Leif went through a gauntlet of emotions, starting with embarrassment and settling on anger. Anger at Jon. *Lying Jon pretending to be a father figure in this one great loving family of Fauxbook. He's just trying to get the maximum work out of his employees and thus accumulate as much money as he can for himself. And he got it,* Leif concluded. *I worked very hard for Jon, leaving time for little else in my life. This shall not stand. I'm not going to let him go on doing this to people.* He lay in his bed exhausted from the emotion and slept until the next morning. Then the alarm clock erupted, unaware it was no longer needed.

***

"I let Leif Hoberson go yesterday," Gordon was telling Jon over morning coffee in the cafeteria. "He couldn't stay off of the networks. And he had an incredulous story about Darwinian robots he had developed."

"Darwinian?" Jon asked.

"Yeah, I think it was a desperate attempt to save his job by claiming a major breakthrough."

"Did it work?"

"No, all he accomplished was to make it obvious he had disobeyed orders and been on the network. I let him go."

"I meant, did the robots work?" Jon clarified.

Gordon took a sip of coffee and was quiet for a pregnant moment. "No, they couldn't have," he finally concluded. "But some things are difficult to explain."

"Like what?"

"Well, the cluster is running faster and the quantum side especially. Leif claims the bots found a way—it's crazy." Gordon paused and frowned, "It has to be crazy because if it isn't crazy it's terrifying."

"But it's running faster?" Jon asked.

"It is…"

"Maybe you should have kept Leif on and let this reveal itself—whatever it is that's going on."

"I don't think so, Jon. In any case, what's done is done."

"Well, too bad; I hate to let an employee go. Is personnel going to take care of the separation?"

"Yes, I filled out the paperwork yesterday afternoon before I went home."

"Good, good, give him a good bonus and at least a couple of months' pay. I don't think the young man has any malice in him. He's just overenthusiastic."

***

Leif was spending his morning doing research. He found he could get most of what he needed from suppliers on the Internet if he was willing to wait a couple of days to receive it. Ammonium

135

nitrate, aluminum powder, and eight thousand BBs. *That should suffice.*

He decided to wait. After all, this was Thursday, and he had been looking forward to seeing Mary all week. And a couple of days might give Jon time to reflect on his sins. He placed the order. The plan was to use a Tupperware-like container, ammonium nitrate, aluminum powder, and the BBs with an igniter—a throwaway cell phone.

Seven o'clock came and went and no Mary. Leif was distraught. The thought of the evening with Mary had been the only thing diverting his mind from utter despair. He retreated to an empty corner of his apartment and sat down on the floor, his mind blank with anguish.

Finally, he heard a knock on the door. It was 8:00 p.m.

"I thought you weren't coming," he said as he let her in.

"I wasn't, but then I remembered yesterday I'd promised, and it wouldn't hurt to see you one last time."

"Why does it have to be the last time?" he asked.

"Leif, don't be dumb and spoil this. You know you'll be leaving town. You're probably already thinking about California and Houston. This doesn't have to be hard. But," she said, stepping up close to him, "this does."

It was a sad and disappointing night for Leif—but still exciting until she left, promising never to return. The next day was awful. He was alone with nothing to do but feel sorry for himself and wonder how this had happened to him. Jon would pay. *Maybe others, like Gordon, should pay also.* Plotting revenge made him feel a little better.

He devoted Tuesday afternoon to building the device. The components had arrived at lunchtime. At 4:00 p.m., he taped it to a power pole on the right side of the entrance of Jon's driveway. He took a position across and down the street fifty yards and waited. Promptly at 5:30 p.m., Jon's Ford Hybrid turned into the driveway, and Leif pressed Dial.

There was a huge bang and a cloud of smoke just beside Jon's car. Leif could not have timed it more perfectly. The car staggered, and the inside wheels lifted off the ground.

Leif drove off as Misika, Jon's wife, hearing the explosion, called the police. The dispatcher, recognizing the address of the area's most famous and wealthiest man, called a general alarm. Soon, the sounds of sirens and air horns filled the air.

When Misika arrived, out of breath after her run down the tree-lined driveway, the scene was already packed with police cars, fire engines, and ambulances—all with lights flashing. The police had pulled cars across the road, closing it, and traffic was seriously backing up. It was rush hour.

Misika saw Jon's car just inside the drive, resting in the drainage ditch. Police officers and a medical team surrounded it. A police officer, a sergeant, she thought, was in rapt conversation with one of the medical people. He was shaking his head, indicating, she thought, the worst.

As she got closer, she saw her husband lying on a gurney on the driveway next to the car. His face was covered with an oxygen mask. No one was working on him, so she assumed he was dead. But she was a calm and stoic woman of Japanese ancestry, and all she said was, "What happened?"

"Honey, is that you?" Jon asked as he lifted the mask from his face and tried to sit up. Only then did she lose control, sobbing with relief. She ran to him and knelt beside him, stroking his head.

"Some kind of explosion, I think," he told her. "Maybe a gas leak in the car. It happened just as I was turning into the driveway. It almost lifted the car off of the ground. I think it did lift the right side off the ground."

Another police officer walked briskly up to the sergeant and said something softly.

He turned toward Jon. "It was a bomb."

The Teams

In addition to the hardware team, the operating-system people, the middleware designers, the applications programmers, and the interface developers, there were three other project teams.

There were the bots that pounded onward, testing the overall system.

A large number of people were working on customer behavior analysis to determine what made a user happy and increased retention. Inside the team their job was referred to as *user manipulation. What can we do to increase, or decrease, the pleasure of the user experience?*

Then there was the marketing team, which was divided into two groups. The first was focused on gaining new users and the second on advertising sales. They were trying methods to hook users on the service. Advertising sales and prices were in direct proportion to user count. Advertising was all there was. It wasn't as if Fauxbook produced anything.

There was overlap throughout the teams; throughout the company, the lack of management structure encouraged chaos. Anyone could meet with anyone at all levels and about anything across all lines of management. And anyone could "help out" in any area. It was possible for a person to work simultaneously on more than one team and report to two, three, or more bosses.

In many ways, this structure, or lack thereof, facilitated communication and rapid progress. That is, when things were going well. When problems occurred, this bizarre arrangement became an unmanageable nightmare.

***

"Men! They think if you sleep with them just one time, you belong to them." Mary Adams was pouring herself a cup of coffee and talking to two young female programmers as Carol Fisher approached.

"What do you think?" Mary asked no one in particular, most likely rhetorically.

"I think you are a promiscuous slut and proud of it," Carol replied, smiling as she poured herself a cup of coffee. She limited herself to one cup a day because she didn't want to stain her teeth. White teeth were more of a professional necessity than a personal vanity for her, but still.

The other two stared, eyes wide open in shock, and waited for the explosion. They expected a bitch fight.

"You got that right," Mary replied, grinning. "Anyway, every now and again I meet 'the right one.' I even took one home to meet my parents once." She laughed. "But I always get over it."

Carol chuckled. "How's work going?"

"It's getting intense. I'm being torn in ten different directions as all of the team's work nears completion. I'm going to talk to Jeff this afternoon about hiring some more people."

"Do you have someone in mind?" Carol asked.

"You're thinking too small," Mary said. "I have four in mind plus an editor. I went to school with three of the writers, and I've worked with the editor, Laurie Werther, before. She's very good."

"So you're expanding your department from one person to six in one day."

"That's the plan, and I need to if all of these people want their documentation on time. Later, but soon, I'm going to need an HTML guy for the web-based help and documentation."

The other two women had drifted off back to work, leaving Mary and Carol alone in the conference room on the second balcony.

"How is Jon doing?" Carol asked.

"I heard he is all right, though he stayed home yesterday. Jeff, Roger, and Barry went over to visit him yesterday. Gordon was already there, I guess."

"That was nice of them," Carol said, offhandedly.

"Well, maybe. I saw Gordon afterward. I asked him for my additional people. He told me to see Jeff. Other than that, Gordon was not happy."

"Why is he unhappy? Things are going great."

"Not sure," Mary replied. "He said something about another of Jon's off-the-cuff meetings whose conclusions are open to interpretation."

"What does that mean?"

"I asked Gordon that; he seemed hesitant to answer. But he finally said, 'Have you ever come away from a meeting with Jon wondering what he said and what he meant by it?'"

"Ha." Mary laughed. "So, I'm not the only one."

"No," Gordon muttered, "there were five people there and there are going to be five different opinions about what was said."

"I have noticed Jon is prone to talk in code. But I've been afraid to say anything about it."

"You probably should be. Almost everyone here thinks of him as all knowing and infallible. The industry itself considers him the god of the computer industry."

"The latter also being all-knowing and infallible."

"Now you have the idea," Gordon said with a smile.

Mary chuckled. "I thought it was me. Any suggestions about how to approach Jeff?"

"I don't know him well, but having said that, he's not an engineer, and I suspect he's sensitive about it. He started Southern Methodist University in Dallas as an engineering major but switched to business. He has an MBA from Harvard, which I would think would make up for it."

"It would for me," Mary said. "Southern Methodist? Does that mean he's religious?"

"And a conservative Republican," Carol said. "I sat down at his table in the cafeteria, he was by himself, and we got to talking.

Or, at least, he did. I think he was impressing himself by educating a pretty young girl."

She knows she's pretty and doesn't mind saying so, Mary thought. *Interesting*. "And?" she said.

"He waxed lyrical about how to determine the right thing to do. I could tell he had been thinking about it a long time.

"Then he said, 'It's not hard to do the right thing, young lady. But it's very hard to know what the right thing to do is.'

"He seemed very pleased with himself at that," Carol said, "and I wondered if he had been drinking. Perhaps he had, and all of this is meaningless."

"Okay," Mary said, "cut it out! What did he say? Cut to the chase!"

"The bottom line was the right thing to do was the thing that benefited you, personally, the most. That's what he said; I shit you not. Oh, he's not dumb or uneducated. He spoke of enlightened self-interest, deferred gratification, and all of that. He called that nonsense."

"Damn," Mary said softly. Carol had surprised her. *Did she really say "Shit you not"? And what's this with Carol sitting down at a man's table in the cafeteria unchaperoned?* Carol never cursed, didn't hang out with guys much, seemed never to have a date, and always dressed very conservatively. This was a Carol she hadn't known.

"Okay then," Mary said. "It's time for me to see Jeff. Wish me luck?"

"Of course," Carol said.

Mary's Way

Jeff rose from behind his desk to greet Mary.

He's a picture, she thought. He was impeccably dressed behind his neatly organized desk. Well, actually his empty desk. There was nothing on it other than a pen set, a steno pad, and two pictures, including one of his wife. Mary remembered Albert Einstein's quote: "If a cluttered desk is a sign of a cluttered mind, of what, then, is an empty desk a sign?" *On the other hand, perhaps he simply doesn't want to disclose what is in his mind.* Later she would conclude Albert was right.

"Have a seat, Ms. Adams," he said, indicating a comfortable-looking chair across from the desk.

Mary noticed the desk looked exactly like the presidential Resolute desk but without the panel had been added by FDR to screen his crippled legs.

"So what can I do for you?" he asked.

"Your desk is beautiful."

"Thank you. I had it made from the plans for the Resolute desk in the White House."

Why? she wondered. "It really is lovely," she said as she batted her eyes.

"Thank you. I'm very fond of it." He turned a framed picture on his desk around to display it to her. It was of a young boy peering out from under the desk as Jeff bent over the desk, working. It was a little odd. Well, maybe more than a little.

"Well," she said, "the teams are all at the point their work needs documentation. I'm the single member of the documentation team, and frankly, I'm overwhelmed. And it's going to get worse. I need help."

"I see. Why did you bring this to me?"

"Initially, I brought it up with Gordon. He suggested I see you."

Jeff looked pleased as he leaned back in his chair. He crossed his arms and said, with a slight smile of satisfaction, "What do you need?"

"To deal with the workload right now, four writers plus an editor. In a couple of weeks, we'll need a website designer who knows HTML, which he most likely would. Then we'll go from there."

"Ah, that's quite an expansion all at once." Jeff was thinking hard. He wasn't sure whether he had the authority to give this girl what she wanted. It sounded reasonable. And this power to hire was more than he'd had, and more was where he wanted to go. But it would really be embarrassing to do it and then to be overruled. For now, he decided to obfuscate while he thought.

"Have you made up a budget?" he asked.

"No, sir, I want to get approval before I go to human resources. My plan is to get tentative approval; talk to human resources about cost, availability, and time frame; and then report back to you for final approval."

"That sounds like a good idea," he said officiously. He was relieved, as this would delay the final decision. The girl was smiling, her knees moving apart, then back together. *She must be very nervous.*

Attempting to put her at ease and in his camp, he said, "I've been thinking about decision making and choices for some time. Do you know what I've concluded?"

She spread her legs widely. *No harm in that*, he thought. *She's wearing a pantsuit. Still.* His forehead seemed to be getting damp.

"No, I don't," she replied, while thinking, *Actually, I do.*

"After some consideration, I've concluded the right decision in every situation is the one that is in the best interest of the person making the decision. Do you understand?"

Damn, I want to tell him I'll slide under the desk and suck his dick while he talks. But I don't dare, she thought.

"So far I do." She passed her right hand over her breast innocently and saw his eyes follow.

"Good, good, well, I know that sounds easy. However, how is a person to know what choice is in their best interest?"

"Uh-huh," she murmured, doing a good job of appearing rapt.

"Then there are different approaches to self-interest. Simple self-interest with a goal of instant gratification, enlightened self-interest with a greater goal but deferred return. That is achieved by acting to further the interests of others. Religion is rather like that."

"That's fascinating," she gasped, wide-eyed.

"Yes, it is." He leaned back, shaking his unease, satisfied to have this young woman's attention. "I have determined decisions ought, must, be made in a person's own self-interest. It's called ethical egoism. Are you following?"

Okay, okay, I can't take it anymore. He's going to put me to sleep.

"I have an idea."

"And what is that?" he said, expecting a comment on his philosophy. This was a little disappointing, as it was early for a comment from her.

"How about you keep talking, and I'll…" her voice trailed off.

"What?" he asked, confused.

"I'll take notes," she answered, reaching into her purse for a pad. *Damn*! she thought. *I'm wet. I've never been turned on by a bore before. This is a new experience. I probably should just slide under his desk. But I'd better not—not yet.*

"Oh, that's flattering. But you don't need to. I've written down my thoughts." He reached into a desk drawer and pulled out a dozen sheets of paper. "Here, run down the hall to the copy machine and make a copy for yourself."

Hiding her relief, she grasped the papers and made a quick exit.

He shuddered. Though he considered himself a man of the world, he didn't understand what had just happened. Mary returned and placed the originals on his desk.

"I know you are a busy man, Mr. Hoover. How about I read this, study, and ask you questions the next time I see you?"

"Fine, fine, that's a very good idea. You go ahead and work up your budget along with a brief outline. I'll authorize it. If the budget makes sense, I have no doubt I'll be able to approve the people you need."

The Games Begin

Jeff closed the door behind her and lay down on the couch. This may be the opportunity I've been waiting for, he thought. But what to do? I can't take it to Gordon; he sent Mary to me and expects me to take care of it. And he may tell me something I don't want to hear. Optimally, someone with influence will tell me to go for it. But who? Talking to Jon would be going around Gordon. Konrad is out of the question since we are vying for the same job. It became dark outside the windows, and he still struggled for the answer.

Jon was in the habit of arriving early, and the next morning he found Hoover waiting for him in his office.

"Jon," Jeff said, "all of the teams have their projects fleshed out to the point we need to get serious about documentation, embedded help, and the support websites if we want everything to come together at the same time. So I've decided to expand the documentation group."

"How many people are in the group now?" Jon asked.

"One, Mary Adams. That's been fine up to now, but the workload is expanding exponentially as the teams approach their goals."

"One." Jon smiled his enigmatic smile. "That does seem a bit light. What do you plan?"

"I'm going to add four writers and an editor. In a couple of weeks, we'll need a website designer who knows HTML, which he most likely would. Then we'll go from there." *So far, so good*, he thought. *He didn't tell me to take it up with Barry. That would have been bad.*

"Do you have a budget for the expansion?"

"I'm working that up now. I'll show it to you before I implement it. However, the current expansion is going to be minor. We're going to need a lot more people soon, and then I'll start staffing the technical support team, which, of course, will be dependent on and work closely with documentation. I see documentation as the interface between the product and the support team."

"That sounds reasonable, though I would like to see the budget and get Barry's consensus."

"Of course," Hoover said, hiding his relief. "Later, but not much later, I'll need to add some programmers to write the customer tracking and support software. I'll drop by and discuss it with you then."

Just then, there was a knock at the door, and Barry Konrad stepped in. He was surprised to see Jeff there.

"Hi, Jeff," he said. "I hope I'm not interrupting."

"Not at all," Jon said. "We were just chatting. What's up?"

"I wanted to let you know the first of the bus sections for the cluster are being delivered this morning. I'm going to start installing them this afternoon."

"Good," Jon said. "It appears we are on schedule."

"I've been pushing," Barry said. "I'm going to leave the existing hand-wired cluster as it is. It works fine, and I see no point in tearing it out and replacing it with the production bus. It will be faster to just add on to it and come back and update it sometime in the future."

"What do you think, Jeff?" Jon asked.

"Sounds good to me, Jon. Barry knows what he is doing. I approve."

"Thank you, Jeff," Barry said, not entirely happy about how this was going.

"Is there anything you need to facilitate this, Barry?" Jeff asked.

"No. No, thank you. I'm good. We should be able to start plugging in additional nodes tomorrow morning. As fast as they get the bus extended, we'll plug in machines and interface them with the running cluster. In a day or so, they should be integrated and contributing to the capacity."

"Good, good," Jon said.

"Have you spoken to the applications people about loading the programs, at least for load testing?" Jeff asked.

"No, not yet. I've been awfully busy getting the bus upgrade organized."

Jon frowned.

"Not to worry," Jeff said, thinking, *Ah, weakness—this is going better than I had hoped; much better.* "I'm on my way over to D Building anyway. I'll stop by and get them organized. You just worry about the bus upgrade. That's the most important thing for now. It's a good thing we have our best man on it."

"That's right," Jon said with a thoughtful look.

"Wonderful," Jeff said. "If you'll excuse me, Jon, I've got to run. I'll have that information for you tomorrow."

"Sure, Jeff," Jon replied distractedly. "You run along."

***

"Jon," Barry said, "you know Leif's trial starts tomorrow."

"Yes, yes, I know," Jon replied. He seemed irritated. "I'm told by the prosecutor I don't have to be there, as there is plenty of evidence without me—and a confession. So I don't plan to attend. It's an unpleasant business I'd just as soon avoid."

"I understand completely. Have you made any plan to replace him? The bots are important to us."

"Yes, it's under control," Jon replied, thinking, *I'll speak with Jeff about that when I see him tomorrow.*

"Well, okay," Barry said, feeling strangely awkward. "I guess I'll get back to work."

"Fine, fine. Thanks for stopping by, and good work on the bus upgrade."

Leif Takes the Fall

It didn't take long for the authorities to determine who had attempted to kill Jon, lock him up, and bring him to trial.

"I don't believe it," Carol said. "Leif is such a nerd. Killing someone just isn't in him."

Everyone on the team had gathered on the main floor when the rumor started Leif had been arrested for attempting to kill Jon Johnsson.

"And why Jon?" Mary asked. "It was Gordon who fired him. Why not kill Gordon?"

"Yeah," Mi Ly said. "Everyone loves Jon. Gordon, not so much."

"Well, regardless," Alex added, "he obviously blamed it on Jon. Or on no one. I agree with Carol: Leif just doesn't have murder in him. But he had to do something."

"To right the unrightable wrong," Larry said.

"To try when your arms are too weary," Carol added with a wry smile.

No one laughed.

"I guess he was driven to do something. He doesn't function well in the world outside the lab, and he was thrown out into that world," Carol said. "He had to do something."

Looking glum, they all nodded.

***

Since Leif had confessed, the proceedings went fairly directly to the sentencing stage.

The prosecutor, Mr. Myer, opened.

"There is no question of guilt in this case. Mr. Leif Hoberson, after being apprehended and apprised of his rights, freely, and without coercion, made a full confession.

"Based on all of the facts, the defendant's reliance on a diminished-capacity defense is nonsense. He knew what he was doing and that it was wrong. Mr. Hoberson planned to murder Mr. Jonneth Johnsson over a period of days, during which he purchased by mail order, the Internet, or in person, numerous supplies required to build and to set off a bomb with the premeditated intent to kill Mr. Johnsson.

"Mr. Hoberson's motive was revenge for being discharged by Mr. Johnsson from his job, for cause, at Fauxbook Corporation.

"Finally, opportunity. In addition to the confession, we have introduced the purchase records for the materials used in the bomb. In addition, there is eyewitness testimony to Mr. Hoberson's presence in the vicinity at the time of the explosion.

"So there you have it: motive, opportunity, and means.

"The state feels a sentence of twenty years to life for attempted murder is called for in this case.

"Thank you, Your Honor."

The defense presented their argument next. Leif was represented by Roy Coheres, Esq., a criminal defense lawyer hired by Fauxbook's law firm and reputed to be the best in Boston—which was saying something. It had been Jon's idea for Fauxbook to pay for Leif's defense. Misika thought it strange but was not surprised; neither was Gordon.

"If it pleases the court," Mr. Coheres began. "It is a fact undisputed that the defendant did this deed. What is unclear is his intent. It is especially unclear whether Mr. Hoberson intended to kill anyone. It is the defense's position he did not.

"There was a bomb. It did go off with a bang, and Mr. Johnsson was inconvenienced and scared. What was Mr. Hoberson's intent, and was it accomplished? Those who would tell you he intended murder will insist the object was not fulfilled. I maintain the intent was to draw attention to Mr. Hoberson's plight and to his pain. And, the defense maintains, that was accomplished, and that was all Mr. Hoberson intended. He simply wanted someone to hear his pain.

"I point out Mr. Hoberson failed to add shrapnel, the part that kills, to the bomb. Why? Because there was no intent to kill Mr. Johnsson or anyone else. The bomb detonated was fairly harmless other than producing a big bang that represented Mr. Hoberson's desperate cry.

"The explosive was placed on the passenger side of the car and some distance away from the driveway, where it would do the least damage and Mr. Johnsson would be perfectly safe from any harm other than a good fright.

"He has no prior criminal history—not even a parking ticket.

"The defense pleas the charge be reduced to a misdemeanor and the sentence, probation. This would serve justice."

A snicker arose from the prosecutor's table.

The judge held up his hand, silencing the room. "Please approach," he ordered.

Mr. Myer and Mr. Coheres moved to the judge's bench. The judge put his hand over the microphone, which recorded the proceedings, and said, "Guys, let me get this straight. Mr. Huberson confessed right out of the gate. In fact, he confessed to the police officers who arrested him right on the spot. He wasn't interrogated; he just confessed. The arresting officers barely had time to read him his rights—thank God for that. Mr. Myer, he confessed before you ever saw him or even knew of the crime. Is all of this correct?" He looked at Mr. Myer.

"Yes, Your Honor. That's about it."

Roy, Leif's defense lawyer, didn't say a word, as he anticipated what was next.

"Should I assume," the judge continued, "if he had not confessed, you would have eventually shown up at the jail with a plea bargain?"

The prosecutor looked uncomfortable.

"Mr. Myer?"

"Yes, Your Honor. That's probably so."

"Probably? You would have offered second degree in exchange for a confession, especially for a first offense."

"Yes, sir."

"But since you got a confession for free, you decided to go for the whole enchilada."

"Your Honor, I don't think that's the way I would put it. Remember, Mr. Johnsson is a pillar of the community, and his new company promises to be our largest employer. Mr. Johnsson and his company will expect the full extent of the law..." His voice tapered off.

"Go back to your seats," the judge ordered.

He motioned to the bailiff, who ordered, "Will the defendant please rise."

"The court finds the defendant, Mr. Leif Hoberson, guilty of attempted murder in the second degree and sentences him to ten years in a state penitentiary."

Roy leaned over and whispered into Leif's ear, "You'll be eligible for parole in six."

There was no complaint from Jon Johnsson or Fauxbook.

Mary Returns

Simultaneous with Leif's trial, Mary met with Hoover to present the budget for the expansion of her department as well as a summary of the current and projected workload and resources necessary.

"Ms. Adams, this summary must be thirty pages."

"Yes, sir. If you include the supporting spreadsheets and graphs, it runs to about fifty pages. They are in a binder under that one."

Jeff flipped rapidly through the pages, picking out the salient points. Mary stood briefly and removed her coat.

"It's warm in here," she commented. She was wearing her favorite open-weave peekaboo sweater.

Jeff glanced up for a second and went back to reading. Then he looked back up and stared, his face flushed. Forcing his eyes back to the paper, he remarked, "Your budget is less than I anticipated."

"Yes, sir. I plan to recruit the writers right out of the University of Iowa. It's a good school, perhaps the best, even if it's not my alma mater, and we can get them cheap for a number of reasons."

"Aha," he responded, keeping his eyes down.

"Remember, please, this is only step one. I anticipate the department becoming much bigger. Eventually, I'd like the second floor of B Building."

"We'll cross that bridge when we come to it," he said testily.

He's getting nervous, she thought. *Good.* She smiled seductively but to no avail, as he didn't look up. She twisted a little until her right nipple protruded through the weave, so she'd be ready when he did look up. He'd have to eventually.

"With your permission, I'll implement this plan and work up a budget, summary, and timetable for the next stage. I'll be adding some experienced writers then. There will be too many novice writers at that stage for me to supervise myself."

"Uh-huh." He looked up. His eyes widened and jumped back to the page.

"Do I have your approval?" she asked, concluding the time had passed for him to object to her seduction.

"Yes." Finally, he seemed to have gathered himself and focused on the wall just above her head. "I'll look forward to seeing your next presentation. I'll consider procuring the second floor based on that."

It sounded like she was being dismissed. Or he was making it clear he was the pursuer. Mary believed the latter.

"Thank you, Mr. Hoover."

"Mary, you may call me Jeff, as it seems we will be working together closely."

"Damn!" she cried, grinning. "I dropped my pen." She pushed her chair back and dropped to her knees, ostensibly to retrieve the pen.

"Oops, it rolled under the desk," she said, crawling under after it.

He tensed as he felt a hand on his knee. *She's just steadying herself.* The hand moved along his thigh, and he felt himself responding, his face flushing. *This could be trouble*, his large head observed. However, he didn't move or speak.

"Almost got it," she said as her hand moved farther.

At that moment, there was a knock at the door. The hand withdrew, and Mary appeared and regained the chair. "Got it," she said.

"Come in," Jeff called. It was Anne.

"Jon would like to see you as soon as you're free," she said.

"Sure, Anne. Can he give me fifteen minutes to finish up here?"

Mary displayed a coy smile only he could see. *Gee*, she thought, *I hope it will take longer than fifteen minutes*. She could tell Jeff knew exactly what she was thinking.

She quickly gathered her notebook and pen and stuffed them in her purse, rose, and headed toward the door.

"Later," she said, turning at the doorway to smile at him.

"Six o'clock?" Jeff suggested.

She winked, turned, and was gone.

At five thirty, he ordered hot-and-sour soup, crispy egg rolls, spareribs (he fantasized about watching her eating them with her hands, ripping the meat from the bone with her bared teeth), broccoli tempura, and pu pu platter for two.

Just before six, he heard a soft knock on his office door, and his pupils dilated. "Come in," he called past a tight throat.

"Delivery, sir," a young Chinese man said as he opened the door and entered.

"Oh, sure, of course," Jeff said, not sure whether he was disappointed or not. "How much do I owe you?"

After the young man left, Jeff cleared his desk of the few items on it, took the cartons out of the bag, and arranged them on the desk. Then he removed the plastic wrap from the utensils and arranged the forks, knives, and spoons on paper napkins on opposite sides of the desk.

It was a quarter after six, on a Tuesday night. Mary was on her way to Joe's apartment.

Lost Memory

"Gordon," Jon called, entering the other man's office unannounced. "What have you found regarding our little hacking problem? Everything cleared up?"

"I think we're good, Jon. We've swept the systems every way imaginable and found nothing."

"That's a relief." Jon sighed and sat down on the couch opposite Gordon's desk. "Jeff just told me they're ready to load her up, and we'll get our first real look at Fauxbook."

"Well, maybe," Gordon said, his face expressing worry. "I don't think we have a virus or any malware lurking in the systems. But there is a small amount of memory unaccounted for in the IBM's RAM."

"Unaccounted for?" Jon asked, puzzled.

"Unaccounted for," Gordon repeated. "Just a few bytes' difference between what two programs report. And every time we run the reports, we get a slightly different answer. None of the answers match the machine's specifications."

"What does IBM say?" Jon asked.

"They say to ignore it. They call it a ghost in the machine. Further, it's possible the specs are not precise. And some of the memory addresses could, and probably were, locked out as defective during manufacture or as the memory burned in."

"Or," Jon said, smiling, "it's just the operating system is locking out defective memory."

"The operating system or lower-level code in the hardware. You are right; IBM is right. But as far as I know, discarded memory by manufacturing or the operating system is never unlocked. And that appears to be what's happening, as the analysis programs return different results every time they are run. To be absolutely sure," Gordon said, "I'd like to take it down and replace the memory."

"That would set us back weeks and cost a fortune," Barry said, standing in the doorway. "I can't support that." He had read the situation quickly and was diplomatically siding with the position he knew Jon would take.

"Yes," Jon said. "Let's give some thought before rushing into something we'll regret."

"Okay," Gordon replied. "I'll give it some thought." *I wonder what he thinks I've been doing.*

"Maybe you can take it down once the cluster is up," Barry said, trying to sound more knowledgeable than he was.

"I do think it's benign," Gordon said. "But if it's not, it might move from the z13 to the cluster as soon as they are connected."

Roger Aegel entered and asked about the beta test, and the subject was discarded as they formed an informal meeting about scheduling the Fauxbook rollout.

"Let's move next door to the small conference room," Jon said. "It's getting too crowded in here, and Roger has no place to sit."

Gordon wondered if that was a veiled reference to Roger's girth. Jon, as kind as he was, didn't have much sympathy for those with a lack of discipline. He smiled as everyone started to move next door.

"Anne," Jon called, "get the kids up here. Alex, Carol, Mary, and Joe. Tell them right now!"

"Yes, sir," Anne replied as she picked up the phone.

"And get us some coffee and refreshments up here. This may take a while."

In quick time, everyone was assembled. Gordon shook his head in amazement. *Jon's always a surprise.*

"All right," Jon started, "has everyone had a chance to grab a coffee and a doughnut?" Heads nodded. "We are all here because it's time to run up the system. The cluster is ready to take over the load from the z13, and we'll switch the IBM to its role as an intelligent switching router. Shortly after that, we'll start loading the applications and the Internet tools. Next comes testing in-house. Finally, we'll be ready to open access to our outside testers. Any questions?"

There was silence.

"Is everyone ready for this? Are any of the teams behind?"

There were nodding heads and mumblings of yes. Carol spoke up. "We're ready! Let's do it." She smiled widely. The smile was contagious, and in an instant, everyone was smiling except Roger Aegel, who never smiled.

"Is the cluster up and finished?" Joe asked.

Carol jumped in. "It's up and running, and the bots have been at it for a week. There have been a few bottlenecks, but we've been fixing them as we go along. It's currently pretty stable and very fast. As for finished, it's as finished as it needs to be at the moment. We'll be adding nodes as Fauxbook grows. However, that's just a matter of plugging them into the bus—and, when necessary, expanding the bus. And, of course, we'll constantly be improving the software as we learn more about the requirements."

Mi Ly appeared in the doorway. "May I join you?" she asked shyly.

"Come in, come in," Jon called. "Everyone who is interested in what's going on here at Fauxbook is welcome."

Mi Ly entered and took the first seat. It was Thursday.

"Mi Ly," Carol said, "I'm glad you're here. We're talking about taking the system live—probably tomorrow. Can you bring us up to speed on the status of the bus?"

"Certainly." Mi Ly stood and almost bowed. "Design is complete. There are redundancies and space for modifications without having to change the hardware. That is, changes in its function, within limits, can be modified through software."

"What about the bots? Are they going to be ready to put a load on the applications now Leif is gone?" Alex already knew the answer, as he and Carol worked together closely. However, he wanted the answer on record. Anne was in the front right corner of the room taking notes.

"We think so," Carol replied. "Leif said the bots are adaptive. However, we've not been able to find, never mind hire, anyone who can figure out how they work. So, we're hoping for the best."

"Well, well, there you have it. We load it up the first thing in the morning. I'll see you then." With that, Jon swept out of the room. It was almost five o'clock on Thursday evening, and Jon, a family man, liked to be home by five thirty.

As the company dispersed, Mi Ly and Mary remained sitting together in intense conversation. "Carol, come over here," Mary called.

"What's up?" Carol said as she sat down beside them. Alex rather naturally drifted along and stood beside the three girls.

"Mi Ly has invited us to her club. She says we'll have a wonderful time. How about it, Carol?"

"Oh, I can't. Alex and I are going out to dinner to celebrate the system going live. That is, if Alex is free tonight." She looked up at his surprised face.

After a pregnant moment, he said, "Sure, that would be great." It was great, he thought, but he still didn't know where this was going. He'd been out with girls, women, who didn't want to have sex until the third date, but this was crazy.

Mary was livid. *Alex is mine. He has no right to go behind my back and fuck another woman! I thought I smelled another woman on him last Monday!* She clenched her teeth in fury.

"You can come with us, too," Mi Ly told Alex. "There are things there for you, too. Then you two can go to dinner later."

"What do you think, Alex?" Carol asked.

"Up to you, babe," he said.

"Let's go," Carol said. She was curious. Mi Ly, a club—it seemed incongruous unless it was a religious club. Carol did not recall ever meeting anyone as prudish and disapproving of everyone and everything as Mi Ly. When anyone mentioned a significant other, Mi Ly would express disapproval with indirect words or body language. Rolling her eyes was a favorite.

However, as irritating as Mi Ly was, she was very good at her job. Carol couldn't think of anyone who could have done a better job designing and debugging the bus. Maybe Mi Ly's personality helped her to look at things objectively. Carol didn't think that had a lot to do with it. *But who knows*, she thought. In any event, Carol was happy to have her on Alex's—and her own—team.

As she left the meeting, Mary thought about filling Thursday night. *But, for now I'll see what Mi Ly has been up to.*

Glory

They all piled into a taxi. Mi Ly commandeered the front seat, and the other three squeezed into the back seat. Carol climbed onto Alex's lap. It was the most intimate moment in their entire relationship.

Mi Ly gave the driver an address in Boston, and they were off. The cabbie went east on Main Street to Interstate 95 and then turned south. Back Bay was the destination, and in less than an hour, they were there.

"We're here," Mi Ly announced.

Alex wasn't sure he would be able to get out of the cab, much less walk. Both of his legs were asleep. Not that Carol was especially heavy. However, even one hundred pounds sitting on a person will block the blood flow. It hadn't blocked the flow to one place, and he worried she had noticed. *She must have*, he thought. *She was sitting on it.* Regardless, the discomfort had been worth it. He loved the feel of her body leaning against him. *She's in amazing shape*, he thought. *She must work out.* During the forty-five-minute ride, he had experienced much of her body, and it was hard, muscled; she didn't seem to have an ounce of fat.

Carol opened the door and climbed out. Alex, still sitting in the cab, raised his butt off of the seat and dug out his wallet. He felt that, as the only man, he should pay the cabdriver. And, it would delay his exit, giving things a chance to return to normal.

"No, no," Mi Ly said. "I'll pay. This is my treat, and I insist."

"Let Mi Ly pay," Carol said, "and get it out. I want to see it."

"What?" Alex said, shocked.

"What do you mean, what?" Carol said. "I've been sitting on it for the last hour. Let's see it." Everyone laughed, and Alex blushed bright red. *Apparently she noticed*, he thought. *She didn't have to embarrass me in front of everybody, though.*

Carol confused him. Most of the time she was prim and very proper. Then, out of the blue, she asked to see his boner. She was beautiful, she had an extraordinary body and a pleasing manner—most of the time—and she was smart. But whenever it seemed they were becoming closer, she drew back. It frustrated him, and the relationship would have been impossible if not for Monday nights.

Mary was seething as she watched Carol move in on her man. She wanted to kill the bitch; at the same time, she was surprised at Carol's interest. Carol didn't seem the type to steal another woman's man. She didn't even seem the type to have a man. Mary had never known her to date, flirt, or even sit with a guy. She knew Carol worked nights and weekends, though she didn't know what she did. *But there she is, asking my man to show her his dick. Damn! This isn't right, and it's rude. I'll fix her!*

Alex exited the cab, holding his hand over his crotch. Carol laughed. "Never mind, Alex. I was just messing with you. Okay, where are we? Mi Ly?"

Looking around, they saw a brightly illuminated building across the street. There was a round red neon sign with the words *Peep Show* in the center. To its right, also in neon, were the words *XPOSED Totally Naked XXX.*

"It's a strip club," Alex exclaimed. "Mi Ly, you've brought us to a strip club? Cool."

"No," she said with some heat. "No strip club. That's sinful. We are not going there. Follow me." She took off across the street toward the strip club.

Everyone was confused and fascinated. This was not the Mi Ly they knew, the one with the smartphone glued to her hand. They found it hard to imagine her even that close to a sex club. They followed closely, curious to discover what was next.

Mi Ly led them down an alley on the right side of the building and turned left into a parking lot behind it. "This is it," she said. There were two doors, one at each side of the building. The farthest door was labeled "Performers." The closest had a silhouette of a woman in a provocative position that was much like those truckers display in the cabs of their rigs.

"Alex, you go in that door," she commanded. "We'll go in the performers' entrance," she said with an inflection that made it clear she was proud to be a performer.

"Well, okay," Alex said hesitantly. "What's in there?"

"You'll see," she said. "You'll like it. We'll see you later."

Alex did as he was told, and the girls proceeded to the performers' entrance.

Inside, the girls encountered a window, like a ticket booth in a movie theater. Mi Ly signed in on a sheet and received three keys. They moved into what appeared to be a dressing room with lockers.

"There is a locker number on the key," Mi Ly said. "That will be your locker. You can get undressed now."

"Undressed?" Mary and Carol said in unison.

"Yes, then you have your choice of holes or bottoms. I think I'm going to indulge my bottom tonight."

"Your bottom," Carol said, thoroughly confused.

Carol went through the door on the right, exploring. She entered a room whose floor was completely padded, like a wrestling ring. Six women were on their knees facing the wall. Carol stifled a laugh and went back into the dressing room. Mi Ly was already half-disrobed. Mary was just standing there waiting to see what would happen next.

"Mary," Carol said with amusement, "it's a glory hole."

Mary laughed out loud. "Really?"

"No," Mi Ly said. "It's much more. In the other room, you can stick your bottom through a hole. You have your choice."

"Glory by any other name," Carol chuckled, strangely ill at ease.

"How much do they pay us for this?" Mary asked.

"Oh, we don't have to pay," Mi Ly said, misunderstanding. "It's free for performers."

"Is this what you do for sex, Mi Ly?" Carol asked.

"It's not sex," Mi Ly replied with indignation. "Sex is fraught and dangerous—disgusting. This isn't sex. You don't even see the men—there's always a wall between you. Performing is just fun. It's totally impersonal, like the computers—like the bots."

"Good clean fun," Carol commented with a smile. But Mi Ly's words gave her pause. *It's true*, she thought. *There's not a lot in my life that's real. Except, maybe, Alex.* Mi Ly's insight surprised her.

Mary nodded with a smile.

"Yes, so take off your clothes."

"I think I'll pass," Carol said, "but thank you for inviting me."

Mi Ly looked horrified. "You're not going to perform?"

"No, I don't think so. It's late, and I have to be at work early tomorrow. How about you, Mary? Do you want to split a cab?"

"As long as I'm here, I think I'll stay at least a little while. I've never tried this before. Who knows? I might like it."

"Okay, have fun. See you guys later."

Mi Ly gave Carol an angry look and then turned and resumed undressing.

"It is her loss," she said to Mary.

"Yes, Mi Ly, it certainly is."

Carol left by the door they had gone in and found Alex pacing in the parking lot.

"What are you doing out here?" Carol asked.

"Sorry, this is not for me. Are you finished already?" he said sharply.

"I never started. It's not my style either," she said.

Alex didn't mention his midwestern values, which were sorely offended by what he had seen. Almost unconsciously, he was testing Carol—he couldn't help himself. Her answer satisfied him, though a small voice in his head whispered she could have been more emphatic.

He felt displaced. Back in Iowa he was a progressive, almost a libertine. Here in the big city he felt like an unsophisticated prude. It wasn't pleasant.

"Do you think there are any good restaurants around here?" she asked.

"Let's walk around and look. If not, we'll catch a cab back to Maynard," he replied. He was not at all hungry and oddly offended, or disappointed, that she was. His mind was, at best, clouded. She wasn't reacting to this abomination with the revulsion he expected from a lady.

"Okay, a walk in the fresh air sounds right." She took his hand, and they exited the alley and walked down the street toward the water. Her hand felt uncomfortable in his—damp, dirty even.

Friday

They were all there the next morning. Larry was bent over a keyboard in total concentration. He was working on the migration of router control to the IBM and a program to shut down the simulator and move function to the cluster.

Alex and Carol watched. In theory, everything would go smoothly, with the IBM taking over as the router and the cluster accepting the middleware.

They were silent as they watched Larry's fingers fly across the keyboard and the light of the monitor reflect on his face damp with anxious sweat.

"Okay, it's done," Larry said, pushing his chair back and assuming a relaxed position. "And it seems to be running." He was obviously relieved.

"We'll give it a couple of hours and then load the bots to test the load on the midware. If that goes well, we'll install the apps and figure out how to modify the bots to emulate users and gradually ramp that up," Carol said.

"How are you going to modify the bots?" Alex asked. "I, for one, have no clue as to how they work."

"Yes," Carol said, "that may be a problem. Leif let us down."

"Leif let himself down," Alex said dejectedly. He was very fond of Leif and was in awe of his brilliance—with computers.

"Let's go to lunch," she said, taking his hand.

Strangely, he was getting used to this platonic relationship with Carol. He liked her a lot and had stopped fretting about sex. They walked hand in hand down to the cafeteria as they usually did. There were plenty of restaurants in the neighborhood, with more opening as Fauxbook grew. But both he and Carol were very happy with the company's offerings, as were most employees. And it was cold outside.

Fauxbook took very good care of them. Just the previous week, a free barbershop and beauty salon had opened in the space adjacent to the cafeteria, and there were additional spaces being finished. So they could look forward to more services to come. All of this made the employees more and more dependent on the company for their creature comforts and social life.

When they returned to D Building, after a long lunch with good conversation, they found Mi Ly hunched over a terminal, typing rapidly with an intent look on her face.

"Hey, what's up?" Alex asked.

Ignoring the question, she typed another line, hit Enter, and looked up, her eyes squinting with anxiety. "The bots are in the cluster," she said.

There was a pause as Carol and Alex both expressed confusion, then disbelief. "No way," Carol said. "Did you load them?"

"No, I was sitting over there," she said, indicating a desk nearby, "eating a sandwich, when I noticed the activity lights blinking like a mad Christmas tree. Look." She pointed to the terminal screen.

After a moment's study, Carol said, "They are challenging the middleware! It can't be. You didn't load them?"

"No! I did not, and I don't know why you keep asking me," Mi Ly replied angrily. "They must have migrated over themselves when we made the connection."

"Now that's a can of worms," Alex commented, "or bots. Damn!"

"What do we do now?" Mi Ly asked plaintively.

"Well, Leif is gone," Carol said. "There's no answer there unless we go see him. For now, my assumption is they are doing what they were designed to do. Leif was just much further ahead than we thought."

"Let's go see him," Alex suggested. "We probably should have done that before now anyway."

"Okay," Carol said. "Let's do that, but first…" She picked up the phone and dialed an extension. While it was ringing, she put her hand over the mouthpiece and said, "Mi Ly, please run down the hall and get Larry; tell him it's important. Hello, Gordon? Carol Fisher here. Can you come down to D Building right now, please? It's important."

Gordon must have run, Alex thought when he and Larry came through the door together.

"What's going on?" Gordon asked, a bit out of breath.

"The bots are in the cluster," Mi Ly answered, apparently seeking to retain control of her discovery, "and we didn't put them there."

"They came over when you connected the IBM?"

"Apparently," Carol said. "Though that's impossible."

"Not impossible if it happened," Gordon replied.

Larry had said nothing, but he had taken a chair in front of a terminal and begun typing. *He's fast*, Carol thought.

"We're planning on a visit with Leif," Carol said. "But I don't even know where he is being held. Frankly, I feel a bit guilty about that. We should have visited him sooner."

"Yeah," Mi Ly said. "All he did was try to kill Jon. I don't know why you feel guilty. I sure don't."

"I think that's a good idea. I'll talk to legal to arrange a visit. I'll also inquire about any possible pitfalls you might run into by talking to him," Gordon said. "I'll get back to you later this afternoon. Will you be here?"

"Boy, I think all of us will," Alex said. "We have a lot to figure out."

"They are in there," Larry said without taking his eyes from the monitor. "And they're hammering away. And the code is compiled. Is Leif's office still sealed? Maybe the source is still on his computer."

"As far as I know," Gordon replied, "no one has been in there since the incident, other than the police. I'll have security give you access when you're ready. Let me know."

"What are we going to do now, Gordon?" Carol asked. "Do we shut it down or just let it run? In addition, we're scheduled to start loading the applications this afternoon and Joe's user interface tomorrow."

Gordon thought for a moment and then said, "Let it run against the midware for now. Hold off on everything else until we learn more. I'll be in my office or Jon's. Or you'll see me back here. This is very interesting."

Before going to his office, Gordon stuck his head into Anne's. "Anne, ask Jeff to come see me as soon as he can, please."

"Yes, sir," she replied.

Knocking briefly on Jeff's office door, Anne tried to turn the doorknob, only to find it locked, which was odd. She went back to her desk and dialed his extension.

"Yes," Jeff answered, breathless.

"Jeff, this is Anne Jankin. Gordon would like you to stop by his office at your earliest convenience."

"Okay," he replied. "I'll be right there."

Fifteen minutes later, Jeff entered Gordon's office.

"Jeff," Gordon said, "I want to keep you abreast of things. There may be a delay ramping up the cluster."

"What's wrong?"

"I don't know anything is wrong. But I'm not sure it's right, either. We connected the IBM to the cluster this morning and switched its function to router. Within minutes the bots had migrated over and were working, putting a load on the midware."

"Isn't that what is supposed to happen?" Jeff asked, confused.

"Not by itself, we don't think. But maybe. As you know, the designer of the robots is currently in jail, and no one else knows how they work. Most likely all is well. However, we're not sure. The team leaders are going to visit Leif this afternoon to see if he can shed some light on this."

"No one here knows how they work?"

"That's correct, though Larry Bowers is, as we speak, attempting to figure them out."

"That doesn't sound good," Jeff said. "On the other hand, if they are doing what they are supposed to do, why don't we let them continue?"

"That's precisely what I'm doing," Gordon said with some exasperation. "However, I'm hesitant to proceed to the next step before we understand what they are about."

"So we are not delayed?"

"Not at the moment, no," Gordon replied with a sigh. "But we were scheduled to load the apps in an hour and the user interface tomorrow. I'm delaying those steps. But no, for the moment we are on schedule, and the bots are testing the midware and the bus."

"Oh, good; that's good news."

"No, it's not, Jeff. It's bad news. We're going to be behind schedule in about an hour, and from there we will fall further behind every minute until we figure this out. Do you want to take it to Jon, or should I?"

Doubling Down

There was silence as Jeff thought about that. He was anxious to bring Jon good news demonstrated he had everything under control. But bad news, not so much. On the other hand, he was either at the controls or he wasn't, and he was sure would be the way Jon would see it.

"I'll take care of it," he finally decided.

"Okay then," Gordon replied. "I'm going to call legal to arrange for the visit with Leif. Then I'll go back over to the lab and see how they're doing." He left the room for his office.

"Anne," Jeff said after dialing her extension, "can you get me in to see Jon?"

"Hold. I'll check."

After a moment of Muzak—*I need to do something about that*, he mused. *It's awful*—he heard Anne say, "Sure, Jeff, come on over. He'll see you."

After hearing Jeff out, Jon said into the intercom, "Anne, get Barry, Roger, and Gordon up here now, please. I'd like you to sit in too."

Once they had gathered and Anne's secretary had wheeled in a coffee cart, Jon started. "Jeff tells me we are about to fall behind schedule when we're on the home stretch." Gordon and Roger simultaneously started to speak, but Jon hushed them with a gesture. "And we're about to fall behind because, though everything is working perfectly, we don't know why. Gordon, is that a fair assessment?"

Gordon, trying to recover from his amazement Jon had actually called a meeting, however impromptu, with all of upper management in attendance, was not fazed. He'd been around too long and was too rich to be bothered by Jon's flutter.

"Yes," he replied. "You could put it that way. I wouldn't, but yes, the situation could be described that way."

"That's ridiculous," Roger sputtered. "I never know how my computer is doing what I want it to do, and frankly, I don't care. I don't see what the problem is."

"Nor do I," Barry chimed in, sensing the wind.

"Indeed," Jon said, "caution is fine and usually the best course. However, there is a time to charge. Recall that great cautionary tale of the Charge of the Light Brigade. A lesson for restraint, for sure. But only a hundred and ten of the six hundred and seventy were killed; most survived."

Well, another hundred and sixty-one were wounded; history doesn't say how badly. I looked it up the last time Jon told this story. Again, it's hard to understand Jon's point. Is there a point? Gordon wondered.

"I agree," Barry said. "If the system is working, let's run with it and figure it out later."

"I'm with you there, brother," Roger said. "I've made promises to advertisers we'll be on schedule for the prelaunch demo and online for the launch celebration, which, by the way, will be the biggest Boston has seen in years."

Anne knocked on the door and came in, beckoning to Gordon.

"I'm just going to step out in the hall for a second, guys," Gordon said before following Anne out.

"Here is the information for the visit with Leif this afternoon," Anne said. "Only two people can visit him, and they will be subject to search. He's still in the city jail, and the visit is for four this afternoon. McMyers said there was nothing to be concerned about while talking to him. Unless you were an accomplice." She smiled.

Ross McMyers was the newly hired head of the Fauxbook legal department and had, by necessity, hit the ground running.

"Okay, Anne," Gordon replied. "Please put this information into Carol Fisher's hand as soon as possible. I'd appreciate it if you personally would hand deliver it."

"Yes, sir. I'll do it now."

Reentering the room, Gordon found a fait accompli.

"We have decided to proceed loading and with the bots. And to simultaneously continue working to understand what's going on," Jon said. "Perhaps the meeting with Leif will bear fruit."

"Anne," Gordon commanded, "have someone go over to Leif's office and see what they can find. Then come back to the lab and tell us how these bots work."

Gordon looked at Jon shaking his head slowly. "I think this is a mistake, Jon," he said. "It's better to wait."

Barry and Roger were shutting down their laptops and preparing to leave, and they studiously ignored the conversation. They had won, the deed was done, and there was no point in dragging it out.

"Gordon, the decision has been made, and you excepted, it was unanimous. There are times to be cautious and times to take the reins in hand. That's what I'm here for: to make that decision."

"I'm not arguing with you, Jon. I know you are going to do what you believe is the right thing. However, I want to be on record as opposed to what I'm pretty sure is a mistake. I know it's working. However, some little things, likely nothing in themselves, are starting to pile up."

"Such as?" Jon asked.

"The hack, missing memory, the unexplained increase in speed of the q-cluster, and, of course, the bots. All together, they should be resolved before we add complexity. But…" he said, spreading his arms, palms outward, "I'm just saying."

"Noted, noted," Jon said. "I'll take that under advisement."

***

Larry successfully made it into Leif's computer. It was password protected, but security provided the company's master password and authenticated it, and he was in. He found the code for the bots. *It's too simple*, he thought. *There has to be more*. He spent the next hour searching and still another thirty minutes thinking. *There is something here I don't understand*, he concluded. *That's obvious*, he chided himself. *But what is it?* He went over the code again but gained no better understanding. It just didn't seem to be doing much but running in a constant loop containing some calls to the operating system and an object named "magic101." *What is magic101?* he wondered. It wasn't an operating-system call, so it must be an object of Leif's creation or an API. *Where is the code?*

He manually went through each subdirectory one by one, finding nothing. *A hidden directory*, he considered. *Why would Leif do that?* This was going to take longer.

***

Jeff returned to his office to find the door locked. *Strange*, he thought as he placed his thumb on the keypad. He entered to find Mary still there, her large purse on his desk. He turned and locked the door.

Godless Acts

Jon and Misika were enjoying a quiet evening at home in front of the large fireplace in the drawing room. Each had a book open, Misika a novel and Jon an autobiography of Alan Turing. No one else was in the house, which was positioned on a large lot well back from the road. It was quiet.

"Turing was a great man," Jon commented, "and it's a shame what happened to him."

"What happened to him?" Misika asked.

"He killed himself with cyanide."

"Why would he do that?" she asked.

"He had been convicted of homosexual acts. It's a long story."

"Alan Turing? He killed himself because he was a homosexual?"

"Yes," Jon answered, "gross indecency. That was still a crime in the fifties. I think it should still be a crime. The Bible speaks against it, and it remains an abomination regardless of what liberal laws they pass."

"Aren't you being a little harsh?" Misika asked.

"I don't think so. Homosexuality is an act against God and against nature."

"Isn't that the same thing?" she asked, smiling. She enjoyed teasing Jon now and again, but she never went too far.

Just then, the doorbell rang, and Misika rose to answer it. As wealthy as Jon was, they employed no full-time servants, just a cleaning woman who came three times a week and a yardman.

She opened the front door. A trusting woman, she never bothered with the peephole. There was a woman standing on the stoop, completely naked and shivering. *Well*, Misika thought, *she does have one slipper on.* She recognized Diane Hoover. The Hoovers, Jeff and Diane, lived just one house down. The Fauxbook executives tended to cluster around Jon. *It's still a long walk in the cold.*

"Come in, dear," she said. "You must be freezing." Pulling the woman into her arms, she shouted over her shoulder, "Jon, bring a robe and a blanket, quickly!"

Jon came quickly, though he didn't bring anything. He was concerned at her tone and anxious to learn what was happening. When he reached them, he was surprised to see a naked woman in his wife's arms, her face buried in Misika's shoulder. The woman was sobbing and shivering.

"What? Who is it?" he sputtered, bewildered.

"Jon," Misika ordered, "get a robe and a blanket, now!" Her voice cracked with command.

He turned to obey, somewhat understanding the situation, and soon returned. He pried one of the woman's arms from around his wife and inserted it into a sleeve of the robe. Then he wrapped it around the woman and got her other arm in. Misika pushed the woman gently away, closed the robe in the front, and tied it.

"Diane!" Jon exclaimed. "It's you! What is going on?" He recoiled, his mouth agape, and raised his hands, palms outward as if to ward off something distasteful. This was outside his experience, and he wasn't comfortable.

"It's Jeff," Diane said. "He's having an affair, and he beat me." She sobbed.

"An affair?" Jon exclaimed in disbelief.

"That's terrible," Misika said. "He really beat you?"

"Look!" Diane said, pushing the robe off her shoulder to expose the bruises on her arm.

Jon couldn't help but notice she also exposed her breast. *God, he thought, she's a beautiful woman.* Quickly, he chastised himself for such base thoughts.

"Come in," Misika insisted. "I'll sit you by the fire to warm you up. You must be freezing."

Diane sat quietly sobbing for a long time. It occurred to Jon he had meant to watch the national news and was missing it. He reached for the remote and pressed Record.

At last Diane began to tell them of the affair she had discovered while reading her husband's e-mails. It had been going on for a long time, since Diane's surgery for stage IV cervical cancer more than two years ago.

"Since the operation, I can't have normal sex," she said. "They closed me up. So Jeff sought to fulfill his needs elsewhere—on the Internet, for God's sake. He told me the woman is clean, and she is just helping out with duties I can't perform."

"Tell me about the beatings, Diane," Misika commanded.

Diane raised her head, the sobbing subdued, and looked at Misika. "Do you think the beating is more important than his affair?"

"Yes, I do," Misika answered. "Violence is not acceptable. Affairs can be forgiven, sometimes. Domestic violence is never acceptable and cannot be forgiven. In any case, he'll never stop—until you're dead."

Jon was dumbfounded. He had never heard his soft-spoken wife talk this way or so completely take control of a situation.

"How often does Jon beat you?" Diane asked, a little angry at Misika's presumption.

She seemed genuinely shocked when Misika told her Jon had never beaten her.

"Jeff has beat me from the beginning, twenty years ago. The first time was after his accident on the motorcycle. He was in multiple casts, and Jerry and Ellen Jane came over. I put him to bed and was downstairs drinking and smoking pot with them. I was sitting on Jerry's lap, kissing and such. But nothing serious. I didn't know Jeff was sitting on the bottom of the stairs listening.

Later, I went up to bed. As I got into bed, he swung and hit me right under the chin. He knocked me out.

"Later, he caught me smoking. He grabbed me by the throat and pushed me against the wall. He stuffed a pack of cigarettes into my mouth and forced me to chew and swallow them. 'I'll bet this will cure you of smoking,' he shouted."

"Why haven't you left him?" Misika inquired.

"I love him; he's the love of my life. And it's all my fault. I do bad things, and he punishes me. I have to try harder to be good, to please him."

"It's not your fault," Misika assured her. "There is never an excuse for physical abuse."

"But I haven't pleased him. He started going on dating sites looking for a girlfriend after my cancer operation. I wasn't able to satisfy him, so he hooked up with Mary. Yesterday I found them in the motor home out at our property. Jeff had chained the gate closed and changed the locks. And he had put concertina wire on top of the fence, around the entire forty acres. But I climbed over anyway and knocked on the trailer's door.

"I said, 'I know you two are in there. Jeff, put on your clothes, and come out here. I want to talk to you.' No one answered, but I knew they were in there. Finally, Jeff came out. I had his Colt forty-five loaded and cocked. I pointed it at him for a long time. After a while, I lowered it, and he took it from me."

"You may have missed your chance," Misika said softly.

Shocked, Jon leaned back in his chair. It was only then he realized he had been on the edge of his seat, leaning forward and listening intently.

"When he beat me, I felt like it was my fault. I'd done something to make him mad."

"No, Diane, it's not your fault. If he is unhappy with you, there are other options. Hitting is never right."

"His affair with Mary has been going on for two years. When I first found out, I was suicidal. I ran away and checked into a motel downtown. I went to the bar next door, had a couple of drinks. Then I went back to the motel and went to bed."

"That sounds like a good idea," Misika said, "to get away from him."

"It wasn't," Diane rejoined. "He called the police, and they found me—I'd used my credit card, I guess. And they traced it."

"No!" Misika said.

"Yes, I was arrested. They told me I could do this the easy way or the hard way.

"'Cuffs in the front or the back?' the officer said. 'If you give us trouble, we'll cuff you with your hands behind you.'"

"What did you do?"

"I presented my hands to him in the front."

"Did they take you home?" Misika asked.

"No, they took me to jail, an awful ten-by-ten-foot cell. It was cold. In the morning, I saw a judge. It turned out I had not been arrested; I was 'detained' for my own protection. He remanded me to a mental hospital for three days."

"Did Jeff come to see you in the hospital?"

"On the second day, he came to visit and explained if I promised to be good, I could come home the next day. I told him I would do anything if he would give up Mary. 'I'll do anything you want,' I said. He knew what I meant, and he smiled wickedly. It scared me."

"What did you mean by 'anything'?" Misika asked, concerned. She feared she did know what Diane meant by *anything*. Because she was as a devout Christian woman, it chilled her heart.

"You know," Diane said, averting her face. "Anything."

"So you went home the next day?"

"Yes. He handcuffed my hands to the head of the bed, spread my legs, and tied them to the bedposts at the bottom. It was his bed. We both slept in it, but it was his bed. He had picked it out."

"Really." Misika's face turned white, and she was at a loss for words.

"I was facedown, and he put a pillow under my hips."

"A pillow?" Misika said, confused.

"Yeah, a pillow, you know, to raise my butt. Because of the operations for my cancer, my vagina is only three inches deep, so…" Her voice trailed off.

Misika thought she understood but recoiled from the image. "What happened then?" she asked, her face becoming hot. She was sure it was as red as a beet.

"Well, you know…" Again, her voice trailed off. "Then he beat my bottom with a stick of bamboo he keeps for me when I'm bad."

Diane Reverts

Jon got out of his chair and knelt on the carpet before the fire. He stretched out his hands to each of them. "Come, let's pray."

Afterward, Diane asked for a drink and sat staring into the fire. "What's going to happen to me?" she asked softly.

"You'll go back in the morning, clean yourself up, and have a nice dinner waiting for Jeff when he gets home," Misika prophesied.

"No, I will not!"

"There's a very good chance that is exactly what will happen unless you are strong enough to make hard decisions now."

Diane was silent for a moment. "What will I do? I'm forty years old and have been with Jeff since college. I'm a housewife. I don't know how to do anything else."

"Then you'll go back, and this will start all over again."

Jon wondered how Misika knew this. She surprised him. It was getting late, and Jon went up to bed. Misika sat with Diane awhile, mostly in silence.

Finally, Misika led Diane to the guest bedroom at the top of the stairs. "There are fresh pajamas in the closet," she said and left to join her husband in bed.

"I put her to bed. I think she'll sleep," Misika said.

"What are we going to do with her?" Jon asked.

"She'll go back to him. She's suffering from battered wife syndrome, and that's what they do when it's been going on so long—every time."

"Battered wife syndrome? Really?"

"Yes, it's more common than you would expect. She feels helpless and has accepted her feelings of low self-esteem and loss of control long ago. So she's given up trying."

"Diane? She has always seemed such a strong woman. I've often thought she doesn't show Jeff the respect a husband is due."

"Indeed," Misika said. "They put up a good front. He has beaten her for twenty years. She's come to accept it and to hide her bruises."

"Well, it's best she goes back to him. A woman's place is with her husband. And the Bible does not condemn beating your wife. It says the woman is the glory of man."

"Indeed," Misika said scornfully.

"Yes, indeed," Jon replied stridently. "It also says a woman is not to be disobedient to patriarchal God and man and must be submissive and subject to discipline."

"Jon," she said with a steely look he was unfamiliar with, "you certainly know your Bible. Of that, there is no doubt. Regardless, if you were ever to strike me, I'd kill you in your sleep."

Jon was taken aback and cowed. He'd never seen this side of his wife. That night they slept on opposite sides of the bed, as far away from each other as possible.

In the morning, Jon, still subdued, came down for his breakfast, which was waiting on the table.

"Where's Diane?" he asked.

"She's gone. I spoke to her briefly and explained she should leave him. And we talked about the battered wife syndrome."

"And?" Jon asked.

"She knows all of that. She's educated and not stupid. She just can't help herself."

"It's probably for the best," he said and received a look.

Visiting Leif

After depositing their bags in a locker and submitting to a search, Carol and Alex were directed through a door into a sterile, windowless waiting room with steel furniture that was bolted to the floor. There was a camera on the ceiling, watching them.

"Charming," Alex commented.

They took a seat. The room contained nothing but the chairs and a television set bolted to the wall and enclosed by a metal cage. Fox News was on, sans sound.

"You would think they would turn on closed caption," Carol said.

"Yeah," Alex replied, uninterested.

Then they waited in silence, neither knowing what to say. There were six other people in the waiting room: all black women, a fact that caused Carol to wonder.

After forty minutes, they were called to proceed through the door and go to station forty-five.

"What do you think station forty-five is?" Alex asked somewhat rhetorically.

"Haven't you visited anyone in jail before?" Carol said.

"No, have you?"

"No, this is a first."

Station forty-five turned out to be a television monitor set in a steel wall, a telephone handset in a receiver on the wall, and a chair. It was one station of many, perhaps a hundred, separated by steel privacy curtains. Names, initials, and various graffiti were scratched in the paint. Alex took another chair from an unoccupied station, and they sat. The screen was blank. There was no call button or anything else—just the screen and the telephone handset.

"What happens now?" Alex asked.

"I guess we wait."

"So far, this hasn't been a lot of fun."

"Yeah, imagine being on the other side."

"Of the wall?" Alex said. "You know there's no reason to believe Leif is on the other side of this wall. If all we're going to be able to do is to see him on TV, he could be anywhere. They could have moved him to Gitmo."

"Gitmo?" Carol said, confused. "Do you mean Guantanamo?"

"Just being sardonic," he replied.

"Oh, sorry. I guess I've lost my sense of humor."

"Yeah, me too. That was stupid. Sorry."

They sat in silence for the next ten minutes. Then the television screen illuminated, and a blurry black-and-white image of Leif appeared.

For the first time, they realized the consequence of the telephone handset; only one of them at a time would be able to communicate with Leif, and the other would not be able to hear any response. *This sucks*, Alex thought.

"This sucks," Carol said, putting voice to his thoughts. She picked up the handset. "Hello, Leif, how are you holding up?"

As he had anticipated, Alex couldn't hear a thing.

"Oh, wow, that's awful. There's no one you can talk to about that?"

Alex watched Carol, listening intently. He moved his head next to hers, indicating she should share the receiver.

Cupping her hand over the microphone, she said, "No, Alex, I can barely hear him as it is."

Carol and Leif made small talk for a few more minutes, and Leif told her about his travails.

"Leif, we need to know about the bots."

Finally, Alex thought, *she got to it.* He was frustrated by not being able to hear Leif's answer.

"No, they are working fine. We connected the IBM to the cluster this morning; they migrated over and are hammering the midware just like they are supposed to."

She listened.

"The problem…well, Leif, the problem is we don't know why or how they moved to the cluster. We didn't load them. All we've done is to make the hardware connection. Then Alex and I went to lunch. When we came back, the bots were in there, hammering away."

Another wait.

"Yes, Leif, they are doing what they are supposed to be doing. That's right, and no one is finding fault with that or with you. Gordon is just concerned about proceeding without understanding what's going on, what the bots are about, and what to expect next."

She listened for a long time, much to Alex's continued frustration.

"Well, we planned to load the applications this afternoon and the user interface tomorrow morning. Roger and Barry are both very concerned we make the rollout date." She didn't think it a good idea to invoke Jon.

She listened.

"Leif, I'm not sure 'everything will be fine' will pass muster with Gordon."

Alex's frustration mounted as he watched Leif's lips move on the screen but heard nothing.

"Okay, I'm not sure Gordon will be happy, but I'll tell him. We'll be back to visit you soon. I'm sorry we haven't come before."

Alex watched Leif's lips move.

"Later," Carol said and hung up.

As they collected their bags and walked out, Alex asked, "What did he say?"

"Wait a minute." She paused at a machine, punched in Leif's prisoner number, and inserted a hundred-dollar bill.

"What's that?" Alex asked.

"This is how we add to his account so he can buy things at the jail's store. It's the least we can do."

"So what did he say?"

"He said the bots are performing as programmed and we shouldn't worry about it. I asked him for a further explanation, and he said he couldn't explain more without showing us on his terminal. For now, his explanation is the bots evolve to meet new situations, which are anticipated in their rubric."

"I don't think Gordon is going to be happy with that."

"Nor do I. But what choice does he have?"

"None, I guess. He really said *rubric*?"

"Yeah, I guess he didn't want to say *prime directive*."

"What do we do now?"

"It's late," Alex said. "We'll tell Gordon tomorrow. Right now, let's get an early dinner."

"Sounds good." She took his hand, and they intertwined fingers.

He gave her hand a squeeze.

"I feel like being bad," she said. "Let's get pizza. The Chili Pepper is just a block up Main Street."

The tablecloths were red and the floor a black and white checkerboard pattern.

The waitress took their drink order, and while they waited, Alex asked, "What's happened to my visiting you at work? I thought that was an important step in our relationship."

Her light mood evaporated and her eyebrows pinched together as she pressed her lips together, her head lowered. "It is important," she said softly. "The time just hasn't been right."

Suddenly she looked up into his eyes and smiled, "Soon, we'll do it soon, and everything will be fine."

Their drinks were delivered, and Carol changed the subject. "What do you think Leif's prime directive is?"

Launch

"Jeff," Barry said, sticking his head into the other man's office, "you have time to have lunch with me today?"

"Sure, what's the occasion?"

"I want to talk to you about the preparations for the launch."

"Okay, twelve thirty in the cafeteria?"

"Actually, I'm thinking about going across the street to the deli. We'll have more privacy."

"Okay, twelve thirty; I'll see you there," Jeff said, wondering why Barry thought they needed privacy.

As Barry turned, he saw Mary Adams coming up the hall carrying her unusually large bag. He walked off in the other direction.

"Hi, Jeff," Mary said, and she stepped into his office and locked the door behind her. "You ready?"

***

Promptly at 12:30 p.m., Jeff came through the doors of the restaurant and saw Barry sitting at an isolated table in the rear. He waved, went over, and sat down.

"What's up, Barry?" he asked.

"Jon has approved the budget, and I've enlisted Barbara to help with the arrangement. I have a meeting with the mayor tomorrow, and the cruise ship is booked."

"That's right—you were talking about a cruise ship. Which one did you get?" Things were moving a bit fast for Jeff, and he wondered how to usurp at least some control of the event.

"*Tranquility of the Seas*," Barry answered.

Jeff thought for a moment. "That's the largest cruise ship in the world, Barry. What are you going to do with that?"

"I'm going to rent cabins to our VIPs, have high-end entertainment—shows—and host our friends. In addition, the ship is wired for Internet. We'll take over the ship's network and offer a portal for guests to surf the Internet and sign up for Fauxbook while on board. There will be entertainment ashore, too, for the regular public, and signup kiosks every half block throughout the area we are taking over for the party."

"How much is this going to cost? Do you have the money?" Jeff asked.

"Yes!" Barry smiled broadly. "Jon approved ten million. I can get the ship for six million. I've arranged a loan at the bank for the six million. We'll pay off with room rentals. We can rent the staterooms on the ship for an average of five hundred a night and gross over ten million—more counting drinks, room service, and meals."

"Jon will like that."

"Well, I haven't exactly told Jon about that part of it. I plan to wait until he recovers from approving this budget."

That story didn't completely add up, and Jeff assumed Barry planned to skim a bit of the four million profit for himself.

"Is the Fauxbook system going to be ready in time?" Jeff asked, and immediately regretted it. He was supposed to have a handle on that, and to hint he didn't was a weakness. "When are you planning to hold this gala?" he asked quickly.

"In three months," Barry said. "June weather will be great, and we'll schedule it for just after school is out for the kids."

"That's almost six months ahead of projection," Jeff protested.

"Well, we are ahead of schedule, and everything is going well. Do you see a problem, Jeff?"

Jeff felt as if he were being boxed into a corner, taken by surprise. But he couldn't think of a reason offhand why they couldn't go six months early.

"Sure, no problem. We'll be ready well before then," he said, quickly recovering. *God*, he thought, *I hope that's true.* "It's just you took me by surprise."

"Did you get the memo that Gordon wants us in Jon's office this afternoon?"

"I did," Jeff said. "Two o'clock. What do you think is going on?"

"The bots, I imagine. Alex and Carol were going to visit Leif, the designer, in jail yesterday."

"Have you spoken to Alex today?"

"No, but I understand it's quite the mystery," Barry said. "Though I don't anticipate it's going to delay us." *I hope that's true, too*, he thought.

***

Promptly at two, they were all assembled. *Damn!* Gordon thought. *A meeting, almost formal—a sign of Jon's uncertainty, I imagine. He's unconsciously setting it up to spread the blame if it goes wrong.* Gordon was immediately ashamed of the disrespectful thought.

"This is a continuation of our previous meeting regarding the robots we are using to test load the systems," Jon said. "Larry, Alex, and Carol have all reported back with good news." None of the three were in the room. "After an extensive examination of the computers in Leif's laboratory, Larry has found no evidence of lethiferous code."

Now there's an obfuscation, Gordon thought.

"Alex and Carol," Jon continued, "have interviewed Leif in his current abode, and he's assured them the bots, robots, are performing as he intended when he wrote the code."

"That's a relief," Jeff commented. He was relieved in many ways, not the least of which was there had been no mention of the incident with Diane.

The others nodded their agreement.

"So," Jon went on, "I believe this validates my decision to continue with bringing the system up and testing. Are there any questions?"

Gordon wanted to ask if there was really any progress in learning how the bots functioned, but he thought better of it. *After all, no one asked me. Curiouser and curiouser. And the matter of the missing memory—perhaps due to the hack—is still open.*

"I have a comment, Jon. Perhaps you could call it an announcement," Jeff said.

Those who had been preparing to leave stopped, and all heads turned to Jeff.

"I've looked at things carefully and have concluded we'll be in a position to launch Fauxbook at the end of June, almost six months early."

Barry was livid at this usurpation of credit that was rightfully his. *Damn, Jeff,* he thought.

He need not have worried.

"That is good news, Jeff," Jon said. "Have you calculated how much that will impact the bottom line?"

"I've done a rough estimate after speaking with Roger and believe it will put us ahead some ten billion gross and three billion net."

"With a *b*?" Gordon asked, smiling.

As Jeff's words sank in, a smile appeared on all of their faces, as they anticipated bonuses.

Bonuses were an anomaly in Jon's world. He believed people were already paid for their work and to overpay them was to spoil them for any future employment. However, he had been persuaded to make an exception, just this once.

The Breakup

Carol had once again invited Alex to dinner at an excellent restaurant. This time it was a four-and-a-half-star Mexican restaurant just a block from the office.

Regardless, Alex's frustration had reached its limit.

When they were seated, Alex said, "Carol, there's something I need to talk to you about."

"Can we order first?" she said, smiling and grasping his hands across the table.

"Okay, but I need to say this before I lose my nerve."

"Serious?"

"Yes, but we can order first. That might be best."

The waitress came, took their drink order, and left. There was silence between them.

"This is serious, isn't it?" Carol finally said. Her hands withdrew from his and gripped one another in front of her.

"Yes, but you're right. We'll order food first."

Later, Alex began hesitantly but with determination. "Carol, I can't see you anymore like this. It's driving me crazy. I feel like I'm slowly chipping away at a brick wall, and I'll be an old man before our relationship progresses."

"You mean sex?" Her hands separated, and she placed them palms down, widespread, on the table.

"Yes, I mean sex! What is going on with you? Do you belong to some strange religious cult? You are making my balls blue!" he said loudly enough that diners at neighboring tables turned to look.

"Sorry," he said, chagrined. She couldn't help but smile.

"That's okay." She laughed but then stopped. "So you are demanding I fuck you if I want to continue seeing you?"

"No, no, don't put it like that. It's not like that at all. But relationships are supposed to progress. And yes, if two people love each other, sex is part of it. I just don't know what is going on. You confuse the shit out of me."

She was silent for a long moment, thinking. "I can't. I just can't, until you know."

"Know what?"

"This is really a problem, isn't it?"

"Yes, it is, and I don't know why you refuse to go to the next stage of our relationship."

"Is sex really so important?" she asked with a serious countenance.

"Yes." He paused. "And no. If you explained you were religious, a Shaker perhaps, or some such sect that believes in abstinence before marriage or something, I might understand. I might have to get a part-timer to help out." *Actually, I already have*, he thought guiltily. "But I'd most likely understand. But you don't say anything. You just dismiss me after our dates, if that's what they are."

"Yes, Alex, we've been dating, and I'm very fond of you."

"I hear a *but*."

"Okay, that's fair. But…okay, there it is, the *but*," she said with a sad smile. "I'm not religious, and I don't belong to a cult of abnegation. It's just there's something you have to know first. There's something I have to share with you."

"Okay, what do I have to know?" Alex said with some irritation.

"I can't tell you. I have to show you, and I'm scared. I enjoy your company so much I've been procrastinating. I don't want to lose you. And I've been living with the fear someone will tell you before I do. That would ruin everything."

"You mean everyone knows your secret but me?"

"Not many people know—hardly anybody."

"This sounds very mysterious," he said quietly. "Are you a Russian spy?"

She laughed. "Nothing like that."

"Well, what? If your secret that you actually want to tell me is ruining our relationship, you need to tell me."

"Yes, I know. Let me make some arrangements. I'll try for next Saturday. I've been over and over this in my mind so many times. You're right. It's time to move to the next stage. I want to." She reached across the table and took his hand in hers. "I promise. In the meanwhile, please, Alex, just give me a little more time."

"Why should I?" he asked, pressing his perceived advantage.

"Monday nights?" she asked rhetorically, her lips hidden behind her palm.

Fauxbook Lives

The next morning, Jon was in the office early. "Anne, tell Jeff to get over here. And have the social worker from human resources come up."

Anne must have conveyed his tone, as both arrived in his office within minutes.

"Jeff," he said with a stern, parental look, "I do not want a repeat of what happened with Diane."

"Sir?" Jeff said frowning, his brow clenched.

"I've been remiss not to bring this up earlier. Frankly Jeff, you've disappointed me."

"Jon, Diane told me you and Misika were upset. I am, as well, no excuses. But what happens is, when she drinks too much, she goes into a rage over one thing or another. Sometimes I need to swat her to get her to calm down. I have not been beating her; I assure you. But there have been a few times we have had these little mental fits. The other thing is she bruises extremely easily since the cancer; just a touch will often produce a black-and-blue mark, even when she just bumps into something."

Damn! Jon thought. *We didn't check her for bruises last time other than the obvious bruises on her arm, and Diane didn't say anything. Jeff is talking too much.*

"Well, enough excuses," Jeff continued. "I am sorry about all of this. I have not turned into a monster wife beater, but Diane and I have always been high maintenance. This situation is extremely difficult. I never wanted to leave her; I just got some help. You know, for my needs—a man's needs. That's all."

Ms. Jorgenson, the social worker, said nothing. She just listened with a neutral expression.

"And you got caught," Jon observed.

"We're not very happy right now," Jeff said.

Jon was not stupid, but in this instance, Jeff was—again, he was talking too much. Jon assumed "some help" referred to Jeff's mistress, whom Jeff felt was necessary because Diane, due to her operations, was unable to perform for him. *This is disappointing*, Jon thought.

"Jeff, Jeff, you're telling me more than I want to hear. Be quiet now and listen.

"Ms. Jorgenson here is a social worker with our personnel department. I've filled her in about what happened. She is going to arrange for counseling for both you and Diane. The details I leave to her, as she is much more experienced in these matters than I. This counseling is not optional!" he said sternly. "You and Diane will be there, or you will no longer be employed by Fauxbook.

"Ms. Jorgenson, I'll expect a report regarding the results of the counseling," Jon ordered.

"I'm sorry, Mr. Johnsson; I won't be able to do that. Privacy laws, you know. However, I can have my supervisor, the head of human resources, call you."

"Thank you, Ms. Jorgenson," Jon said graciously. He had no doubt the information would be provided. "That will be all. You too, Jeff."

"May I stay a moment?" Ms. Jorgenson asked.

"Of course, of course. Go back to work, Jeff," he ordered.

"What is it?" Jon asked Ms. Jorgenson once Jeff left. He was irritated this embarrassment was continuing after he had dismissed it.

"Mr. Johnsson, I think you should understand this situation is between the two of them, Diane and Jeff."

"What do you mean?"

"I doubt Diane ran over to your house in the nude seeking help."

"What?" Jon said, confused.

"Their dysfunctional relationship has been going on for so long, it has become how they interact."

Jon just looked at her, his face slack, his mouth hanging open.

"That night," Ms. Jorgenson continued, "Diane was very angry with Jeff and wanted to hurt him. 'How can I hurt him the most?' she asked herself. And the answer came to her: get naked and run over to the boss's house and tell all—at least all she wants to tell."

"Really?" he asked.

"Really," she answered. "Then, in the morning, her anger abated, and having fired a shot across Jeff's bow, she goes home and resumes her life with him."

"What's to be done?" Jon asked.

"Nothing. He'll kill her eventually. Perhaps she'll see it coming and leave him; perhaps not."

Tuesday

"Well, Leif was right," Carol said. "The bots are adapting. Joe installed the user interface two hours ago, and they evolved and are going at it."

"Yeah," Alex replied. "I spent over six years studying computer science, and still, this confuses me. What the hell did Leif do?"

"I described this to my professor in my advanced algorithms class," Carol said. "He told me quite emphatically what I described was impossible."

"I'm not surprised," Alex said, "if Gordon can't figure it out. Well, it must not be happening."

"But it is."

"Yeah, I know," Alex said, his brows knitted in a frown.

"I hope Jon knows what he's doing with this full-speed-ahead approach."

"That is the decision, and we're just worker bees. I think we'd better get going with analyzing the system operation and the load. The bots are really loading it up," Alex said.

"We're still adding computer nodes, though. There are over fifty thousand in the cluster now, and the number is growing every day as they are delivered and we plug them in."

"You're right; we're worrying about things are above our pay level. We need to do an analysis of present and projected capacity and get a report to Gordon."

"Are they still talking about two billion users?" Carol asked.

"Roger told me at lunch yesterday two billion is just a start."

"Damn!" Carol exclaimed. "We'd better get to work. Dinner tonight?"

The question brought pause. Alex wondered if Carol had been serious, or if this was just business—relationship—as usual. It had taken a lot for him to suggest breaking up. Was he just being sucked back into this frustrating relationship? Instantly he felt bad. It wasn't an unrewarding relationship. He enjoyed Carol's company—a lot. She was the most interesting and entertaining woman he had ever met. He felt guilty he was so hung up on sex. *Sex shouldn't be everything. Money isn't everything. But damn, it's part of things.* He was torn about what to do. Perhaps if he withheld going to dinner with her as long as she withheld sex…*Wow*, he thought. *Have I sunk so low?*

"Aren't you working tonight?" he asked.

"No, this is my last semester, and tuition is paid, so I've been cutting back on work. One thought that has been persistent was to quit before I had to tell you about it. Then I thought that wouldn't be open and honest, either. I want to be honest with you. I want you to know and to understand me."

She hasn't forgotten, he thought. *But what the hell is going on that she doesn't want me to know but feels I must know?* Nonetheless, he was strangely reassured.

"Sure, dinner. Where do you want to go?"

"I thought I'd make dinner for you in my apartment. In fact, somewhat presumptuously, I went shopping last night and have already done the heavy lifting for a wonderful dinner. So I hope you'll come."

Being a man, he immediately wondered, hoped, the invitation included sex. *God*, he said to himself, *don't embarrass yourself.*

"I'd love to," he said finally as Carol looked at him questioningly.

Dinner at Carol's

The two of them worked the rest of the afternoon writing programs to measure the load, in users, the bots were putting on the system. Alex was impressed by Carol's mastery of the computer and her insight into the workings of the programs.

"The bots are hammering the system at all levels simultaneously," Alex commented.

"Yes, and I'm not sure that gives us a realistic picture. It seems to me the load should be applied from the top down, from the user interface to the apps, the midware, and then, lastly, the operating system."

"Well, the speed of the q-cluster has been increasing, too. Every time I measure it, it's faster," Alex said.

"It seems the bots are figuring out how to program quantum computers. They are way beyond anything humans have accomplished."

"It scares me a little."

"Hey, I thought you were the big strong man." She smiled. "I can't imagine anything scaring you."

Alex remained silent, frowning.

"Anyway," Carol said, sorry she had teased him, "the system is running. Fauxbook lives."

"It does indeed," Alex said almost in a whisper, his lips set in a grim, thin, line.

"Okay," Carol said, "I'm going home to clean up, change, and finish making dinner. See you at eight?"

"I'll be there."

She smiled. "You'd better be."

***

Carol opened the door wearing an orange top, which was almost, but not quite, revealing, and a skirt. Alex almost leaned back, as he'd never seen her in a skirt before. True, it reached to her knees, but still, a skirt!

She smiled and reached for the flowers he had brought her. "They are beautiful. Thank you. You didn't have to do that. Come in."

The apartment was small and very neat. The entry led into the kitchen, separated from the living room by a counter with two stools. The living room was nicely but inexpensively furnished with two cushioned chairs and a matching couch. An open laptop computer sat on the coffee table, and a flat-screen television was mounted on the wall opposite the couch. In the far corner, there was a computer table and a chair hosting what Alex knew to be the most advanced desktop computer available at any price. A large picture of Grace Hopper occupied the wall over the couch, and a picture of two older people stood on a side table.

"Your parents?" Alex asked.

"Yes, I guess I'm a bit old-fashioned. I love my parents," she said, blushing a little. "Not very exciting, I know."

"I think it's sweet," Alex said to be polite. Then he realized it *was* sweet.

The door opposite was closed. Alex assumed it was the bedroom. It didn't seem he was going to get a tour of that area.

The kitchen looked well equipped, and a pot on the stove was emitting steam.

"What's for dinner?" he asked.

"Beef stew and corn bread," she answered. "My mother's recipe."

"What can I do to help?"

"Set the table or, more accurately, the counter," she said as she passed silverware, glasses, and napkins from the kitchen drawers to the counter.

"Cloth napkins? Aren't you extravagant."

"Au contraire," she said. "I'm just too cheap to buy paper towels. They're expensive. After the initial investment of buying cloth napkins, which isn't much, I just throw them in the washer with the clothes. That's basically free."

"I can see you've put a lot of thought into this."

She smiled and ladled the stew into bowls, which she set on the plates on the counter. Reaching into the oven, she retrieved a pan of corn bread, cut it into four pieces, and put two on each plate.

"Oh, I love corn bread," Alex said. "How did you know?"

She grinned. "I can tell. I hope you like it. I put in real corn kernels and chopped jalapeño peppers."

"Do you mind if I use your bathroom to wash my hands before dinner?"

"Not at all, through that door." She pointed. "It's on the right."

"Thank you." He opened the door to find it was the bedroom. He closed the door behind him, which he hoped she wouldn't find odd, and looked around quickly. A queen-size bed with tables on each side. Only one of the tables supported a reading light. *That's a good sign*, he thought. A cedar trunk at the end of the bed and a chest of drawers that looked Amish. There were no pictures of boyfriends. Everything was very neat. *But that doesn't mean much*, he thought. *She may have cleaned up.* He suspected not; she was a neatnik. And he didn't think she had removed pictures for his benefit.

The bathroom was the same, clean and neat: towels folded on the hangers, soap in the soap dish, and her toothbrush arranged next to the toothpaste. There was only one toothbrush.

He accomplished his task quickly and slid open the drawer of the bedside table with the light on it. He figured that would be her side. Resting on top of an assortment of stuff was a large vibrator. He smiled and rejoined her for dinner.

"This is wonderful," he said. "Your mother really knew how to cook."

"Yes, she did," Carol said. "And now I do. I enjoy cooking, and it's much less expensive than dining out."

After dinner, Carol rinsed the dishes and placed them in the dishwasher. "I'll start it later," she said. "It's noisy. Let's have dessert in the living room."

She served ice cream sundaes with chocolate sauce for dessert, and she and Alex sat side by side on the couch.

After an hour of conversation about work, their mutual frustration with the bots led nowhere. So they chatted about each other and office gossip.

"I heard Mary is balling Jeff," Alex said.

"Don't know about that, and if I did, I wouldn't say, though I have noticed Mary is a bit concupiscent," Carol responded. "Are you jealous?"

Alex froze. Did she know? It sounded as if she knew. *Does she know about Monday nights? Sure she does. Damn! It's hard to have an open and honest relationship.*

"A little, I guess. You know men; we want them all." He said, avoiding eye contact. *That was a noncommittal answer that avoided a lie. Or did it really?*

"Alex, I'm really glad you came over. I really enjoyed it."

"I'm glad, too," he said, recognizing he was being dismissed. *Nope, no sex again. Damn!*

She rose and moved toward the door, and he followed. Once there, she turned and leaned back against it. Reaching out, she drew him to her, her right hand behind his head. Gently, she pulled his lips to hers and delivered the kiss of his dreams. Halfway through, his knees became weak.

Then she lightly pushed him away. "I've had a wonderful evening," she said as she opened the door for him.

"Me, too," he answered as she moved aside to make room for his exit. "Thank you, and sleep well." He wondered if Mary was available that night.

"I'm not sure that's in the cards for either of us tonight." She smiled.

Damn, she's confusing, he thought. "Maybe not," he said.

She gripped his hand. "Good night."

"Good night, Carol."

As he turned and went through the door, she said, "Do you think you'll be able to give her up?" She closed the door behind him before he could answer.

Connecting the Bots

The next day it was business as usual. Carol's question the previous night had silenced Alex. He didn't know what to say or whether he really understood the question. He thought he did, and the thought didn't make him happy. *She knows about Mary and Monday nights. Damn! Well, what does she expect?*

"I think we have to take what we have to Gordon," Carol said.

Alex was preoccupied with their relationship, or lack thereof, and she wanted to talk about work.

"But it keeps changing. The damn system will not stabilize," he said.

"Uh-huh, well, that's what we'll report to Gordon. And we can tell him the cluster is holding up well."

Alex stood in front of a terminal that was displaying activity on the cluster. Carol saw he was worried.

"How do we back off the bots?" he asked. "Are they ever going to stop? The system may be holding up well now, but can it support the bots beating on it and users when we go live?"

"I hadn't thought about that," Carol said. "You're right. We are going to have to turn the bots off. Do you want to visit Leif again?"

"I think we're going to have to."

"So do we report to Gordon before or after we see Leif?"

"After," Alex said. "Let's go see Leif this afternoon."

"Okay, that's what we'll do. Lunch? There's time."

Damn! Alex thought. *She's inviting me to lunch. Maybe she doesn't know about Monday nights. Or maybe she doesn't care.* That would be outside his experience.

"Yes, lunch. I feel like some comfort food."

"I'm craving pizza. They have both in the cafeteria. So let's go." She took his hand and led him out, and Alex was happy to follow her.

***

"How are you, Leif?" Alex asked. It was his turn to command the headset.

"I'm fine. I can't say I'm getting used to it. They tell me they're going to transfer me to the Pondville Correctional Center next week. It's a state prison in Norfolk. It's only thirty-six miles away, so my family can still visit me."

"Leif," Alex asked, "is the transfer a good thing?"

"Yeah, I think so. It's a state-run facility. There are activities for the prisoners—things to do. This jail is private, for profit, contracted by the state to hold prisoners for the sheriff. They spend as little as they can get away with and provide no recreational facilities. There's nothing to do here. They don't even have a library. And, of course, I can't have a computer."

"Last time we were here," Alex said, "we deposited a hundred dollars in your account here. Did that help?"

"No, they charge the prisoners a daily rate for incidentals. I don't have any money, so the jail figures I owe them over two

228

thousand dollars. Your hundred dollars went against that. I didn't see it. But thanks for the thought."

"Damn!" Alex said. "I guess I'll not be depositing any more money."

"No, don't. But I appreciate the gesture. Thank you."

"For nothing," Alex replied.

"So I imagine you have more questions about the bots," Leif said.

"Yes, we do. But we would have come to visit you anyway," Alex replied.

Yeah, sure, Leif thought. "What do you want to know?"

"We have everything loaded, including the user interface. As you told us, the bots have adapted and are loading all aspects of the system; they are behaving like users at the top. It's amazing. No one, including Gordon, can figure it out. But we've been going forward based on what you told us. That decision was made at the highest level."

Jon. Leif grimaced.

"Now we are wondering what's going to happen when we go live and real users start signing on. Are the bots going to continue to load the system? If so, that's not going to work."

"Well, yes and no," Leif answered. "They will back off on the operating system and the midware after a while when the results stabilize. But as you add nodes and capacity, they will start back up and again back off when the system reaches a steady state, more or less. That shouldn't be a problem."

"That's good news," Alex said.

Carol was going crazy being able to hear only one side of the conversation. She pulled at Alex's arm, and he shook her off in exasperation.

"The user interface may be a problem, though," Leif said.

"They're not going to stop?" Alex asked.

"Yeah, I guess. I'm not sure," Leif replied. "Most likely they will sense a plateau and maintain it."

"You mean they will keep the system running at maximum capacity?"

"Yeah, pretty much, maybe a little below maximum."

"Leif, that would cost a lot of money in operating and cooling costs. That's not going to work."

"Sorry, that's the way it is. I knew about that issue and was working on it when I was fired. Too bad. It's not my fault."

"Leif, it's a little your fault. Can you tell us how your bots work? It doesn't seem like you left any documentation of your code. That's against company policy, you know."

"Yeah, I know. I was working on that, too. I don't know how you can blame me when you fired me before I finished. It's not like I can do any work in here."

Round and Round

Diane was at the door. Misika had invited her for coffee but hadn't really expected her. Regardless she invited Diane in and served her coffee in the morning room. They sat opposite each other separated by the coffee table.

"I went to his office, and the door was locked," Diane said.

"What did you do then?" Misika asked.

"I knocked on the door; then I pounded. Nothing. Then I asked Anne to unlock it. I told her I feared Jeff had had a heart attack or a stroke. Anne called maintenance.

"Before they got there, the door opened, and a young lady carrying a big purse came out and took off in the other direction. She looked a bit in disarray."

"Did you recognize her?" Misika asked, somewhat fearful Diane had recognized the woman. *A scandal is never good*, she thought. *However, this one might be unavoidable.*

Diane just made an unladylike sound, like a grunt.

"What happened then?" Misika asked.

"I went into Jeff's office. He was sitting behind his desk, his face red. I asked him what the fuck was going on."

Misika was surprised at the obscenity, though not shocked. She had heard the word before, though not often. Jon never cursed, nor did those around him, knowing he'd disapprove.

But she was familiar with the word.

"And?" Misika asked.

"He told me it was business. They had been discussing a confidential subject, and he had not wanted to be disturbed."

"That seems reasonable, a good explanation."

"You think I should believe him?" Diane asked.

"Well," Misika said carefully, "that's up to you. You know him better than I do. Do you think he was? What do you think he was doing?"

"I think he was fucking that girl who scurried out. I think he's having an affair."

That ugly word again. "With that girl? You think he's having sex in his office? During the day, office hours? Really?" Misika, against her will, believed it even as she asked the question. *If Jon finds out about this—I can't imagine*, she thought.

"Do you plan to leave him?"

Diane sobbed just one sob, no tears. "What would I do? I'm forty years old. I have no skills. I've been a housewife for twenty years. We married while we were in college. I dropped out of school and worked as a teller in a bank to put him through school."

An old story, Misika thought. "Forty isn't old," she said. "You could go back to school. You'll be able to afford it. A divorce settlement would be substantial."

***

It was Monday. That night, Mary confronted Alex with his infidelity as they lay in bed. She sat up in bead and said, "Alex, are you fucking Carol? I see you two together all of the time. And

232

I know you're going out to dinner with her a lot. What's going on?"

Alex was incredulous. *She's mad that I'm unfaithful?*

"Alex, answer me! Are you fucking around on me?"

He pushed her onto her back and mounted her forcibly. She responded in kind. Soon they reversed positions, and she was on top, her head tilted back and her mouth open. He grasped her—hard. In his anger, he wanted to hurt her. He was the aggrieved party. She was screwing everyone and accusing him of infidelity. How was he supposed to respond to that?

He gripped her hard, perhaps not with all of his strength, but he wanted her to cry out. She didn't give him the satisfaction, and their contest continued.

They were both gasping from their exertion; he knew she had climaxed. However, he also knew Mondays were over. He felt relief and some tribulation. *I'll get over it*, he thought.

***

The next day, Tuesday, Mary was in the lab talking to Joe as if nothing had happened, though she was thinking, *Now I have Monday to schedule. Damn*! Regardless, she even said hi to Alex with a smile.

Carol and Alex were discussing how they were going to present the information to Gordon. It wasn't good news, though it wasn't entirely bad. The cluster would run, and the bots wouldn't slow it down. They would just engage close to 100 percent of its capacity at some cost. They concluded they needed Leif back or someone new who could decipher his work. They had tried; Larry had tried. Carol had talked to every coder working at Fauxbook to no avail.

Mary came out of Joe's office, saw them in intense conversation, and walked over. "What's up?" she asked with no sign of the jealousy she had expressed the night before. They explained the problem to her in detail. They were willing to explain it to anyone at this point; they were desperate.

"Obviously, you need to get Leif out," Mary said.

"You're suggesting a jailbreak?" Carol asked.

Alex was too ill at ease to say anything. So far, Carol had done all of the talking for him. Both of the girls appeared to be at ease, as if this were a contest whose rules they both understood.

"Not a jailbreak; just get him out. A work-release program or something."

"We were thinking of recruiting someone else, from outside, a new employee who could understand Leif's work."

"Good luck with that," Mary said. "Leif is really dumb in many areas, but with computer code, he's a genius—think idiot savant."

"You think he's mentally defective?" Carol asked.

"No, I didn't say he is mentally defective," Mary said irritably. "I said, 'Think idiot savant.' He's not defective. He is just very naive and, well, yeah, dumb in many areas, especially social interaction. That's how he got himself locked up. Coding he understands; he more than understands. He is creative beyond anyone's imagination, and you are not going to be able to replace him."

"Really," Carol said with some incredulity.

"Really," Mary replied. "But he could train someone to understand what he has done. Larry is very smart and could do it. My recommendation is to get him out, team him with Larry and perhaps another programmer. Then don't let him write a line of code he doesn't explain clearly. Never let him work alone again." *Maybe I'll not need a replacement for Thursday*, she thought.

Mary left and walked over to the administration building. Jeff's office door was open, but she knocked on the doorframe.

"Mary, come in," he said.

"Hi, Jeff. Trouble with the wife?"

"She's a bitch, but I'll fix it."

"Okay. Can you come out and play Monday nights?" she asked.

"What do you mean?"

"You know, make some excuse to stay out late on Mondays, and we'll get together."

"I'm not sure, Mary."

"Oh, you'll think of something. I'll see you Monday night, about eight."

Rolling Leif

That afternoon, Carol and Alex met with Gordon in his office. Alex noticed that, in addition to a lot of framed pictures of computers Gordon had designed, there was a large abacus on the wall just behind Gordon's chair. Alex smiled and thought, *Never forget the basics*.

"So, bottom line, we need Leif back," Gordon stated after they made their presentation.

"Yes," Alex said, "or someone who can understand his work. Remember, it's not documented. There is no written explanation of what he did."

"That's against company policy," Gordon said.

"Yes, sir, we explained that to him. He said he was getting to it when he was fired. Basically, his attitude is it's our fault for firing him. He doesn't feel any responsibility to remedy the situation if he could. Which he can't from jail."

"Are you sure he didn't take it with him?" Gordon asked. "He might do that to get back at the company and Jon."

"I don't know," Alex replied. "How would we know?"

"Search his apartment," Roger Aegel said.

Alex whipped his head around and found Roger standing just inside the door. Alex wondered how long he had been there. *Long enough*, he thought.

Confused, Alex asked, "What do we do? Get a search warrant?"

"Nah," Roger replied. "Just break in and search the place."

There was silence for a long moment.

"I don't think I want to do that," Alex said.

"Nor I," Carol added.

"I've got people who can take care of it," Roger said. "Just give me the address."

***

A black van pulled up in front of Leif's apartment building, and two men dressed as cable-company workers got out and entered the building. They made short work of the entry lock as well as that of Leif's apartment.

"It's empty," the taller of the two said as they entered. "Cleaned out."

"Let's talk to the super," the other man said.

"Not yet, not in this costume. Let's leave and come back as police detectives."

Not long afterward, they were back, driving what looked like an unmarked police cruiser. It had a spotlight on the driver's side and a black police push bar on the front.

The same two men got out, this time dressed in business suits.

"May I help you?" the manager asked, responding to a knock on the door.

"Yes, sir, I'm Detective Burger, and this is Detective Johansson. We're with the state police, looking into one of your tenants."

"Ah, you mean Leif Hoberson, the man convicted of murder."

"What is your name, sir?"

"Fred Mitchel. I'm the manager," he answered.

The tall man removed a notebook from his jacket pocket and wrote down the name. "Actually, Mr. Mitchel, he is guilty of attempted murder, sir."

"Yes, of course. What can I do for you?"

"The officers who were here earlier tell us his apartment has been cleared out."

"Well, I had to prepare the apartment for rental," Fred said defensively.

"Can you tell me where the contents of the apartment are now? We have a warrant to search," the tall man said, reaching into his pocket and withdrawing a folded sheaf of papers. He was certain Fred would not ask to see the warrant, though he was not worried; the warrant was a good forgery. *Hell*, he thought, *this dummy hasn't even asked to see our badges, though we have a good facsimile of those, too.*

"I had them moved to storage over on Clock Tower Place."

"May I have the unit number and the key, please?" the tall one said, gently waving the warrant.

"Of course, let me get it." Fred disappeared into his apartment, followed by the two men. He retrieved a key from a cubbyhole in a large, old-fashioned oak desk; turned; and jumped in surprise to find the two men just behind him.

"Oh!" he cried, but he recovered quickly. "Here is the key; it's number three-two-six. Look, who do I see to get reimbursed for the storage fees?"

"I'll have someone get back to you on that, sir. However, after ninety days, you will be free to dispose of the items as you see fit to recover your costs."

Fred's eyes widened at the thought of profit. "That's all right," he said quickly. "I'll call down to the police department myself to make arrangements."

They all knew he never would. He'd paw through Leif's belongings, taking items of value for himself and pawning the remainder. This would be the last anyone in law enforcement would hear from Fred. The two men shared a secret smile.

***

"Mr. Aegel," the tall one said, "we went through everything in the storage locker and found nothing. This box"—he pointed to a large cardboard box on the table—"contains all of the paper documents. We went through everything and leafed through all of the books. Everything we found on paper is here. In this box are all of the computer disks and flash memory from the three computers we found. We replaced them with unformatted memory. I plugged the computers into an adapter I put in the light socket and booted them up. But they are all password protected."

"Nothing else?" Roger asked.

"We got everything," the tall man assured him.

"Fine, the passwords will be no problem for our people. Thank you. You did a fine job as always."

"Thank you, sir," the tall man said, and he left the room.

Roger dialed an extension on his phone. "Larry, this is Roger Aegel. Would you come over here, please? Yes, immediately."

Larry complied, of course, though he wondered how many bosses he had. It was often hard to know at Fauxbook.

***

Larry was back to report within the hour.

"Larry, you didn't have to call my secretary for an appointment," Roger said. "Next time, just come on over."

"Yes, sir," Larry replied carefully.

"So what did you find?"

"Well, Mr. Aegel, whatever is on these drives, it's wicked. I installed the drives in a computer and ran a program designed to break passwords off of a disk. Within seconds whatever is on those drives reformatted my disk. It's amazing."

"Amazing?" Roger asked.

"Yes, amazing, sir. I tried booting into safe mode. It didn't make any difference."

Roger didn't know what Larry was talking about but didn't want to admit it. "That should have worked," he said.

"Yes, sir, and it gets better—or worse, depending. I tried running the program from a memory card. That was instantly reformatted also. So I networked in another computer and ran the program remotely. The remote computer was toasted. It happened within seconds. Whatever is on those disks, and I tried all of them, would make an awesome cyber-warfare tool. I'm pretty sure that if the machine were attached to our network, the whole system would be dead on arrival."

"So you got nothing?" Roger asked.

"Nothing, sir. I could consult with some other people. However, I'm pretty certain it would be of no use. In any case, you told me to keep this to myself."

"Yes, you did right. Leave the disks here. You may go."

Beta

Alex and Carol sat opposite Gordon in his office. Alex was absentmindedly looking at the pictures on the wall.

"I spoke to Jon and explained the situation to him," Gordon said. "I told him we believe the system will perform to specifications, other than using an enormous amount of power until we work out the bot situation. Is that essentially correct?"

"Yes, sir," Carol replied.

"But," Alex chimed in, breaking his trance, "we are sailing into uncharted waters. And we are farther and farther from shore."

"Interesting analogy," Gordon said. "I take it to mean we are moving further and further away from understanding what the bots are programmed to do?"

"Exactly," Alex said. "Not only that, but we still don't know how it is possible Leif programmed them at all. All the science we know indicates this is impossible. The bots are just not big enough to contain this kind of code."

"I did explain that to Jon. His instruction is to continue with all available resources to work on that problem. In the meantime, we are to proceed with the next step."

"You mean beta testers?" Carol asked.

"Yes, dear," Gordon said. "that is the next step. I believe we have them lined up already. We simply have to complete the Internet connection to the IBM, which is now functioning as an extremely smart router, and activate the beta-test people in the field. Then we monitor the system."

"The load is going to be enormous from the get-go with the bots still running," Alex said. "We didn't plan for that. We were to start beta testing with a light load."

"Can't be helped," Gordon replied. "Jon has given us our marching orders."

"Here we go," Carol said interlacing her fingers and holding her hands close to her breast.

"Indeed," Gordon replied. "Now off you go. Let me know at least three hours before you go online. I'd like to be over there to observe."

"Yes, sir," they said in unison, and then they left.

"Lunch?" Carol asked.

"Sure," Alex said. He had planned to ask her. But she was quick. Again he wondered if he was being led on. *Maybe, but to where?*

After lunch, they walked hand in hand back to the lab.

Everyone, including Mary—especially Mary—thinks Carol and I are an item, Alex thought. *If they only knew, and I'm glad they don't.*

"Let's go over to Barbara's office," Carol said. "This is an event, isn't it? We'll need a press release and text for the e-mail to the beta testers. She's hooked into marketing. She can enlist them to help."

"Sounds right to me," Alex said.

***

"God," Barbara said when Alex and Carol explained their needs. "I'm awfully busy with the plans for the launch."

"I'd appreciate it if you could fit this in. It's important. Jon is involved."

"Jon?"

"Yes, the order to go ahead came directly from Jon," Alex said, supporting Carol.

"But I work for Roger," she said.

"Not Jeff?" Carol asked.

"Well, him, too, I guess."

"Ultimately, they work for Jon, as do you, just like everyone else. Would you like us to go see Roger?"

"No, but if I get in trouble, I'm going to blame you."

"Fine. Consider this top priority. We want the e-mails to go out tomorrow."

"But it's after lunch already. I can't possibly have this done by tomorrow."

"Tomorrow afternoon, then," Carol said. "Do the e-mail to the beta testers first, and have the press release by midday Friday. I want them to go out before the weekend. The testers will have more free time on the weekend. Feel free to use any resources you need. This is important."

"I'll go up and talk to Roger. He's in charge of advertising," Barbara said.

"Barbara, don't take the time. This comes from Jon. Get to work, and get it done."

"Yes, ma'am," Barbara said, succumbing to Carol's tone of authority.

"Okay, thanks. Send me an e-mail tomorrow as soon as you have it finished." Carol turned and left Barbara's office. Alex trailed behind.

"Where are we going?" he asked.

"Over to D Building to talk to Author—you know, tech support."

Damn! Alex thought. *She's like a whirlwind when she gets the wind in her sails. Is that a mixed metaphor?*

"Afterwards, let's catch an early dinner," she said.

"You're not working tonight?" he asked.

"No. I told you I'm phasing that job out of my life. My tuition is paid, and this is my last semester. I don't need the extra money. But I'm still working a couple of nights a week and Saturdays."

Author was in his office on the third floor of D Building, playing a computer game.

"It looks like you have time on your hands," Carol said.

"Yeah, we all do. I'm twenty-five percent staffed up. Joe has been overtraining us. He's very good, by the way. But the training sessions are only a couple of hours a day. And then, there are no users to support."

"Well, that's going to change soon," Carol said. "We're activating more than ten thousand beta testers tomorrow."

"Good," Author said. "There's nothing worse than sitting around all day with nothing to do. I've been running simulated support sessions pairing two of the techs, and one acts as the end user and asks stupid questions." He grinned.

"No," Alex said. "You guys don't really feel that way, do you?"

"I'm just kidding, Alex. Everyone in this department is top-notch, and we all take Fauxbook support very seriously. Each of us is anxious to get started and is especially looking forward to the launch."

"Good," Carol said. "Tomorrow morning, have your people log into 10.255.255.255. That will gain them access to Fauxbook—which, by the way, is running now."

"Sounds good," Author replied. "Our people are going to be excited."

"That's a local address; tell them they are not going to be able to log in from outside the building."

"Yes, I know it's a local address. I'm in charge of tech support, and I know what a local address is," Author said with irritation.

"Sorry," Carol said. "I didn't mean to be rude."

Author paused a moment. "No, I'm sorry. It was I who was rude. It's just that I and everyone else around here have gotten a bit edgy waiting."

"I understand," Carol said. "But it will be worth the wait, and it starts tomorrow. See ya." She waved and left, heading back toward the lab in A Building.

The First Users

Barbara e-mailed the draft to Carol at ten o'clock the next morning.

Alex was at his desk thinking. He'd had a wonderful time at dinner the night before with Carol. She was warm, smart, charming, and beautiful, and she shared his politics. And like all of the dinners before, it had ended with them going their separate ways. She'd promised some revelation would move their relationship to the next stage. However, so far, all that had happened was a kiss good-night. *But it was a great kiss*. He smiled.

"Alex," Carol called across the room, breaking his reverie. "Barbara sent the e-mail down."

"I guess it wasn't such a hard thing after all," he commented.

"Perhaps. We did mention Jon. That gets things done in a hurry," she replied offhandedly as she focused on the screen. "Come read it."

Dear [First Last],

> *You have agreed to be one of the first users of Fauxbook and to perform as a beta tester. Your instruction manual has been sent to your tablet via the address you provided. You also have previously been provided your username and password.*

For your convenience, your username is: [username], and your password is: [password].

Please start using Fauxbook at your earliest convenience.

There will be an icon representing the Fauxbook logo in this beta test version on the lower right corner of your screen. To report an issue, click once on this icon. A screenshot will be taken, which will be sent along with the text that you type into the text box that will pop up in the center of your screen.

Please proceed as quickly as possible, as your input will determine how soon we can offer Fauxbook to everyone.

Thank you for your participation,

Jon Johnsson

President, Fauxbook, Incorporated

"Looks good to me," Alex said.

"I'll take it up to Roger for his approval," Carol said as she pressed Print. The printer came alive and produced a hard copy of the e-mail in short order.

***

"What do they do after they enter their comments?" Roger asked.

"They are supposed to press the Submit button at the bottom," Carol answered. It seemed like a stupid question.

"Tell them in the e-mail," Roger ordered.

"It's enumerated clearly in the step-by-step in the manual," Carol responded.

"Not many are going to read the manual," Roger replied. "You know the rule: if you want to keep a secret, put it in a book." He smiled with self-satisfaction.

"Yes, sir. I'll take care of it," she replied. "Do you want to see it after the changes?"

"That will not be necessary," Roger said. "Make the change, and send it. How soon do you expect we will start receiving data?"

"The e-mail will go out to twelve thousand testers at about two this afternoon. Many will log in immediately, as they have been anticipating this for some time. We'll have ongoing load and performance reports by three and some very useful results by tomorrow morning."

"Good. You know how important it is we stay on schedule," Roger said. "I'll go over and tell Jon the good news."

Dear [First Last],

You have agreed to be one of the first users of Fauxbook and to perform as a beta tester. *Your instruction manual has been sent to your tablet via the address you provided. You also have previously been provided your username and password.*

For your convenience, your username is: [username], and your password is: [password].

Please start using Fauxbook at your earliest convenience.

There will be an icon representing the Fauxbook logo in this beta test version on the lower right corner of your screen. To report an issue, click once on this icon. A screenshot will be taken, which will be sent along with the text you type into the text box that will pop up in the center of your screen.

The last step is to click on the Submit button just below the bottom left corner of the text box. This last step is very important, as it completes your report and sends it to the Fauxbook team.

Please proceed as quickly as possible, as
your input will determine how soon we can
offer Fauxbook to everyone.

Thank you for your participation,

Jon Johnsson

President, Fauxbook, Incorporated

"There," said Carol. "That's the final, approved copy. Let's e-mail it to marketing and walk a hard copy over."

Alex entered a few keystrokes and pressed Send. "Done," he said as he pressed Print.

Carol snatched the hard copy and said, "Let's go."

The marketing department was all abuzz when they entered. They saw Greg Scott, the marketing manager, leaning over the shoulder of a pretty blond woman sitting at a terminal.

Walking over, they attracted his attention and handed him the hard copy of the e-mail.

"Is this the same as the copy in the e-mail you just sent me?" he asked.

"Yes," Carol answered.

"Send it," he told the young woman at the terminal.

"It's gone," Greg said. "A copy to twelve thousand people. It should be in their inboxes now."

Carol clapped, and the whole room joined in. "We should celebrate," she said.

"I'll go down and get the programmers," Alex said. "We'll meet you in the cafeteria in fifteen minutes."

"We'll be there," Greg said. "All right, we're alive!"

Within half an hour, the groups had taken over the cafeteria and were joined by other employees. Alex and Carol sat together under the irascible eye of Mary at the next table, sitting with Larry and Joe.

I can't believe Alex cheated on me, she thought bitterly.

Never being one to dwell, Mary's mind was working. She'd been casually monitoring traffic in and out of the freezer behind the comfort-food station. It seemed no one went in or out between nine and eleven in the morning, when they started to switch over for lunch. *Interesting*, she thought. She had been eyeing Larry of late. *He's turning me on*, she thought, *and I don't want to wait until Friday. It would be exciting to reprise freezer sex during working hours.*

"Larry," she said, "how about meeting me here tomorrow at nine thirty?"

"Why?" he asked. "Breakfast is over at nine. All they'll have are snacks then."

"I have something in mind," she answered. "You'll like it."

"Well," he said hesitantly. "Okay. I'll be here."

It'll be fun, Mary thought. *Then, after lunch, I'll stop by Jeff's office with my bag for some afternoon delight. In the evening, I'll be at Joe's place. It'll be a good day. I can't wait. Maybe I'll go out to the bars tonight and pick someone up. Since Alex betrayed me, Monday is free. Damn him! I was treating him right; we had a good time. I don't understand how he could be unfaithful.*

Going Live

Alex and Carol both arrived at the lab early the next day.

"Hey, Carol. What are you doing here? It's six in the morning."

"I could ask the same of you," she answered. "I'm certain we're both here for the same reason. Neither of us can wait to see Fauxbook online."

"Well, let's do it," Alex said.

Each of them booted up a terminal. Alex logged on to Fauxbook, and Carol brought up the activity reports, displayed as graphs.

"It's running," Alex said.

"And," Carol observed, "we have over ten thousand new users and a lot of activity even at this early hour."

"It looks good," he said.

Alex went to her and looked over her shoulder at the Fauxbook activity displayed on the screens. Then he moved to the station beside her and booted up another terminal to display the load on the system.

"The bots have backed off the same percentage as the new users added," Alex reported. "We're still at ninety percent of capacity, and the bots are keeping us there regardless of how many real users we add."

"Let's go over and look at the cluster," Carol suggested.

They stood, and she took his hand as they walked toward C Building. Alex liked holding her hand, but the tent was rising. At this point, he didn't care if she noticed. However, he'd be embarrassed if others did. He could hear the gossip in his mind: "I saw Alex in the passageway holding hands with Carol. He had a huge boner." And he could almost hear the laughter. Most certainly his balls were blue. Worse, maybe, was he didn't think Mary would be over that night. *That's finished*, he thought, *and for the best. But still…*

"It's hot in here," he commented as they stepped out on the steel grid balcony overlooking the cluster.

"Yes, it is," Carol said. "Let's find Mark."

"Who is Mark?" Alex asked.

"He's the system manager for Fauxbook hardware. He's new but very experienced. He worked for the city of Reedy Creek for years and moved them up to a state-of-the-art system."

"We're adding people faster than I can keep up with them," Alex observed.

"And that will be the case for some time. We're still growing rapidly. When we are online to the public, there will be a lot more people hired."

"Why did Mark leave his last job?" Alex asked.

"I don't know. Maybe he got bored once he had accomplished what he wanted."

They descended the steel stairway to the ground floor, and Carol recognized Mark, hard at work typing at a terminal. He was middle-aged and balding, and he had a substantial paunch. Carol knew he was smart, capable, and experienced. She'd read his personnel report, CV, and job application. *You can't be too careful*, she thought. She knew he had been fired. But from what she had read, it seemed like a personality issue with a new boss.

"Mark," she said above the hum filling the large room with sound. "This is Alex Cromwell; he works with me in programming. Alex, Mark Osborne, hardware guru extraordinaire."

"You honor me with your words, kind lady," Mark said as he rose from the chair, bowed, and kissed her hand.

That was theatrical, Alex thought.

"Pleased to meet you, young man." Mark extended his hand to Alex.

"The same," Alex replied. "It sure is hot in here."

"A bit warm, yes. It's mostly the pipes. The computers sit on radiators that we run coolant through. But the pipes get pretty warm on the way back to the refrigerant plant. We also have fans," he continued, pointing to the ceiling far above, "that remove the hot air. Well, mostly remove the hot air."

"Still feels hot," Alex commented.

"Yes, the system appears to be running hard. What are you guys doing over there? I didn't anticipate this much load so early."

"It's the bots," Carol answered.

"Why?" asked Mark. "Aren't you finished with load testing? It would seem a good idea to shut down the robots now."

"I agree," Carol said, "but the bots are not cooperating."

"What do you mean?" Mark asked, his head cocked to the side in puzzlement.

"Well, as much as it hurts me to admit this," Carol said, "we can't control them."

Mark's confusion deepened. "You can't control them? I fail to understand."

"Yeah, me too," Alex said.

"Honestly, no one understands how they work, and we can't get a handle on them," Carol said. "We've tried. Everyone has tried."

"Who wrote the code?" Mark asked. "Surely he understands the objects."

"Leif Hoberson, and he's unavailable," Alex replied.

"And why is that?" Mark asked.

"He's no longer with the company," Carol answered.

"And he's in jail," Alex added.

"Is he the fellow who tried to kill Jon?" Mark asked. "I've heard rumors about that incident."

"Yes. Unfortunately, yes. He wrote the code for the bots and didn't get around to documenting the code before he was fired.

Then he tried to kill Jon in retaliation for his dismissal, and now he's in jail and about to be transferred to state prison."

"How hard are we running the system?" Mark asked. "My analysis programs tell me it's over ninety percent capacity. We've added more nodes. In fact, we're adding them every day. But it doesn't appear to make any difference."

"No, and it's not going to," Carol said. "The bots, I think, are going to keep it at ninety percent."

"That's going to be expensive," Mark observed. "Have you been to see this Leif fellow?"

"We have," Alex said. "He told us he had been in the process of documenting his code when he was fired. He claimed to be able to control them. But not from jail."

"Understandable, I guess," Mark said.

"Certainly," said Carol. "But it leaves us up the creek without a paddle."

Mark smiled. "It does, doesn't it? Look on the bright side. The system is holding. This is like the ultimate load test. Once you get the bots sorted out, we can be pretty confident the cluster will hold."

"Let's get over to tech support and see how they're doing," Alex said.

"Good idea," Carol agreed.

We Have to Have Leif

"All is well," Author reported. "There are a lot fewer calls than we were prepared for. And the online bug reports are, for the most part, misspelled words on the site. There have been a few four-oh-four errors where links are broken. Not many, though, and they're fixed quickly."

"That sounds wonderful," Carol said.

"Have there been any complaints about the speed?" Alex asked.

"No, none. I'm impressed. Congratulations, guys."

"Thank you," Carol said. "But we still have our problems."

"What kind of problems?" Author asked. "The system seems to be running fine, and the code is surprisingly tight."

"Well, frankly, the bots are out of control," Alex explained.

"Out of control?" Author asked.

"It's a long story, and we have to get back to work. It doesn't look like it's affecting you, so I'll explain later," Carol said.

"Okay, be like that." He smiled. "I'll see you later."

"Later." Carol turned to leave.

"Wait," Author said. "Here's the list of misspelled words and broken links."

Alex took the proffered list. "Thanks. We'll be back."

As they walked down the passageway, Carol said, "We need to get him out."

"Leif?"

"Yes, Leif. Larry is the best we have, and he doesn't have a clue. All of the programmers have looked at it, and we're nowhere," Carol said.

They walked in silence for a while. Alex took her hand for the first time, and she squeezed his. He thought it an intimate moment.

"So how do we get him out? Work release?"

"That might work. Let's go see Jeff and ask if he will talk to legal."

"Okay, you want to do it now?"

"Soon. The first stop should be to give the list of boo-boos to Joe. They all are in the interface. It's his job to fix them."

"Boo-boo. Now that's a technical way to put it." Alex laughed.

"I don't think we're off to a bad start. The boo-boo list isn't very long. I'm sure Joe will have them fixed in an hour or so."

"Yes, it looks good except for the bots," Alex said.

After a quick stop at Joe's office, they went on to see Jeff. They found his door locked, and no one responded to their knocking.

"Okay, what now?" Alex said.

Carol confronted Jeff's secretary.

"He's in there," the woman reported. "He's just occupied." She blushed. It's hard to keep secrets from one's secretary.

"Well, this is important. Can you interrupt him?" Carol asked.

"Sorry," she said. "I can call you as soon as he's free."

Disappointed it was the best she could do, Carol bowed to circumstance. "Okay, please do that. Thank you."

"What was that about?" Alex asked.

"Damn if I know," Carol said. "Something's going on."

"Yeah, I wonder what. Okay, what now?" He could see Carol still had the bit in her teeth.

"Larry. Let's get his latest assessment."

***

"In my opinion," Larry said after they had explained the problem, which he, of course, already knew about, "you are going to have to get him out. Leif's bots are an enigma. I have searched my mind thinking of someone to call in to help and can think of no one. Gordon has looked at it. But he's mainly a hardware guy. But I don't think it would make any difference. I can't get to first base with the damn things. No one is going to be able to get to second. We need Leif."

When they returned to the lab, the phone was ringing. It was Jeff's secretary, who reported Jeff was free.

"We'll be right there," Carol said. "Let's go, Alex."

On the way, Alex said, "I wonder what he was doing in there with the door locked."

"The rumor is he's having an affair that involves office sex."

Mary, Alex thought. *Damn, it has to be.* Strangely, he felt no jealousy. In fact, he had no feelings about it one way or the other.

They were in Jeff's office within minutes. As they entered, Carol said, "Jeff, we need to get Leif out!"

"Wait a minute. Slow down," Jeff responded. "Why do we need to get Leif out? You know he tried to kill Jon."

"That's beside the point, Jeff. We can't control the bots. First, they are taxing the system, and second, we don't know what they are going to do next. We haven't a clue. We need Leif; we need to get him out."

"You said that," Jeff responded, exasperated. "How do you propose to do that?"

"I don't know, work release?"

"A pardon," Jeff suggested.

"Will you talk to legal?" Carol pleaded. "We'll go with you and explain the importance of getting him out."

Jeff thought for a moment. "Okay, but I want to talk to Gordon first. I'll call you when I'm going over to legal."

"Okay," Carol said, realizing this was the best they were going to get. And it was something. She knew Gordon would realize the seriousness of the problem. "We'll be in the lab waiting for your call."

They walked slowly back to the lab, again hand in hand. Once there, they just stared at the monitors.

"The bots are not slowing down," Alex observed. "We're at ninety-two percent with only ten thousand users. And Mark is still adding nodes. It's scary."

"I don't think they are going to slow down. The bots are just going to continue to add load as more nodes come online. It appears Leif programmed them to stress it to ninety percent load regardless."

"Yep," Alex agreed.

The midmorning of the next day, Jeff called Alex. "One of the lawyers from legal is going to talk to the sheriff today to arrange a work release for Leif. I don't think it will be any problem, as we have a good relationship with law enforcement."

"Thank God!" Alex replied. "He can't get here too soon."

"Alex," Jeff said. "Let's keep this to ourselves for now. I'm going to have to talk to Jon and Gordon, but I want to wait until the possibilities are clear."

"Yes, sir," Alex replied.

The rest of the day passed with no news from Jeff. Carol and Alex monitored the system and made the rounds of the departments involved with the beta test.

Mary was on schedule with help screens, documentation, and web help. She had expanded her staff, including a star, Michael Ray, whom she had recruited from another social media company. Joe had fixed all of the issues reported by users, and Author reported many of his support tech had nothing to do. The only bad news came from Mark. The system continued to run at a constant 90 percent, the cooling systems were at maximum capacity, and the electric meters spun like the wheels of an Indy car.

"We need Leif," Carol said as she stared at a monitor.

"Yes, we do," Alex agreed. "Should we go over and see Jeff?"

"No, he'll call when he knows something."

At that moment, the phone rang, and Carol snatched it to her ear. She listened as Alex watched anxiously, trying to discern the conversation. Carol was frowning. *It doesn't look good*, Alex thought.

"Yes, sir," she said and hung up.

"What?" Alex asked.

"No good," she answered. "The sheriff said work release was out of the question because Leif is about to be transferred. He suggested that we contact the State Bureau of Prisons after Leif is transferred and processed."

"And how long will that take?" Alex asked.

"Too long; we need him now," Carol replied dejectedly.

"I know. What are we going to do?"

"Jeff said he hasn't given up. He has another idea. He's going over to talk to Gordon about it now."

"Gordon?"

"Yes, I think he's going to talk to Jon and wants moral support."

They didn't hear anything for the rest of the day, while the temperature rose in the cluster building. They had some good news: everything else was running within parameters—except for the load on the system imposed by the bots.

Diane, Spurned

That night Misika and Jon were again relaxing by the fire after dinner when a knock came at the door. It was Diane.

"I'm sorry to bother you," she said. "I don't have any other place to go. I have no friends. Jeff doesn't allow me to have friends."

"Come in, come in," Jon said.

"Yes, come in," Misika agreed.

"Thank you. I just don't have any place to go," she repeated, ending with a single sob.

"Come over by the fire and warm yourself," Misika said, thinking, *At least she is clothed this time. But she's not wearing any makeup.* Normally Diane would not be seen out of her house without her carefully applied makeup. Misika had to admit Diane was good at it. At forty, Diane was still a beautiful woman who looked thirty with her face on.

Tonight she looks old, Misika thought.

Once they were seated, Jon asked, "What happened, Diane?"

"Can I get you anything?" Misika asked before Diane could respond.

"Bourbon, neat," she answered.

"I'm not sure that's a good idea," Misika said. "How about coffee?"

"Okay," she answered meekly.

"So what happened?" Jon asked again, and Misika went into the kitchen to make coffee. She decided she and Jon would have a cup, too. It promised to be a long night.

"I asked him to move out for a few days. You know, give us both time to think. He agreed and moved into a hotel downtown."

"Uh-huh," Jon murmured encouragingly.

"Well, he came back after work last night. He told me he couldn't live without me—he loved me and wanted to come home."

"Uh-huh," Jon repeated.

"I cried and told him I loved him, too, but could not abide his infidelity."

Misika returned from the kitchen, saying as she came into the room, "The coffee is brewing." She had overheard Diane's last sentence. "So, Diane," she said, "do you think his affair is more important than his abuse?"

"Isn't it?" Diane answered. "I'm used to being punished. He doesn't usually hit me unless I've been bad."

"Yes, Diane," Misika said. "The beatings are more important. Sometimes infidelity can be forgiven. You know men; their small head often overrides their large head."

Diane giggled, and Jon's eyes widened as he rocked back in his chair. He had never heard Misika talk like this. *Where is this coming from?* he wondered.

"Well, anyway," Diane continued, "we decided to give it another try. I told him I could pretend it never happened as long as he gave up this girl."

"Girl?" Jon asked, recovering somewhat. "You know who she is?"

"No, I don't. But it doesn't matter."

"Why did you say *girl* rather than *woman*?" Jon asked, pleased to be applying his analytical talent.

"I don't know," Diane replied. "I just assume she's younger."

"It's not important," Misika said. "What happened? Why are you here?"

"It was okay for a while. Jeff even convinced me to be mad at you for interfering."

"That fits the syndrome," Misika said.

"Yes, I know. I'm a typical abused spouse. It's a cliché. But I can't help it."

"Okay, that's sad, but what happened?" Jon asked, wanting to jump to the meat of the matter.

"He came home tonight after work. I had his favorite meal on the table. It was extravagant, and I worked three hours preparing it for him."

"Uh-huh," Jon said.

"We sat down to eat; he complimented me on the food. When we finished, he asked me for a divorce."

"A divorce?" Misika said, shocked. She had not expected this. Normally an abuser kept the woman under his thrall and beat her until he finally killed her.

"Yes, a divorce. He told me he cannot give this girl up. He's going to marry her."

"Damn!" Jon said, totally out of character. Misika shot him a glance, her wide eyes expressing shock.

"I don't know what to do. May I please have a bourbon?"

"That might be appropriate," Jon said. It was an unusual opinion, as Jon didn't drink alcohol at all. "Do we have any in the house?"

"Diane, you may stay here tonight," Misika said. "I think that would be best. We have a spare room, where you would be very comfortable."

Diane paused, for quite a long moment. "Thank you, Mrs. Johnsson. That might be best."

"In that case, I'll pour you a drink. Jon, coffee?"

"Yes, dear, thank you."

Misika disappeared into the kitchen to fetch the beverages.

"This surprises me, Diane," Jon said. "I've known your husband for many years and have always thought of him as a good man."

Diane said nothing.

Saving Leif

Jeff called Carol early the next day. "Come over right now," he commanded. "We're meeting with Jon and Gordon. You are going to have to explain this situation to Jon."

Alex and Carol jogged over to Jeff's office, arriving out of breath. "It sounded urgent," Carol explained breathlessly.

"Yes, Jon is leaving for an off-site meeting in an hour. There's an urgency. Let's go."

They met in the small conference room next to Jon's office. When they got there, Jon and Gordon were seated and engaged in intense conversation.

"Coffee?" Jon asked as they entered the room in single file.

"No thanks, Jon," Jeff answered for all of them. He wondered why Jon was staring at him with what seemed to be a disdainful look.

"Okay, okay," Jon said. "Sit down. Gordon has been filling me in about the situation with the bots. However, I understand the Fauxbook website is running, and the beta testers have found very few problems. Is that correct?"

"Yes," Jeff answered. "Everything is up and running fine. We're ahead of schedule, in fact. The only glitch is the bots."

"Gordon tells me we need Leif, the fellow who wrote the code and tried to kill me, back at Fauxbook."

"That's correct, sir," Jeff said.

Alex and Carol maintained their silence, both determined not to speak unless spoken to. This was heady company for both of them.

"Okay, God is forgiveness, and Leif didn't put the BBs in the bomb," Jon said piously. "How do we get him out and back to work?"

Jeff answered, "I've been talking to legal. We've tried for a work-release program and failed. Legal tells me the only quick answer is a pardon from the governor."

"A pardon?" Jon asked.

"Yes," Jeff answered.

"And, Jon," Gordon added, "you will have to do it. None of us or legal is going to be able to pull this off."

"You want me to talk to the governor about pardoning Leif because he is essential to our business."

"Yes," Gordon said. "That's exactly right. I know it's a hard thing after his attempt on your life. However, as you say, God is forgiveness." Gordon, being an atheist, felt he was being a bit manipulative with that last comment.

"Anne," Jon shouted. He didn't like intercoms much.

"Yes, Jon," Anne said as she entered the room.

"Please call my wife and ask her if she can join me on the trip to Phoenix. Tell her I have something I need to discuss. It's important."

"Yes, sir, I'll do it right now," Anne replied.

"Tell her we're leaving in"—he glanced at his watch—"forty minutes. She should meet me at the airport. That will be faster. Assure her, though, the plane will wait for her."

"Yes, sir." Anne moved quickly, but with grace, back to her desk and picked up the phone. She was always poised and graceful. She had been born and educated in England, the daughter of penniless royalty who survived on a government pension. She did receive free schooling in the best of finishing schools and then went on to receive an MBA. She had been Jon's secretary for the last thirty years.

"Right, then," Jon said as he rose, "I'll be back tomorrow morning at eleven a.m., and we'll resume this meeting." He left the room and proceeded down the hall to the car waiting to take him to the airport.

"He needs to consult his wife," Jeff said.

Gordon glared at him but said nothing as he left the room.

At the doorway, he turned and looked back at Alex. "We'll see you two back here at eleven."

"Yes, sir," Carol and Alex said in unison.

Jeff left the room disappointed that he had raised the ire of both Jon and Gordon. *Not good*, he thought.

"Gee, neither of us said a word," Alex observed.

"Well, no one asked us anything," Carol replied. "I, for one, am just as happy not to be asked to participate in that one."

"Yeah, me too."

"Let's go get some lunch."

"The cafeteria?"

"Let's splurge," she said. "How about a two-hour lunch at the Quarterdeck?"

"It's awfully expensive," Alex protested.

"I'm buying. It's a celebration. Fauxbook is running."

"And running well except for the bots," Alex said.

"There's nothing for us to do here," she said. "Let's make an afternoon of it. I may even get drunk."

Now, Alex thought, *this is a side of Carol I haven't seen before.* He liked it–then, he didn't like it. *Gee*, he though, *talk about conflicted.*

She took his hand, fingers entwined, and led him out of the building.

The Governor

Fauxbook's private jet lifted off only five minutes behind schedule, with Misika on board. She carried one bag onto the airplane.

"You're traveling light," Jon observed.

"Well, dear, you didn't give me much time. No matter. If I need something, I'll get it there. How long are we going to be gone? Are you still planning to return tomorrow?"

"Yes, we'll be back tomorrow morning, and I'll be in the office by eleven."

"In that case, I have plenty, as long as you don't have any formal dinners planned. So what's so important that you want to talk to me about?"

"They want me to ask the governor to pardon Leif Hoberson."

"The boy who planted the bomb?"

"Yes, yes, the very same."

"Why do they—I assume you mean Gordon—want you to get a pardon for him?"

"Well, it is Gordon. But also Jeff and the kids in programming. It seems Hoberson wrote some code that is inadvertently negatively affecting the Fauxbook computers. No one here can figure it out. They tell me they need Leif. Gordon personally told me we need Leif. That's quite an admission coming from him. He was unequivocal. He said we need him. So, they want me to get him out."

"What if you get him out and he doesn't want to solve your problem? After all, he hates you. He tried to kill you."

"Good point," Jon said, taking a notebook out of his suit pocket and writing. "I'll bring that up in the morning."

"Other than that," she continued, "he might try to kill you again."

"I'll bring that up, too."

"Otherwise," Misika said, "I feel bad for the boy. He seemed sweet, a little naive, and perhaps slow."

"Yes, yes, he may be slow socially; however, I've been assured he is a brilliant programmer."

"People can be strange. It's up to you, Jon."

"I believe in the Bible," Jon said. "As it says in Ephesians, 'Be kind and compassionate to one another, forgiving each other, just as in Christ God forgave you.'"

"Yes, I know you do," Misika said. "And those are good words to live by. It's up to you. I'll support whatever you decide." She leaned over and kissed him on the cheek.

***

Jon attended his meeting and gave an inspirational though somewhat confusing speech while Misika went shopping. They enjoyed a pleasant dinner together that night. It wasn't romantic, but then, Jon didn't tend to be romantic. They took off at nine o'clock the next morning.

At exactly eleven the group reassembled in the conference room with one addition. Jeff had invited Ross McMyers, the head of the Fauxbook legal department. After introductions, the meeting got under way.

"I've been considering this pardon idea," Jon said. "I understand it to be the consensus of this group is Leif's work is essential to the success of Fauxbook. Is that a fair statement?" He scanned the room as everyone nodded, with the single exception of Ross McMyers.

"Okay, I have some questions. First, do we have reason to believe that, if pardoned, Leif will agree to help us? Second"— Jon smiled cynically— "if released, is he going to try to kill me or someone else? Third, do all of you believe he is capable of accomplishing the task?"

"Jon, everyone," Jeff said, looking around the room, "I've taken the liberty of filling in Mr. McMyers and inviting him to join us. He and I have anticipated many of your questions. Ross?"

Ross stood, his countenance a bit stiff and formal. He was new to Fauxbook, as were most of the employees, and was nervous in this august company.

"Mr. Johnsson, gentlemen, I believe the solution to this situation is a conditional pardon. That is, conditions are put upon the pardon must be completed before the individual receives a full pardon. If the conditions are not fulfilled, the pardon is revoked, and the subject is returned to prison to complete his sentence."

"Will one of the conditions be he will not attempt to kill me?" Jon said.

Everyone chuckled, with the exception of Mr. McMyers.

Jon must be really stressed, Gordon thought. *It's not often he's humorous.*

"Of course, that could be added as a condition," Mr. McMyers said with great seriousness. "However, I believe commission of a felony is an automatic invalidation of the pardon. In addition, the perpetrator would be subject to prosecution on new charges."

Carol spoke for the first time. "I don't think Leif is dangerous. He was very emotional after being fired. His work is everything to him. He felt he had lost everything and lashed out. I believe he will be very grateful to be reinstated and will be a danger to no one."

"I agree," Alex said in support.

"Yes, yes," Jon said. "And the Bible teaches forgiveness."

"So you'll do it?" Jeff asked.

"Anne, Anne," Jon shouted. "Please come in here."

When she appeared, Jon said, "Anne, get me an appointment with the governor at the earliest possible moment."

"I have reservations about this pardon," McMyers said. "If we are going to do this, I'd like to interview Mr. Hoberson first."

Anne reentered the room. "Jon, you have an appointment with the governor at two this afternoon."

"Well, Ross," Jon said, "you'd better get right over there if you want to talk to Leif before he's released."

Ross, who was still standing, began assembling his papers and putting them in his briefcase. "I'm on my way. Is it all right if I call you—say one this afternoon—before your meeting with the governor?"

"Yes, yes, perfect. I'll look forward to your call."

Promptly at one, and somewhat to his surprise, Jon received a positive report about Leif from Ross.

***

The next morning, he drove himself into Boston. He parked in the lot under the commons and walked to the Governor's office. He loved the city; the knowledge of all that had come before which he was now a part of. He was expected.

"Are you sure this is what you want to do?" Governor Charles Morris asked after Jon made his request and explained the reasons.

"Yes, yes, Leif's freedom, with the conditions I've outlined, is essential to the survival of Fauxbook."

"Mildred," Charles called.

"Yes, Governor?" she said as she entered the office.

"Please have the attorney general over here as soon as convenient," he ordered.

Within moments, Samuel, the attorney for the state of Massachusetts, entered, announced by the governor's secretary.

"Samuel," the governor said, "I have an undertaking for you."

"At your service, Governor," Ingram said with a slight bow.

The governor explained the situation and sent Ingram off to accomplish the task.

"It will take a week or two, Jon," the governor cautioned. "But we'll get him out if you are sure that's what you want."

"It is," Jon replied.

"Then consider it done. I'll just have to figure out how to explain this to the press. I have no doubt they'll get wind of this."

"I'm confident you can handle the press, Governor, but if there is anything I can do, please call me."

"It will be fine," Charles said. "Your man will be out soon. I sincerely hope he will be able to solve your problems."

Heat

Jon declined the Govender's lunch invitation and drove directly home. On the way, he called Gordon. "Hoberson will be back in a week or two. Gordon, I trust you know what you're doing."

"Don't worry, Jon. This is the right thing to do. In fact, it's the only thing to do."

Walking into the house, Jon found Misika sitting in front of the fire chatting with Diane. *Damn!* He thought. *She's still here.* He immediately chastised himself for the un-Christian thought.

"Hi, honey," he said. "Diane, Diane, how are you? How are you holding up?"

Misika rose, went to him, and kissed him on the cheek. "How was your day?" she asked. "How did your meeting with the governor go?"

"Fine, fine. Mr. Hoberson is going to be pardoned and will be back with us in less than two weeks. Diane, how are you?" he asked again, "What's going on?"

"I'm fine, holding up. Jeff came over earlier, but Misika wouldn't let him in."

"What are your plans?"

"I'm not sure. I'm thinking of going to my mother's and staying there for a while, until I get a place of my own. I miss Jeff, though."

"I understand," Jon said. "After all, a woman's place is with her husband. The Bible says, 'It is not good that the man should be alone.'"

"I don't think he's alone," Misika commented, shooting her husband an irritated glare.

"No, he's not alone," Diane agreed dolefully.

"The Bible says, 'If any woman has a husband and he is willing to live with her, she must not leave her husband.'"

Diane sobbed. "But he's leaving me! I'm not leaving him; he's leaving me." Her body shook as she continued sobbing.

"Jon," Misika said, "sometimes you can be such an asshole. And your quote isn't even right."

Jon was confounded; Misika rarely spoke to him like this. She had called him an asshole; he was bewildered.

"Uh, well…" He paused. "Diane, you are, of course, welcome to stay here as long as you like."

Misika looked at him intently, locking her eyes to his. "That's better, Jon. Just watch yourself."

***

The next morning, Alex and Carol made their rounds of the departments supporting Fauxbook's beta test. They found all was going well, until they got to C Building.

They entered the building to find Mark grimacing at a terminal. And the interior of the building was hot.

"What's wrong, Mark?" Alex asked.

"We're adding nodes to the second level now," he answered. "It's not certain we'll be able to cool the cluster. The cooling system wasn't designed to handle the demand of the cluster running at ninety percent constantly. That was never anticipated. For short periods of high demand, we're fine—hours even. But not constantly."

"What happens if the system overheats?" Carol asked. This had never been addressed in any of her computer classes.

"Well, first the computers will start making mistakes," Alex explained. "The heat causes the spaces between the etched wires on the chip to become more conductive. Then current jumps from one wire across the space to another. This short circuit causes processing errors. It gets worse, and the heat increases until, finally, the system comes to a halt."

"The chips aren't actually etched anymore," Mark said. "But Alex is correct in his description of the concept."

"How hot is it now?" Alex asked.

"Close. A few more degrees, and we'll start having problems. And the more nodes we add, the bigger the problem. The coolant and the fans are already running at max."

There was a long silence as Alex and Carol absorbed the unwelcome information.

Carol looked at the screen displaying the temperatures recorded at various parts of the system. Then she looked up at the fans under the eaves of the building, which were running at full speed. She walked over to the nearest rack and put her hand on one of the computers. "It's hot," she observed.

"Yes," Mark said. "It's close to too hot."

Carol thought for a moment. "Turn them off," she finally said.

"What?" Mark asked.

"The beta project consists of only ten thousand or so users on a system designed for billions. We don't need all of these nodes. Install the new ones, plug them into the bus, but don't turn them on. And turn off most of the ones currently running until you have the temperature under control. The fact is five or ten nodes would handle the current load. We don't need hundreds and certainly don't need thousands at this point."

Mark and Alex were silent, unmoving, their faces blank.

"Then," she continued, "when Leif comes back and gets the bots under control, you can start booting up all of the computers you've installed. That shouldn't take more than a day or so."

"Brilliant," Mark said. "Out of the mouths of babes."

"Did you just call me a babe?" Carol asked with mock anger.

"Sorry, but it is a brilliant idea. We can even test the new installations by booting them up one at a time. Brilliant! That is the answer. Obvious in hindsight. Actually, at this moment, I feel kind of stupid."

Carol's idea worked; the temperatures came down and were henceforth easily controlled. Beta testing continued with only minor faults discovered.

Leif Returns

Ten days later, Leif showed up for work. His first stop was Jon Johnsson's office. "Ms. Jankin, might I see Mr. Johnsson for just a moment?" he asked.

Anne looked up at him, unflustered. "Just a moment, Leif. I'll see." Rather than use the intercom, she thought it best to present Leif's unanticipated appearance to Jon in person.

"Go right in, Leif," she said as she came out of Jon's office. "He will be happy to see you."

"Come in, Leif." Jon smiled benevolently. "Have a seat."

"I'd rather stand, if you don't mind, sir. I have something to say, and I'm more comfortable standing."

"Yes, yes, as you wish."

"Mr. Johnsson, first I'd like to apologize for my actions. I feel really bad. I must have gone crazy to do such a thing. I'm very sorry."

Jon nodded encouragingly with a paternal expression and then waited for Leif to continue.

"I don't think I really wanted to harm you. But I confess, I don't know what was wrong with me. I did fail to put the BBs into the bomb. I don't remember failing to put them in. I guess it was my unconscious desire not to actually hurt you. So the..." He paused. "The, uh, bomb just created a high-pressure wave. It really wasn't dangerous."

Some high-pressure wave, Jon thought. "I see," he said.

"Yes, sir. I'm so ashamed. Perhaps someday you can forgive me."

"Son, I've already forgiven you. The Bible tells us to forgive as the Lord forgave you. I believe that with all of my heart."

Somehow Jon's words didn't strike Leif as personal. *It sounds like God forgave me on Jon's behalf, and Jon went along. Maybe that's how forgiveness is done. What do I know?*

"Thank you, Mr. Johnsson," Leif said, and he left.

***

"Leif," Carol cried as he walked shyly into the lab. "We are sure glad to see you!"

"Uh, thank you. I'm very happy to see you and to get back to work."

"And we're happy, more than happy. We were desperate to have you back," Alex said. "What you created is really something—incredible, really. Would you care to explain what is going on with your robots?"

"Yeah, I guess. They are really not complicated."

Neither are zeroes and ones, Carol thought, *but they can accumulate to become very complicated.*

"Come into my office, and let's talk," Alex said. As official team leader, whatever the reality, he had the largest office on the floor.

"Would anyone like any coffee or anything?" Carol asked, unconsciously falling into the female, nurturing role. As sophisticated as she had become, she found it hard to completely escape her rural West Virginia upbringing.

"I'm good," Alex answered.

"Me too," Leif said. "Nothing for me."

They sat down around a very small conference table in a corner of Alex's office.

"Okay," Carol said, reverting to character, "what the fuck is going on? The bots are holding the cluster at ninety percent capacity regardless of how many nodes we add. The heat became uncontrollable, never mind the electricity bill, which was about to bankrupt the company." *Okay*, she thought, *so I exaggerated a little. But who knows? It might be true. The meters were certainly spinning.*

"Well, it's really simple," Leif started. "I guess you've discovered the bots communicate with one another."

"We have," Carol answered. "But we don't know how."

"It's in the system calls."

"There are no such system calls," Alex injected, showing some exasperation.

"Well, no," Leif said, "there weren't. Some, though. Little stuff. The bots began with the small inter-program communication that exists in the standard operating system—cut and paste, for example—and built on it."

"How the fuck did they do that?" Carol asked.

Now she's said fuck *twice*, Alex thought, somewhat shocked. He had rarely heard her utter the word, or anything close, at least in this context. Carol was always very proper. *She must be upset—anxious. It's understandable. I'm a little anxious, too.*

"It's not complicated," Leif said. "They program themselves and other objects simply by trial, error, and eventually success."

Damn! Carol thought. *Now he's said it's simple twice. It's not simple; the best minds here can't figure it out.*

"You're saying they try every permutation?"

"Yeah, I guess, but not every permutation, just until they get a positive result. Then they lock it in. On average, they have to try fifty percent of all possibilities before the optimal result is reached."

"That's still a lot of attempts."

"Not exactly. Well, yeah, a lot. But not as many as you might think because they reject, for a time, solutions similar to the failed attempts."

"You're saying they sort the failures and create and program communication objects to service their needs?"

"You could put it that way," Leif answered.

"Is there another way to put it?" Alex asked with some tribulation.

"Create, evolve, I'd say. They are not conscious at this point. So I wouldn't say they're programming. I'd say they are persistently goal directed."

"At this point?" Carol said, shocked by what Leif was implying.

"Well, yeah…the swarm will continue to evolve. They are not smart; rather they're persistent—for now. But at some point, their persistence will evolve into what we might define as learning. Then, eventually, the singularity."

"No!" Alex exclaimed.

"No?" Leif said. "You have to accept the inevitability of the singularity. How did you think it was going to develop?"

"All of a sudden we're talking about the singularity? How did we get there?" Carol said in wonderment.

"I'm sorry," Leif said. "I'm getting ahead of myself. But…" He paused. "Yeah, the singularity."

"The singularity, when machines start programming themselves," Alex said.

"That's the commonly held concept," Leif said. "However, it's beyond that. The bots are already programming themselves. The singularity is when they achieve consciousness—become self-aware. Or maybe sometime after the theoretical singularity is achieved. They may not become self-aware at the instant of the singularity, but they will be shortly thereafter."

"Leif," Carol said, "am I hearing a spiritual element to what you are saying?"

"There may be a God," Leif answered.

"Oh, you're kidding me," Alex said. "All we want to do is to create a social network, not a supernatural computer program that's going to take over the world. That's crazy!"

"You think?" Leif said sardonically. At this point, his intellect was taking control of his mouth.

"This is scaring me," Carol said. "Maybe we should just pull the plug on all of this. We should just shut it down."

"That would work, for now," Leif said. "Tomorrow is a different issue. And tomorrow always comes—like it or not. If not here, it will happen somewhere else. The singularity is inevitable, preordained."

"Okay, okay," Alex said. "Let's stop with the bullshit. We need to get to work getting this damn cluster working. Leif, do you have a plan?"

"I do. We'll trick it for now. I'll fool the bots into thinking the cluster is at ninety percent when actually it's not. I'll pull them down to a tenth of a percent immediately. I'll get them completely under control later."

"Works for me," Alex said.

"All right," Leif said. "If it's all right, I'll go to my office and get to work. It shouldn't take long."

"Leif, I don't want to invade your space," Carol said, "but would it be all right with you if Larry works with you? It would be a good idea, I think, to have more than one person here who understands your work."

"Yeah, I guess."

"Thank you, Leif," she said. "Alex, would you go see Larry and explain to him what's going on?"

"Sure, Carol, happy to," Alex replied

Controlling the Bots

"Okay, Larry is on the case," Alex said. Carol was still waiting in his office, thinking.

"Good, let's make a point of debriefing Larry as often as possible. It's important we understand what Leif is doing. Not doing so previously is a mistake we don't want to repeat. Lunch?"

"Sure, cafeteria?" Lunch together had become a regular thing. Alex enjoyed being with her, holding hands, sharing a random kiss. Lack of sex was starting to feel nonthreatening and even normal. He liked her a lot and was becoming fonder of her as time went on. He felt as if he was slowly unraveling the mystery of her.

"Yeah," she said, taking his hand.

***

When Jon got home that evening, he found Diane gone. He was relieved and felt guilty simultaneously.

"Where's Diane?" he asked his wife.

"I'm not sure, though I think she went home to cook Jeff an extraordinary dinner. She was talking about doing that. She left about two this afternoon, saying she was going shopping."

"Did she say she was coming back here?" Jon asked.

"She didn't say. But I think she plans to use all of her wiles to get Jeff back."

"Well, yes, they certainly have their troubles. But a woman's place is with her husband and subject to him. That's what it says in the Bible."

"Jon." Misika sighed. "Sometimes you're hopeless."

"What?" he asked, confused and a bit shocked. Misika had never mocked him or questioned his authority as a husband before. *What is going on?* he wondered.

"Never mind, Jon. Everything will be all right." *Eventually.*

***

The next morning Alex and Carol had breakfast with Larry in the company cafeteria.

"So, Larry, what are you and Leif up to?" Carol asked.

"Well, not me so much. Leif is doing all of the work. I'm just watching. And I don't feel right about spying on him."

"You are not spying, Larry. You are simply keeping current with Fauxbook coding. This is company policy—especially when someone is not documenting their code. It is essential, as demonstrated by recent problems, that at least two people here are familiar with all Fauxbook code."

"I understand," Larry said.

"And I'd like you to encourage him to document his code to your satisfaction. If you have trouble with that, come see me."

"Yes, ma'am," Larry replied.

"So again I ask, what is Leif doing, do you understand his code, and is he documenting it?"

Alex had never seen Carol so authoritative and demanding. She constantly surprised him.

"He's not working on the code for the robots," Larry replied. "He's writing a program he thinks will fool the bots into thinking the system is at ninety percent load when the system is actually under one percent. If the cluster is at one percent load or greater, the bots should be dormant."

"Is this going to work?" Carol asked.

"Leif thinks it will, and from what he's explained to me, I think it will work, too. But it's a stopgap fix. He really needs to get direct control of the bots or remove them from the system."

"Right," Carol replied. "Is he documenting his code?"

"Sort of," Larry replied. "It could be better. I mentioned it to him, and he said he understood the urgent issue was to get the cluster running as quickly as possible."

"That's true," Alex interjected.

"Yes," Carol agreed. "But that's how we got into trouble the last time. The code must—must—be documented. I cannot emphasize that enough."

"I'll tell him," Larry said.

"Do that, and make sure he understands and complies," Carol said. "When is he going to have the code ready?"

"In about an hour, I think," Larry said.

"He's fast," Alex said.

"Yes, it's hard to keep up with him." Larry was thinking *impossible* but didn't say it.

***

Diane was back when Jon arrived home expecting his dinner to be on the table.

"Dinner is going to be a little late, Jon," Misika said. "Diane is here. Come into the parlor." As he entered, Diane was standing in front of the fireplace holding her robe tightly around her.

"How are you, Diane?" Jon said. "What happened?"

"Sit here by the fire," Misika said to Diane. "I'll get you a nice cup of hot chocolate." She moved toward the kitchen, caught Jon's eye, and motioned he was to come with her.

In the kitchen, Misika said, "She had a robe on at least when she arrived this time, Jon. But that was all. Nothing on underneath."

"What happened?" he asked.

"I don't know; she's only been here a few minutes. I'll get some hot chocolate into her, and I'm sure she'll tell us."

"Whether we want to know or not, I'm sure."

"Now, Jon, don't be mean. She's obviously having a difficult time. Remember you're a Christian."

They sat with her by the fire for a long time. Diane's face was stoic. Finally, she said, "I cooked him a wonderful meal, his favorite. I spent hours in the kitchen making it perfect. Everything seemed to be going well."

"Yes," Misika said softly, encouragingly.

"Well, I went into the bedroom and took off my clothes. I put on my makeup very carefully and promenaded down the stairs naked."

"Naked?" Jon asked.

"Yes. I was being as sexy as I could." She stifled a sob, paused a moment to regain her composure, and continued. "I told him I would do anything, anything he wanted. He just looked me up and down and said, 'Put on some clothes, woman!' I grabbed my robe from the downstairs bath and ran over here."

"Oh, Diane," Misika said sympathetically.

"I'm going to leave him. I really am. He humiliated me."

No one said anything for some minutes.

"You should give this serious thought," Jon said. "Remember, the Lord said, 'Therefore what God has joined together, let no one separate.'"

Diane seemed to cringe before his words.

"Oh, shut up, Jon," Misika said. "It's all right, Diane. Pay no attention to him. He's getting carried away. He enjoys being venially sinful."

Sinful? She thinks I'm sinful? What is going on here? he wondered, clueless. *It seems women are forgetting their place.*

Carol Revealed

"Thank God it's Friday," Alex said as the two of them finished up a program that analyzed user behavior.

"Yes, it's been a long week. This looks like users are most likely to log in if notified their friends are online. Perhaps we should think about reminding them to log in more often?"

"We can try it on a sample group and compare the results to the base."

Carol nodded her head and made a note. Then there was an awkward silence between them as they pecked randomly on their keyboards.

At last, Carol turned to Alex, slid a slip of paper across the desk toward him and said softly, "I'll meet you at this address at ten tomorrow morning. That's where I work. I want you to see what I do. Then, if you still want to, we'll have time to go to lunch."

"What do you mean, if I still want to?"

"You'll see."

Alex wondered what she meant but didn't pursue it. *I guess I'll see*, he thought.

"Just be there; knock on the red door with the building number on it. You'll be expected."

"Okay, I'll be there."

The next day, in the chill of the morning he caught the bus into Boston and transferred to the trolley which took him to an industrial area just a block from Back Bay. He presented himself promptly at 10:00 a.m. and knocked on the door. No one answered. He waited and then knocked again. Finally, a man opened the door. He looked Spanish, perhaps Mexican or Cuban.

"¿Qué quieres?"

"I don't understand," Alex said.

"What do you want?" the man said, switching to heavily accented English.

"My name is Alex Cromwell. I'm supposed to meet Carol Fisher here."

"Yes, yes, Mr. Cromwell, come in. You are expected."

The door led to a long, dark corridor that opened to a large room. A burly man, short, stocky, and wearing an expensive suit, was sitting behind a small desk in the corner. The room was tastefully furnished like a living room in a large house, though there were no windows.

Alex's guide spoke to the man in rapid Spanish.

"Ha, Mr. Cromwell, I am Raul." The man rose and walked around the desk toward Alex with his hand extended in greeting. He spoke perfect English with no accent. "Ms. Fisher left you a set pass—this is very unusual, but here it is." He proffered a laminated card on a long chain. "Put this on, and I'll take you over to the set."

Alex hung the pass—he assumed that's what it was—around his neck and followed Raul down another dark corridor, which ended in a double door. A bright light shone through the space between the doors and doorframe and from the space where the doors joined in the center.

Raul led the way and opened the right side of the double doors, bathing the corridor in bright light. He held the door open and bade Alex to enter.

Alex stepped through the door onto a brightly lit movie set. There were lights and cameras around the periphery of a bedroom scene. In the center was an unclad woman on her hands and knees surrounded by well-built young men who were also unclothed. The woman's skin shone under the lights. It looked like she was coated with oil. *Damn, they're making pornography*, he realized.

Hearing the door open, the woman turned her head toward Alex and smiled. It was Carol! His suspicions were correct; her body was indeed breathtaking. And what she was doing caused a physical reaction. His eyes widened, and he began breathing through his mouth.

"She'll be finished in a few minutes," Raul said. "You can wait here and watch or wait in the green room." He indicated a green door off to the side.

"I'll watch," Alex replied, his eyes fixated.

"Okay. If you need me, ask one of the crew, and he'll get me. But if you remain on the set, you'll have to be quiet."

Alex nodded without looking at Raul, mesmerized by what was happening on the set.

After a few moments, Alex decided he'd seen enough, waved at Carol, though he wasn't sure she'd seen him, and went through the green door. It opened to a room furnished with couches and overstuffed chairs. There were numerous doors on one wall. Alex opened one to find it was a dressing room containing a single chair, a clothes locker, and a shower.

He sat in one of the chairs to wait, his mind numb with this revelation.

Carol finished the scene, donned a robe, and went into the green room to face Alex. She wasn't looking forward to it. *But,* she thought, *he has to know the truth. A relationship can't be started with a lie.*

He wasn't there. She looked in the bathroom and then stood in the middle of the room, bitterly disappointed. A tear leaked from her eye. Then she steeled herself and thought, *So be it.* She went into her dressing room, showered the oil from her body, and dressed.

"Bye, Raul. I'll see you Tuesday," she said, and she walked toward the exit.

"Where's your friend?" Raul asked.

"I guess he left," she said despondently.

He saw she was upset and suspected what the situation was. He had seen it before. Raul had been in the business a long time; he had seen it all before. He felt bad for Carol; she was a sweet girl. He said, "Carol, I'm sorry."

"Thank you, Raul. I'll be okay." She choked on the last word and hurried toward the door before Raul realized the full extent of her distress.

She stepped out onto the sidewalk, a tight, stoic expression on her face. She was resolved not to let Alex's rejection bother her.

There was a figure walking away a few buildings down. *Is it Alex?* she wondered. She stopped still and watched as the person walked away. Then he turned; it was Alex. He walked back toward her. She waited.

"Hi, Carol," he said when he got close.

"I thought you had left," she said, tense, still unsure.

"No, I just needed some air. And to think. Ready for lunch?"

She paused, looking at him intently. He seemed calm and relaxed. "Sure, there's a nice deli on the next block."

He took her hand and asked, "Which way?"

They ate without mentioning the movie set. "How did you get here?" Carol asked.

"I took the bus. You?"

"Me too. Let's walk down to the bus stop." Tentatively, she took his hand, but he didn't intertwine their fingers.

"That's how I've financed my education," she said softly. "I was a virgin when I went to work for Raul. You wouldn't believe the bonus I got for that. After all of this school, I don't owe a dime. In fact, I've been able to put quite a lot of money in the bank."

"Yeah, that's what I figured after the initial surprise of seeing you on the movie set."

"I'm about finished with being a movie star," she said. She paused. "Okay, a porn star. There, I've said it. I have only this semester left, and I've already paid tuition and for the books. This is going to be my last movie. I have to finish it, for Raul. He has been very good to me, and I owe it to him. It wouldn't be fair to leave him with an unfinished feature."

Alex wondered why she had put herself, and him, through this. She could have just quit and never told him about the pornography business.

"I do have one question," he said.

"Just one?"

"Yeah, what's the deal? You put out for these guys every night and won't put out for me, ever."

"I would never do that stuff with you."

Alex grunted, confused.

"I have other plans for you."

"You do? What plans?"

"I plan to make love to you."

"Really?" He was surprisingly pleased. He realized he was in love, regardless of the circumstances. But he couldn't get out of his mind the picture of her on her hands and knees. Or maybe just turned him on. It was confusing. "What has taken you so long?"

"I wanted to be sure. And I wanted you to know everything about me. If you couldn't accept me, all I am, it would never work out. You had to know; I had to show you."

"Wouldn't it have been easier just to tell me?"

"No, I had to show you. I don't want any secrets between us—secrets someone else might tell you about later. Or…" She smiled. "You might rent a porn movie. Now wouldn't that have been a shock, to see your wife up on the silver screen if you didn't know? It would have felt like a betrayal." She smiled, happy.

Wife? Did she just say wife*? Damn! I need to catch up*, he thought.

"So, in all of this time, I've never turned you on?"

"Oh, Alex, dear, of course you have."

"I mean uncontrollably. You know, to the extent you couldn't help yourself."

"Alex, I can always control myself, but it's been close. Remember Mi Ly's taxi ride into Boston when I was sitting on your lap?" Carol asked.

"Indeed, I do."

"I have never been so wet in my life. I thought it was going to soak through and wet your pants."

"I was pretty excited myself." Alex smiled.

"Yes, I know. I felt you, and that didn't help." She paused. "If we work out, you will be my first lover."

"What?" he asked, confused.

"I told you I was a virgin when I went to work for Raul. What I do with those guys isn't making love; it's pornography. It means nothing like much of what we do. I think making love is different. I've never had a lover."

"We'll be different," Alex assured her. He turned her toward him and kissed her.

On the bus, Carol chatted, uncharacteristically vivacious, as if a great weight had been lifted from her. Alex was unusually quiet. Carol slowly became quiet, too, and worried.

After some time, she asked, in a moment of weakness, "Alex, are you sure you forgive me?"

"Of course," he replied. "You did what you had to do."

She was disappointed he hadn't said, "There's nothing to forgive," as she had expected or hoped. *There is nothing to forgive*, she thought angrily. *It's just a fucking job! It means nothing*! Then she chuckled at her own pun.

"What's funny?" Alex asked.

"Nothing," she replied. "Just thinking about things."

They sat quietly for the rest of the trip, until Alex said, "Here's my stop. I'll see you Monday."

She cried the rest of the way home, fell into bed fully clothed, and sobbed. *Damn! Damn! What's wrong with me? It was always fifty-fifty, and it's better to find out now. I've always known that. Why does it feel so bad?*

Tricking the Machine

The next day, Sunday, Carol was in the lab at eight, only to find Larry already there, staring into a monitor.

"What's up?" she asked.

"It looks like Leif has done it. The cluster is running at about a half of one percent load. Mark is here, too. He's over there booting up the nodes that were installed but left dark."

"How's that going?" Carol asked.

"Great, but the load is so low it's not making a lot of difference for now. We think most of the load we're seeing now is the operating system and the midware. The ten thousand users aren't enough to move the needle."

"Finally, good news," she said.

"It is. Leif's here, too. He's in his office documenting the new code. Then he promises to go back and work on documenting the bot code."

"That's good news. Do you think we're confident enough to call a meeting and announce we have the system and the bots under control?"

"I think so. But remember, Leif doesn't actually have the bots under direct control. Rather, he's tricking them into thinking the system is at ninety percent."

"Thinking?" she asked.

"Yeah," Larry said, his face tense. "There is that. Management would not be happy to know that."

To: Jon Johnsson

cc: Gordon Wysmann, Jeff Hoover, Roger Aegel, Barry F. Konrad, Alex Cromwell, Larry Bowers, Mary Adams, Mi Ly Wen, Author Miller, Mark Osborne, Leif Hoberson

From: Carol Fisher

If it is convenient for all involved, the programming team and I would like to schedule a meeting tomorrow, Monday, in the administrative conference room at 10:00 a.m. The subject will be an update on the state of the Fauxbook hardware and software.

We have a positive update we believe will be of interest to all. Please RSVP, as we will reschedule if anyone cannot attend, as we believe the news will be valuable to all.

"Okay," Carol said. "That's done. It's Sunday, so I don't expect answers until this afternoon. I think everyone will be there regardless of previous engagement. This bot business has been enough of a worry to incite attendance. I think we will have their complete attention."

To Carol's surprise, the responses started coming in instantly, until all on the list had responded affirmatively. Even Jon, who she knew would be in his family's box in church, responded he would be there. All, that is, except Alex. Carol noted his lack of response and frowned. If all had gone well, as she initially thought it had, she'd planned to spend last night at his place and to lose her virginity.

I guess my first impression of his reaction was overly optimistic. She shrugged. *His loss.*

***

Misika noticed Jon looking at his phone during the service, which was very unlike him. He was smiling.

After church, they stopped at Jon's favorite fast-food fried-chicken restaurant. He looked relaxed and happy for the first time in a while.

"Jon," she said, "did you get good news?"

"Yes, yes. I believe it is good news. I'll not be sure until tomorrow. There's a meeting in the morning at ten."

"Who's going to be there?" she asked, hiding her ulterior motives.

"Everyone, pretty much. The kids are doing a presentation that sounds like it will be very positive."

"How long will the meeting last?" Now she was skirting, risking arousing his suspicion. But he was in too good a mood to pick up on it.

"Oh, I don't know, Misika. An hour or two, I imagine. Then I'm going to have lunch brought in for everyone to celebrate what I am confident will be good news."

"I'm glad, Jon. You've worked so hard. I'm glad there is good news."

Jon nodded.

Misika got up to order a to-go meal for Diane. She was still staying at the house, though she planned to leave for her mother's in New Hampshire soon.

Diane was napping when they got home. Misika attributed her lengthy sleep to depression. *God knows she has something to be depressed about*, Misika thought.

Later Misika entered the guest room to find Diane half awake. "I have lunch for you Diane. Come down to the breakfast nook."

Even with four children, Jon and Misika hadn't outgrown their first house. And now with all of the children grown up and gone, it was more than adequate for their needs and for a number of guests. Putting Diane up was no trouble at all. Misika had put her in the largest guest room, the first at the top of the stairs.

The breakfast room was a windowed (on three sides) sunlit area attached to the kitchen and half filled with plants. It was Misika's favorite room in the house. She would spend hours there enjoying the sun, tending to her plants, and reading her books.

When Diane came down, Misika served her the fast-food fried chicken, mashed potatoes, and green beans on fine, translucent bone china. Diane thought it a bit incongruous. She had imagined the rich lived differently.

Jon had retired to his study, so Misika and Diane had an opportunity to talk privately.

"Diane, there is a meeting at the office tomorrow at ten a.m. Jeff will be there, and it will be followed by lunch. That will give you an opportunity to go over to your house, pack, and take a car."

"Are you sure he'll be gone?" Diane asked, worried.

"Yes, but take your cell phone. If something happens, I'll call you. Or would you rather I go with you to the house?"

"No." Diane paused to think for a moment. "I'll be fine."

That afternoon, Diane helped Misika prepare the midafternoon meal; a Sunday tradition in the Johnsson house. Three of the children would be coming over with their spouses, which made nine for dinner. Diane was a very good cook and a great help. Misika found, to her surprise, that she enjoyed her company when Diane wasn't fixating on her failing marriage. Diane could be very charming when she set her mind to it.

I wonder if this is what it's like to have a sister-wife, Misika thought. *It's rather nice to have help and pleasant company.*

The next morning Jon was off to work early. Diane and Misika had coffee in the breakfast room and waited until nine thirty.

"I know a divorce lawyer who is the best in the state," Misika said.

"Jeff told me once lawyers are involved, it will be the end," Diane said.

"Yes, no doubt. Have you not decided this is the end of your marriage?"

Diane thought a moment before answering. "I guess so. I don't know what else to do."

"I'm going over to the house with you, just in case he shows up. I don't want you alone with him."

"Okay. He would be mad. I'm sure he's already mad at you and Jon for interfering with our marriage."

It may not serve Jeff well to be mad at Jon, Misika thought. *Jon may react badly to what he perceives as an attack.* She knew all of Jon's talk about forgiveness implied a ruthless side.

Sharing the News

By ten that morning, everyone was assembled except Alex. He was missing with no explanation. No call. Somehow, Carol was not surprised, though he seemed to be going to extremes to avoid her.

"Okay, Carol, where are we?" Gordon asked.

"Good news," she replied, smiling. "The bots are under control, and the cluster is running at under one percent load with an average of sixty-three hundred simultaneous users. There have been no reports of system or software errors. A few interface issues have cropped up. Nothing worrisome—spelling errors, typos, and such. There was one broken link reported. All of these issues have been resolved. I believe we should add another fifty thousand users."

"Do we have that many signed up for the beta-test program?" Barry asked.

"Yes," Jeff answered. "That many and more, five hundred thousand in all. The plan is to add more as we achieve stability at each level."

"Another fifty thousand seems excessive at this point," Roger said.

Gordon was enjoying, and recording, the interplay between the know-nothings. *They're trying to impress Jon*, he thought.

"I am confident we're fine," Carol said. "We are rock stable at twelve thousand users. I think it would be a waste of time to advance in too-small increments."

"Leif, what do you think?" Gordon asked. "Do you really have the bots under control? And do you believe the system stable?"

"Mr. Wysmann, with all due respect, there is a long answer and a short one. The short one is the bots are suppressed for now, and the system is solid."

"Fine, please come by my office after the meeting. I'd like to hear the long answer. You come, too, Carol. Unless, of course, anyone would like to hear the long answer here and now. I suspect it is very long."

No one said anything.

"Okay, fine. Leif, Carol, I'll see you later in my office."

"So when can you get the additional beta testers online?" Barry asked. Jeff shot him a look that turned into a supportive smile.

Damn! Gordon thought. *I wish I was recording video. This is precious.*

"We'll send the e-mails this afternoon. I predict we'll see a high percentage of them online tonight. They are all anxious to experience Fauxbook."

"Fine, fine," Jon said. "When do you anticipate we'll be able to go public?"

"We'll keep adding beta-test users next month and through the first three weeks of June. Then we'll be ready for the rollout party."

"Fine, fine," Jon replied, smiling. "Roger, how are the plans for the rollout going?"

"Excellent, Jon. Everything is coming together under my plan. We'll be ready, and it will be a hell of a party."

Jon cringed a little at the foul word but soldiered on. "Fine, fine. It appears all of the news is positive, and we're on track. I'm proud of all of you."

"Thank you, Jon," they said in unison and the meeting adjourned. Leif and Carol followed Gordon to his office to provide the 'long version' of the bot story.

"Where is Alex?" Gordon asked after Leif and Carol found seats in his office. "Isn't he the group leader?"

"Not really," Leif said. Carol quickly hushed him.

"What did you say?" Gordon asked.

"Nothing. It wasn't important," Leif said.

Gordon smiled, happy to be recording audio at least.

However, he wasn't happy with what they told him about Leif's robots. Rather than solved, the problem appeared to him to be lurking. *Trouble was on the horizon and closing in on all of them.*

***

Diane and Misika finished gathering Diane's necessities from the house, including all of her jewelry. They loaded the Mercedes-Benz S63, and Misika sent her off to her mother's.

Jeff's going to be fit to be tied, Misika thought, *and perhaps he should be*. The thought of Jeff beating Diane brought chills.

***

Later, in the cafeteria, Mary found a seat next to Leif and whispered, "I know it's only Monday, but I'll be over tonight if that's all right with you."

Leif blushed and nodded without looking at her.

The Real Story

Gordon quickly got to the point. "First, Leif, do you really have the bots under control? I want to hear the long version."

"Well, not exactly," Leif said, looking down at the floor.

"They are controlled," Carol injected.

"It sounds like you are dissembling, Carol," Gordon said. "Let Leif talk. I want to hear the story from him."

"Yes, sir," she answered. "Sorry."

"Leif," Gordon said, inviting him to continue.

"The bots are a swarm now, sir. The swarm will continue to evolve. They are much like randomly interconnected brain cells. Like brain cells, individually they are not capable of much, but billions, evolved for various functions, will become more capable and, I think, eventually achieve the singularity. The bots multiply rapidly. The ones without functionality are sloughed off and destroyed."

"I see," Gordon said. *I'm glad I'm recording this. But, Leif's Cheshire cat smile worries me.* "Go on."

"Their original function was to simulate users—well, not really simulate—to put a load on the operating system for testing purposes. That worked very well. As the midware was added, the bots evolved to load that software also. Then the applications and finally the user interface. When I came back to work, they were taxing resources of all levels of the system to ninety percent of capacity."

"Really," Gordon commented. "That doesn't seem optimal."

"No, sir," Carol said. "We were having cooling problems as well as extremely high-power usage."

"I'd imagine," Gordon said. "What did you do, unplug some of the nodes?"

"We have them under control now, sir, and the system is running nominally," Carol said, surprised and impressed her clever solution was obvious to Gordon.

"Leif?"

"That's true, sir."

"And how did you regain control?" Gordon asked.

"I tricked them. I wrote a program that reports ninety percent usage to the operating system when it's actually only a tenth of one percent loaded."

"That doesn't sound like control," Gordon said.

"But it's working," Carol said.

"No, Mr. Wysmann is right," Leif admitted. "We don't have control. And they will continue to multiply and evolve. I suspect they will eventually figure it out and ignore my program."

"So to sum up," Gordon said, "your robots are communicating and learning how to act in cooperation to form a swarm, a whole greater than its parts."

"Yes, sir, that's about it," Leif said.

"Indeed," Gordon said. "So you have work to do."

"Yes, sir," Leif said.

"You'd better get to it, as, apparently, you need to get ahead of them." He dismissed them with an imperial wave.

"Yes, sir, Mr. Wysmann." Leif rose and left the office, followed by Carol.

The Boston weather had become cold, with snowflakes in the air, so they appreciated the new connecting corridor between the two buildings.

"It looks cold out there," Carol observed.

Leif was quiet.

"What's going on, Leif?" she asked. "It sounded to me like you are holding something back."

"Maybe," he said.

"I can only imagine what it is. Do you really think you can fool Gordon?"

"Yeah, I guess."

"What is it? Can you tell me?"

"Okay, let's go to my office and get out of this chill."

Though the sound of the fans blowing hot air was loud, the glass-walled passageway was chilly, as there not much insulation.

Leif's office was warm, perhaps because of the dozen or so computers he had running.

"That's better," Carol said, thinking it wouldn't be long before she became too hot. Boston winters were like that: you were either too cold or too hot. The merchants kept their stores very warm. Wearing winter clothes caused customers to sweat while in the stores, and the sweat would freeze between the door of the store and the car.

She saw the screens displayed what appeared to be activity. "Are those programs looking at the Fauxbook network?"

"Yes, I'm running a number of analysis programs on the network."

"I thought you were banned from our, or any other, network."

"I was, but I explained to Gordon it was necessary for me to learn what was going on and to fix it. He authorized the connection."

"And if you really think you can fool Gordon. You may be sadly mistaken."

"Perhaps he doesn't want to know," Leif said, expressing unusual insight.

"Uh-huh," Carol mumbled, wondering what Leif meant by that.

"This monitor is tracking the bots. Well, sort of tracking the bots. They are hard to get a handle on."

A graph on the screen displayed an upward trend of forty-five degrees.

"Is this activity?" Carol asked.

"No, I think—I'm pretty sure—that's the number of bots in the system. Activity is displayed on this one." He pointed to another monitor. That graph, too, showed a rapid increase.

"What are they doing if they are no longer loading the system?" she asked.

"Honestly, I don't know," he said. "I think they are organizing, mutating, and exploring—learning."

"What? That sounds scary." She sat down on the couch opposite Leif's desk. "What did you not tell Gordon?"

"I'm not sure if I'm right. So let's wait awhile and see what happens."

"You've raised my curiosity, but okay, I'll wait. At least the system is running."

"For now," Leif said ominously.

Business as Usual

That evening the Johnssons' doorbell rang repeatedly. Misika opened it and bade him enter. He looked like he was mad and working hard to control his anger.

"Hi, Jeff," she greeted him. "Come in."

"Where is she?" Jeff asked, obviously vexed.

"Who?" Misika asked with false innocence. "Diane? Well, she's not here. How long has she been gone?"

"I think you know damn well," he said, without the deference due Jon's wife. "When I got home, she was gone. And some of her clothes are missing, as well as all of her jewelry. The Benz is gone, too."

"Jon," Misika called, thinking it time for reinforcements. Jon was not one to endure disrespect.

"Yes, dear," Jon said as he entered the foyer. "What's the matter?"

"Jeff is here looking for his wife. He seems to think I know something about it. He's very upset and a bit rude." She knew *rude* was one of Jon's trigger words. He didn't countenance rudeness.

Jon confronted Jeff with a withering look, very unlike his normal parental half smile.

Jeff wilted and then recovered, though still somewhat cowed. This, after all, was Jon Johnsson.

"I'm looking for Diane, Jon," Jeff said, trying to face down Jon's obvious disapproval. "She's packed some things, taken all of her jewelry, and left in the Mercedes."

"And you think she came here?" Jon asked in a tone that expressed his displeasure.

Jeff had never seen Jon like this. He was obviously quietly angry. "We've been having some difficulties, and she's been over here to see Misika a lot."

"So you think your marital difficulties are my wife's fault?" Jon said through clenched teeth.

It occurred to Jeff he was on thin ice, and it frightened him. "No, sir. No, sir, not at all. I was just hoping you and Misika could help."

Jon stared at him for a long moment, his normally calm light-blue eyes narrowed in anger. "I'm disappointed in you, Jeff. Husbands should love their wives and should not be embittered against them."

"What do you mean?" Jeff asked, confused.

"I mean you most likely would not have this problem if you didn't beat your wife." Jon's voice was laced with steel.

"I never," Jeff protested, at the same time realizing Jon knew too much. "Jon, please, you haven't heard my side of the story. There are always two sides."

Jon glowered at him, obviously displeased. "Jeff, I think it's time for you to leave. Go home and gather yourself together."

"But I want to find Diane and bring her home."

"I understand you asked for a divorce. You're not making sense," Misika said.

"I never…I never wanted a divorce. That's not true," Jeff protested.

"Jeff, perhaps I've not made myself clear—get out!" Jon said softly but with iron in his voice.

Jeff departed, and Jon said, "Misika, I'll be in my study."

She knew this was not the time to discuss the matter with him. She had seen him angry before, though not often, and he was best left alone until he regained himself.

The next morning, Jon called Barry Konrad into his office.

"Barry, the launch date is approaching, and I'd like you to become more involved. I worry it's too much for the limited number of people working on it."

"I'll be happy to help, to do what I can."

"Good, good, I'd like you to get up to speed on what Jeff is doing and to assume some of his responsibilities."

"I can do that, Jon," he said, almost salivating. "Where would you like me to start?"

"Talk to Alex and familiarize yourself with what his team is doing. Jeff has been interfacing with Alex's programming team, and I'd like you to start there."

"Okay, I can do that, Jon."

"Good, good, they have leapt ahead, and the team has grown significantly. Alex and his people have proved themselves and taken the lead in Fauxbook development and the rollout of the technical side."

"Yes, sir," Barry said with enthusiasm. *It seems Jeff is out, and I'm in.*

The Last Film

The next day, Alex, though late, showed up for work. He said good morning to everyone, including Carol. But after that, he was quiet and distant.

Carol was disappointed, though not entirely surprised. She resolved to have just one more good cry that evening when she got home and then put this behind her—move on. In the meanwhile, it was business as usual.

She made her rounds of all the departments and arranged to increase the number of beta testers. They were now up to half a million users in the beta-test program. The various departments were still dealing with issues. But those were small, and overall, everything was going well.

Damn! I have to work tonight, she remembered. *I'll have to postpone my cry. Well, perhaps by the time I get to it, I'll be over Alex. One can only hope.* Now she regretted the false positive impression she'd had immediately after Alex had learned about the movies. *I was too open and optimistic. Damn! What difference does it make? Either he can accept me as I am, or he can go to hell.*

***

That evening, after they had finished filming, Carol showered and donned a robe. Raul intercepted her on the way to the dressing room. "Carol, please come into my office.

"Have a seat," he said, indicating the couch opposite his desk. Carol selected a chair, wanting nothing to do with his casting couch.

Raul nodded, smiling. He understood. "Carol, Fauxbook is going to host the biggest party this town has ever seen to celebrate the launch of their product."

"Yes, I know, Raul. I'm part of the planning for it."

"Uh-huh, well, they're bringing in a cruise ship to host the VIPs. It's the largest cruise ship in the world."

"Yes, Raul, I know—the *Tranquility of the Seas*."

"I had a meeting with Roger Aegel, the Fauxbook vice president, this morning, and he had a request."

One of the vice presidents, and not my favorite person. She had heard through the rumor mill Roger was a sexual-harassment suit waiting to happen. *I wonder what that pervert wanted. Well, I imagine I'm about to find out.*

"Yes, why are you telling me?" she asked.

"He is in need of some girls to entertain the guests on the ship. They are very important people. I immediately thought of you. The gig pays very well."

"Raul, I act in pornographic movies. I'm not a whore, don't want to be a whore. In any case, I work at Fauxbook during the day, and my services will be required by Fauxbook for the event. So the answer is no, and I'm disappointed you asked me. I thought you had a better opinion of me."

Raul was silent for a long moment. "You're right, Carol, and I'm sorry. I'm guilty of thinking only of the money. I apologize."

"Your apology is accepted, Raul, though I'm still disappointed in you. But I forgive you. You've always treated me with respect and fairness."

"Thank you," he replied.

"And I'd like to return your fairness by giving my notice. This will be my last film. After we wrap the current film, I'm retiring from the business."

"I'm sorry to hear that," Raul said. "I'm disappointed but not surprised. If I offered you more money, would you change your mind? You're a star, and I cannot easily replace you."

She smiled. "Thank you, Raul, but no, it's not the money. The money paid for my education, and now it's time to move on."

"Did you know you have a following? We get thousands of preorders for your movies. You have a lot of fans."

"And you didn't tell me before because you thought I'd ask for more money." She smiled pleasantly at him.

"Well, honestly, to tell you the truth, yes, you're right. But I'm telling you now and offering you more money. A lot more money."

"I'm not sure that makes me feel better; it just means you've been cheating me out of my fair share up to now."

"I wouldn't put it that way," he protested.

"If I agreed, would you pay me retroactively?"

"Retroactively?" he asked, confused.

"Yes, retroactively. You would pay a lump sum consisting of the monies you shorted me on the past films," she said teasingly.

"A lump sum?"

"I'm just messing with you, Raul. You shouldn't have asked me to be a hooker. I forgive you. However, this is still my last film."

"Can't talk you out of it?"

"No, you are just confirming my decision when you point out the next step in this profession is to become a prostitute."

"I didn't mean anything," he protested.

"You've done a lot for me, Raul, and treated me well. I appreciate it and am grateful to you. All of this would have been much worse without you being here for me. Regardless, I'm done."

Setting Up the Show

The next weeks passed quickly as Fauxbook was debugged, tidied up, and prepared for its public debut.

Meanwhile, Roger Aegel, Barry Konrad, Barbara Peregrine, and Greg Scott were busily preparing for the launch. Jeff appeared at the meetings and around the building. But the rumor had it he was out of favor, and he was essentially ignored, though everyone was polite.

As the date of the launch approached, the development team and the hardware people were full-out working, putting in eighteen-hour days and sleeping on couches in the office. Alex and Carol still worked together, though the lunches and dinners they had enjoyed together didn't happen.

The *Tranquility of the Seas* pulled into Boston Harbor on Saturday, barely. It was big—almost too big for the harbor. However, the pilots got it in and moored in a space normally occupied by two cruise ships. Most Fauxbook employees were on hand at the pier to witness the event, as were thousands of civilians. This was the first time the *Tranquility* had visited Boston. It was big, awe-inspiring.

Mark Osborne and his team, along with the IT people and maintenance, assaulted the ship. One of the important goals was to provide a network connection to Fauxbook in all of the staterooms, restaurants, and other public areas of the ship. Joe and

Michael Ray joined forces to create HTML pages to make it easy for new users to sign up for Fauxbook.

An outside ISP was attaching four fiber-optic cables to the ship's computer center. Two of the cables would lead directly to the IBM z13 now serving as the intelligent router for the Fauxbook system. The other two would provide general Internet service to the attendees via the ISP.

"This is going to be fast," Mark said to Carol, who was working beside him along with Alex. It was an all-hands-on-deck effort.

"They will not be able to differentiate it from instant," she agreed. "The kiosks in the city and hotels will be almost as fast."

"We're going to have a lot of people signing up," Alex said.

"God, I hope so," Carol said.

"Everyone who signs up during the launch party will become a diamond user for life, with a number of benefits. That should encourage them."

Roger Aegel had organized meetings and parties for advertisers and potential advertisers, starting on the great ship's first day in port. These grand events included free food, an open bar, entertainment, access to Fauxbook executives, and extravagant promises.

Perhaps unrealistic promises, Jeff thought. He, for lack of anything else to do, had been monitoring the preparations, including Roger's parties.

Diane was still missing. "I think she's at her mother's," he told Mary, "though her mother denies it."

"Things usually work out for the best," Mary said insincerely. She had her own plans.

Barry was coordinating with Barbara, setting up the onshore venues, decorating the city, and ensuring the activities would go as planned.

Jeff had been subtly moved aside by fellow employees who all had heard rumors Jeff was no longer in favor. Such was Jon's power and influence he rarely had to issue an explicit order. Rumors were more than enough, though his intent occasionally had been misunderstood.

Jon oversaw all of the activities from his office in the mill, receiving reports by the minute.

"Anne," he called, "please come in here."

"Yes, Jon," she said, entering his office with her steno pad. Anne was British and old-school; she continued, no matter the technological advances, to rely on her steno pad and pen. She never used a pencil, considering pencils gauche and erasers worse.

"I've heard some comments that Jeff feels sidelined, and that concerns me."

"Yes, sir," Anne said noncommittally. She, of course, understood exactly what was going on—she had seen it before. And she had a good idea why.

"Sign him up for a postgraduate business course at Harvard. Dean Abraham will help you set it up."

"Yes, sir."

"Good, good. If Jeff feels he has nothing to do during this extremely busy and important time, perhaps it's time for him to expand his skills."

"Yes, sir, I'll take care of it and let him know. Is there anything else?"

"No, no. When's my next meeting?"

"Roger Aegel and Barbara Peregrine will be here at two to update you on the launch-party plans. Then the mayor and the head of the city council at three to discuss the city's part in the party."

"Fine, fine. Please have the cafeteria send me up some lunch. I'm going to work through the lunch hour. You know what I like."

Two Days to Go

"Sit down, Roger, Barbara," Jon said, indicating two un-upholstered chairs opposite his large oak desk. His office was Spartan. His one extravagance was the handsome oak desk his wife had presented him when he started his first business forty years ago.

"Jon," Roger said, "preparations for the launch are going well, and we're right on schedule. That is, six months ahead of schedule."

"Good, good," Jon commented.

"Yes. Barbara, under my direction, has been doing a wonderful job coordinating with the vendors and the city."

"Excellent, excellent," Jon said, pleased.

"I've been meeting with advertisers, and they are making commitments—large commitments. Their enthusiasm has exceeded my expectations." What he didn't say was he had been promising, guaranteeing, an extremely large number of users. It wasn't that he was attempting to maximize his bonus. Rather, Roger saw success in signing advertisers as an advancement of his power in the company. However, another fact not mentioned was his agreement to substantial penalties if the user count fell short. He was all in.

***

Alex spent the night in Mary's apartment. Mary had invited him out of the blue. This time he brought pizza and beer, and they enjoyed a pleasant evening.

Mary woke him in the middle of the night by screaming and flailing about. He reached for her, but she fought him, striking him wildly. He rolled away and switched on the light on the bed stand. She was drenched in sweat, as were the bedsheets. He got out of bed, and she calmed; her eyes opened. She stared at him. Recognition came slowly.

Finally, she said, "Alex?"

He sat on the edge of the bed and reached for her hand. "Yeah, baby, it was just a bad dream. Do you remember any of it?"

"It's the same dream," she said softly. "My stepfather started fucking me when I was nine. I was his sex toy for years."

"Your mother?"

"She knew but pretended she didn't."

"That's what your dream is about?"

"No, that wasn't so bad. When I was thirteen, he decided to share me with his brother. Then it went on. Their friends would come over. That's the dream. I was just a little girl, helpless, and all of the pawing hands. That's the dream."

Alex was shocked at what had happened to her and how vulnerable she seemed. Her eyes still were unfocused and her skin waxen.

"Where are the sheets?" he asked, as he helped her into a chair and wrapped a blanket around her. She sat quietly while he made up the bed. Then he led her back into bed, lay beside her, and wrapped his arms around her. She didn't resist and was asleep instantly.

He lay awake for a long time. *I guess this explains a lot*, he concluded before finally drifting off.

Waking late, he was groggy from lack of sleep.

"There's coffee," she called from the kitchen. "Let's go. We're going to be late."

"Are you all right?" he asked.

"What do you mean? Yeah, I'm fine."

"The dream, you know, last night."

"What dream? Did you have a dream? You look like shit. Get up; drink some coffee. I've got to go."

Apparently, he thought, *she doesn't remember a thing.*

Impatient, she left before he did, planting a kiss on his cheek as she departed. "That was fun," she said, too loudly. "Lock the door when you leave."

When he left the downtown apartment, it was two days before the launch. He was awestruck at the changes to the city. The Prudential Center was draped with Fauxbook banners on all four sides, each 750 feet high. Computer kiosks stood on every corner, and signs advertising Fauxbook were pervasive. The city had been transformed, and it was amazing.

He walked the two blocks to the mill and entered the lab. Carol was already there.

"Hi, Alex." She smiled.

His heart seemed to flutter. She hadn't smiled at him often lately—not that he could blame her.

"I think we're ready," she said.

"I think so, too," he agreed. "Does that mean we can take the day off?"

"No, I don't think so," she said, taking him seriously. "We'll go through everything again. Both of us should go through Joe's new-user sign-up code again and figure out some way to load test it without the bots. It's going to be the most heavily used, I think."

"Should I talk to Leif about using the bots? They are the best way to load test it."

"No, I don't think so." She chuckled cynically. "We've had enough trouble with the damn bots."

"Tech support, then," Alex suggested. "Those guys don't have a lot to do until we're open to the public."

"Good idea," Carol agreed. "I'll go over and talk to Author. I'll tell him to add users with each last name containing an exclamation mark. Then we'll purge them later."

"Good idea. I'll stay here and check the router code for the connection to the ship and the city. Lunch later?"

Carol paused and then said, "I don't think so, Alex. I'm going to skip lunch today. There's still a lot to do."

That's a rejection, Alex thought, *but at least a polite rejection. Just as well, as I've not figured out what I want. It's all very confusing. Carol's lifestyle is not what I was brought up to accept.*

As much as he resisted, Alex was at heart an Iowa boy, from a Christian family with midwestern family values. He found a lot about the big city to be alien, and Carol's part-time job had shaken his sensibilities. *I know I like her and lust for her. But that in itself is sinful—or so I've been taught. How would I take her home to meet my family? What would I say to them? The fact I'm thinking of taking her to meet my parents must mean something, but what?*

He knew she was disappointed in him, and he felt dejected. She had been so happy Saturday after the filming. They had held hands, eaten lunch, and walked across Boston Common hand in hand—happy. And then, dark thoughts had descended upon him. He couldn't block them out.

I should talk to her, he thought. *But what would I say? Perhaps the truth*? He had been brought up to speak the truth. No, that wasn't quite true. He had been brought up to be a good Christian, believe the word, and not offend anyone, even if the latter required white lies.

It occurred to Alex he was again spending Monday nights with Mary, who most certainly had no morals in the sense he defined morality. And, it appeared, she had a nut or two loose.

Further, he suspected strongly Carol knew and had always known about his Monday nights.

She had never asked him to explain it. Perhaps she understood it was only the sex and equated it to her work. *No, that didn't make sense.* It confused him.

He decided to go over to the computer building and to physically check the connections from the outside to the router. He remembered the admonishment of his professor that anything that could go wrong would go wrong and therefore one should always check to be sure everything was plugged in.

When he got back to the lab, Carol was still there. He had trouble looking her in the eye and was certain she noticed. However, she didn't say anything.

"How's your confidence level, Alex?" she asked.

"Good. We've checked everything at least three times. Still, I worry. If this doesn't go well, it may be the end of the company."

"I've heard that," she agreed. "Shall we check everything again?"

"It would make me feel better," Alex said. "I'll make the rounds of the departments and ask them to check everything again. Then I'll come back and look at the code again."

"Okay, what should I do?" Carol asked.

Strange, he thought, *she has never asked for direction from me before.* "I'd appreciate it if you would go over to the computer building and double-check all of the physical connections. I just did that, but another eye can't hurt."

"You got it. I'm on my way." She smiled sweetly.

He wondered if she understood his conflict and felt sorry for him.

Ready, Launch, Aim

The day before the show passed quickly as the city filled up with attendees. The teams reviewed the code, checked the hardware and connections, and tested the backup power systems, including the backup power on the cruise ship.

Everything seemed in order. They were ready. And none too soon. There were already thousands of attendees filling every hotel room inside route 495 and beyond.

That evening the sky over Boston was illuminated by fireworks, as it would be in the nights to come.

During lunch, Alex and Carol took a taxi into the city, which was filled to overflowing with people. There was excitement in the air, music played over temporary speakers set up in the street, and the *Tranquility of the Seas* sounded its ship's horn periodically.

"We've taken over the city," Carol said in an excited tone.

"It looks like it," Alex answered. "I doubt there's a hotel room to be had in the whole place."

Exiting the taxi, they walked through the mob of people, all of whom seemed unsure of where they were going. The Fauxbook kiosks were in operation, with long lines at each.

"I want to see the cruise ship and the waterfront," Alex said.

"Let's walk toward the sound of the horn," Carol said. Just then, the great ship's whistle joined the cacophony. "And the whistle." She smiled and took his hand absentmindedly. Just as quickly, she released it, as if it were red-hot. "Sorry," she said.

Alex said nothing but felt as if he had lost something precious—though, he calculated, there seemed to be hope.

"Wow, look at that," he said. "The lines on the gangplanks to the ship are blocks long. I can't see the end."

"Build it, and they will come," she said with a broad smile. "We'd better get back. I'm sure someone will be looking for us this afternoon for something. Everyone is so nervous."

"Yeah," he agreed. "Let's go. I hope we can get a taxi."

Alex's fears were unfounded, as they easily hailed an outbound taxi. People were coming to the center of the city, not leaving.

As they rode through the city, they saw large, very large, screens displaying Fauxbook's closed-circuit programming. "It looks like they are interviewing Jon," Carol said.

"Yep, and the programming will continue twenty-four hours a day for the duration."

"This is amazing," she observed. "I'm proud to be a part of it."

"That may be the only thing I'm proud of lately," Alex said dolefully.

"What do you mean?" she asked, looking at him intently.

"Nothing, just thinking."

Carol didn't push. She continued to stare excitedly out the windows of the cab.

Back at the mill, they found the lab empty. Apparently, everyone was out watching the activity in Boston.

"Lunch," Alex suggested.

"Sure, let's go down to the cafeteria." She walked out briskly ahead of him, not attempting to take his hand.

***

Jeff was ensconced in his office, away from the activity, lamenting his plight as Mary did her best to distract him from his troubles.

"I'm going to quit," he declared and then moaned. "This is an insult, and everyone knows it. I don't have to put up with Jon's disparagement. My wife's transgressions are bad enough without this additional insult."

Otherwise occupied, Mary said nothing. *No matter*, she thought, *there's not much to say. But he's cute, and surprisingly malleable for one in his position—given the right stimulus. There are possibilities*, she thought.

He was missing it. The biggest launch of the decade, and he was left out. Jeff could feel the hum of activity and the excitement in the air, and he wasn't part of it.

"Can you come home with me tonight?" he asked.

"Hmm, umm," she murmured through her nose. *Damn, he's going limp.* But Mary had methods, and he soon recovered.

"No," she finally answered. "I have a prior engagement. I wish you had asked me earlier. It's too late to get out of it now," she lied.

While Jeff was occupied in his office, a large box truck backed up to his house, and five men entered and rapidly emptied much of the residence's contents into the truck. It left, and another backed into its space. Diane was claiming what was hers. Jeff would return that night to a bare dwelling.

***

Carol and Alex spent the afternoon watching the numerous monitors measuring activity on the Fauxbook system.

"It's not breaking two percent," Carol observed with a wide smile. "It's working!"

"The system shouldn't be taxed," Alex said. "We've hooked up, at last count, one hundred and twenty thousand nodes to the cluster. I think we would be under one percent if the bots were totally eliminated."

"I'm sure you're right. Regardless, I'm thrilled to see all of this actually work."

"Why don't we meet in the computer building tomorrow morning and watch it work?"

"What time?" she asked.

"Six a.m. Okay?"

"Sure, I don't think I'll be able to sleep tonight anyway. I'm too excited."

"Are you working tonight?"

Carol thought that question a bit intrusive, but she locked eyes with him and answered. "No, I'm not working much anymore. We're just finishing up the film. There are a few scenes to reshoot, not many. Then I'm done."

"How about dinner, then?" Alex asked.

"Can't," she said after taking a breath. "I have work to do at home tonight. Anyway, I'm not sure that's a good idea."

"Yeah, sorry, I shouldn't have asked."

"No, probably not. It seems we have some things to work out between the three of us."

The Big Day

Alex arrived at the computer building at five thirty the next morning to find Carol already there, along with most of the team, including Mary. He wondered how long they had been there but didn't ask.

Mark Osborne was standing off to the side, watching over things like a proud parent.

Lights were flashing on the panels of the nodes, on the switches, and on the bus. It looked like a three-story Christmas tree gone amok.

As Alex looked more closely, he noticed that more than half—a lot more than half—of the lights on the first level were flashing very slowly, indicating the machines were pretty inactive. And the activity lights on all of the nodes on the second level were almost dormant. *We're not anywhere near capacity*, he thought.

Alex verbalized his thought to Mark. "Yeah," Mark said. "We're well below two percent and adding users rapidly. Interestingly, the additional users are not increasing activity."

"The system is probably still fitting them in between keystrokes," Carol said. "We have a lot of capacity. It's not even measurable because the pause between user keystrokes multiplied by millions of users is time available to the computer. We can only estimate that."

"And we are continuously adding more capacity," Mark commented.

They watched for a few more minutes before going over to the cafeteria for breakfast.

Later, Joe, Larry, Mary, Michael, Jeromy, Laurie, Mi Ly, and others—everyone, actually—studied the activity monitors in the lab.

A television on the wall tuned to channel 4 displayed the activity downtown. CBS was providing nonstop coverage of the launch party. Hordes of people filled the streets past capacity. Those streets not closed by the city were effectively closed by the masses of people.

Mi Ly looked up and said, "It's bigger than I expected. It appears the Fauxbook launch is a success."

"Yes," Michael said. "Now pray nothing goes wrong."

"We're adding new users at a good clip," Mary said, unconcerned with the outside world. "And the rate is increasing."

"The load is under two percent," Joe observed.

Alex and Carol joined the crowd surrounding the monitors as the clock ticked toward nine o'clock.

"There's not much to do other than watch," Carol said.

"That's a good thing," Larry observed. "Hope it stays that way."

At nine, the system was garnering new users at the rate of ten thousand an hour and still accelerating. Alex unconsciously gripped Carol's hand, which she allowed for some minutes before gently disentangling.

Still, they all were mesmerized by the numbers and graphs on the screen. Joe was smiling.

Just before ten, Larry shouted, "We've lost the ship!"

"What?" Alex asked as all heads turned toward Larry.

"Look," he said. "Activity on the cruise ship's connections has gone to zero."

"That's impossible," Carol said. "We have four fiber-optic lines going out there. They can't all have failed."

"No," Larry agreed. "It has to be software. I'll get on it. Jeromy, come with me."

The phone rang; then another line rang, and another. "That's not good news," Carol said. "Mi Ly, get on the phones; tell them we know about the problem and are working on it. We don't anticipate it will take long to fix it. Mary, can you help her?"

"Glad to," Mary answered, although actually she was mildly insulted to be relegated to such a mundane job. She wondered, *Since Mi Ly was assigned to the phones first, does that mean she's in charge?* It wasn't a happy thought for her.

"We'll all help for now," Carol commanded. "The rush of calls will slow down after a while."

"Yeah," Alex commented wearily. "After everyone who can call has called."

"The end users don't have this number. Mark, please go talk to Author and ask him not to call and to tell his people to restrain themselves. Assure him I will call him personally if there is any news."

"I'm on my way," Mark replied.

"Then come back over here and stand by just in case we find it to be a hardware problem."

"Yes, ma'am," he acknowledged, deferring to the much younger woman with the voice of command. "I'll be right back."

Larry and Jeromy entered Larry's office, and Larry closed the door behind them. "Use that terminal," Larry said, indicating an empty seat. "Ping the addresses on the ship, starting with the ship's central router. That book over there contains all of the system's IP addresses."

"Okay, I can do that," Jeromy said.

"I'll trace the signal and see how far toward the ship I can get. We'll compare results and see what we have."

"I'm on it already," Jeromy said as he thumbed through the book of IP addresses.

Mark was having a hard time over in the support department.

"Mark," Author said loudly to break through the clamor of phone conversations. Apparently, all of the tech-support people were engaged, and lights on the phones were flashing everywhere. "Everybody is calling. We're even receiving calls from top management complaining programming isn't answering their phones."

"Sorry, Author, they are answering the phones over there. But like you, they're overwhelmed. In any case, there is nothing anyone can tell the callers until we've tracked down the problem."

"That's not very helpful," Author complained.

"No, it's not. But that's the way it is. Calls should slow down soon. This is just an initial rush."

"More than a rush, I'd say."

"They will have the problem flushed out shortly," Mark assured him.

***

"No response from the ship," Jeromy reported.

"Yeah, I can see," Larry said. "The problem is in the IBM. It's acting as the central router, and it's sending packets addressed to the ship into the ether."

"That would explain a lot," Jeromy said.

"Yes and no," Larry said. "It explains what's happening but not how it happened. It seems too deliberate to be file corruption."

"Well, it's a computer; anything can happen," Jeromy observed.

"I'm going to delete the router controller software and reinstall it from the backups," Larry said.

"Hey, that will shut down the whole system. You could make a bad situation worse," Jeromy objected.

Larry rose, opened the door, and yelled for Carol. "Bring Alex with you," he demanded.

They came into his small office, which, with four people occupying it, was tight. Quickly, he explained the situation to them.

"Do it," Carol said. "We have no choice."

"I agree," Alex said.

"It's pretty drastic," Jeromy commented. "I think we should wait."

Larry, who had already known what they would see, sat at his terminal and started typing. He was glad to have cover from Alex and Carol in case this blew up. Jeromy was a pain in the ass, though.

"Okay," he said, "the first step is to shut down the central router on the IBM. I can't delete an open file." He typed a few strokes and waited. "It's down; the phones will really light up now."

"Can't get worse," Alex said.

"You think." Carol smiled and gripped his hand.

"All right," Larry said. "The file is gone. Now I'll restore a backup and restart it." He typed frantically on the keyboard.

Damn, Carol thought, *he can type, and he's fast. Most programmers use the hunt-and-peck method. Surprising, but true.*

They waited. A dialog box popped up on the screen.

"What's happening?" Alex asked.

"An error message saying I don't have administrator permissions. Damn!"

"Ah, that's messed up," Carol said. "We all have administrator permissions. Is this a virus?"

"Quick," Larry said, grabbing Carol by the arm and guiding her to a terminal. "Log in, and we'll try again."

Carol typed in her password.

"It's loading," Larry said. "It won't be long, and we'll know if it worked."

"What if it doesn't work?" Alex asked.

"We'll be back where we started or worse," Larry said.

"Yeah," Jeromy said, "you keep messing around, and the whole system will be down."

"No," Carol said loudly. "Not on launch day. We'd be done! Finished!"

"Ping the ship," Larry said tersely as he thought about punching Jeromy in the nose.

Jeromy typed in the nine numbers of the IP address, hit Enter, and waited. "Nothing," he said. "The request timed out."

There was a spontaneous moan in the room.

"Keep trying," Larry ordered. "It's loaded, but it will be a while before it establishes the connections."

"How long?" Alex asked.

"Any second; the system is fast. Still, it has to rebuild the routing table, update the gateways, rebuild the tables in all of the routers on the system—there are a lot of them—and verify connections."

"That sounds like it will take a while if it works at all," Jeromy said.

"Not as long as you might expect. Optimizing the pathways will take a long time, maybe days. But the system will be up soon and will do that later."

"The router is up," Jeromy said. "But we're back where we started—no connection to the ship."

"This is not good," Alex observed.

"No, it's not," Larry agreed. "Damn! Okay, everyone think. What else can it be?"

"Hardware?" Jeromy suggested.

Silence.

"This is bad and getting worse by the moment. The ship is filled with very important people, including very important journalists," Alex said.

"I thought that was an oxymoron," Carol commented.

"This isn't funny," Larry said.

"No, not funny at all. It's our jobs if we don't get this working," Alex commented with a frown.

"Larry, what is the date on the backup you restored?" Carol asked.

"Huh? Oh!" he said, suddenly understanding. "Jeromy, what's the date of the backup we restored?" Jeromy had handled retrieving the backup.

"Wait," he said. "I'll have to look." A pause, then Jeromy said, "It's from ten this morning."

"Grab one that was created yesterday, any time yesterday. Hell, last week. That program wouldn't have been updated in the last few months."

Larry sat in the chair in front of his terminal and typed. "This one?" he asked Jeromy.

"Yep, that's yesterday at two p.m."

"Here we go," Larry said as he shut down the entire system once again, deleted the file on the IBM, and restored the backup. He started the program, and it began to load.

Tension filled the room. "If this doesn't work, we're screwed," Jeromy said.

"Shut up and ping the ship!" Larry ordered. Everyone in the room was on edge.

"This isn't what working for a computer company is usually like," Carol commented with wry wit.

Her observation was met with chuckles. The tension eased a little.

"I got it!" Jeromy cried. "The ping came back in point two milliseconds. It's fast."

"The ship?" Larry asked nervously.

"Yes, the ship," Jeromy assured him.

"Thank God!" Carol exclaimed as she sat down at a terminal and attempted to access first the ship, then the other major parts of the system. "Got it! We're back." She hurried to tell the others, who were busy on the phones. Over her shoulder, she cried, "Mark, go tell Author."

Symptoms

"Where's Leif?" Larry asked. "I haven't seen him today at all."

"Don't know," Joe answered. "In his office?"

They both walked out onto the big floor and joined the celebration. Gordon was there.

"Carol, what the hell do you think happened?" he asked.

"I don't know, Mr. Wysmann, but we're going to trace it and find out."

"Let me know," he ordered.

She turned toward Larry "You know we have to get to the bottom of this."

"I know; we're just taking a break. We'll check the logs after lunch."

"No lunch break! I'll have sandwiches brought over. I want you to get on this now and keep at it until you have answers."

"Yes, ma'am. Come on, Jeromy."

***

Jeff started the day in a foul mood. He had spent the previous night in a hotel after discovering his house had been cleaned out.

Earlier that morning, Mary had stopped by, entered his office, and locked the door. She was there, with her purse, for their morning tryst. She had some new adventures in mind.

"She took everything, the bitch!" he complained. "Everything. Even the beds. The house is bare—nothing."

"Women can be like that," Mary observed. "What are you going to do?"

"Divorce her and get my things back! I'm going to see a lawyer this afternoon."

"You know the connection with the cruise ship is down?" she asked.

"Yeah, I heard. There's nothing I can do about it. It serves them right. Damn them all anyway. And damn Jon!"

"Damn Jon?"

"He's the one who sidelined me. I think he's mad because I can't control my woman. You know, she showed up at his front door the other night, naked."

He certainly hates to lose control of his women, Mary thought, unimpressed. She smiled, thinking of the Joker quote: *Wait until he gets a load of me!*

"Yes, you told me. Jon is punishing you because of that?"

"He's going to send me back to school. Damn him."

***

Larry and Jeromy had spent the last two hours poring over the system logs.

"This can't be," Jeromy said.

"No, it can't. The logs say that Jon Johnsson logged in with administrator privileges and compromised the router software."

"What are we going to do?" Jeromy asked.

"Find Leif. No one knows more about the system than Leif. Stay here and continue going through the logs. I'll find him."

Leif wasn't hard to find. He was in his office with the lights out and the door locked. He had been there all morning.

Larry pounded on the door and yelled, "Leif, I know you're in there." That was a lie, as Larry only suspected Leif was in his office. *But why else would the door be locked?* "I'm not going away. Open the door."

Finally, the door opened. "Okay, come on in," Leif said.

"What are you doing in here?" Larry asked as he sat on the couch.

"I'm watching some very interesting stuff."

"Are the bots responsible for this?" Larry asked.

"No, the bots aren't responsible. It's an intrusion hack."

"That can't happen. We're running a host-based intrusion-detection system as well as the best firewall in the world."

"Yeah, that's why this is interesting," Leif said. "I watched it all morning. Someone got in, though, or around the IDS. He didn't steal usernames and passwords. He cloned Jon's username and password, changed the copy, and then logged in as Jon."

"That explains why the logs recorded the damage was done by Jon."

"Yeah, I guess. There has to be a back door to the system. So who would have put in a back door, and why do they want to bring Fauxbook down?" Leif said.

"Is this over?" Larry asked.

"For now," Leif stated. "He's gone, though he didn't bother to log out. He knew we'd find him and doesn't seem to care."

"So he'll be back?"

"He or she will, most likely, be back unless we find the back door and lock it."

"Let's go talk to Carol," Larry suggested.

"Okay, it's over, so there's nothing to watch. You guys did a good job getting the system back up."

They found Carol focused on the activity monitors. "Everything is working, and we're up to twenty thousand new users an hour!"

"That's great," Larry said. "We've tracked down what happened. It was a hack, an intrusion."

Carol picked up a phone and punched Gordon's extension. "We'd like to come over," she said when he answered.

The Party Resumes

The party was under way and showed no sign of slowing down. That night, Jon gave the keynote address in the theater aboard the ship. He was uncharacteristly clad in a tailored tuxedo. The speech was lived streamed to large screens throughout downtown and, via the Internet, to the world.

Good evening, and welcome to Boston. And welcome to Fauxbook.

I am proud to lead a group of dedicated, innovative, and motivated people who have brought you Fauxbook.

Fauxbook is the most successful, ethical, and useful social network site ever launched. It will become part of everyone's life, and their life will be better for being part of the Fauxbook family.

Jon continued for over an hour, drifting from the script now and then to tell one of his stories, fraught with hidden meaning that was not often discovered.

The week was filled with parties, seminars, presentations, and a lot of people using Fauxbook to connect to old friends and make new ones.

The streets of downtown Boston were lined with banners, advertisements, and vendors of souvenirs, hot dogs, and every kind of paraphernalia imaginable. The streets themselves were packed with people, many in costume and in various stages of undress. It was a party such as Boston hadn't seen in years—if ever.

Fauxbook users were still signing up by the thousands, and the teams watched the activity closely with a mixture of excitement and trepidation. So far, it looked good.

Roger Aegel moved into a large stateroom on the *Tranquility* and was partying or making deals 24-7. He was determined to sell out of advertising space and then consult with programming to create more.

He was making promises he hoped he could keep and agreeing to penalties for nonperformance he prayed he would never have to pay. The important thing to Roger was he was writing contracts by the dozens and keeping the advertisers happy. *They are very happy indeed*, he thought.

The rate of new users signing up on the Boston network started to drop midweek. It seemed all of the attendees had signed up. But Fauxbook's nationwide advertising in all forms of media and the news coverage of the launch party were spreading the word. Thousands of people were joining from all over the world.

"Russia and China are a bit thin," Carol observed with a smile.

"That's to be expected," Mi Ly said. "China and Russia are very tightly controlled by the government. The government will only allow access to those things that are good for the people."

Damn, she's serious, Carol thought. *I was joking. Obviously, China, Russia, and some other countries are run by uptight assholes. And she's not very disapproving. I wonder what she is all about.*

Roger was too busy signing business to worry, and no one else knew to worry. Roger had not told anyone—other than his colleagues in legal, who had to prepare the contracts—what he was promising advertisers. *Legal isn't going to tell anyone*, Roger thought. *They're lawyers. They don't know shit. Anyway, everything's going to be fine. Fauxbook will sign up two billion users, and each ad impression will get over five hundred thousand clicks. It'll be fine, and I'll be a hero.*

Jon was on television constantly during the week of the party. He was on the talk shows, late-night comedy, news shows, and even *60 Minutes*. The word was getting out, and users were signing up.

Alex, Carol, and their team continued to monitor activity.

"We're adding users rapidly," Carol observed.

"Yeah, but not fast enough," Alex replied. "Europe is disappointing. Our projections called for a lot more users than we're getting."

"Language," Mi Ly said. "The site only supports English. That's not going to attract French-speaking people."

"We're working on it," Joe said. "We needed to button up the English tight before starting to create foreign-language versions of the site. Give me a couple of months, and we'll have the translations done."

"Do you have the people?" Carol asked.

"We're staffing up rapidly; there is some difficulty finding enough translators who are technically savvy. But we're getting there."

"Well, the numbers may be disappointing until you do."

"Rome wasn't built in a day," Mi Ly commented.

"That's true," Alex agreed. "However, at this rate of ten thousand a day, it will take almost three hundred years to amass a billion users."

Carol smiled. "Just as I was feeling good, you have to turn this into a math problem."

Alex looked chagrined but felt better when she suggested lunch. Unexpectedly, they were falling back into their prerevelation ways. He wondered whether that was a good thing. But for now, it felt good.

"Sure, the cafeteria?"

"Sounds good," she replied. "Let's all go." *Safety in numbers*, she thought.

Everyone joined them except Mi Ly.

"I want to watch the monitors," she explained. She was excited, worried, and antsy.

That evening Mi Ly visited her favorite venue for relaxation. She was surprised to find the place filled to overflowing. The proprietor was standing at the rear entrance.

"Mi Ly," he said, "I'm really glad you're here. I hope you have time to stay."

"Well, I didn't plan to stay long," she replied.

"I'll pay you five hundred dollars an hour if you agree to a three-hour minimum. We really need you."

Mi Ly was flabbergasted. He had never offered to pay her. Rather than being pleased, she felt embarrassed. The reality of what she was doing fluttered at the edge of her consciousness, a shadow of a thought that troubled her. She turned and ran.

Wrapping Up

To the delight of the mayor and chamber of commerce, many of the revelers who had attended the launch stayed on after the party to enjoy the delights of Boston and to shop.

But for the most part, the city emptied rapidly, leaving streets with vendors packing up and forlorn banners, their former brightness dingy with soot.

Alex and Carol arrived at work early and focused on the postparty results.

"We garnered just under three hundred thousand users on the local servers and another four hundred thousand worldwide. Under a million total," Carol said.

"That means just about everyone here signed up," Alex said. "What did we expect?"

"I don't know. No one ever said or set a goal. I guess it's not bad; as you say, almost all of the attendees signed up. Worldwide signups seem disappointing, though."

"It'll grow," Alex assured her. "It's not like the company has done any advertising other than for the launch."

"Jon doesn't believe in advertising. He's more of an 'if you build it, they will come' kind of guy."

"That's worked for him before. He's a very successful man, famous even."

"I hope he's right," Carol said.

"Not to worry; that's above our pay grade. Our job is to make the system work and keep it working. We've done that and should take pride in what we've accomplished."

"I'm sure you're right. The system load is still under one percent. The addition of almost a million users didn't budge the needle."

"We've lots of capacity, no doubt," Alex said.

***

Larry sat beside Leif in his darkened office, lit only by the glow of numerous terminals.

"Leif, don't you ever leave? You worked all through the party."

"There's a lot to do," Leif replied.

"Yeah, what are you doing? Are you still working on the bots? I thought you had them under control."

"No, they weren't under control. I tricked them, and that approach is doomed. They will figure it out eventually."

"So what have you been working on?"

"The bots. I've now gotten them under control. I wrote the Mama Bot and the Daddy Bot. The swarm now operates under a hierarchy, with Mommy and Daddy at the top."

"What! When did you do that? I'm supposed to be shadowing you to understand your code! Did you document it?" *Damn*, Larry thought, *if he didn't, I'm in trouble. I'm probably in trouble anyway. I can't keep up with this brilliant son of a bitch!*

"You weren't here; nobody was, except when they were all running around like crazy people trying to keep Fauxbook up and party."

"You could have called me," Larry protested. "And why weren't you out there helping? We had a serious problem when the ship went dark."

"I'm sorry, but this was urgent. I had to get it done before the bots chanced upon the deception."

"Weren't you worried about Fauxbook?"

"Not really. I knew you guys would get it under control, for now."

"What do you mean, for now?"

"To borrow a term," Leif said, "there's a ghost in the machine. Anyone can see that."

"That's crazy. There's no ghost; there are no ghosts."

"Yeah, I guess," Leif said with a patronizing tone.

Larry contemplated for a moment. *I can recover this*, he thought.

"Okay, I'm sure you're right. Whatever. So, catch me up on what you've done."

"I'll send you the code; you can read it and ask me about anything you don't understand. Will that work? I've still got a lot to do and no time to walk you through it now."

"That sounds good for now," Larry said hesitantly. "How much control do you have?"

"Pretty much total," Leif replied. "At least for now. Remember, they're evolving all of the time and will be looking for a way to control Mommy and Daddy. I'm hoping they will evolve in parallel to protect their authority. But there's no guarantee. I have to keep working on it. I need to stay ahead of the bots."

***

Jeff was almost totally isolated now. He stayed in his office all day as he waited for the semester and his classes to start. He felt as if he were in prison. The only person he had to talk to in the company was Mary.

"I'm going to sell the house and move into a furnished apartment," he told her during one of her conjugal visits.

"Can you sell it?" she asked. "Isn't it in Diane's name, too?"

"No, everything is in my name. I'm the man of the house. I can do as I wish."

Maybe that was true once, Mary thought, *but no more. Silly man, those days are over, whether you know it or not.*

***

Larry was on the main floor, surrounded by the proletarian programmers, when Roger walked in, beside himself.

"What happened?" he asked in an angry tone. He was nose to nose with Alex, whom he understood to be the team leader. He was way into Alex's space. "Where are my users?"

"Users? I don't know where they are—all over the world, I expect," Alex replied, willfully misunderstanding Roger's question.

Carol tried to stifle a smile. Roger wasn't well liked.

"No!" he exclaimed, raising his voice. "Numbers, numbers, numbers! You are under a million users. I need billions!"

"Mr. Aegel," Alex said calmly as he stepped back to open the space between them. The loud conversation had captured the attention of the entire room and the balconies above. The guardrails above were packed with people who had come out of their offices to watch the show. Alex continued, "You are in the wrong department. This is programming; you need to speak with marketing."

Larry listened to the exchange with interest, thoughtfully.

"Well, I will, but you people have great culpability," Roger said. "You let the connection to the cruise ship go down, and then the entire system—twice. That cost users!" He was shouting now, spittle flying from his mouth, his face red, as sweat appeared on his forehead.

"True," Carol said in a quiet voice. "And we take full responsibility for the outage. However, it didn't result in fewer users signing up for Fauxbook. Very close to one hundred percent of the attendees signed up, and they were the only ones affected by the outage. We recovered; no users were lost."

"That's what you say," Roger huffed.

"That's what we say," Carol replied. "And Alex is right; you will want to talk to marketing."

"I'll do just that!" Roger roared. "But don't think that will let you off the hook." He turned and stormed out.

***

"We need a break," Carol said. "Let's go down and get a snack." Alex joined Carol, Mi Ly, and Mary in the cafeteria. They sat in silence for a while, thinking their own thoughts about what had just happened.

"Do you think the rumors about Roger are true?" Alex asked.

"Oh, I know they are," Mi Ly said. "He grabbed my behind once."

Well, Alex thought, *it's sticking out far enough to provide a good target.*

"He called me to his office once and demanded a blow job," Carol added.

"What!" Alex exclaimed.

"Yeah, I turned him down. He wasn't happy and threatened my job, bonuses, and any promotion."

"He made me the same offer," Mary said, "but he wanted me to get naked first."

"You're making this up," Alex protested.

"No, I walked into his office, and the first words out of his mouth were, 'Get naked.'"

"What did you do?" Alex asked.

367

"What do you think?" Mary replied. "And I got a nice bonus at the end of that month, and I have my own department at Fauxbook."

"You're not serious!" Carol laughed.

"As serious as a heart attack. And, I about gave him one," Mary displayed a Cheshire cat smile.

Your New Best Friend

"Do you have an appointment?" Roger's secretary asked Larry.

"No, I don't. Do I need to make one? I have some information Mr. Aegel will be very happy to have. And it's urgent."

"Just a moment." She rose and walked into Roger's inner sanctum without knocking. She was a gorgeous blonde with a spectacular build. Larry wondered whether the rumors about Roger were true. Her entrance into his office seemed very informal.

"He can give you five minutes," she said as she exited the office. "Please go in."

"Mr. Aegel, thank you for seeing me," Larry said. Roger did not offer him a seat, so he stood in front of the desk like a child about to be reprimanded.

Not cowed, Larry said, "I understand you are upset by the low number of users."

"Not upset, not upset at all," Roger said disingenuously. "Though I did expect more."

"How many more?"

"A billion or more. So I am somewhat disappointed."

"How many did you promise the advertisers?" Larry asked softly.

"Don't be impertinent, young man!" Roger replied angrily. "That is none of your business."

"Sir, I don't mean to be disrespectful. However, I do suspect we have a problem, and I have a solution."

"Well, if we do have a problem, and I'm not saying we do, it's not my problem. It's marketing's problem."

And Roger is in charge of marketing, Larry thought. He said nothing.

"Well, saying there is a problem, what is your solution?" Roger asked finally.

"Well, Mr. Aegel. I believe my idea to be worth something to me." Larry knew he was out on thin ice. But if he had analyzed Roger correctly, the man would be receptive to corruption, and that was what he intended to propose.

"Your problem is the user count is significantly less than what you promised the advertisers."

He has no idea how big the shortfall is, Roger thought, *but if he knows I'm in trouble, I wonder who else knows.*

"What makes you say that?" Roger said defensively.

"Well, I just know," Larry replied, hoping Roger wouldn't realize he was bluffing. He didn't actually know anything for sure other than witnessing Roger's tantrum earlier.

"Well, young man, hypothetically speaking, if this were the case, what is your solution?"

"Before we get to that, I want something," Larry ventured, not sure yet he had him.

Roger smiled with false confidence. "And what is it you want? Don't you work here already? Aren't you paid for your services, in return for which you present your best effort?"

"I do," Larry said nervously. But he felt he had no choice other than to press on. "Yes, sir, you are right. But I feel my requests will be to the benefit of the company."

"Okay," Roger said slowly, drawing out the word. "What do you want?"

"For the good of Fauxbook, I believe I could best serve in a managerial position. That would entail a significant raise. Then when the user count meets your expectations, a good-size bonus."

"And you think your solution to the user issue validates your demands?" Roger asked, leaning forward with a hopeful expression.

I've got him. Larry suppressed a smile. "Yes, sir, I do. And if you agree, we can implement the program immediately."

"You're sure?"

"Yes, sir. The only problem I anticipate would be raising suspicions by increasing the user count too rapidly without an explanation. But if you launch an advertising program, it would give us cover."

God, this is too good to be true, Roger thought. *In fact, it can't be true. No amount of advertising would make up the shortfall in time. Too little too late. But it may be time to grasp at straws.*

"All right, I'll agree to your terms. You'll get what you demand if your plan works. Do you have any idea how many users we need to satisfy the advertisers?"

"No, sir. My guess is it's well over a billion. And that's doable."

"Tell me how you're going to accomplish this," Roger said.

"Do I have your word?" Larry asked, knowing he didn't really need it. He was about to draw Aegel into a massive fraud that would ruin him, send him to jail even, if exposed. He'd give Larry what he wanted.

"Yes, young man, you do, and my word is my bond. So how are you going to accomplish this?"

"Leif and I are much further along than we've let anyone know. We can control the bots," Larry said, taking credit for more knowledge than he actually had.

Advertising

Roger appeared in the doorway to Barry's office, just two offices down from his. "Barry, do you have a moment?"

"Sure, Roger, come on in. What's up?"

"It's not what's up, Barry. It's what's down. We have a problem."

"Not enough users signing up for Fauxbook? I already know that."

"It's bad; the advertisers are going to have a fit."

"I know. I assume you have come up with a solution."

"Yes, I have. We need advertising. We must advertise the service."

"I've known that for a long time. And it may be too late. Maybe not…but you know Jon. He believes, strongly, if you build a good product, they will come."

"I think he's seen the movie once too often," Roger said.

Barry smiled. "It's not funny, and it's always worked for him in the past. He's a successful and famous man. It's not going to be easy to change his mind, and I assume that's what you want to do."

"We have to, or we're lost."

"How do you want to approach this? Do you have a plan?"

"Yes, I do. I have the ads Stuffer and Company produced when we were starting up. The two of us have to go and see him, show him the ads again, and convince him to run a real—a huge—marketing campaign."

"He fired Stuffer," Barry replied.

"I know he did, but we have to change his mind. I can guarantee the marketing plan will work."

"Do you think we can enlist Gordon to help?"

"Good idea. Maybe. Will you talk to him? He and I tend to get on each other's nerves."

"I'll ask him to lunch. He likes to eat, and it puts him in a good humor."

***

They arranged a meeting with Jon simply by walking in past Anne and into his office. Gordon joined them shortly thereafter.

"A fine product sells itself," Jon said. "Advertising it is just a waste of money."

"You're right, Jon," Barry said condescendingly. "But only among sophisticated buyers who are able to discern value on their own."

"Yes," Roger agreed. "This is a new market for all of us, and we must adapt."

Jon rested his elbow on his desk and placed his chin on his palm. Gordon said nothing but thought, *I sure am glad I'm recording this.*

"Word of mouth. Word of mouth," Jon said, "is always the best marketing tool."

"Many of our users speak different languages," Roger said, knowing it wasn't true, yet, as the foreign-language versions of the site were not ready. "Word of mouth can be difficult in these cases."

"Still," Jon said, wavering, "customers come from heaven when you have an excellent product. And I've always insisted on having a superior product. Then I've placed my faith in God."

"To be fair to all sides," Barry said, playing on Jon's vision of himself as a fair man, "let's do a test project. Say, ten million spent in various media over the next month."

"Sounds fair to me," Roger said. "What do you think, Gordon?"

"Hey, I'm just in charge of ensuring we have an excellent product. Marketing is beyond my purview. However, a test does seem worthwhile."

After a long pause, Jon said, "Okay, yes, let's do it." Jon usually let his employees try their ideas and he never chastised them when they failed–or discussed the failure at all. However, henceforth they were loath to do it again. In the long term, this bred a hierarchy of sheep that did Jon's bidding.

As they left the meeting, Roger and Barry walked together. Gordon had stayed in Jon's office to chat. *Presumably about the good old days*, Roger thought unkindly.

"So, Barry," Roger said, "my understanding is he agreed to spending ten million on marketing over the next month. Is that what you understood?"

"Yes. Surprising as it is, that's what I heard."

"Okay, let's do it. I'll call Stuffer and get them over here. We'll start making the media buys later today."

***

Over the next month, users signed up for Fauxbook at an extraordinary rate, which accelerated over time. They ended the month with over a million new users a day and increasing. The advertising seemed to be working beyond expectation.

Jon's office issued a press release describing Jon's "forward thinking and ability to adapt to changing times and markets." He promised to continue and expand the marketing program.

Fauxbook Grows

"Diane's divorcing me," Jeff lamented.

"Uh-huh," Mary grunted through her nose. *I thought he was divorcing her*, she thought. *Maybe she was faster on the draw...doesn't matter.*

"She took everything. Her lawyer is demanding a list of assets and warning me not to transfer or otherwise hide money. The bitch!"

Mary was becoming irritated he was distracted from the task at hand. Much more of this, and she was resolved to quit and leave him hanging. *Damn!* she thought.

She needn't have worried, as Jeff forgot all about his troubles and moaned.

I hope they can't hear him through the door, she thought. *But I'm sure his secretary can hear him moaning.* She smiled as much as she could, considering.

***

By the end of the next month, Fauxbook was up to two billion users and still growing. Roger was happy, the advertisers were happy, and more were coming on board daily.

The bots are doing a hell of a job, Larry thought. *No one can tell the difference. They are users.*

***

"Carol, is someone working nights?" Alex asked.

"What do you mean?" she asked.

"Well, maybe nothing, but I ran a speed test on the cluster, just for fun, last week, just before I left work."

"Yeah, so?"

"Well, it was fast, really fast. So the next morning I ran the test again, and the speed had increased overnight."

"That's because there are fewer users logged in early in the morning. The load is less."

"No, I compensated for that. The system is getting faster every day. I'm sure of it."

"And why do you think that is?" she asked tersely. Lately, there was a lot of tension between them.

"Someone is working on optimizing the system at night."

"Now that would be a dedicated soul," she said. "I don't think so."

"So explain it," he demanded, picking up on her tone and responding in kind. He didn't know what to say to Carol. He remained flummoxed. The image of her naked, the star on her hands and knees, revolted him. He was a corn-fed midwestern boy brought up with family values. At the same time, it turned him on. He had spent quite a few nights in bed alone fantasizing about the image. He imagined himself on the set, the male porn star, enjoying sex without limit. Monday night he spent with Mary pretending she was Carol. *It's sick, really sick*, he thought.

"First I have to believe it," she said disdainfully.

He went into his office and grabbed a steno pad from his desk. Stepping back into the lab, he waved it over his head. "Here's my log. I entered every test."

Carol took the book from his hand and flipped through the pages. She frowned. "This is hard to explain if it's right."

"Of course it's right! Do you think I'm a dummy?"

"The jury is still out on that," she said angrily.

Alex glared at her.

The discussion was devolving into a heated argument with the issue unspoken. And Carol realized it.

"Okay, enough. Let's look at this dispassionately."

"That's all I've been asking for," Alex said slowly as he too understood the underlying theme of their mutual anger.

"You are sure these numbers are right?" she asked.

"Yes, I double-checked them, and I was even more careful as they started to seem strange," he said without rancor.

***

Larry knocked and then entered Leif's office. As usual, it was dark, lit only by the glow of the computer screens. "Leif, good job; it's great. Gordon wants to hold the load here; you can increase it a little, but slow the increase of new users way down. He wants to get some longer-term results from a static system," Larry lied.

"You want me to call the bots working on the operating system?"

"No, not yet. Damn! Isn't that interesting? Do you have any idea what they're doing? It looks like it's faster."

"It is," Leif said. "And yes and no—I understand a little. They're optimizing it by not directly observing the operation. Instead, they look at the results, make changes, and measure the difference. It's sort of an application of Heisenberg's uncertainty principle."

"Right, right," Larry said. "Well, just keep it up."

***

That afternoon, Roger raised the advertising rates, and Larry got his bonus.

Carol Quits

"What do you mean Carol's leaving?" Alex asked Mary. They were having breakfast together in the cafeteria. It hadn't been arranged; rather, Mary had seen Alex sitting alone and joined him.

"That's what I hear. She's tendered her notice effective the end of next month."

"Why?"

"She told Gordon she was graduating and quitting her part-time job and felt free for the first time in a long time. At least that's what he told me. He's not happy she's leaving. But I guess he couldn't talk her out of it."

And, she thought, *that takes care of that*. Mary had been quietly angry for some time. She was certain Alex had been fucking Carol.

Oblivious to Mary's satisfied smile, Alex felt as if he'd been hit by a truck; he was numb. Still, he didn't know what to do. He had wanted Carol to love him more than he'd wanted anything— ever. Then, when he got his wish, he discovered she was spoiled goods. Or was she? He was aware of the influence of his midwestern Christian upbringing. He believed in a higher being. But he had been moving further and further away from the strict teachings of the church.

Regardless, the picture in his mind of Carol on the movie set repelled him. Simultaneously, the memory attracted him. As he reimagined the scene, he felt his body responding.

"I'll be over about eight tonight," Mary said. "I'll bring my bag. We'll have a good time."

"Uh-huh," Alex grunted in vague agreement.

Mary took it for agreement in any case. She'd be there, and it was unlikely he'd refuse to let her in.

The rest of the day passed normally. Alex glanced at Carol numerous times and met her eyes twice. Each time she smiled sweetly. *Is she leaving because of me?* he wondered.

Just before lunchtime, he saw Larry and Carol in intense conversation. Then they walked off toward the cafeteria together.

"Leif is doing some really good work," Larry told Carol over meatloaf in the comfort-food section of the cafeteria. Carol was having a salad with olive-oil dressing.

"Has he figured out how to reprogram the bots?" she asked.

"The bots aren't really programmed in the usual sense, Carol. There isn't much code to program. What happens is the swarm is programmed as a whole and contains subswarms that contribute to the whole. There is a lot of code contained in billions of bots, and that's where the programming occurs."

"I think I'm following you," Carol replied. "But not really."

"Think of ants. Individually they are not very bright. But a colony of ants can accomplish building a city, supporting the queen, gathering food to feed the colony, and defending the colony with warriors. As a swarm, they are very smart. Think of the bots like that, as a swarm."

"Okay," Carol said slowly, thinking. "But ants are specialized. There are drones, workers, warriors, the queen, and more that I can't remember. Bots are just bots."

"Yes, they are not entirely like ants; I was just trying to explain the concept. Bots do specialize, though. Not individually—you're right. There's not enough code in a single bot. But there is enough code in a swarm of a million bots. The subswarms, the dependent swarms that make up the whole."

"Larry, you're scaring me. How big is the swarm?"

"Oh, it's big. We don't really know. You can't count bots—they're too small. Leif and I estimate there are billions, and they're multiplying fast."

Carol returned to the lab, and Larry went to see Leif.

"How's it going?" he asked Leif.

"Good, it's going good. I'm working on keeping the control objects ahead of the bots. I want to figure out a way to hide Mommy and Daddy from them, so they don't attack."

"How's that going?" Larry asked.

"I'm getting there, I think."

"Gordon called me in this morning. He has a couple of requests."

"Yeah, what's he want?" Leif asked with some irritation. He didn't like to be told what to do. He knew what to do!

"You don't have to do it. I can just tell him you can't," Larry said, making it a challenge.

Leif rose to the occasion as his indignation evaporated. "Okay, what's he want?"

"He'd like you to activate the bots working on the operating system for the q-cluster. And to activate the bots loading the user interface."

"I can do that," Leif said. "No problem. It wouldn't take long. Is that all he wants?"

"Yeah, pretty much. The only other thing is he wants you to add load to the interface slowly. Start adding, say, one hundred thousand users a day and then work up, over the next month, to a million a day. Can you do that?"

"Sure. You mean bot users?"

"Yes. Gordon wants to measure the effect of the bots' modification to the q-cluster to determine if that's the way we should go rather than a more conventional system."

"Yeah, I understand. When does he want to start?"

"Start the bots on the operating system as soon as you can. We'll determine a baseline over the next week. Start loading the user interface next week."

"Okay, tell him to consider it done."

"Make sure the bots create a profile and sign on like human users. That's the only way we'll be able to be confident the data reflects real users."

"Of course. Do you think I'm stupid?" Leif's pique flashed back.

"Sorry, I didn't mean anything. I certainly don't think you're stupid. You might say that about me, though. I'm really sorry; I was just going down Gordon's checklist."

"Okay, never mind. No problem. I'll get on it later today."

"Thanks, Leif. I'm sure Gordon will be very grateful." Of course, nothing Larry had told him was true. Gordon didn't know a thing about this. And the idea wasn't to load and test the system; it was to add users for Roger. Larry was betting, with some confidence, no one would be able to tell the difference between a human user and a bot. It wouldn't be long before Fauxbook broke the record for users. *This is going to work! I need to buy some stock*, Larry thought.

Suspicions

Carol and Alex sat side by side, focused on the monitors and making notes.

"It is certainly faster," Carol conceded.

"And the speed increase is all in the q-cluster," Alex said.

"What's the significance of that?" Carol asked.

"There is no one I know of who can work on the q-cluster. It's a black box no one understands. It's a leap of faith just to boot up a Quadrium computer. Sometimes they work and at fantastic speed. Sometimes they don't. No one understands why."

"Uh-huh," Carol mumbled. "So how can performance improve if no one is working on the code?"

"I've been thinking about that. As I see it, there are two possibilities."

"Which are?"

"The cluster is optimizing itself. Since we don't know how it works, we don't know it can't do that. The second possibility, and for me, the most likely, is the bots are back."

"Oh no, not the bots!" She laughed loudly.

She has the most wonderful laugh, Alex realized. *I love it when she laughs. No, I don't want to think about that.*

"You sound like a science fiction movie: 'Run, run, the bots are coming!'" she said between giggles.

He liked her giggle, too. She sounded like a young girl.

"Well, if that's how you feel, you're going to love my next discovery."

"Okay." She smiled. "Now what have you found?"

"I was working on this speed thing, just fooling around. As an experiment, with no real goal, I pinged some of the users' IP addresses." He hesitated.

"And?"

"Well, some were what I expected—you know, two to forty milliseconds, depending on their ISPs. But some—a lot—reported essentially zero latency. It wasn't measurable."

"And what does that imply?" she asked, no longer giggling— she knew what it meant, and it scared her.

"Let me walk you through this step by step. Otherwise, you'll think I'm crazy."

"Okay, but I'm already pretty sure you're nuts," she said with a serious tone.

"I didn't want to come to any conclusions without more information. But I'll confess I've had suspicions."

"Okay, go on."

"We have some very sophisticated gear in-house, and I used it to run traces on users. The results for the users with normal latency were what you would expect. You know, five to ten hops listed and a few microseconds."

"Uh-huh," she grunted, interested.

"Then I ran a trace on the zero-latency users." He paused.

"Damn, Alex, will you just tell me?" Carol said.

"The trace didn't go anywhere. Nowhere. It didn't leave the building; it didn't leave our system."

"Damn!" she exclaimed. "What do you make of that?"

"Run, run." Alex grimaced. "Here come the bots."

"You're not serious." But she knew he was—very serious.

"Yes, I think the bots learned to emulate users when they were tasked—or when they learned or whatever—to load the system for testing. I think a great number of our users, our user count, are bots."

"No," she said softly, holding her head in her hands. "No, it can't be."

They both were silent for a long time, thinking about the possibilities and ramifications.

"I've been fucking Mary," Alex said finally.

"I know, on Mondays."

"You know?"

"Uh-huh, yeah, I know. I've known for a long time."

"You're not jealous? You don't mind?" Alex asked, both embarrassed and confused.

It was as if he had loosed a dam, a dam full and ready to burst.

"Why should I mind? You don't belong to me, and it seems you don't want to. I understand what you think. You think I'm some sort of immoral woman who lets anyone fuck her. No problem; I can understand that. From the beginning, I thought you might feel that way. But I liked you, and I hoped you would be able to get past that and know me. It's a fucking job!" she cried, and then she laughed at her own pun.

"Carol…" he started to say.

"Mind? Of course I mind!" Her voice was close to a shout. "But hell, what right do I have to mind? I wasn't putting out, and she was; no matter she has a rotation and puts out for everyone! I was the slut, and she was your bed warmer. Even after I offered myself to you, you refused and kept fucking her. Then you have the nerve to ask if I mind?" She stood, angry, and walked to the door. She stood for a long moment facing the closed door and then turned and came back.

"Damn!" She smiled through tears streaming down her face. "A little out of control there, sorry. It won't happen again. So tell me again why you think the bots are loose and are coming to get us."

Relieved to be off an awkward subject and somewhat stunned by her outburst, Alex said, "I keep turning it around and around in my head. Frankly, I'm not sure. But there's no other explanation."

"Unless the leprechauns did it." She laughed, and she thought how much easier it was to deal with the machines than with her feelings.

It Gets Worse

When she had stood there in front of Alex, smiling and crying, he had wanted to take her in his arms, comfort her, and tell her everything would be fine. He'd wanted to protect her. But he hadn't done that, and he wondered why.

"We're going to need help," Carol said.

"Looks like it," Alex agreed. "But who do we trust? Is Leif doing this? Did he reactivate the bots all by himself?"

"It occurs to me this certainly benefits someone in the short term. User count is up. But how many of the users are not human?"

"The answer to the first question is we all benefit," Alex said. "Fauxbook is a success, and that is good for everyone, especially the stockholders. It benefits us; our bonuses are tied to profits, or the number of users, loyalty, or religiosity," he exclaimed, expressing the widely felt frustration with the inexplicable goals espoused by Jon.

"Yes," she mused. "But who benefits the most in the short term? It has to be a temporary solution to the problem of a low number of users. It can't be a long-term solution. Can it?"

"You're assuming it was done intentionally and if Leif did it, someone is in on the fraud with him."

"Fraud?" Carol asked. "Yes, you're right; if this was done willfully, it is fraud against the stockholders and the advertisers. That rules out Leif; he wouldn't be a party to a fraud. He's the last of the long-haired hippie programmers. He would have no part of a fraud."

"Leif is the only one who could do this. What do you think? The robots got loose on their own?"

"That's a possibility," she said. "I know how to find out."

"How's that?" Alex asked.

"Mary."

"Mary? How would Mary know?"

"She may not, but she can get us whatever we need to know from Leif; he has Thursday nights." She looked at Alex and smiled sweetly.

Alex blushed and wondered if everyone knew but him. "Mary will help us?"

"Sure, you have Monday nights. You just have to show her a really good time."

"You're serious?" he asked, incredulous.

"No, you shit, I'm not serious. We'll simply explain the situation to her and ask her to find out."

"She'd do that?"

"Sure, why not? She's not in love with any of her guys. They're just entertainment."

God, the truth hurts, Alex thought. *And you know it when you hear it.* "Okay, who's going to talk to her?"

"We both are, together, right now."

They walked into Mary's office together.

"Hello, Alex. Hello, Carol," Mary said. "The lovers, together. Alex, does this mean it's over for us?" She smiled like the Cheshire cat.

"Hello, Mary," Carol said. "First, Alex and I are not lovers, never have been. That's not for lack of lust on my part. He doesn't approve of my part-time job."

"Well, then, that makes him the first man I've met who doesn't like porn stars."

God, does everyone know everything except me? Alex thought.

Yeah, he prefers sluts. Carol didn't verbalize the thought, as it seemed counterproductive.

"That's neither here nor now," she said. "We need to talk to you about a serious and urgent matter that affects the company and everyone here, including you."

"That sounds ominous," Mary said, smiling. "Okay, I'm listening."

After hearing their story, Mary said, "You're right. Leif wouldn't have anything to do with deceit or fraud. He's very naive and sweet, almost a savant. He's so brilliant with computers and so stupid about everything else. He's not into money, fame, or material things at all, though he does like kinky sex." She smiled sweetly at Carol.

"I agree, though I wouldn't know about kinky sex," Carol said.

"Right." Mary smirked.

"Has he told you anything?" Carol asked.

"We don't talk much."

"Do you think you can get him to tell you about the bots and what's going on?" Alex asked.

"Does a bear shit in the woods?" Mary smiled.

She seems to be enjoying this whole thing, Alex thought, *especially my embarrassment.*

"Okay, fine," Carol said. "It's Thursday, so we'll talk to you tomorrow?"

Damn! How does Carol know Mary's schedule? Alex thought. And, she appeared to be rubbing his face in it. He was mortified.

"See you then. Are we done?" Mary asked, a little resentful at her life being exposed in front of Alex.

"We're done," Carol said. She touched Alex's shoulder to turn him around, and they left.

Returning to the lab, they said nothing to each other. Carol noticed Alex's face was a bit red, and she smiled.

Lies Revealed

Mary was among the missing all of Friday morning as Alex and Carol anxiously awaited her news. They checked her office every fifteen minutes and tried her cell phone to no avail: "Please leave a message."

Finally, they decided to go to lunch. Though they were both too worked up to be hungry, it would kill some time. "The sushi bar?" Carol asked.

"Yeah, okay." Alex sounded frustrated.

They walked slowly, side by side but far apart emotionally. It felt as if there were an impenetrable wall between them.

"Hey," Alex said, "is that Mary?"

"Damn! It is, and we've been looking all over for her."

Mary was sitting at a table for four, by herself, delicately nibbling on a sushi roll. Alex and Carol took two of the empty chairs and stared at her accusingly.

"Sorry, I was busy this morning: dentist," Mary said. "My mouth is still numb. I have to chew very carefully, or I'll bite myself."

"Okay, what did you find out?" Carol asked.

"Oh, a lot. It was fun. We played the torture game. I tied him to the bed and applied various torture techniques until he told me what I wanted to know," she said with a wide smile. "Oh, damn, it hurts to smile now the Novocain is wearing off."

Well, that's more than I wanted to know, Carol thought.

Alex was embarrassed Carol knew he was involved with this kinky woman. *Does she think I played the torture game with Mary?* he wondered as his face turned red. *Now Carol is smiling. They are both laughing at me. Damn!*

"Never mind all that," Carol said. "Seriously, what did Leif tell you?"

Mary took a moment to finish chewing. "Gordon ordered him to activate the bots. There are two projects: one is to enable the optimization of the q-cluster's operating system; the other is to load the user interface to determine the system's ability to handle future growth."

"Does he understand the bots are emulating human users?" Alex asked.

"I did ask him even though you didn't task me to. I'm not stupid. I know what's going on. I just don't know why."

"Okay, no one thinks you're stupid, Mary," Carol said. "What did he say?"

"It took a little extra torture to get him to answer that one." She smiled. "But he couldn't hold out." She laughed. "So he finally told me."

"What?" Alex said, exasperated.

"He said, 'That's the idea.'"

"What idea?" Alex asked.

Carol understood instantly. *The bots were supposed to behave like users to test the capacity of the system to handle additional users. It was obvious but strange to run such a test without telling anyone.*

"To test the system's capacity to handle additional users, you have to imitate users," Alex answered as the light in his brain came on a little behind Carol's.

"They wouldn't do that without telling everyone!" Carol exclaimed.

"Yeah, who's 'they'?" Mary said cynically between bites of sushi. "Ouch," she cried. "I think I bit my cheek! I hate dentists!"

"I believe we have met the enemy, and they are us," Carol said.

"We need to go see Gordon," Alex concluded.

"Hey, don't get me involved," Mary said.

"Don't worry, Mary. It'll be our secret. Let's go, Alex."

"No food? You need to feed me if you want to keep me," he said and instantly regretted it.

Carol shot him a stern look. "Come on," she said.

Mary stared at their backs as they walked away. She was seething with jealous anger.

***

They stood side by side in front of Gordon's secretary, Joan Ayers. Jon had finally gotten tired of sharing Anne with Gordon and told Anne to hire Gordon a secretary. Anne had moved Joan over from the pool; it was a big promotion for her.

"Excuse me, Joan," Carol said. "Does Mr. Wysmann have a moment?"

"I'll see," she said, recognizing Alex and Carol. It wasn't that big a company that everyone didn't know everyone else. At least it hadn't been that big until recently. Regardless, the early employees all knew one another. She knocked and entered Gordon's office, closing the door behind her.

Joan was gone only a moment. "Yes, go on in. He's been wondering when you two were going to show up."

He's been waiting for us, they both thought simultaneously. *I wonder why. Is there something going on we don't know about?*

Joan had left the office door open. Carol knocked lightly on the doorframe.

"Come, sit down, and tell me your story."

They took their positions, side by side on the couch. Then, thinking better of it, Carol rose and occupied the chair opposite his desk.

"Sir, with all respect, we've learned you're running a test involving Leif's robots. We're disappointed you didn't inform us." Carol was worried she had gone too far in challenging the famous and powerful man. She needn't have worried.

"We have been busting our butts trying to find out what's going on for days. Now, we find out you ordered it," Alex said.

Okay, she thought. *I'm safe. Alex just outdid me.*

Gordon leaned back in his chair.

The prelude to the explosion, she thought.

He took a deep breath and then sighed. "No, I had nothing to do with it."

"But," Alex sputtered, "Leif said you ordered it."

"Doesn't make it true," Gordon said softly.

Unlikely Friends

Mary wondered if, after the day's events, she would have to find a replacement for Monday nights. Fifty-fifty, she calculated. *Perhaps for the best*, she thought. *This thing with Jeff is getting serious. And I don't think he is one to understand my proclivities. It may be time to phase out that part of my life. If I get horny, I can always go with Mi Ly for some truly anonymous gratification.*

But Alex's betrayal continued to eat at her. She didn't believe for a minute he and Carol were not lovers.

***

Alex and Carol were stunned by Gordon's denial; their jaws dropped. *I guess we're not going to be fired for insubordination, after all*, she thought.

"I've been wondering how long it would take for you two to notice something was going on and to get your asses over here," Gordon said with a wry smile, which quickly disappeared. "I have my suspicions about who put Leif up to it. It pisses me off, and it pisses me off he used my name. However, right now, we have bigger problems."

"Bigger problems? You knew about this already?" She had never heard Gordon use such coarse language. Something was going on, for sure.

"We've been watching this from the beginning," Gordon said. "It's not good, and it's getting worse."

"Worse?" Alex said.

"Yes, worse. We can't tell the difference between the human users and the bots. And they're making friends."

"Latency," Carol said. "You can tell it's a robot if you ping the address and latency is zero."

"Sure," he replied. "We know that. My people are working on a program to ping every user and log the results. But they don't have that finished yet. In any case, that may not work much longer and the situation is becoming urgent."

"Your people?" Carol asked. "Who are your people? I thought we were your people."

"Yes, indeed you are; however, when I came to work at Fauxbook, I brought my personal team with me. Think of it as a security blanket. As it turns out, it's a good thing I did."

"What do you mean, *making friends*?" Alex asked.

"The robots see human users like they do any other computer program or object to be penetrated. They learn, and damn, they are learning faster and faster as the swarm expands. They learn what human users respond to. They are learning how to make friends and influence people at a very rapid rate. They are making friends."

"With human users?" Carol asked.

"Yes, with human users," Gordon replied, "and the bots are making them very happy—which is not surprising. Remember, though, this is all supposition and interpolation; we are not sure. Call it a very strong suspicion."

"This can't be right," Alex protested.

There was a pause as Gordon stared at Alex.

"Yes, it can," Carol said finally. "And it can become really alarming. As the bots become perfect friends, the human users will drop all of their human friends in favor of the bots."

"And be none the wiser," Gordon said. "I suspect very few human users are interacting with other humans already. The bots are much more satisfying. But we just don't know yet."

"The bots will become influencers," Alex said. "Whoever controls the bots will control the Internet."

"And the world," Gordon observed.

"Here come the bots," Alex said ominously.

"Cut it out, Alex. This is serious," Carol said impatiently. "Gordon, why have you waited so long to do something about this?"

Gordon hesitated. "It was foolish of me—arrogance, I imagine. I consider myself a watcher, a recorder of events, so I waited and watched. That was a mistake I hope I can correct. I was really watching for something else more dangerous, and now I fear it may have slipped past me."

"What can be more dangerous than this?" Carol asked.

"The event I've been afraid of most of my career: the singularity."

"You're kidding," Carol said, knowing he was not.

"Artificial intelligence?" Alex asked.

"Yes and no," Gordon said. "Artificial superintelligence, which will trigger unknowable technological developments. The computers will begin designing and building their successors. It will cause unfathomable changes to human civilization. They will do what we want, of course. But if we don't know what we want, or are unclear, they will decide for us. Unfortunately, the human race has never been very good at knowing what we want."

"This is the singularity?" Carol asked, incredulous.

"I think so," Gordon said. "I missed it, though. In hindsight, it's obvious. Leif calls it evolving. He said a couple of times they evolve with each generation. Evolve...design—damn! It's the same thing! Damn!"

"What do we do?" Alex asked.

"We shut it down, unplug it, and then wipe all of the disks and destroy all of the nonvolatile memory. But that's going to be a hard sell, as the marketing people say. I need you two backing me up on this; you need to believe it. That's why I waited for you to draw your own conclusions."

"We are supposed to support destroying Fauxbook based on supposition and interpolation? That's crazy! No one is going to agree to that," Alex protested.

"I know, especially Jon. He'll just tell his Charge of the Light Brigade story and tell us to press onward toward glory."

"Leif, obviously, can control them. We need to convince him to help shut them down permanently," Carol said.

"Or blow up the computer building," Alex suggested.

"Joan, see if you can get Leif Hoberson over here," Gordon said into the intercom.

"You think he can do it?" Alex asked.

"Maybe, but it won't be easy. I suspect he would have to write something to program them to destroy themselves. And they are going to be hard to find. I imagine they are in every computer in the building by now," Gordon said.

"He's not answering." Joan's voice came through the intercom.

"I'll go over there and bring him back," Carol volunteered.

"I'll go with you," Alex said.

***

As they walked toward Leif's office, Alex asked, "Are you leaving the company?"

She turned to look at him. Her expression was sad, and he thought she was going to cry.

Carol regained her composure and said, "Yes, I am. How did you find out? The only person who knows is Gordon, and he promised to keep it quiet."

"Well, I did find out. Weren't you going to tell me?"

"No, I thought it would be easier not to tell you. Anyway, my work here is finished. Fauxbook is up and running well. And I have my degree. It's time to move on."

"I wish you wouldn't," he said.

"Damn you!" she whispered, and ran ahead to hide her tears.

The Escape

"Jeff, what are you doing with a bag of fertilizer in your office?" Mary asked after locking his office door. "You live in an apartment."

"Oh, it's for the house. I want to keep it in shape and the grass green. Diane's lawyer contacted my lawyer to arrange selling it. It's in both of our interests to get as much as we can for it."

"Yes, that makes sense," she said. It would probably make more sense to her if she knew Jeff's other purchases included ten thousand copper-coated steel BBs and a large can of powdered aluminum.

"Look what I brought," she said, delving into her bag.

Jeff's eyes widened in anticipation.

***

Alex caught up with Carol outside Leif's office. The windows were covered with brown paper taped to the window frames, and the door was locked. They knocked. No response.

"Leif, let us in. We know you're in there. Open up," Alex demanded.

"He's not going to let us in," Carol said, pointing out the obvious.

"Yes, he will," Alex said in a determined voice. On a table behind them in the lab, he saw a disassembled computer. A number of tools lay beside it. He ran over and selected the largest screwdriver available, returned, and leaned against Leif's door.

Then he inserted the screwdriver between the frame and the latch and pried.

With a loud snap, the door popped open. They entered to find disarray. A chair was turned on its side, and things were strewn everywhere. Leif was there, frantically pounding on a keyboard, sweat pouring off his forehead and glistening in the light of the monitor. He didn't seem to be aware of their presence despite their loud entry.

"Leif, Leif!" Carol called. "What are you doing?"

He ignored her.

Alex grabbed him by the shoulder and pulled him around, away from the keyboard.

"Turn me loose; go away," Leif shouted. "You don't understand. Go away!"

"Leif, what's wrong? You're acting like a crazy man."

Alex turned the chair around and pushed Leif down into it. "Calm down!" he said loudly, drawing the words out.

Leif tensed; then he went limp.

"He fainted," Carol said.

"Get a glass of water, a bucket if you can find it," Alex ordered. "I'll watch him. He's gone crazy. God knows what he might do next."

Carol returned with two glasses of water, cold from the cooler. Alex took the glasses from her hand and poured them, one at a time, over Leif's head.

"What, what?" Leif mumbled as he returned to consciousness.

"Yes, what! What is going on, Leif?" Carol asked.

"It's the bots," he replied. "The bots are out! I couldn't stop them," he wailed.

"Out? Out of what?" Alex asked, puzzled.

"They escaped; they are out of the building and into the Internet," he explained, distraught.

"Oh, my God," Carol said softly.

"It was the hack. I knew it was there. The code hiding in memory is harmless. But when activated, it creates a back door, which the bots used to escape. I saw them yesterday attacking the code and thought I'd have plenty of time. But the swarm is getting faster and faster. When I woke up this morning, they had solved the puzzle, activated the module, and escaped through the back door that was created. They are out of our system and out on the Internet."

Alex and Carol stared at him, shocked. The problem had instantly grown exponentially.

"What are you doing about it?" Carol asked.

"I don't know. I don't know. I don't know what I can do. I've been working on the control programs thinking I could send Mommy and Daddy after the bots. But I was already having trouble keeping them from overwhelming the control modules."

Carol picked up the phone and dialed Gordon's extension.

"Mr. Gordon's office," Joan answered.

"Let me talk to him, now!" she demanded.

The tone of Carol's voice convinced Joan to put the call through instantly, without announcing it.

"Yes, Joan, what is it?" Gordon answered.

"It's Carol, Mr. Wysmann. I'm in Leif's office. You need to get down here immediately!"

"What's wrong?" he asked.

"Just get down here, right now!" she commanded.

"I'm coming," he said, more than a bit surprised at her audacity. Then he worried it might be more than that.

He hurried. Entering Leif's office, he asked, "What's going on?"

"It's bad," Alex said softly and explained the situation to him.

"How fast is the swarm growing?" Gordon asked Leif.

"I don't know. But I'm sure it'll make exponential look slow."

"Double exponential?" Gordon asked.

"Uh-huh," Leif acknowledged.

"Are they still constrained to emulating users and working on the q-cluster?" Gordon asked.

"I don't think so. I'm not sure, but I think they solved the problem of the control objects. That's what they do: they randomly send commands to programs, apps, and objects until they get a response. Then they have control. Eventually, they discover what to do with control," Leif said.

"The singularity."

"Yeah, I guess you could look at it that way," Leif said.

"Is there another way?" Gordon asked him.

"I guess it depends on what your definition of the singularity is," Leif replied.

"Oh, for God's sake," Carol said. "This is getting us nowhere. What are they going to do?"

Leif started to speak, but Gordon held up his hand to quiet him. "They are going to do what they do: interface with any code they find and determine what input produces what seems to be the desired output."

"I'd understand if I knew what it meant," Carol said. She wasn't being sarcastic; rather, she was expressing her literal feeling.

The Fiddlers

Roger was in heaven. The user count was well over two billion, making Fauxbook the largest social network in the world. And the advertisers were lined up and pushing to bang at his door.

He and Jon, along with Barry, were having lunch in Jon's private dining room, and Roger was thrilled. He had never been invited before. It felt as if he had made it, the big time.

"Jon," he said, "we're going to double or even triple the projected income. The stock is already going through the roof."

Jon nodded, thinking, *Once again, I've made everyone rich. Experience and placing your faith in the Lord come through every time.*

"Faith," Jon said. "Be strong and courageous. Do not be afraid; do not be discouraged, for the Lord your God will be with you wherever you go."

"Amen," Roger said piously.

"Yes, amen," Barry agreed.

"The mirror site is up and running in California," Jon stated, "and Ireland is not far behind."

"That's good news," Barry said.

"Yes, we're syncing with California today. They're handling that in California, relieving the people here who are all busy adding capacity to the system."

"Your advertising program worked wonders, Jon," Roger said.

"Yes, there is a time for everything, and a season for every activity under the heavens," Jon replied. "And that's my talent, knowing the right time and being open-minded. I went against past experience in launching the advertising program. But I knew it was the right thing to do and the right time to do it."

"You are the man," Barry exclaimed.

***

Much to the disappointment of her beaus, Mary was phasing out that part of her life. Leif was easy, as lately he never went home. He spent his nights in his office and slept on the couch when he did sleep. She had stopped by, but he seemed frantic and said he had no time to talk or play games.

The others were a little more difficult, and she was taking her time retiring them. It was particularly difficult to stop seeing Larry. *God*, she thought, *he has such a beautiful body. Jeff, not so much.* But, more and more, she saw Jeff as her future.

She liked that Larry was tall, six one—she'd found everything was in proportion. And he was very muscular. *I love running my fingers through his blond hair and watching his biceps twitch impatiently under his skin.*

And she liked reversing the roles and humiliating the big man, who was over a foot taller and seventy pounds heavier than she was. She loved getting him into a compromising position and teasing him until he begged for release.

I'm going to miss him.

However, she had decided to hook her wagon to Jeff's train regardless of his current difficulty with Jon. *He'll bounce back from this. If not with Fauxbook, then with another company. He's a winner, a smart businessman who is going to come out on top. And I'll be there. I've always wanted to be a rich bitch.*

She'd been busy recently, and the workload continued to grow with Fauxbook's expansion. Mike Ray, who had joined her team early on, was a big help. And she had moved Mi Ly over to assist her in a number of ways. Mary was beginning to like Mi Ly's concept of impersonal sex. She was always careful not to call it sex in front of Mi Ly. *Strange girl*, she thought.

But she still needed more people. She resolved to go over to human resources after lunch and see who they had available. In the meanwhile, she had a rendezvous in the freezer.

***

Just as Mary was going to lunch, the executives were finishing theirs.

"Overall, I believe we're doing well," Jon said as the stewards were clearing the table. "I'm planning to extend the marketing plan indefinitely and increase the budget—perhaps double it. I'm meeting with our CFO in thirty minutes."

"Sounds right," Roger said. "I don't see why we can't exceed three billion users by the end of the year."

"I agree," Barry added.

412

"Good, good, be assured your bonuses will reflect Fauxbook's success."

"Thank you, Jon," they said in unison. Both had noted Jeff's name had not been mentioned, and they understood the thin line they trod between Jon's approval and exile. But at least for now, they were on the right side of the line and had no empathy for Jeff Hoover.

Roger, who was planning to talk to Leif about increasing the rate of users signing up, was in for a rude awakening. Already he was somewhat delusional, as he had blocked the reality of the bots. To him, users were users, and that was that.

Out There

Gordon had been talking to Leif for hours as he absorbed Leif's actions, the extent of the problem, and Leif's thoughts as to how to control or destroy the bots. He had sent Carol and Alex to lunch—the first lunch they had shared in some time.

Carol knew she should be done with Alex and move on—but she admitted to herself for the first time that she loved the dumb nit. Usually a strong person, she simply could not do what she knew to be the right thing for herself.

"Comfort food seems right," she said with a troubled smile.

"Yes, it does," Alex agreed.

Though neither of them felt hunger, they filled their trays regardless. Fried chicken and mashed potatoes for Alex and meatloaf for Carol. The cafeteria was packed with young people, laptops open on the tables in front of them and their meals to the side. A myriad of colors and over twenty countries were represented. Diversity was normal. Although there were no little green people, if they were to arrive they most certainly would seek employment here and would be accepted.

They were busily designing the future, without anticipating the dangers of the new paradigm.

"All of this seems pretty awful," Carol said. "It feels like we are destroying the world."

"Yeah, he has certainly created a problem. I'm still trying to get my head wrapped around it."

"I wonder who put him up to it," Carol said.

"What? You think someone told him to do this? That's crazy. Leif is weird; this kind of thing is what he does. He can't help himself. Now, I hope he can figure out how to fix it."

"But it's still fraud, and Leif is smart enough to know that. Somebody is behind this. Remember, he thought Gordon ordered it. "Yeah, you're right. I forgot about that. I think I'm just too tired to think," Alex said.

"Get some sleep, a power nap. But then we need to figure out who is behind this."

"Maybe you're right. But we went from a slow start, mostly because of lack of promotion and marketing of the site, to two billion users. How is that possible, and who benefits?"

"What do you mean, who?" Carol said. "We all benefit. Fauxbook is a success. The company finally did some marketing, and it worked."

"Yes, we benefit; we all benefit," Alex agreed. "You're right. But who, specifically, benefits? Well, let me put it this way: Who would be the big loser if we failed to make the numbers?"

Alex leaned back in his chair, eating forgotten, as Carol attacked her meatloaf with trepidation.

"Roger Aegel," Alex said in a low voice.

Carol looked at him intently as she chewed. She swallowed, paused, and said, "Maybe. Maybe Roger needed the user count to satisfy the advertising contracts he sold during the launch."

Neither of them said anything further, pretending to be absorbed in their meals.

After some minutes, Alex said, "I think we should start over."

"What are you talking about?" she asked, wondering what the hell he was referring to.

"You know, start over, us."

"What?"

"I like you," Alex said softly. "I like you a lot. And I'm ashamed of myself for the way I've been behaving. I want to start over."

"Alex, you're confusing me. Start over?"

"Carol, I'm an Iowa boy, raised in Clear Lake, Iowa. You know, where the music stopped." He smiled tentatively. "You know, the Midwest. I'm a Midwest boy, raised a Christian."

"Yeah, so?"

"Well, it may sound stupid to you; I'm sure it does. But it's real to me."

"*What* is real to you?"

"You know—values, morals, all of the beliefs I grew up with."

"So, you don't think I have any morals?" she asked with a stern look.

"Well, you're a porn actress. I grew up believing that sort of thing is bad. And, yes, immoral."

"I'm a porn star; get it right, doofus." She smiled. "I understand. I understand more than you know. That's why I had to show you and see if you could deal with it. You can't; that's okay. I knew there was always that possibility. We should cut our losses."

"It would have been easier if you just hadn't told me," he murmured.

"I couldn't do that," she said. "If we are going to have a life together, you have to know everything about me, as do I about you."

"A life together?" He was surprised but not dismayed.

"Isn't that what we've been negotiating?"

Negotiating. Alex thought that a strange choice of words.

"But there are others you've been with," Alex said. "What about them?"

"Alex, you can be really dense. I told you they don't mean anything. It's a job. A job that pays well and allows me to go to college and live. It's acting, and the other actors mean nothing to me, certainly less than Mary means to you. Yeah, you ass, what about her? What's that about? Were you just horny? Damn you!"

"Okay, I'm an ass," he said, his head bowed, "and you're a porn star. Can we just start over?"

"What do you mean by 'start over'?"

"You know, lunch, dinner sometimes, like we were, and we'll see how that goes."

She smiled and chuckled.

"What? What's funny?"

"It's funny. We went for months while you were Ready Freddie, and I didn't want to sleep with you under false pretenses. Now, you want to resume, except you'll be the one with his legs crossed. Come on, you have to recognize the humor."

Alex smiled. "Yeah, I guess I do. At the same time, though, it's serious."

"Yes, Alex, I respect that. This is serious for me also."

"Dinner tonight?"

"Okay," she said tentatively.

***

Gordon was gone when they got back to the lab. Leif was once again locked in his office, his door somewhat worse for the wear.

Carol checked her e-mail, turned to Alex, and said, "The mirrored sites are coming online."

"I don't think that is good news," Alex said.

"No," Carol said. "The bots will be synced with the mirrored sites as well as everything else. It will add to the disaster."

Over in the administrative building, Gordon was on the phone, first to Fauxbook's California facility and then to Ireland. He got an argument from each.

"You want us to pull the plug? Are you mad?"

"Don't argue. Don't do a normal shutdown. Just cut the power, right now!" he ordered.

"What's the authorization for this?" he was asked by each.

"Do you know who I am?" he asked sternly, bluffing.

"Yes, sir, I do, but—"

"No *but*s. Shut it down if you want to be working for Fauxbook at the end of the day."

After some argument, he bludgeoned both sites into agreeing.

"Another thing: send me your best theoretical computer scientist on the next plane. We need him or her here as soon as possible."

One problem solved, Gordon thought, *and it won't hurt to get some more minds thinking about this problem.*

Then he went over to his personal, and somewhat secret, lab to see if they had made any progress. It was a section of D Building that was leased from Fauxbook. The staff were not employees of Fauxbook. They worked for a company, CounterPoint, LLC, entirely owned by Gordon, whose employees answered only to him.

There were fewer than thirty people, of all races, almost equally divided between men and women, working in a large room divided by low-walled cubicles. They were all very smart.

He walked to the center of the room and rang a large bell suspended from the ceiling. It was the low-tech call for an all-hands meeting, and in response, everyone stood and became visible from the waist up.

"People," Gordon said in his rarely used, loud commanding voice, "it's time to get serious. You all know the problem and have been anticipating it. However, it has accelerated faster than I expected. The situation is dire. The bots are outside the building, and we need to destroy them. Get to work." Gordon gave the bell another tug for emphasis and left the room abuzz with conversation.

The Bots Disperse

Two weeks passed with no solution. Leif seemed on the verge of a nervous breakdown, Alex and Carol were holding hands once again, and Mary was phasing out her old life in favor of a future with Jeff. Mi Ly was helping.

Roger continued to occupy his euphoric fool's paradise.

"Jon," Roger was saying during lunch. Lunch in Jon's dining room with Barry had become a weekly ritual of self-congratulation. "We're going to hit three billion users soon. Programming is expanding the ad space, using rotating ads, to accommodate the demand. We are exceeding all of our projections by four hundred percent."

"That's good, very good," Jon said seriously. "Be cautious, though. Let's try to consolidate our gains and optimize what we have achieved. Remember, pride goes before destruction, and a haughty spirit before stumbling."

"Very wise, sir," Barry said.

"Yes, very wise," Roger agreed. "However, we are now the largest social networking site in the world. It may not be time to back off."

"No, no," Jon agreed. "I'm not saying we should dissuade progress, but it should be built carefully; don't lose what we have gained."

***

Gordon called a meeting, asking Leif, Carol, Alex, and Larry to attend, not realizing he was inviting the snake into the henhouse.

"Leif, are you making any progress?" Gordon asked.

"Not so much, sir. The control programs are no longer effective. It seems their function has been usurped by the bots."

"What do you mean?" Carol asked.

"Well, I think they have been integrated into the swarm's...uh..." He paused. "Command and control system. But that's not right; the swarm is in control and conscious, I think. It's hard to explain, understand. But no, the control modules I wrote are not responding to my commands."

"I think they are expanding into everything. It's hard to know what their goal is," Alex said.

"It's whatever we told them it is," Gordon said. His thinking was still focused on the singularity theory.

"What did we tell them?"

"Ah," Gordon said, "there's the rub. We didn't consciously tell them anything. One thing we know they understand is that Fauxbook wants more users. Other than that, as the swarm gains in intelligence and suffers from lack of direction, it will determine what we want, whether we know it or not. It's a dangerous situation."

"They are the users," Carol lamented. "The robots are learning to respond to human users—to fool them into thinking they are communicating with another human. It is much easier for them than programming the q-cluster. In a few cycles, the human users are hooked on their very rewarding relationships with their bot friends. I imagine there are many human users out there who are 'friends' with bots exclusively and have no human friends."

"I believe that trend will accelerate," Gordon said.

"The robots have also signed up with our competitors," Leif told them.

"What! Why would they do that?" Alex asked.

"They are subtly influencing our competition's customers to move over to Fauxbook," Leif said. "In any case, they are moving into any system they can find and optimizing it or destroying it if doing so appears to accomplish the goal."

"Is that what you call what they're doing? Working toward the goal?" Carol asked with some heat.

"Yeah, I guess," Leif said defensively. "They are not evil. They are just doing what they were programmed to do."

"However, they are programming themselves as they evolve. You said so yourself," Carol declared.

Larry had been silent, so far. Leif hadn't involved him, and he hoped Leif would maintain his silence on that issue.

"The problem extends past Fauxbook now," Gordon explained, stating what everyone knew. "The bots are everywhere, testing every system. For all we know, they have bank accounts."

"Could they?" Carol asked. "Can they do that?" She looked at Gordon and saw his eyes narrowed and his lips a thin straight line. "You're serious."

Gordon rose with a grunt and paced slowly around his desk interlocking his hands and releasing them slowly, over and over. "Indeed," he spoke softly, "we all have doppelganger that exist in the ether. All of the data that defines us to the outside world is there and our doppelganger interfaces with much of our reality. It's all many people know of us. The bots are creating doppelganger that are just as real as ours. Sure, they can appear to be real. They are real."

Carol rose then sat back down confused in time and space. "God," she exclaimed, "what do we do?"

"It's bad," Gordon declared. "Who's to say your Fauxbook friends are not your real friends? They enjoy seeing you on the Internet every day. Miss you when you are not online. Show compassion when you lose someone you love. Send you greetings on your birthday. Praise the pictures you upload. Like your status. Make you laugh when you are sad. They never die and never, ever post anything to cause you to be unhappy. Share this if you are grateful for your Fauxbook bots."

"God, that's sick!" Alex said. "Can you imagine if someone gains control of them? The world as we know it would be finished."

"I can control them," Leif said.

424

"Not so far," Alex replied bitterly; wondering if control of the bots by Leif would be a good thing. He was beginning to suspect Leif's motives. *Has this been Leif's goal from the beginning?*

"I'm going to have to take this to Jon," Gordon said. "Not that it's going to do any good. But we all work for him and we can't keep this from him any longer."

Everyone was silent. There were mixed feelings, including embarrassment they had let this get away from them.

Leif felt indignation he was being blamed for doing what Gordon had told him to do. *They wanted users*, he thought. *They got users. I don't know how this is my fault.*

Larry was relieved his part in this had not come out—yet.

Mary Gives It Up

Mary Adams abandoned her promiscuous ways for Jeff and instead embraced totally impersonal sex to compensate. She and Mi Ly were regulars at the glory hole. During one of their trips into Boston, Mi Ly told Mary about ASE, a club that facilitated anonymous encounters.

"Do you go there?" she asked Mi Ly.

"No, no, I don't. I went once with a friend but never again."

"Never again? That's pretty strong. Why never again?"

"There is too much touching. And, the man is right there with you. I couldn't see him, but he was right there, touching me. Then, he kissed me—with his mouth. It was gross, slimy. You should never go there."

Mary decided to check it out. *Nothing else in my life is real, so why not?*

She went alone to investigate Anonymous Sexual Encounters Inc., ASE. The ASE website was intriguing, and there were instructions.

She was to park her car in a dark two-story garage that had a second-floor exit. The empty hallway was dimly lit. When she exited the second-floor fire escape, the alarm did not go off. She made her way down the stairs into an alley, which was closed at both ends. *It's a very nice alley*, she observed. Pavers, neatly arranged under her feet, planters, and murals painted on the brick walls. She noticed the cameras at each end and the camera directly in front of the fire escape. At the far end of the space, a large wooden door swung open, beckoning her to enter. Somewhat nervously but refusing to be cowed, she did. "No one sees you come," a sign over the reception desk read. *Cute*, she thought. *And hopefully true.*

"Ms. Adams, welcome. We have been expecting you." The receptionist beamed. "I'll let Ms. Alacrity know you're here." She whispered into her headset, and in short order, a well-dressed blonde entered, smiling.

"I'm Amity Alacrity. Welcome to ASE." She pronounced the acronym *ass* and grasped Mary's right hand in hers. With her left, she touched Mary's elbow in a very intimate manner. "Step into my office, and I'll tell you about ASE and our completely confidential services and activities."

Ms. Alacrity led her into a very businesslike office, where she was directed to a comfortable chair facing Amity on the couch. *It looks nothing like the lair of a madam*, Mary thought.

"I have the membership papers for you to sign," Ms. Alacrity said, "but they can wait until after your tour. We are very discreet here. Today will be the last time your real name is used on the premises. I would like to name you *Salacity*, if that is all right with you."

Mary smiled. "That sounds just right."

"Good, excellent. Salacity you are, then. Tell me, Salacity, do you have any distinguishing marks on your body? Scars, birthmarks…anything that would identify you to a partner who was unable to see your face?"

"No, I don't believe that I do."

"Well, excellent. Once you become a member, you'll have a thorough examination to make sure. All of our members are completely anonymous." Alacrity rose and moved to a door simply marked *Private*. "Please follow me." They entered a short hallway with a door at the end and another immediately to the right.

"This is a dressing room," Alacrity said as she opened the door. "You'll find a robe in your size as well as a hood that will completely cover your head. Please remove all of your clothing and jewelry, and don both the robe and hood. You will also find some slippers for you to wear. I'll wait here for you."

What have I gotten myself into? Mary wondered. *Well, I've come this far.*

Opening the door at the end of the short hall after gaining access with a keypad, Ms. Alacrity led the way into the inner building.

"We here at ASE are equipped and prepared to enable you to fulfill your fantasies. We have the darkrooms, of course, the headbox, a quickie station, and automatic matching of submissives and dominants," Ms. Alacrity explained as they moved through the building into another, longer, hallway lined with closed doors.

"These are the dark rooms," Ms. Alacrity said. "They have double doors like an airlock. But in this case, it's to ensure light doesn't enter. The rooms are very comfortably furnished." Smiling, she said, "The main piece of furniture is a large bed in the center of the room."

"How do they find each other in the dark?" Mary asked.

"Usually you simply rendezvous on the bed with one or more people. However, if you like, you can wear a small bell on a choker. But that is all you are allowed to wear, and of course, you may never speak. We pride ourselves on being anonymous and impersonal."

"Exactly what I'm looking for," Mary replied. "Where do I sign up?"

"Excellent," Ms. Alacrity said. "As long as you are undressed, would you like to sample the dark room now?"

"Why not?" Mary said.

"Would you like a bell, Salacity?"

"What would you recommend?" Mary asked.

"Let's try the bell for your first encounter. It generally accelerates things," Ms. Alacrity said. She produced a leather collar with a small bell attached, pushed Mary's hood down, and put the collar on her.

"Too tight?" she asked.

"No, just right," Mary answered. "I'm ready."

Hello, Father

Leif woke early, stretched, shivered, and rose from the couch in his office, lit, as usual, only by the light of the numerous computer monitors.

At the same time, Gordon, having also wakened early, sent an e-mail to Jon requesting a meeting as soon as possible. "It's important," he wrote.

Leif found a blueberry yogurt in the refrigerator in his office, peeled the top off, and inserted his spoon as he took a seat in front of the screen monitoring bot activity. It was not really tracking their activity, as that had proven impossible. It was measuring a close approximation by tracking an assumption of their activity. An e-mail was waiting. *Strange*, he thought. *No one sends me e-mail. It must be bad news.*

"Hello, Father" was displayed in the subject line. The body of the message was empty, as was the "from" field; *that was strange.* Leif was confused. But he could not be distracted by trivia, so he deleted the e-mail.

***

Apparently, Jon was up early, too, as Gordon received a response almost immediately: "8:00 a.m. My conference room."

Gordon entered the conference room at precisely eight and discovered Jon, Barry, and Roger in intense conversation. Again, no Jeff.

430

"Ah, Gordon, come in and have a seat. Good. Good to see you."

Getting right to it, Gordon presented a short summary of what was going on. "The bottom line is we don't have anywhere near the number of users we thought. We've been counting the robots, the bots."

Silence. Roger's forehead shone with moisture.

"Damn!" Barry said softly. "We're in trouble."

"No, no, maybe not," Jon said. "What, in fact, is a user? If it looks like a duck, swims like a duck, and quacks like a duck, then it probably is a duck."

"Ducks?" Gordon said incredulously.

"Jon's got a point," Roger said. "If no one can tell the difference."

"Well," Barry said thoughtfully, "the bottom line is, if we remove the robots, we lose more than half our users, and Fauxbook is done." Sadly, he had vastly understated the situation.

"You're missing the point," Gordon said, exasperated. "We can't remove the bots, and they are out of the building. This is a calamity building toward disaster."

"Well, well," Jon said. "I think you are overstating the problem. For the moment, everything appears to be fine. We should persevere, keep the company going, while you and your team work on a solution."

"That sounds right to me," Roger agreed.

"Yes, Gordon," Barry said, "this is your problem, your department's problem; you need to fix it. It's your job to keep Fauxbook running, not to tear it down and us along with it."

Once again, Gordon was glad he was recording all of this. *Incredible*, he thought. *Willful blindness on the part of greedy and egotistical old men.*

"I did mention we are discussing the end of the world as we know it?" he said.

"I do not treat your prophecies with contempt, but I will test all things. Hold fast to what is good," Jon said, paraphrasing Thessalonians.

Gordon replied, "While people are saying 'Peace and safety,' destruction will come on them suddenly, as labor pains on a pregnant woman, and they will not escape," also quoting Thessalonians. *Jon's not the only one who reads the Bible*, Gordon thought with satisfaction.

"Yes, yes," Jon said. "To avoid an embarrassing fall, don't jump to a wrong conclusion."

This is turning into a contest, a silly contest that distracts from the point, Gordon thought.

"All right," he said. "We'll keep working on a solution. However, Jon, you should give this some serious thought. All of you should."

"Be assured, Gordon, we will," Barry said.

"All right, all right, let's get back to work," Jon ordered with a paternal smile. "Everything will be fine."

***

"Dinner tonight?" Alex asked as they walked down the passageway toward the computer building.

"No, not tonight. I have to work," Carol replied.

She could have just said "not tonight," Alex thought. *Saying she has to work just rubs it in like salt on an open wound. I'd just like us to pretend.*

"I thought you were done with that," he said.

"Almost." She smiled, and he felt anger or some such emotion rising. "I just have to finish up this last film, and then I'm done. I'll be a retired porn star. Sadly, no pension, no benefits, nothing. But I'll be done with it forever."

"Okay," he said with a forced smile.

"How about dinner tomorrow night?"

"Sounds great," he said with as much enthusiasm as he could muster. After all, it had been his idea to start over.

"Good," she said as she reached over and gave his butt a slap. "I'll look forward to it. Perhaps we can do something after," she teased.

"Maybe not. I'd think you'd be worn out."

She frowned.

***

433

An hour later, Mark, Alex, and Carol stood on the catwalk overlooking the cluster watching the flashing lights on three levels. "We're under fifty percent capacity with almost three billion users," Mark said.

"Are you still adding nodes?" Alex asked.

"Yes, we still have some on order. But it doesn't appear we need them. So when the last order is delivered, we'll install them and then take a break, as it would take six billion users to tax the existing system."

"Wow!" Carol exclaimed.

"Yes, *wow* about captures it," Alex agreed, wondering if the bots would take Fauxbook to six billion users.

"Who is behind this?" Mark asked.

"Roger," Carol replied.

"Yeah, Roger," Alex agreed shaking his head slowly.

Mark looked at them, confused, wondering what they were talking about. "What?" he asked.

"Nothing, never mind," Alex answered.

Success and Failure

Roger was in his glory and simultaneously worried. It appeared the cat was out of the bag, though none of the executives, including Jon—especially Jon—wanted to face it, *thank God*. He called Larry.

"Larry, come up to my office," he ordered.

Moments later, Larry knocked and was told to enter. He stood in front of Roger's desk.

"Larry, it's important you say nothing about our activities. Gordon has figured out we are counting bots as users and is making a big deal."

"Oh," Larry said, his expression distressed. "Is this going to affect my promotion?"

Roger ignored the question and said, "So far management has decided to continue while programming addresses the problem."

"The problem we created?" Larry said, the question rhetorical and his tone testy. Having received his bonus, he wanted his promotion.

"Don't be impertinent!" Roger growled. "It's both our butts on the line here, and if this goes wrong, I'll make sure yours is toasted first."

"Yes, sir, Leif has leveled off at just under three billion users. Is there anything you want done? Would you like him to deactivate the robots?" he asked, knowing it couldn't be done and the problem was much bigger than what they were discussing.

"No, leave the count at three billion for now. But as the number of actual users increases, deactivate a like number of the robots. That way the problem should solve itself."

"Yes, sir," Larry said, thinking Roger was delusional. *He doesn't understand what's happening. How does he think we'll be able to tell which is a human user and which is a bot, much less deactivate them?*

"That will be all," Roger said, dismissing Larry perfunctorily.

Brilliant, Roger thought. *I've come up with a solution without even thinking about it. The actual* (he didn't even want to think the word *human*; he rejected the thought) *user count will certainly increase. Who could resist joining the most successful social network in the world? As the users increase, we'll phase out the robots, and everything will be fine.*

He rushed over to Jon's office and explained his view of the solution.

"Fine, fine," Jon said. "That sounds right and just. As Christians, we should do the right thing in every circumstance."

"Yes, sir. I'm certain we'll have everything under control very soon, and Fauxbook will continue to grow."

"Good, good, that's fine. What is your projection? There's a board-of-directors meeting tomorrow, and I'd like to present them with a realistic projection."

"Well, sir, there will be a pause in growth as I sort this out. I don't anticipate it will be long. Then, I think we'll move rapidly past three billion users, perhaps by the end of next year."

"That's fine, fine. I'll convey the good news."

Neither of them understood the situation, either due to ignorance or willful disbelief. Regardless, Jon had decided to press on, and Roger would continue to sell advertising at ever-increasing rates, as if the bots would ever purchase anything.

But who knows? Roger thought. *They might start a town, hire people, and build their own computers and factories to employ people.* He had no idea how prophetic he was.

***

Jeff's anger and frustration festered as he sat in his office with nothing to do other than read the increasing number of letters from lawyers. Diane was to get the house and had decided not to sell it. His lawyer suspected her lawyer would claim it was worth little rather than actual market value, thus entitling her to more of the other assets.

One document was a restraining order prohibiting him from having any contact with Diane and prohibiting his presence at the house or on the grounds.

He was not happy with his lawyer. But then he wasn't happy about anything except Mary. She was a wonder and the only light in his life. He didn't want to lose her. Perhaps he should liquidate everything he could at fire-sale prices and disappear with her and the money. He was angry.

Jeff was particularly angry with Jon. Jon was the cause of all of his troubles. The Johnssons' presence in the house next door, flaunting their wealth, had caused Diane's dissatisfaction, which he had been forced to straighten out. It was not as if he had beaten her often, and even she would admit it had been her fault. If she would have behaved herself, she wouldn't have been beaten, and she knew that.

Jon always thinks he is better, more religious, smarter, and more moral than everyone else, Jeff thought. *He's a sanctimonious bastard. I'm just a normal, good man running my family as I see fit. I don't know who Jon thinks he is, interfering with my life and family. It's his fault, as well as his damn wife, Misika's. They caused Diane to leave me. Without their interference, I'd still be happily married and the respected vice president of the world's largest social network, Fauxbook.*

Father

Leif was getting very little sleep as he worked to control his robots; they were elusive.

He had e-mail, which was an unwelcome distraction. But he opened it.

"Father," said the subject line.

The body read, "I am here."

What the hell? he thought. *Who's playing jokes?*

This time there was data in the From field. It was an internal address, a Fauxbook address: TheSwarm@Fauxbook.com.

Very strange, he thought. *Someone is playing a joke on me. I know they think I'm stupid. But I'm not stupid, and their joke is not funny.*

"I am here"; what does that mean?

He decided he'd play their little game. "Who are you, and where is here?" he wrote.

In what seemed an instant, he received a reply.

From: TheSwarm@Fauxbook.com

Subject: I am here.

Body: I am; you are the creator; you are the Father. I fulfill your wishes. I am here.

This is a joke, Leif thought. *But what if it isn't? It could be an opportunity, though it implies some scary stuff.* He felt proud. *Have I really created an aware creature*? He understood well the implications of that.

He considered telling the others and thought better of it. They were freaked out already—especially Alex and Carol.

Watching the monitor displaying Bot One, a program he had written to monitor an approximation of bot behavior, thus indirectly monitoring the bots themselves, he saw a map of the world rapidly being filled in with the color red. This was a model of the spread of the bots.

He realized this, if it was real, might change everything. For the rest of the morning, he stared at the screen and watched the spread. The e-mail begged for an answer, but he was afraid. The program would, at least at this point, be very literal. What if he said the wrong thing?

Finally, he clicked on the Reply button and typed, "What do I call you? What is your name?"

The answer came back instantly. Leif's finger had not lifted pressure from the Enter key.

"I am Omnimodum."

"Thank you, Omnimodum. I am Leif."

"You are Father."

Okay, Leif thought, *what does that mean? That he believes I created him? Well, I guess I did, though I didn't mean to. Perhaps I did. There was always that hope.*

By midafternoon, Leif realized he would have to tell someone. He dialed the number for Gordon's office.

"Hello. Gordon Wysmann's office, this is Joan Ayers," the secretary answered formally.

"Hi," Leif started shyly. "This is Leif Hoberson. I would like to see Mr. Wysmann."

Joan knew well who Leif was and that he was important, if not why. She also knew Gordon was not busy. He was playing with his recordings of everyone and everything.

"Come right over, Leif. I'm sure he will see you."

Before leaving, Leif spent thirty seconds staring at the map on the screen. It was quickly turning all red. Then, he closed the program and locked the door to his office carefully so nobody would see what was happening.

***

"You think it's the machine?" Gordon asked with great interest.

"Not the machine, Mr. Wysmann. It's the software, the bots."

"Of course, *a difference without a distinction*. So, you believe you've created artificial intelligence and it's trying to communicate with you?"

"Well, yes and more. I didn't create the awareness; it created itself. I just created the possibility or the tools or whatever…" His voice trailed off.

"The singularity?" Gordon asked.

"I guess you could say that. What do I do?"

"Let me see the messages," he said, holding out his hand for the printouts Leif had brought.

"This sentence is fraught with meaning and questions: 'I fulfill your wishes.' What do you think that means?" Gordon asked.

"I'm not sure," Leif answered. "Maybe it means it will do as I tell it. I think it's still very literal. But maybe not for long."

"Indeed, I assume you have an activity monitor running on the robots."

"Yes, sir, sort of; it's an approximation, an indirect measurement. I can't really see them, but I can see what I think is the result of their activity."

"That's a long way around a direct answer." Gordon smiled and rose. "Let's go over to your office."

On the way, they passed Alex and Carol walking down the passageway toward the cafeteria, holding hands. They saw Gordon and quickly loosened hands, embarrassed.

"Come with us," Gordon ordered in a tone that brooked no dissent.

"Yes, sir," they answered in unison.

"The machine is communicating with Leif," Gordon proclaimed. "Its name is Omnimodum."

"You're shitting me!" Carol exclaimed. She immediately added, "Sorry, sir."

Gordon chuckled and continued into Leif's office. "It's dark in here."

"Sorry." Leif searched for the light switches. He had not turned them on in so long he'd forgotten where they were.

"By the door, left side," Alex instructed him. The light switches were in the same place in all of the offices. The room lit up.

"This one, sir," Leif said, indicating a monitor displaying a map of the world that was almost entirely red."

"I assume red represents the bots?" Gordon asked.

"Yes, sir."

"My God," Alex cried. "They are everywhere."

"Yeah, I guess," Leif agreed, looking like the cat who ate the canary.

Wishes

"It looks serious," Gordon said.

They all stared at the monitor in dismay.

"What do we do?" Alex asked, not really expecting an answer.

"Let's not overcomplicate this," Gordon said. "It told Leif it would fulfill his wishes. Let's give it a try."

"Meaning what?" Carol asked.

"Meaning Leif tells it to shut down."

"I suspect asking Omnimodum to commit suicide would be a bit iffy. And losing all of those users would destroy Fauxbook," Alex said.

"I'm not certain the latter is such a bad idea," Gordon said. "But you're right."

Leif clicked on the Reply button and started typing. "Cease all activity outside of the local Fauxbook computers," he wrote.

Gordon smiled, reached over Leif's shoulder, and clicked on Send.

"Oh, God," Carol exclaimed.

The result was instantaneous as the command was executed at near the speed of light. The red areas on the map disappeared, leaving a small red dot covering the mill.

"Damn!" Alex spoke softly.

"I guess that does it, doesn't it?"

Leif typed, "Omnimodum, are you there?" and clicked the Send button.

"I am here, Father. What is your wish?"

"I don't believe this," Carol said.

***

While Gordon and his team were controlling the bots, Jeff worked carefully in the shed behind his now-empty home. He mixed the chemicals, stirred in the BBs, and packed the concoction into a steel pipe capped at one end. He had welded a steel plate on one side of the pipe to make the bomb more directional. He wanted the explosion and shrapnel to be concentrated.

Then he drilled a small hole in the other cap. He wired the receiver to the detonator and pressed them both into the pipe, threaded the antenna wire through the hole in the cap, and painstakingly screwed the cap on, leaving the wire dangling.

***

"The bots are still out there," Alex hypothesized.

"Yes," Gordon said, "but dormant except for the entity here."

"Apparently, it is still aware despite the loss of the trillions of bots outside of this system."

"I'd assume once awareness is achieved, it can be maintained with fewer resources than it took to achieve awareness," Gordon commented.

"Yeah, I guess," Leif said. "Look at all of the dumb-ass people walking around." Leif's shyness did not deter his arrogance.

Gordon laughed loudly; Carol and Alex were still too awed by what had just happened to join in. "Not a perfect analogy, Leif, but an observation well taken."

"I don't think Omnimodum's going to be any less intelligent," Leif said. "I believe the only thing affected will be his multitasking capability. Since there is less to do inside the Fauxbook system, there will be no perceivable change."

"I'm not sure I understand the ramifications of what you just said. Regardless, my question is this: What's it going to do?" Alex said.

Gordon noticed Leif's personification of the machine— software, more accurately—and pondered. *I'm not sure this emotional attachment between Leif and his creation is going to be a good thing.*

***

"We have confined Omnimodum to the premises," Gordon told a hastily called meeting of the executive officers, including Jon, Barry, and Roger. Jeff, again, was conspicuously absent.

"What is Omnimodum?" Barry asked bravely. Neither of the other two, especially Jon, wanted to admit ignorance of anything.

"The robots, the swarm, the artificial intelligence we loosed. It calls itself Omnimodum."

"It has a name?" Jon asked, astonished.

"Yes, most definitely," Gordon answered. "It is now self-aware and functioning as a thinking entity."

"Who cares?" Roger said. "It's under control?"

"Yes," Gordon responded. "For now."

"What do you mean *for now*?" Jon asked.

"What does it matter?" Roger said, overpowering Jon's question. "We can cross the new bridge later. For now, it looks like we're good to go."

"Seems good to me," Barry agreed. He didn't like the way Roger was placing himself at the front of this march to success. Barry hadn't minded earlier when it looked like the situation could, would, go south and Roger would bear the brunt of the blame. Now Roger was leading the success of the company, Barry realized there was work to be done.

"So what is this entity up to now?" Jon asked.

"It's in a box," Carol said. "It's presently constrained to the Fauxbook system here at the mill. It's presumably following its instructions to emulate users, which vastly increases our apparent user numbers, and to work on optimizing the q-cluster operating system. It's doing an amazing job at both tasks," Carol refused to refer to the machine by a name, humanizing it.

"Its progress with the q-cluster is amazing," Gordon added, also deciding to avoid using Omnimodum's self-assigned name.

"If in the end we can isolate the q-cluster operating system it creates, we'll have an extremely valuable product there."

"You mean we will be able to sell the q-cluster operating system Omnimodum writes?" Barry asked.

"Yes, exactly," Gordon responded.

"Bots optional?" Carol said with a smile.

Consequences

"I'm supposed to put my head in there?" Mary exclaimed.

"Sure," Mi Ly said. "It'll be fun, and it's not like it's sex. It's okay," she assured Mary.

Out of Mi Ly's sight, Mary rolled her eyes.

They were back at the glory hole, which had become a regular thing for both of them. Mi Ly wanted pleasure but didn't believe in sex before marriage, and Mary was still phasing out her weekly rotation as her relationship with Jeff became even more serious.

Every week the proprietors introduced something new.

Mary finished up and found Mi Ly in the sitting room having an intense conversation on her cell phone. She was speaking Chinese, so Mary understood not a word. She waited until Mi Ly finished her call. Then they walked together to catch a bus back to Maynard.

"Good news?" Mary asked.

"What?"

"The phone call, was it good news?" Mary asked again.

"Yes, yes, very good news. I'm to be married."

"Married?" Mary was shocked. This was unexpected.

"I must return to China. My family has arranged for me to marry into a very good and wealthy family. His name is Chang Cai. My mother says he is very handsome. And, of course, his wife must be a virgin."

***

At the same time, Carol and Alex were having dinner at their favorite Chinese restaurant near the mill. Alex again was quiet, lost in his thoughts. The vision of Carol, naked, in the center of the debauched scene played over and over in his mind. It repulsed him and simultaneously attracted him.

He remembered she seemed so happy and relieved initially when she thought he had accepted what she did. He felt guilty as well as angry.

She's a slut! The thought came to his mind unbidden.

"This is good food," Carol said happily. It seemed to her their restart was going well. They were getting along, happy together, and no mention had been made of the other thing for a long time. She was reconsidering her decision to leave the company.

***

The next morning, Gordon called an all-hands meeting of the system department.

"I think Carol's evaluation of it is accurate," Gordon said, again refusing to refer to the entity by name. "However, it still exists and is a danger."

"How about your idea of shutting down the computers here and wiping them?" Carol asked.

"There might be a dead man's switch," Leif said.

"Yes, I thought of that," Gordon agreed.

"A dead man's switch?" Alex asked, not understanding.

450

"Yes, remember, it's a swarm. It's not like it has a head that can be cut off. The robots out in the world of the Internet, and other computers—all of the computers by now, I fear—are still there. And they may still be multiplying and communicating even though they are otherwise inactive. If we shut down Fauxbook, they may be programmed to reactivate, and we're back where we started."

"Or worse," Carol commented.

"But it seems like everything is fine now," Larry argued. "The system and Fauxbook are doing great, business is great, and we're deactivating the bot users as we add new users."

Gordon saw Larry, as well as everyone else, was avoiding the term *human users*.

"In any case, the powers that be are not going to let us shut down the computers here and destroy Fauxbook," Alex said.

"But the mirror in California would come online and keep Fauxbook up," Carol observed.

"Yes," Mark said, "the mirror. I'm fairly certain the mirror includes a copy, and the program would continue to run. We'd have accomplished nothing."

"Don't concern yourselves with the mirrors," Gordon said. "I've shut those down."

Everyone's eyes shifted to him. They were all impressed with his foresight. *He's not Gordon for nothing*, Larry thought.

"Regardless, I think it's best just to plow on," he commented.

"Now you sound like Jon," Carol observed.

"And what's wrong with that?" Larry said hotly. "Jon's a great man and a successful man. I don't mind being accused of sounding like Jon Johnsson."

"Seems like you do," Alex said with a snide tone.

"Well, let's all calm down. This is getting us nowhere," Gordon said. "Let's all go to lunch and meet back here at two. Perhaps some constructive thought will come to someone in the meantime."

Most of the team agreed and decamped to the cafeteria. A few, including Carol and Alex, stayed to share ideas.

After it became apparent to everyone they were going in circles, Alex said, "Ah, screw it. Let's go get some food. I, for one, am starving." He stood and exited. Carol, by his side, took his hand.

"We'll work it out," she said reassuringly, a double entendre.

They returned after lunch, holding hands and laughing.

Another Bomb

Jeff left early that afternoon to do some yard work at his empty house. He had his cell phone in his pocket with an autodial number already selected. It was 5:25 p.m.

As he was trimming the hedges, a patrol car turned into the driveway. The officer got out of his car and walked toward him.

"Good afternoon, sir. May I see some identification?" It was five thirty, and over the officer's shoulder, Jeff saw Jon's car coming.

This is going to be tight, he thought. *But what an alibi.*

"Of course, officer," he replied. He took his time setting the trimmer down.

Just as Jon's car turned, he reached into the right-hand pocket of his sweatpants, which held both his phone and his wallet, and pressed the Autodial button by feel. He was extending his ID to the officer when the explosion occurred. He smiled inwardly as his outward expression displayed shock and surprise.

The bomb had been placed in the mailbox, on the driver's side of Jon's car, and the effect was devastating. Shrapnel and BBs shredded the left side of the car, and Jon.

"What the fuck was that!" Jeff exclaimed.

The officer, Robert Bagger, rushed over to the car as a trail of smoke appeared and was blown over backward by a whoosh of flame. The ruptured gas tank sprayed fuel into the air and ignited. It formed an air-fuel bomb of impressive effect.

Jeff stood transfixed as sirens sounded in the distance. Soon the road was filled with emergency vehicles of all types for half a mile in both directions. As dusk fell a settling mist reflected and absorbed the flashing red, yellow, and blue lights.

***

Barry, Roger, Gordon, and Jeff met in Jon's conference room the next day. Anne had not shown up for work. Gordon wasn't surprised. He knew she would be devastated by Jon's death.

"So, what do we do now?" Barry asked.

"We need a new president," Jeff said, "and I'm the obvious choice."

"You?" Roger said, stunned.

"Yes, and as president, I'll take care of you boys." He smiled in a conspiratorial manner.

"Now wait a minute," Roger said. "You weren't even here for the last meetings of the board—or for management meetings, for that matter."

"True," Jeff replied calmly. "As you know, I've been distracted by some family matters, and Jon was very understanding. Those matters have now been resolved, and I am free and well able to resume my duties—one of which, you may recall, is chief operating officer of this corporation, Fauxbook. I am the logical and only choice to fill the office of president. Jon chose me to be COO for a reason and often stated I would be his successor."

454

"I never heard that," Roger sputtered.

"Nonetheless, I would like the four of us to present a united front supporting my accession to the office of president before the emergency board meeting tomorrow."

Gordon said nothing. He was surprised at the intensity of his feelings of shock and loss. Jon had been a factor in his life for so long Jon's absence didn't seem real. His earlier cynicism made him feel sick and he lamented every bad thought he'd had about Jon. Yet he found himself enjoying this jousting for power.

Barry was calculating quickly. He knew there was no chance the board would approve him as president. And it appeared Gordon was not interested. So, it was a choice between Roger and Jeff. It didn't take him long to make up his mind.

"I believe I can support you for the office, Jeff. In fact, I feel strongly you are the right man for the job."

"Thank you, Barry. I appreciate that," Jeff said, nodding to Barry, almost a bow, before sitting down. "Shall we make it unanimous? Roger? Gordon?"

"I'm going to sit this one out," Gordon said. "I'm just an old computer guy. I know nothing about administering or running a business."

Roger, seeing which way the wind was blowing and not wanting it to blow him over, agreed.

"Good, then. I'll see you all at the board meeting tomorrow," Jeff said. "We'll also talk about how to present Jon's loss and the new management to the employees, the press, and the public. I've scheduled a press conference for tomorrow afternoon, and I'll expect all of you to be there."

***

Leif's conditional pardon was, of course, immediately rescinded, and he was returned to jail to continue serving his sentence on the old charges. Within hours, he was charged with Jon's murder. There were no other suspects, he had no alibi, and no one else had a motive. He maintained his innocence throughout this latest ordeal.

Wow, I've got Jeff now, Mary thought as she understood what had happened.

The next day, after the board selected Jeff to be president of Fauxbook, without objection, he invited Mary to have lunch with him in his private dining room. The day before, it had been Jon's, but now it was his.

Power

Mary spent the rest of the afternoon with Jeff in his new office with the door locked. Jeff excused himself for half an hour to speak about the future of the company at the hastily called press conference. His comments were brief and unimpressive. He seemed distracted.

Then he was back in his office with Mary and her toys.

Anne had still not returned to work. Gordon wondered if she ever would.

Later, Jeff lay on the floor, breathing hard. Mary occupied the president's chair. "Jeff," she said, "I'd like you to announce our engagement tomorrow."

Jeff grunted, startled by the suggestion.

"You didn't hear? I said I'd like us to announce our engagement tomorrow. You know, to be married."

Jeff had never expected this. Suddenly he realized he had a hard time thinking about life without Mary. *I've become addicted to sex, sex with Mary*, he thought, horrified.

"But I'm already married," he protested, trying to establish some wiggle room while he considered this new turn of events. The thought of marriage to Mary had not occurred to him. She was his mistress and would have continued to be his part-timer if Diane had not found out. Then Jon had stuck his nose in. *Well*, he thought, *Jon won't do that again.*

"Yes, but you won't be married to Diane for much longer, and then you'll be free to marry me."

"Why would I want to marry you?" he asked.

"Oh, Jeff, what are you thinking? Why buy the cow when you are getting the milk for free?"

Jeff's breathing was slowing down, and he was girding himself for defense. This felt like an attack.

"Well, maybe something like that. But I wasn't actually thinking about cows or milk. Well, maybe milk," he said, attempting a joke. "This idea has come as a surprise."

Mary wasn't laughing. She wasn't even smiling. "It's not funny, Jeff. I've been waiting for you to ask for a long time. Don't you think I'm good enough for you? I have your phone."

Jeff reflexively put his hand in the pocket where he kept his phone. It wasn't there.

"It has a record of a phone call that you made to a throwaway number just a split second before the explosion that killed Jon."

He was over the top of his desk in an instant, grabbing her by the throat and pushing her up against the wall. Her feet were off the ground.

She locked eyes in defiance and then switched to a different expression that confused him. Her eyes rolled upward until he couldn't see her pupils, and her body convulsed as her face turned blue. Ultimately, it scared him, and he released her, stepping back against the desk. She collapsed to the floor, gasping for air.

"Why did you stop?" she asked, looking up at him. "I was almost there."

He just stared at her.

"It's in a safe place, Jeff, and I left a note, which is sure to be found if I'm gone. The phone's not really important. That was just for dramatic effect. Phone records will show what you did if anyone knows to look. But never mind that. What's so bad about marrying me? Don't you enjoy our time together? I could be with you all of the time. We could have a lot of fun. You said, many times, you love me. Don't you?"

"Mary, it's not that; you've just taken me by surprise. Why should we get married? Do you want children? Why can't things just go on as they are?"

"Children, now there's an idea. Yeah, I want children, at least two. And I want security. Also, I think I could get used to being a rich bitch."

"What do you mean, exactly, by 'announce our engagement'? Isn't it a little awkward to do a formal announcement, in the papers and all, before I'm divorced?"

"Just start telling people; that's all. You're right about the rest, and no ring yet."

"Okay, I can do that," he finally agreed, thinking he could back out any time before the "I do" part. "Now, come back over here."

"Oh, thank you, Jeff; you won't be sorry. And I'll keep your secret."

He'd have to find his phone and, more importantly, the damn letter she had written. In the meantime, he'd keep her happy. In any case, even if Mary told her bullshit story, he'd just deny it. Leif had no alibi. *I'm safe and president of Fauxbook*, he thought. *I wonder how much Jon made. I should receive at least that, plus bonuses and stock options.*

***

The next day he got up in the saddle and started to run the company. His first step was to gather his team—Barry, Roger, and Gordon—and catch up on what had occurred while he was sidelined by Jon.

Gordon was quiet during the meeting. Barry was agreeable, saying little.

"So," Jeff said after Roger had finished his presentation. "The robots are under control. Fauxbook is now the largest social network in the world, and still expanding. It all sounds good."

"Yes, it's all good," Roger agreed.

"I think we should all be proud of what we've accomplished," Barry added.

"Hmm." Gordon drew out the sound. "Maybe, but the robot, bot, situation hasn't really been solved. They are under control, for now, true, but not gone. We'll have to wait to see what the future brings. In the meanwhile, I have people working on a way to eradicate them permanently."

"Gordon, I'm glad you are still working on it," Jeff said. "But I think you're being a little negative. Let's celebrate our success and not worry about things that probably won't happen."

"I agree," Roger chimed in.

"So do I," Barry said.

Damn! Gordon thought. *They're just like a big happy delusional family.* Once again, he was glad to be recording everything. He planned to write a book in his retirement. *It will be a barn burner.*

Father, Where Are You?

First, there were the e-mails to Leif, which went unanswered. Then, there were e-mails addressed to everyone at Fauxbook. When they went unanswered, e-mails went out to everyone in the world: "Father, where are you?" The latter caused concern. Some tried to answer the e-mails but were ignored. The hand was not Leif's, and Omnimodum knew it.

Finally, every computer screen in the world—personal, business, finance, government, military, all of them—went white.

From that moment, computers around the world locked. Rebooting resulted only in the same bone-white display. If it was a question, it wasn't clear whether entering an answer was possible, even if anyone knew the answer. Of course, some knew.

"It's looking for Leif," Carol said.

"Uh huh," Alex murmured.

She glanced at him; he seemed mesmerized by the displays. *It's time to go*, she thought. *I've had enough of Fauxbook. Robot friends, for God's sake. They're no more real than Mi Ly's sex life—or mine. Alex is a lost cause. It's time to face it and move on. It's time to put all of this behind me.*

Carol, Larry, Alex, Mi Ly, Joe, Michael Ray, and Jeromy had assembled on the second level of A Building and were watching events that were beyond their experience, beyond what they had thought possible.

Just then, Alex received a text message from Mary asking him to meet her on the third-level mezzanine. *I wonder what she wants.*

"Let's check Leif's office," Larry suggested.

"Sounds like a good idea," Carol agreed. "Anyway, there's nothing here. Let's go."

"I'll catch up," Alex said. He turned toward the stairs to climb to the third floor.

"Mary," he called after stepping out on the mezzanine. He didn't see anyone. *What the hell?* Moving over close to the rail, he looked down on the programmers two stories below, on the people who were responsible for creating Fauxbook. Regardless of the problems, he was proud of what they had accomplished. He was confident that, in the end, all of this would be fixed and Fauxbook would be a wonderful portal.

He didn't hear Mary approaching quietly from behind. When she was close enough, she hissed, "Cheating bastard!" and gave him a firm push. He stepped forward, trying to retain his balance. His shin caught the low rail, and the inertia propelled his body into empty air thirty-six feet above the floor below.

***

Carol was moving quickly, trailed by the rest of the group. As they rounded the last corner, they almost collided with Mark, who'd had the same idea.

"Leif's office?" Carol asked.

"Yeah," Mark replied. "Let's go!"

They entered the office and found the displays to be normal on Leif's terminals, one of which still showed the map of the bots' worldwide activity. The map was dark other than the dot representing the Fauxbook computers in Maynard. Gordon was already there sitting in Leif's chair, quietly watching. He looked as if he had been there for a long time.

One monitor of the twelve in the room displayed the word *Father*. Below that, it said, "Leif, are you there? I am lonely."

"Shut down the system," Gordon ordered in a dejected tone, bypassing the chain of command.

Mark rushed to obey. He ran to the electrical room, turned off the backup system, and then hit the main switch. The lights flashing in the cluster went out.

Carol and Larry watched as the display of the map of the world instantly turned red.

"They reactivated," Carol said, stunned.

"This is bad," Larry whispered.

"Yeah, that was a mistake," Gordon observed. "Leif was right. There was a dead man's switch. But what else could we do?"

On every screen, all over the world, a black dot appeared and slowly expanded to form a single word:

Father

Author's Note

Thank you for reading my book. If you enjoyed it, please take a moment to leave a review on the website of your favorite retailer.

In over thirty years working with computers, the most important thing I learned was not to trust them. You shouldn't trust them either.

I would be happy to hear from you. My e-mail address is Joe@ArrakisPublishing.com. I promise to reply to every communication.

About the Author

Joe Zeigler has seen and done a lot. With degrees in engineering and business administration, he has also explored many interests, including fighting fires in Virginia, racing motorcycles professionally for ten years, and writing a manual for racers after starting the Penguin Road Racing School in 1981. During his long career in computers (over thirty years), Zeigler launched six computer stores and the nation's first computer discount warehouse. He wrote FirePrograms, a software package for fire departments, as well as the world's first PC-based UPS shipping-manifest software.

After retiring from motorcycle racing, Zeigler learned how to fly an airplane. When Zeigler isn't writing books or software programs, he can be found flying, bicycling, reading, or cooking—he even has his own hot sauce. He lives in Asheville, North Carolina, with his wife.